THE DEBTOR

MORE WILDSIDE CLASSICS

THE DEBTOR

MARY E. WILKINS FREEMAN

WILDSIDE PRESS

THE DEBTOR

This edition published 2005 by Wildside Press, LLC.
www.wildsidepress.com

CHAPTER I

Banbridge lies near enough to the great City to perceive after night-fall, along the southern horizon, the amalgamated glow of its multitudinous eyes of electric fire. In the daytime the smoke of its mighty breathing, in its race of progress and civilization, darkens the southern sky. The trains of great railroad systems speed between Banbridge and the City. Half the male population of Banbridge and a goodly proportion of the female have for years wrestled for their daily bread in the City, which the little village has long echoed, more or less feebly, though still quite accurately, with its own particular little suburban note.

Banbridge had its own "season," beginning shortly after Thanks-giving, and warming gradually until about two weeks before Lent, when it reached its high-water mark. All winter long there were luncheons and teas and dances. There was a whist club, and a flourishing woman's club, of course. It was the women who were thrown with the most entirely upon the provincial resources. But they were a resolved set, and they kept up the gait of progress of their sex with a good deal of success. They improved their minds and their bodies, having even a physical-culture club and a teacher coming weekly from the City. That there were links and a golf club goes without saying.

It was spring, and golf had recommenced for some little time. Mrs. Henry Lee and Mrs. William Van Dorn passed the links that afternoon.

The two ladies were being driven about Banbridge by Samson Raw-dy, the best liveryman in Banbridge, in his best coach, with his two best horses. The horses, indeed, two fat bays, were considered as rather sacred to fashionable calls, as was the coach, quite a resplendent affair, with very few worn places in the cloth lining.

Banbridge ladies never walked to make fashionable calls. They had a coach even for calls within a radius of a quarter of a mile, where they could easily have walked, and did walk on any other occasion. It would have shocked the whole village if a Banbridge woman had gone out in her best array, with her card-case, making calls on foot. Therefore, in this respect the ladies who were better off in this world's goods often displayed a friendly regard for those who could ill afford the necessary expense of state calls. Often one would invite another to call with her, defraying all the expenses of the trip, and Mrs. Van Dorn had so invited Mrs. Lee today. Mrs. Lee, who was a small, elderly woman, was full of deprecating gratitude and a sense of obligation which made it appear incumbent upon her not to differ with her companion in any opinion which she might advance, and, as a rule, to give her the initiative in conversation during their calls, and the precedence in entry and retreat.

Mrs. Van Dorn was as small as her companion, but with a confidence of manner which seemed to push her forward in the field of vision farther than her size warranted.

She was also highly corseted, and much trimmed over her shoulders, which gave an effect of superior size and weight; her face, too, was very full and rosy, while the other's was narrow and pinched at the chin and delicately transparent.

Mrs. Van Dorn sat quite erect on the very edge of the seat, and so did Mrs. Lee. Each held her card-case in her two hands encased in nicely cleaned, white kid gloves. Each wore her best gown and her best bonnet. The coach was full of black velvet streamers, and lace frills and silken lights over precise knees, and the nodding of flowers and feathers.

There was, moreover, in the carriage a strong odor of Russian violet, which diffused itself around both the ladies. Russian violet was the calling perfume in vogue in Banbridge. It nearly overcame the more legitimate fragrance of the spring day which floated in through the open windows of the coach.

It was a wonderful day in May. The cherry-trees were in full bloom, and tremulous with the winged jostling of bees, and the ladies inhaled the sweetness intermingled with their own Russian violet in a bouquet of fragrance. It was warm, but there was the life of youth in the air; one felt the bound of the pulse of the spring, not its lassitude of passive yielding to the forces of growth.

The yards of the village homes, or the grounds, as they were commonly designated, were gay with the earlier flowering shrubs, almond and bridal wreath and Japanese quince. The deep scarlet of the quince-bushes was evident a long distance ahead, like floral torches. Constantly tiny wings flashed in and out the field of vision with insistences of sweet flutings. The day was at once redolent and vociferous.

"It is a beautiful day," said Mrs. Van Dorn.

"Yes, it is beautiful," echoed Mrs. Lee, with fervor.

Her faded blue eyes, under the net-work of ingratiating wrinkles, looked aside, from self-consciousness, out of the coach window at a velvet lawn with a cherry-tree and a dark fir side by side, and a Japanese quince in the foreground.

After passing the house, both ladies began pluming themselves, carefully rubbing on their white gloves and asking each other if their bonnets were on straight.

"Your bonnet is so pretty," said Mrs. Lee, admiringly.

"It's a bonnet I have had two years, with a little bunch of violets and new strings," said Mrs. Van Dorn, with conscious virtue.

"It looks as if it had just come out of the store," said Mrs. Lee. She was vainly conscious of her own headgear, which was quite new that spring, and distinctly prettier than the other woman's. She hoped that Mrs. Van Dorn would remark upon its beauty, but she did not. Mrs. Van Dorn was a good woman, but she had her limitations when it came to admiring in another something that she had not herself.

Mrs. Lee's superior bonnet had been a jarring note for her all the way. She felt in her inmost soul, though she would have been loath to admit the fact to herself, that a woman whom she had invited to make calls with her at her expense had really no right to wear a finer bonnet — that it was, to say the least, indelicate and tactless. Therefore she remarked, rather dryly, upon the beauty of a new pansy-bed beside the drive into which they now turned. The bed looked like a bit of fairy carpet in royal purples and gold.

"I call that beautiful," said Mrs. Van Dorn, with a slight emphasis on the that, as if bonnets were nothing; and Mrs. Lee appreciated her meaning.

"Yes, it is lovely," she said, meekly, as they rolled past and quite up to the front-door of the house upon whose mistress they were about to call.

"I wonder if Mrs. Morris is at home," said Mrs. Van Dorn, as she got a card from her case.

"I think it is doubtful, it is such a lovely day," said Mrs. Lee, also taking out a card.

Samson Rawdy threw open the coach door with a flourish and assisted the ladies to alight. He had a sensation of distinct reverence as the odor of Russian violet came into his nostrils.

"When them ladies go out makin' fashionable calls they have the best perfumery I ever seen," he was fond of remarking to his wife.

Sometimes he insisted upon her going out to the stable and sniffing in the coach by way of evidence, and she would sniff admiringly and unenviously. She knew her place. The social status of every one in Banbridge was defined quite clearly. Those who were in society wore their honors easily and unquestioned, and those who were not went their uncomplaining ways in their own humble spheres.

Mrs. Van Dorn and Mrs. Henry Lee, gathering up their silken raiment genteelly, holding their visiting-cards daintily, went up the front-door steps, and Mrs. Lee, taking that duty upon herself, since she was Mrs. Van Dorn's guest, pulled the door-bell, having first folded her handkerchief around her white glove.

"It takes so little to soil white gloves," said she, "and I think it is considerable trouble to send them in and out to be cleaned."

"I clean mine with gasolene myself," said Mrs. Van Dorn, with the superiority of a woman who has no need for such economies, yet practises them, over a woman who has need but does not.

"I never had much luck cleaning them myself," said Mrs. Lee, apologetically.

"It is a knack," admitted Mrs. Van Dorn. Then they waited in silence, listening for an approaching footstep.

"If she isn't at home," whispered Mrs. Van Dorn, "We can make another call before the two hours are up." Mr. Rawdy was hired by the hour.

"Yes, we can," assented Mrs. Lee.

Then they waited, and neither spoke. Mrs. Lee had occasion to sneeze, but she pinched her nose energetically and repressed it.

Suddenly both straightened themselves and held their cards in readiness.

"How does my bonnet look?" whispered Mrs. Lee.

Mrs. Van Dorn paid no attention, for then the door was opened and Mrs. Morris's maid appeared, with cap awry and her white apron over a blue-checked gingham which was plainly in evidence at the sides.

The ladies gave her their cards, and followed her into the best parlor, which was commonly designated in Banbridge as the reception-room. The best parlor was furnished with a sort of luxurious severity. There were a few pieces of staid old furniture of a much earlier period than the others, but they were rather in the background in the gloomy corners, and the new pieces were thrust firmly forward into greater evidence.

Mrs. Van Dorn sat down on the corner of a fine velvet divan, and Mrs. Lee near her on the edge of a gold chair. Then they waited, while the maid retired with their cards. "It's a pretty room, isn't it?" whispered Mrs. Lee, looking about.

"Beautiful."

"She kept a few pieces of the old furniture that she had in her old house when this new one was built, didn't she?"

"Yes. I suppose she didn't feel as if she could buy all new."

The ladies studied all the furnishings of the room, keeping their faces in readiness to assume their calling expression at an instant's notice when the hostess should appear.

"Did she have those vases on the mantel-shelf in the old house?" whispered Mrs. Lee, after a while; but Mrs. Van Dorn made a warning gesture, and instantly both ladies straightened themselves and looked pleasantly expectant, and Mrs. Morris appeared.

She was a short and florid woman, and her face was flushed a deep rose; beads of perspiration glistened on her forehead, her black hair clung to it in wet strands. In her expression polite greeting and irritation and intense discomfort struggled for mastery. She had been house-clean-ing when the door-bell rang, and had hastened into her black skirt and black-and-white silk blouse. The blouse was buttoned wrong, and it did not meet the skirt in the back; and she had quite overlooked her neckgear, but of that she was pleasantly unconscious, also of the fact that there was a large black smooch beside her nose, giving her both a rakish and a sin-ister air.

"I am so glad to find you in," said Mrs. Van Dorn.

"I was telling Mrs. Van Dorn that I was so afraid you would be out, it is such a lovely day," said Mrs. Lee.

"I am so glad I was in," responded Mrs. Morris, with effusion. "I should have been so disappointed to miss your call."

Then the ladies seated themselves, and the conversation went on. Overhead the maid could be heard heavily tramping. The carpet of that room was up, and the mistress and maid had planned to replace it before night; but the mistress held fast to her effusive air of welcome. It had never been fashionable or even allowable not to be at home when one was at home in Banbridge. When Banbridge ladies went abroad calling, in the coach, much was exacted. Mrs. Morris could never have held up her social head again had she fibbed, or bidden the maid fib — that is, if it had been discovered.

"How lovely your house is, Mrs. Morris!" said Mrs. Van Dorn, affably. The Morris house was only a year old, and had not yet been nearly exhausted as a topic of polite conversation.

"Thank you," said Mrs. Morris. "Of course there are things about the furnishings, but one cannot do everything in a minute."

"Now, my dear Mrs. Morris," said Mrs. Lee, "I think everything is sweet." Mrs. Lee said sweet with an effect as if she stamped hard to emphasize it. She made it long and extremely sibilant. Mrs. Lee always said sweet after that fashion.

"Oh, of course you would rather have all your furniture new, than part new and part old," said Mrs. Van Dorn; "but, as you say, you can't do everything at once."

Mrs. Van Dorn was inclined at times to be pugnaciously truthful, when she heard any one else lie. Her hostess looked uneasily at an old red velvet sofa in a dark corner, which was not so dark that a worn place along the front edge did not seem to glare at her. Nobody by any chance sat on that sofa and looked at the resplendent new one. They always sat on the new and faced the old. Mrs. Morris began absently calculating, while the conversation went on to other topics, if she could possibly manage a new sofa before summer.

Mrs. Lee asked if she knew if the new people in the Ranger place, "Willow Lake," were very rich? She said she had heard they were almost millionaires.

"Yes," said Mrs. Morris. "very rich indeed. Mr. Morris says he thinks they must be, from everything he hears."

"Of course it does not matter in one way or another whether they are rich or not," said Mrs. Lee.

"Well, I don't know," said Mrs. Van Dorn. "Of course nobody is going to say that money is everything, and of course everybody knows that good character is worth more than anything else, and yet I do feel as if folks with money can do so much if they have the will."

"I think that these new people are very generous with their money," said Mrs. Morris. "I heard they about supported the church in Hillfield, New York, where they used to live, and Captain Carroll has joined the Village Improvement Society, and he says he is very much averse to trading with any but the local tradesmen."

"What is he captain of?" inquired Mrs. Lee, who had at times a fashion of putting a question in a most fatuously simple and childish manner.

"Oh, I don't suppose he is really captain of anything now," replied Mrs. Morris. "I don't know how he happened to be captain, but I suppose he must have been a captain in the regular army."

"I suppose he hasn't any business, he is so very rich?"

"Oh yes; he has something in the City. I dare say he does not do very much at it, but I presume he is an active man and does not want to be idle."

"Why didn't he stay in the army, then?" asked Mrs. Lee, clasping her small white kid hands and puckering her face inquiringly.

"I don't know. Perhaps that was too hard, or took him away too far. I suppose some of those army posts are pretty desolate places to live in, and perhaps his wife was afraid of the Indians."

"He's got a wife and family, I hear," said Mrs. Van Dorn.

Both calling ladies were leaning farther and farther towards Mrs. Morris with an absorption of delight. It was as if the three had their heads together over a honey-pot.

"Mr. Lee said he heard they had a fine turnout," said Mrs. Lee.

"Mrs. Peel told me that Mr. Peel said the horses never cost less than a thousand," said Mrs. Van Dorn.

"A thousand!" repeated Mrs. Morris. "Mr. Morris said horses like those were never bought under twenty-five hundred, and Mr. Morris is a pretty good judge of horse-flesh."

"Mr. Van Dorn said Dr. Jerrolds told him that Captain Carroll told him he expected to keep an automobile, and was afraid the Ranger stable wouldn't be large enough," said Mrs. Van Dorn.

"So I heard," said Mrs. Lee.

"I hear he pays a very large rent to Mr. Ranger — the largest rent he has ever got for that house," said Mrs. Morris.

"Well, I hear he pays fifty dollars a month."

"Why, he never got more than forty before!" said Mrs. Lee. "That is, I don't believe he ever did."

"I know he didn't," said Mrs. Morris, positively.

"Well, it is a handsome place," said Mrs. Lee.

"Yes, it is, but these new people aren't satisfied. They must have been used to pretty grand things where they came from. They want the stable enlarged, as I said before, and a box-stall. Mr. Carroll owns a famous trotter that he hasn't brought here yet, because he is afraid the stable isn't warm enough. I heard he wanted steam-heat out there, and a room finished for the coachman, and hard-wood floors all over the house. They say he has two five-thousand-dollar rugs."

"The house is let furnished, I thought," said Mrs. Van Dorn.

"Yes, it is, and the furniture is still there. The Carrolls don't want to bring on many of their own things till they are sure the house is in better order. I heard they talk of buying it."

"Do you know how much —" inquired Mrs. Van Dorn, breathlessly, while Mrs. Lee leaned nearer, her eyes protruding, her small thin mouth open, and her white kid fingers interlacing.

"Well, I heard fifteen thousand."

Both callers gasped.

"Well, it is a great thing for Banbridge to have such people come here and buy real estate and settle, if they are the right sort," said Mrs. Van Dorn, rising to go; and Mrs. Lee followed her example, with a murmur of assent to the remark.

"Must you go?" said Mrs. Morris, with an undertone of joy, thinking of her carpet up-stairs, and rising with thinly veiled alacrity.

"Have you called?" asked Mrs. Van Dorn, moving towards the door, and gathering up her skirts delicately with her white kid fingers, preparatory to going down the steps. Mrs. Lee followed, also gathering up her skirts.

"No, I have not yet," replied Mrs. Morris, preceding them to the door and opening it for them, "but I intend to do so very soon. I have been pretty busy house-cleaning since they came, and that is only two weeks ago, but I am going to call."

"I think it is one's duty to call on new-comers, with a view to their church-going, if nothing else," said Mrs. Van Dorn, with a virtuous air.

"So do I," said Mrs. Lee.

"Good-afternoon," said Mrs. Van Dorn. "What a beautiful day it is!"

Both ladies bade Mrs. Morris good-afternoon and she returned the salutation with unction. Both ladies looked fascinatedly to the last at the black smooch on her cheek as they backed out.

"I thought I should burst right out laughing every time I looked at her, in spite of myself," whispered Mrs. Lee, as they passed down the walk.

"So did I."

"And no collar on!"

"Yes. She must have been house-cleaning."

"Yes. Well, I don't want to say disagreeable things, but really it doesn't seem to me that I would have been house-cleaning such an afternoon as this, when people were likely to be out calling."

"Well, I know I would not," said Mrs. Van Dorn, decidedly. "I should have done what I could in the morning, and left what I couldn't do till next day."

"So should I."

Samson Rawdy stood at the coach-door, and both ladies stepped in. Then he stood waiting expectantly for orders. The ladies looked at each other.

"Where shall we go next?" asked Mrs. Lee.

"Well, I don't know," said Mrs. Van Dorn, hesitatingly. "We were going to Mrs. Fairfield's next, but I am afraid there won't be time if —"

"It really seems to me that we ought to go to call on those new people," said Mrs. Lee.

"Well, I think so too. I suppose there would be time if Mrs. Fairfield wasn't at home, and it is such a lovely day I doubt if she is, and it is on the way to the Carrolls'." She spoke with sudden decision to Samson Rawdy. "Drive to Mr. Andrew Fairfield's, and as fast as you can, please." Then she and Mrs. Lee leaned back as the coach whirled out of the Morris grounds.

It was only a short time before they wound swiftly around the small curve of drive before the Fairfield house. "There is no need of both of us getting out," said Mrs. Van Dorn.

Mrs. Van Dorn alighted and went swiftly with a tiptoeing effect upon the piazza-steps. She was seen to touch the bell. She waited a short space, and then she did not touch it again. She tucked the cards under the door-step, and hurried back to the carriage.

"I knew she wasn't at home," said she, in a whisper, "it is such a lovely day." She turned to Samson Rawdy, who stood holding open the coach-door. "Now you may drive to those new people who have moved into the Ranger place," said she, "Mrs. Carroll's."

CHAPTER II

There are days in spring wherein advance seems as passive as is the progress of a log down the race of a spring freshet. Then there are other days wherein it seems that every mote must feel to the full its sentient life, and its swelling towards development or fulfilment. On a day like the latter, everything and everybody bestirs. The dust motes spin in whirling columns, the gnats dance for their lives their dance of death before the wayfarer. The gardeners and the grave-diggers turn up the earth with energy, making the clods fly like water. The rich play, or work that they may play, as do the poor. Everybody is up and wide awake and doing. The earth and the habitations thereof are rubbed, cleaned, and swept, or skylarked over; the boy plays with his marbles on the sidewalk or whoops over the fields; the housewives fling wide open their house windows, and the dust of the winter flies out like smoke; the tradesmen set out their new wares to public view, the bees make honey, the birds repeat their world-old nesting songs, the cocks crow straight through the day; nothing stops till the sun sets, and even then it is hard for such an ardent clock of life to quite run down.

It was that spirit of unrest which had sent the two ladies out making calls. There was not one where, if the womenkind were at home at all and not afield, but they had been possessed of the spring activity, until they reached the Ranger place, where the new-comers to Banbridge lived. The Ranger place was, in some respects the most imposing house in Banbridge. It stood well back from the road, in grounds which deserved the name. They were extensive, dotted with stately groups of spruces and pines, and there was in the rear of the house a pond with a rustic bridge, fringed with willows, which gave the place its name, "Willow Lake." The house had formerly been owned by two maiden women with much sentiment, the sisters of the present owner. The place was "Willow Lake." The pond was the "Willow Mere," in defiance of the name of the place. The little rustic bridge was the "Bridge of Sighs," for some obscure reason, perhaps buried in the sentimental past of the sisters. And the little hollow which was profusely sprinkled with violets in the spring was "Idlewild." It was in "Idlewild" that the new family, perverse to the spirit of the day, idled when the callers drove up the road in the best coach.

There was in the little violet-sprinkled hollow a small building with many peaks as to its roof, and diamond-paned windows which had been fitted out with colored glass in a hideous checker-work of orange and crimson and blue, which the departed sisters had called, none but themselves knew why, "The Temple." On the south side grew a rose-bush of the kind which flourished most easily in the village, taking most kindly to the soil. It was an ordinary kind of rose. The sisters had called it an eglantine, but it was not an eglantine. They had been very fond, when the weather permitted, of sitting in this edifice with their work. The place was fitted up with a rustic table and two quite uncomfortable rustic chairs, particularly uncomfortable for the sisters, who were of a thin habit of body.

When James Ranger, who was himself not a man of sentiment, showed the new aspirant for the renting of the place this fantastic building, he spoke of it with a species of apology.

"My sisters had this built," said he, "and it cost considerable," for he did not wish to disparage the money value of anything.

When the family were established in their new home, one of the first things which they did — they signifying Mrs. Carroll, Miss Anna Carroll, the daughters Miss Ina and Miss Charlotte Carroll, and the son Edward Carroll, called Eddy by the family — was to march in a body upon the little "Temple," and, armed with stones, proceed with shouts of merriment to smash out every spear of the crimson and orange and blue glass in the windows. They then demolished the rustic furniture and made of that a noble bonfire. Mrs. Carroll had indeed wondered, between fits of laughter, in her sweet drawl, if they ought to destroy the furniture, as it could not be said, strictly speaking, to belong to them to destroy, but she was promptly vetoed by all the others in merry chorus.

"They are too hideous to live," said Ina; "they ought to be burned. It is our plain duty to burn them."

Therefore they burned them, and brought out some of the parlor chairs to replace them. Then Eddy was sent to Rosenstein's, the village dry-goods store of Banbridge, for yards of green mosquito netting, which, the Carroll credit being newly established with a blare of trumpets, he purchased. Then they had tacked up the green mosquito netting over the window and door gaps, for they had forcibly wrenched the ornate door from its hinges and added it to the bonfire, and the temple of the Muses stood in a film of gently undulating green under the green willows, and was rather a thing of beauty.

The Carrolls loved to pass away the time in that retreat veiled with cloudy green, through which they could see the dull glimmer of the pond, like an old shield of silver, reflecting the waving garlands of the willows, which at that time of year were as beautiful as trees of heaven, having effects of waving lines of liquid green light, and the charming violet-blue turf around them.

The afternoon of the call all the female members of the Carroll family were out there. Captain Carroll was in the City, and Eddy, who, being a boy, was more susceptible to the lash of atmospheric influence, had gone fishing.

"I wonder why Eddy likes to go fishing," said Mrs. Carroll, in her sweet drawl. "Eddy never caught anything."

"You don't have a very high opinion of your son's powers as a fisherman, Amy," said Ina, and they all laughed. The Carrolls were an easy-to-laugh family, and always seemed to find delicious humor in one another's remarks.

"Amy never thinks any of us can catch anything," said Charlotte, the younger daughter, and they all laughed again.

Mrs. Carroll was always Amy in her family. Never did one of her children address her as a parent.

They were a charming group in the little, green, gloomy place, each with the strongest possible family likeness to the others. They were as much alike as the roses on one bush; all were, although not tall, long, and slim of body, and childishly round of face, with delicate coloring; all had pathetic dark eyes and soft lengths of dark hair. Mrs. Carroll and her husband's sister, although not nearly related (Mrs. Carroll had married her many-times-removed cousin), resembled each other as if they had been sisters of one family, and the children resembled their mother. The only difference among any of them was a slight difference of expression that existed mostly in the youngest girl, Charlotte. There were occasions when Charlotte Carroll's expression of soft and pathetic wistfulness and pleading could change to an expression of defiance, almost fierceness.

Her mother often told her that she resembled in disposition her paternal grandmother, who had been a woman of high temper, albeit a great beauty.

"Charlotte, dear, you are just like your grandmother, dear Arthur's mother, who was the worst-tempered and loveliest woman in Kentucky," Mrs. Carroll often remarked. She scarcely sounded the *t* in Kentucky, since she also was of the South, where the languid air tends to produce elisions. The Carrolls came originally from Kentucky, and had lived there until after the births of the two daughters. When they were scarcely more than infants, Arthur Carroll had experienced the petty and individual, but none the less real, cataclysm of experience which comes to most men sooner or later. It is the earthquake of a unit, infinitesimal, but entirely complete of its kind, and possibly as far-reaching in its thread of consequences. Arthur Carroll had had his palmy days, when he was working with great profits, and, as he believed, with entire righteousness and regard to his fellow-men, a coal-mine in the Kentucky mountains. He had inherited it from his father, as the larger part of his patrimony. When most of the property had been dissipated, at the time of the civil war, the elder Carroll, who was broken by years and reverses, used often to speak of this unimproved property of his, to his son Arthur, who was a young boy at the time. Anna, who was a mere baby, was the only other child.

"When you are a man, Arthur," he was fond of remarking — "when you are a man, you must hire some money, sell what little is left here, if necessary, and work that coal-mine. I always meant to do it myself, and reckon I should have, if that damned war had not taken the money and the strength out of the old man. But when you are a man, Arthur, you must work that mine, and you must build up what the war has torn down. You can buy back and restore, Arthur, and if the South should get back her rights by that time, as she may, why, then, you can stock up the old place again, and go on as your father did."

The old man, who was gouty and full of weary chills of body and mind, used to sit in the sun and dream, to his faint solace, until Arthur was a grown man and through college, and Anna a young girl at school near by. The little that had been left, with the bare exception of the home estate, the plantation, and the mine, had been sold to pay for Arthur's education. Arthur had been out of college only one summer when his father died. His mother, whose proud spirit had fretted the flesh from her bones and drunk up her very blood with futile rage and repining, had died during the war. Then Arthur, who had control of everything, as his sister's guardian, set to work to carry out his father's cherished dream with regard to the coal-mine. He sold every foot of the estate to a neighboring planter, an old friend of his father's, at a sacrifice, with a condition attached that he should have the option of buying it back for cash, at an advanced price, at the end of five years. The purchaser, who was a shrewd sort, of Scotch descent, curiously grafted on to an impetuous, hot-blooded Southern growth, looked at the slim young fellow with his expression of ingenuous almost fatuous confidence in his leading-strings of fate, and considered that he was safe enough and had made a good bargain. He too had suffered from the war, in more ways than one. He had come out of the strife shorn in his fleece of worldly wealth and mutilated as to his body. He limped stiffly on a wooden leg, and his fine buildings had gone up in fire and smoke. But during the years since the war he had retrieved his fortunes. People said he was worth more than before; everything he had handled had prospered. He was one of those men whose very touch seems to multiply possessions. He was a much younger man than Arthur's father, and robust at the time of his death. He explained to Arthur that he was doing him an incalculable service in purchasing his patrimonial estate, when he announced his decision so to do, after taking several weeks to conceal his alacrity.

"It is not everybodee would take a propertee, with such a condeetion attached, Arthur, boy," he said. He had at times a touch of the Scotch in his accent. His father had been straight from the old country when he married the planter's daughter. "Not everybodee, with such a condeetion," he repeated, and the boy innocently believed him. He had been used, ever since he was a child and could remember anything, to seeing a good deal of the man. The Southern wife had died early and the man had been lonely and given to frequent friendly meetings with Mr. Carroll, who had valued him.

"He's the right sort, Arthur," he had often told the boy; "you can depend on him. He has given his gold and his flesh and blood for the South, although he came on one side of another race and might have sided against us. He's the right sort."

So the Scotch-Southern planter had been one of the bearers at the old Carroll's funeral, and the son, when he had formulated his business schemes, had gone to this friend with them, and with his proposal for the sale of the Carroll property. The boy, who was honorable to the finish, had been loath to ask, in the then reduced state of the property, for a loan on mortgage to the extent which he would require; therefore he proposed this conditional sale as offering rather better, or at least more evident, security, and he regarded it in his own mind as practically amounting to the same thing. He was as sure of his being able to purchase back his own, should he secure the necessary funds, as he would have been of paying up the mortgage. The advance price would about twice cover the interest at a goodly rate, had the affair been conducted on the mortgage basis. Arthur himself had proposed that, and "I will of course pay for any improvements you may have made in the mean time," he said. There was nothing in the least mean or ungenerous about Arthur Carroll. He meant, on the whole, rather more squarely to his fellow-men than to himself.

Then with the money obtained from the sale of his patrimony he went to work on his coal-mine. A very trifle of a beginning had been made on it before the war, so he had not actually to break the first ground. The previous owner had died bankrupt from lack of capital, and his minor daughter had inherited it. It was from the minor daughter that the elder

Carroll had purchased it, partly with a view to assisting the child, who had been left penniless except for the mine, at the death of her father, who was of a distant branch of Carroll's own family. With the proceeds of the sale the girl was supported and educated; then she lost the remainder through the dishonesty of her guardian. That was the year after young Carroll began to work the mine. Then he married her. She was a beautiful girl, and helpless as a flower. He married her without a cent to support her except the old coal-mine, and he worked as hard and bravely as a man could. And he prospered, to the utter amazement of everybody who watched him, and who had prophesied failure from the start. In four years he was looked upon with respect. People said he was fast getting rich. He went to the man who had bought the Carroll place, at the end of the four years, with the money in his hand and proposed purchasing it. He had not a doubt, such was his trust in the friendliness of the man, that he would gladly consent and pat him on the back with fatherly affection for his success; but, to his amazement, he was refused, although still under the guise of the purest philanthropy.

"No, Arthur, boy," he said. "It is best for you to keep the money in your business awhile longer. It will not do, in a big undertaking like a mine, for you to be creepled. No, Arthur, boy, wait until the next year is up. It is for your good."

In vain Arthur offered an advance upon the original advance price. "No, Arthur, boy," he repeated.

"No, Arthur, boy," he continued to repeat. "It is not wise for you to be creepled in your business."

Arthur protested that he would not be crippled, but with no avail. He went away disappointed, and yet with his faith unshaken. He did not know what transpired later on, that negotiations which would materially enhance the value of the property were being carried on with a railroad by the planter, who was himself one of the railroad directors.

About six months after Arthur's attempt to purchase back his ancestral acres, and while he was at high tide of a small prosperity, this same man came to him with a proposal for him to furnish on contract a large quantity of coal to this same railroad. Arthur jumped at the chance. The contract was drawn up by a lawyer in the nearest town and signed. Arthur, trusting blindly to the honesty and good-will of everybody, had hurried for his train without seeing more than that the stipulated rates had been properly mentioned in the contract. His wife was ill; in fact, Charlotte was only a few days old, and he was anxious and eager to be home. There had been no strikes at that period in that vicinity, and indeed comparatively few in the whole country. Arthur would almost as soon have thought of guarding in his contract against an earthquake; but the strike clause was left out, and there was a strike. In consequence he was unable to fill the contract without ruin, and he was therefore ruined. In the end the old friend of his father, who had purchased his patrimony, remained in undisputed possession of it, with an additional value of several thousands from the passage of the railroad through one end of the plantation, and had, besides, the mine. Arthur had sold the mine at a nominal price to pay his debts, to a third party who represented this man. He had been left actually penniless with a wife and two babies to support, but as his pocket became empty his very soul had seemed to become full to overflowing with the rage and bitterness of his worldly experience. He had learned that the man whom he had trusted had instigated the strike; he learned about the railroad deal. One night he went to his plantation with a shot-gun. He approached the house which had formerly been his own home, where the man was living then. He fully intended to shoot him. He had not a doubt but he should do it, and he had always considered that he should have carried out his purpose had not an old horse which the man had purchased with the estate, and which was loose on the lawn, from some reason or other, whinnied eagerly, and sidled up to him, and thrust her nose over his shoulder. He had been used, when a boy, to feed her sugar, and she remembered. Arthur went away through the soft Southern moonlight without shooting the man. Somehow it was because of the horse, and he never knew why it was. The old childish innocence and happiness seemed to flood over him in a light of spirit which dimmed the moonlight and swept away the will for murder from his soul. But the bitterness and the hate of the man who had wronged him never left him. The next day he went North, and the man in possession breathed more easily, for he had had secret misgivings.

"You had better look out," another man had said to him. "You have trodden on the toes of a tiger when you have trodden on the toes of a Carroll. Sooner or later you will have to pay for it."

No one in the little Kentucky village knew what had become of Arthur Carroll for some time, with the exception of an aunt of Mrs. Carroll's, who was possessed of some property and who lived there. She knew, but she told nothing, probably because she had a fierce pride of family. After years the Carroll girls, Ina and Charlotte, had come back to their father's birthplace and attended a small school some three miles distant from the village, a select young ladies' establishment at which their mother had been educated, and they had visited rather often at their great-aunt Catherine's. After they had finished school, the great-aunt had paid the bills, although nobody knew it, not even the elderly sisters who kept the school, since the aunt lied and stated that Captain Carroll had sent the money. Arthur Carroll was called captain then, and nobody knew why, least of all Carroll himself. Suddenly he had been called captain, and after making a disclaimer or two at first, he had let it go; it was a minor dishonesty, and forced upon him in a measure. The old aunt calmly stated that he had joined the army, been rapidly promoted, and had resigned. People laughed a little, but not to her face. Besides, she had stated that Arthur was a very rich man, and much thought of among the Yankees, and nobody was in a position to disprove that. Certainly when the feminine Carrolls visited in the old place, their appearance carried out the theory of riches. They were very well dressed, and they looked well fed, with that placid, assured air which usually comes only from the sense of possession.

The feminine Carrolls had been speaking of this old aunt that spring day as they sat idly in the little green-curtained temple beside the pond. They had indulged in a few low, utterly gentle, and unmalicious laughs of reminiscence at some of her eccentricities; then they had agreed that she was a good old soul, and said no more of her, but gazed with languorous delight at the spring scene misty with green and rose and gold like the smoke of some celestial fire.

Through the emerald dazzle of the trailing willow-boughs could be seen a small, blooming apple-tree, and a bush full of yellow flowers. Miss Anna Carroll and Ina held books in their laps, but they never looked in them. They were all very well dressed and they wore quite a number of fine jewels on their hands and at their necks, particularly Mrs. Carroll. Her stones, though only of the semi-precious kind, were very beautiful, amethysts which had belonged to a many-times-removed creole grandmother of hers, and the workmanship of whose fine setting dated back to France, and there was a tradition of royal ownership. Mrs. Carroll had a bracelet, a ring, a brooch, and a necklace. The stones, although deeply tinted, showed pink now instead of purple. In fact, they seemed to match the soft, rose-tinted India silk which she wore.

"Amy's amethysts match colors like chamellons," said Ina. "Look how pink they are."

"Lovely," said Charlotte, gazing admiringly. "The next time I go to a dance, you promised I should wear the necklace, Amy, dear."

"You will not go to a dance for a long time in Banbridge, sweet, I fear," said Mrs. Carroll, with loving commiseration.

"Somebody will call soon, and we shall be asked to something," said Charlotte, with conviction.

"Nobody has called yet," Ina said.

"We have only been here three weeks," said Miss Anna Carroll, who was a beautiful woman, and, but for a certain stateliness of carriage, might have seemed but little older than her elder niece.

"Somebody may be calling this afternoon," said Ina, "and the maid has gone out, and we should not know they called."

"Oh, let them leave their cards," said Mrs. Carroll, easily. "That is the only way to receive calls, and make them. If one could only know when people would be out, but not have them know you knew, always — that would be lovely — and if one only knew when they were coming, so one could always be out — that would be lovelier still." Mrs. Carroll had a disjointed way of speaking when she essayed a long speech, that had almost an infantile effect.

"Amy, how very ungracious of you, dear," said Miss Anna Carroll. "You know you always love people when you really do meet them."

"Oh yes," replied Amy, "I know I love them."

Meantime, Mrs. Lee and Mrs. Van Dorn were ringing the door-bell of the Carroll house. They rang the bell and waited, and nobody came.

"Did you ring the bell?" asked Mrs. Van Dorn, anxiously.

"I thought I did. I pressed the button very hard."

"I didn't hear it. I think you had better ring again."

Mrs. Lee obediently pressed the bell again, and then both ladies heard distinctly the far-away tinkle in the depths of the house.

"I heard that," said Mrs. Lee.

"Yes, so did I. It rang that time."

Then the ladies waited again.

"Suppose you ring again," said Mrs. Van Dorn, and Mrs. Lee rang again. Then they waited again, straining their ears for the slightest sound in the house.

"I am afraid they are out," said Mrs. Van Dorn.

"So am I. It is such a lovely afternoon."

Mrs. Van Dorn, after they had waited a short time, put out her hand with a decisive motion, and rang the bell yet again.

"I'm going to make sure they are not at home," said she, "for I don't know when I shall get out calling again, and I always feel as if it was my duty to call on new-comers in the village pretty soon after they move in."

Then they waited again, but no one came. Once Mrs. Lee started and said she was sure she heard some one coming, but it was only the rumble of a train at a station two miles away.

"Shall we leave our cards?" said Mrs. Lee. "I don't suppose there is much use in waiting any longer, or ringing again."

Mrs. Van Dorn, who had been staring intently at the door, looked quickly at her companion with a curious expression. Her face had flushed.

"What is it?" asked Mrs. Lee. "You don't suppose any one is in there and not coming to the door?" Mrs. Lee had a somewhat suspicious nature.

"No; I don't think there is a soul in that house, but —"

"But what?"

"Nothing, only —"

"Only what?"

"Why, don't you see what they have done?"

"I am afraid I don't quite know what you mean," Mrs. Lee returned, in a puzzled way. It was quite evident that Mrs. Van Dorn wished her to grasp something which her own mind had mastered, that she wished it without further explanation, and Mrs. Lee felt bewilderedly apologetic that she could not comply.

"Don't you see that they have gone off and left the front door unlocked?" said Mrs. Van Dorn, with inflections of embarrassment, eagerness, and impatience. If she and Mrs. Lee had been, as of yore, school-children together, she would certainly have said, "You ninny!" to finish.

"Why!" returned Mrs. Lee, with a sort of gasp. She saw then that the front door was not only unlocked, but slightly ajar. "Do you suppose they really are not at home?" she whispered.

"Of course they are not at home."

"Would they go away and leave the front door unlocked?"

"They have."

"They might be in the back part of the house, and not have heard the bell," Mrs. Lee said, with a curious tone, as if she replied to some un-spoken suggestion.

"I know this house as well as I do my own. You know how much I used to be here when the Ranger girls were alive. There is not a room in this house where anybody with ears can't hear the bell."

Still, Mrs. Van Dorn spoke in that curiously ashamed and indignant voice. Mrs. Lee contradicted her no further.

"Well, I suppose you must be right," said she. "There can't be any-body at home; but it is strange they went off and did not even shut the front door."

"I don't know what the Ranger girls would have said, if they knew it. They would have had a fit at the bare idea of going away for ever so short a time, and leaving the house and furniture alone and the door unlocked."

"Their furniture is here now, I suppose?"

"Yes, I suppose so — some of it, anyway, but I don't know how much furniture these people bought, of course."

"Mr. Lee said he heard they had such magnificent things."

"I heard so, but you hear a good deal that isn't so in Banbridge!"

"That is true. I suppose you knew the house and the Ranger girls' furniture so well that you could tell at a glance what was new and what wasn't?"

"Yes, I could."

As with one impulse both women turned and peered through a green maze of trees and bushes at Samson Rawdy, several yards distant.

"Can you see him?" whispered Mrs. Lee.

"Yes. I think he's asleep. He is sitting with his head all bent over."

"He is — not — looking?"

"No."

Mrs. Lee and Mrs. Van Dorn regarded each other. Both looked at once ashamed and defiant before the other, then into each pair of eyes leaped a light of guilty understanding and perfect sympathy. There are some natures for whom curiosity is one of the master passions, and the desire for knowledge of the affairs of others can become a lust, and Mrs. Lee and Mrs. Van Dorn were of the number. Mrs. Van Dorn gave her head in her best calling-bonnet a toss, and the violets, which were none too securely fastened, nodded loosely; then she thrust her chin forward, she sniffed like a hunting-hound on the scent, pushed open the front-door, and entered, with Mrs. Lee following. As Mrs. Van Dorn entered, the violets on her bonnet became quite detached and fell softly to the floor of the porch, but neither of the ladies noticed.

Mrs. Lee, in particular, had led a monotonous life, and she had a small but intense spirit which could have weathered extremes. Now her faculties seemed to give a leap; she was afraid, but there was distinct rapture in her fear. She had not been so actively happy since she was a child and had been left at home with the measles one Sunday when the rest of the family had gone to church, and she had run away and gone wading in the brook, at the imminent risk not only of condign punishment, but of the measles striking in. She felt now just as then, as if something terrible and mysterious were striking in, and she fairly smacked her soul over it.

Mrs. Lee no longer shrank; she stood up straight; she also thrust her chin forward; her nose sharpened, her blue eyes contracted under her light brows. She even forgot her rôle of obligation, and did not give Mrs. Van Dorn the precedence; she actually pushed before her. Mrs. Van Dorn had closed the front door very softly, and they stood in a long, narrow hall, with an obsolete tapestry carpet, and large-figured gold and white paper revealing its gleaming scrolls in stray patches of light. Mrs. Lee went close to an old-fashioned black-walnut hat-tree, the one article of furniture besides a chair in the hall.

"Was this theirs?" she whispered to Mrs. Van Dorn.

Mrs. Van Dorn nodded.

Mrs. Lee deliberately removed the nice white kid glove from her right hand, and extending one small taper forefinger, rubbed it over the surface of the black-walnut tree; then she pointed meaningly at the piece of furniture, which plainly, even in the half-light, disclosed an unhousewifely streak. She also showed the dusty forefinger to the other lady, and they both nodded with intense enjoyment.

Then Mrs. Lee folded her silk skirts tightly around her and lifted them high above her starched white petticoat lest she contaminate them in such an untidy house; Mrs. Van Dorn followed her example, and they tiptoed into the double parlors. They were furnished, for the most part, with the pieces dating back to the building of the house, in one of the ugliest eras of the country, both in architecture and furniture. The ceilings in these rather small square rooms were so lofty that one was giddy with staring at the elaborate cornices and the plaster centrepieces. The mantels were all of massively carved marble, the windows were few and narrow, the doors multitudinous, and lofty enough for giants. The parlor floor was carpeted with tapestry in enormous designs of crimson roses, in deliriums of arabesques, though there were a few very good Eastern rugs. The furniture was black-walnut, upholstered in crimson plush; the tables had marble tops; the hangings were lace under heavily fringed crimson lambrequins dependent from massive gilt mouldings. There were a bronze clock and a whatnot and a few gilt-framed oil-paintings of the conventional landscape type, contemporary with the furniture in American best parlors. Still, there were a few things in the room which directly excited comment on the part of the visitors. Mrs. Lee pointed at some bronzes on the shelf.

"Those are theirs, aren't they?" said she.

"Yes, the Ranger girls had some very handsome Royal Worcester vases. I guess James Ranger saw to it that those weren't left here."

Mrs. Van Dorn eyed the bronzes with outward respect, but she did not admire them. Banbridge ladies, as a rule, unless they posed, did not admire bronzes. She also viewed with some disapproval a number of exquisite little Chinese ivory carvings on the whatnot. "Those are theirs," said she. "The Ranger girls had some handsome bound books and a silver card-receiver, and a bust of Clytie on top of the whatnot. I suppose these are very expensive; I have always heard so. I never priced any, but it always seemed to me that they hardly showed the money."

"I suppose they have afternoon tea," said Mrs. Lee, regarding a charming little inlaid tea-table, decked with Dresden.

"Perhaps so," replied Mrs. Van Dorn, doubtfully. "But I have noticed that when tea-tables are so handsome, folks don't use them. They are more for show. That cloth is beautiful."

"There is a tea-stain on it," declared Mrs. Lee, pointing triumphantly.

"That is so," assented Mrs. Van Dorn. "They must use it." She looked hard at the stain on the tea-cloth. "It's a pity to get tea on such a cloth as that," said she. "It will never come out."

"Oh, I don't believe that will trouble them much," said Mrs. Lee, with soft maliciousness. She indicated with the pointed toe of her best calling-shoe, a hole in the corner of the resplendent Eastern rug.

"Oh," returned Mrs. Van Dorn.

"I know it is considered desirable to have these Oriental things worn," said Mrs. Lee, "but there is no sense in letting an expensive rug like this wear out, and no good house-keeper would."

"Well, I agree with you," said Mrs. Van Dorn.

Presently they passed on to the other rooms. They made a long halt in the dining-room.

"That must be their solid silver," said Mrs. Van Dorn, regarding rather an ostentatious display on the sideboard.

"The idea of going away and leaving all that silver, and the doors unlocked!" said Mrs. Lee.

"Evidently they are people so accustomed to rich things that they don't think of such risks," said Mrs. Van Dorn, with a curious effect of smacking her lips over possessions of her own, instead of her neighbors. She in reality spoke from the heights of a small but solid silver service, and a noble supply of spoons, and Mrs. Lee knew it.

"I suppose they must have perfectly beautiful table-linen," remarked Mrs. Lee, with a wistful glance at the sideboard-drawers.

"Yes, I suppose so," assented Mrs. Van Dorn, with a half-sigh. Her eyes also on the closed drawers of the sideboard, were melancholy, but there was a line which neither woman could pass. They could pry about another woman's house in her absence, but they shrank from opening her drawers and investigating her closets. They respected all that was covered from plain sight. Up-stairs it was the same. Things were strewn about rather carelessly, therefore they saw more than they would otherwise have done, but the closet-doors and the bureau-drawers happened to be closed, and those were inviolate.

"If all their clothes are as nice as these, they must have wardrobes nicer than any ever seen in Banbridge," said Mrs. Lee, fingering delicately a lace-trimmed petticoat flung over a chair in one of the bedrooms. "This is real lace, don't you think so, Mrs. Van Dorn?"

"I don't think. I know," replied Mrs. Van Dorn. "They must have elegant wardrobes, and they must be very wealthy people. They —" Suddenly Mrs. Van Dorn cut her remarks short. She turned quite pale and clutched at her companion's silk-clad arm. "Hush!" she whispered. "What was that?"

Mrs. Lee, herself ashy white, looked at her. Both had distinctly heard a noise. Now they heard it again. The sound was that of footsteps, evidently those of a man, in the lower hall.

"What shall we do? Oh, what shall we do?" said Mrs. Lee, in a thin whisper. She trembled so that she could scarcely stand.

Mrs. Van Dorn, trying to speak, only chattered. She clutched Mrs. Lee harder.

"Is there a back staircase? Oh, is there?" whispered Mrs. Lee. "Is there?" The odor of a cigar stole softly through the house. "I can smell his cigar," whispered Mrs. Lee, in an agony.

Mrs. Van Dorn pulled herself together. She nodded, and began pulling Mrs. Lee towards the door.

"Oh," panted Mrs. Lee, "anything except being caught up-stairs in their bedrooms! They might think — anything."

"Hurry!" hissed Mrs. Van Dorn. They could hear the footsteps very distinctly, and the cigar-smoke made them want to cough. Holding their silk skirts like twisted ropes around them so they should not rustle, still clinging closely one to the other, the two women began slowly moving, inch by inch, through the upper hall, towards the back stairs. These they descended in safety, and emerged on the lower hall.

They were looking for a rear door, with the view of a stealthy egress and a skirting of the bushes on the lawn unobserved until they should gain the shelter of the carriage, when there was a movement at their backs, and a voice observed, "Good-afternoon, ladies," and they turned, and there was Captain Arthur Carroll. He was a man possibly well over forty, possibly older than that, but his face was as smooth as a boy's, and he was a man of great stature, with nevertheless a boyish cant to his shoulders. Captain Arthur Carroll was a very handsome man, with a viking sort of beauty. He was faultlessly dressed in one of the lightest of spring suits and a fancy waistcoat, and he held quite gracefully the knot of violets which had fallen from Mrs. Van Dorn's bonnet.

The two stood before him, gasping, coloring, trembling. For both of them it was horrible. All their lives they had been women who had held up their heads high in point of respectability and more. None was above them in Banbridge, no shame of wrong-doing or folly had ever been known by either of them, and now both their finely bonneted heads were in the dust. They stood before this handsome, courteously smiling gentleman and were conscious of a very nakedness of spirit. Their lust of curiosity was laid bare, they were caught in the act. Mrs. Van Dorn opened her mouth, she tried to speak, but she only made a strange, croaking sound. Her face was now flaming. But Mrs. Lee was pale, and she stood rather unsteadily.

Arthur Carroll at first looked merely bewildered. "Aren't the ladies at home?" said he. "Have you seen the ladies?" He glanced at Mrs. Van Dorn's deflowered bonnet, and extended the bunch of violets. "Yours, I think," he said. Mrs. Van Dorn took them with an idiotic expression, and he asked again if they had seen the ladies.

The spectacle of two elderly, well-dressed females of Banbridge quaking before him in this wise, and of their sudden appearance in his house, was a mystery too great to be grasped at once even by a clever man, and he was certainly a clever man. So he stared for a second, while the two remained standing before him, holding their card-cases in their shaking, white-gloved fingers, and Mrs. Van Dorn with the violets; then suddenly an expression of the most delighted comprehension and amusement overspread his face.

"Oh," he said, politely, with a great flourish, as it were of deference, "the ladies are not in. They will be exceedingly sorry to have missed your call. But will you not come in and sit down?"

Mrs. Van Dorn gained voice enough to gasp that she thought they must go. Captain Carroll stood back, and the two women, pressing closely together, tottered through the hall towards the front door.

Captain Carroll followed, beaming with delighted malice. "I hope you will call again, when the ladies are home," he said to Mrs. Van Dorn, whom he recognized as the leader.

She made an inarticulate attempt at "Thank you." She was making for the door, like a scared hare to the entrance of its cover.

"But I have not your names, ladies, that I may inform Mrs. Carroll who has called?" said Captain Carroll, in his stingingly polite voice.

Both women looked over their shrinking shoulders at him at that. Suddenly the hideous consequences of it all, the afterclap, sounded in their ears. That was the end of their fair fame in Banbridge, in their world. Life for them was over. Their faces, good, motherly, elderly village faces, after all, were pitiful; the shame in them was a shame to see, so ignominious was it. They stood convicted of such a mean fault, that the shame was the meaner also.

Suddenly Mr. Carroll's face changed. It became broadly comprehensive, so generously lenient that it was fairly grand. A certain gentleness also was evident, his voice was kind.

"Never mind, ladies," said Arthur Carroll. "There is really very little use in your telling me your names, because my memory is so bad. I remember neither names nor faces. If I should meet you on the street, and should fail to recognize you on that account, I trust that you will pardon me. And —" said Captain Carroll, "on that account, I will not say anything about your call to the ladies of my family; I should be sure to get it all wrong. We will wait, and trust that you will find them at home the next time you call. Good-afternoon, ladies." Captain Carroll had further mercy. He allowed the ladies to leave the house unattended and to dive desperately into the waiting coach.

"Home at once," Mrs. Van Dorn cried, hoarsely, to Samson Rawdy, waking from his nap in some bewilderment.

Captain Carroll was standing on the porch with a compound look of kindest pity and mirth on his face when the Carroll ladies came strolling round that way from the pond. He kissed them all, as was his wont; then he laughed out inconsequently.

"What are you laughing at, dear?" asked Amy.

"At my thoughts, sweetheart."

"What are your thoughts, daddy?" asked Charlotte.

"Thoughts I shall never tell anybody, honey," he replied, with another laugh. And Captain Arthur Carroll never did tell.

CHAPTER III

History often repeats itself where one would least expect it, and the world-old tide of human nature has a way of finding world-old channels. Therefore it happened in Banbridge, as in ancient times, that there was a learned barber, or perhaps, to be more strictly accurate, a barber who thought that he was learned. He would have been entirely ready, had his customers coincided with his views, to have given his striped pole its old signification of the ribbon bandage which bound the arm of a patient after bleeding, and added surgery to his hair-cutting and his beard-shaving. John Flynn had the courage of utter conviction as to his own ability to master all undertakings at which he chose to tilt. An aspiration once conceived, he never parted with, but held to it as a part of his life. Non-realization made not the slightest difference. His sense of time as a portion of eternity never left him, and therefore his patience under tardy fulfilment of his desires never faltered. Some ten years before, he decided that he would at some earlier or later date become mayor of Banbridge, and his decision was still impregnable. After every new election of another candidate, he begged his patrons for their votes another time, and was not in the least disturbed nor daunted that they had failed in their former promises. Flynn's good-nature was as unfaltering as his self-esteem, perhaps because of his self-esteem. He only smiled with fatuous superiority when from time to time, after the elections, his patrons would chaff him about his failure to secure the mayoralty. They did so with more effect since there were always among the horse-players on such occasions a few who would cast votes for the barber, esteeming it as a choice and perennial joke, and his reading his name among the unsuccessful candidates served to foster his delusion and keep Flynn's ambition alive.

One Sunday, shortly after the Carrolls had moved to Banbridge, John Flynn was shaving Jacob Rosenstein, who kept the principal dry-goods store of the village, and a number of men were sitting and lounging about, waiting their turns. Flynn's shop was on the main street in the centre of the business district — his shop, or his "Tonsorial Parlor," as his sign had it. It was quite an ornate establishment. There was a lace lambrequin in the show-window, a palm in each corner, between which stood a tank of goldfish, and below the lace lambrequin swung a gilt cage containing an incessantly hopping, though silent, yellow canary.

Flynn was intensely proud and fond of the establishment, and was insulted if it was alluded to as a barbershop. He himself never even thought of it, much less spoke of it, as such. "Well, I must be going to the 'Parlor,'" he would say when setting out to business. He was unmarried, and lived in a boarding-house.

As Flynn shaved Rosenstein, who was naturally speechless, his landlady's husband, Billy Amidon, was talking a good deal. Amidon was always shaved for nothing, in consideration of the fact that his wife supported him with board money, and the barber had an undefined conviction that it was mean to take it back after he had just paid it. Amidon was a notorious talker, and was called a very "dry sort of man," which, in the village vernacular, signified that he was esteemed a wit.

"Well," he said to another man, who was leaning with a relaxation of all his muscles against the little strip of counter, which contained a modest assortment of hair-oils and shaving-brushes and soaps which nobody was ever seen to buy — "well, John has lost ten pounds since the election, Tappan."

Tappan ran a milk-route between Banbridge and Ardmoor, a little farming-place six miles out. Tappan was an Ardmoor man. His milk-wagon stood in front of the "Tonsorial Parlor." He had a drink of beer at Frank Steinbach's saloon next door, and now was waiting for his Sunday shave before going home. His milk-peddling was over for the day. He was a hard-working-man, and had been on the road since four o'clock. He had a heavy look about his eyes, and he greeted Amidon's facetiousness with a weary and surly hitch.

"Has he?" he replied, indifferently.

But a very young, very small man, sitting in one of the "Parlor" arm-chairs, laughed like a child, with intense enjoyment. "Yep," he said, "I've noticed that. As much as ten pounds has went since election, sure."

"Shet up," replied Flynn, carefully scraping his patron's face. He said "Shet up" with an expression of foolish pride. The postmaster of Banbridge, who was sitting somewhat aloof and held himself with a constraint of exclusiveness (he was new to his office and had not yet lost the taste of its dignity), laughed.

"Let me see, how many votes did you have this year, John?" he asked, condescendingly.

"Five," replied John, with open exultation.

"Now, John, why didn't you get more than that, I'd like to know?"

Flynn laughed knowingly. "Oh," he said, "it's the old story — not money enough."

"But a lot promised they'd vote for you, didn't they, John?" persisted the postmaster, Sigsbee Ray, with a wink of humorous confidence at the others.

"Yep, but damme, who expects anybody to keep an election promise if he ain't paid for it? I ain't unreasonable. What's elections for? You wait."

"Haven't you given up yet, John?"

"Well, I guess not. You wait."

"Say, John," interposed Amidon, "how much did you pay them five what voted for you this year, hey?"

Flynn looked up from Rosenstein's belathered face with a burst of simple triumph. "I didn't pay any of them a penny," said he. "There is damn fools everywhere, and you wait," said he, "an' see ef there ain't more come to light next time. I'll fetch it yet, along of the fools, an' ef I can raise a leetle money, an' I begin to see my way clear to that."

"How's that?" John was asked by the small young man.

"I'm layin' low 'bout that," replied John, mysteriously.

"Now, John," said the postmaster, "you wouldn't lay low if there was a good chance to make some money, and not give us poor devils a chance?"

The postmaster spoke consciously. He expected what came, the buzz of remonstrance at his classing himself in his new office with poor devils.

"You'd better talk about poor devils," growled the milkman, Tappan. "You'd better talk. Huh! here you be, don't hev to git to work till eight o'clock, an' quittin' at eight nights, and fifteen hundred a year. You'd better talk, Mr. Ray. If you was a man gittin' up at three of a winter's mornin', and settin' out with a milk-route at four, an' makin' 'bout half a penny a quart, an' cussed at that 'cause it ain't all cream — if you was as dead tired as I be this minute you might talk."

"Well, I'm willing to allow that I am not as hard pushed as you are," said the postmaster, with magnanimous humility.

"You'd better. Poor devils, huh! I guess I know what poor devils be, and the hell they're in. Bet your life I do. Huh!"

"I'm a poor devil 'nough myself, when it comes to that," said Amidon, "but I reckon you kin speak for yourself when it comes to talkin' about bein' in hell, Tappan. Fur's I'm concerned, I'm findin' this a purty comfortable sort of place."

Amidon was a tall man, and he stretched his length luxuriously as he spoke. Tappan eyed him malignantly. He was not a pleasant-tempered man, and now he was both weary and impatient of waiting for his turn with the barber.

"I should think any man might be comfortable, ef he had a wife takin' boarders to support him, but mebbe if she was to be asked to tell the truth, she'd tell a different story," he said. Tappan spoke in a tone of facetious rage, and the others laughed, all except the barber. He had a curious respect for his landlady's husband.

"Ef a lady has the undisposition to let her husband subside on her bounty, it is between them twain. Who God has joined together, let no man set asunder," said he, bombastically, and even the surly milkman, and Rosenstein under his manipulating razor, when a laugh was dangerous, laughed. John Flynn, when he waxed didactic, and made use of large words and phrases, was the comic column of Banbridge.

Amidon, thus defended, chuckled also, albeit rather foolishly, and slouched to the door. "Guess I'll drop up and git the Sunday paper. I'll be in later on, John," he mumbled. He had the grace to be somewhat ashamed both by the attack and by the defence, and was for edging out, but stopped on the threshold of the door, arrested by something which the small man said.

"Talkin' about poor devils, there's one man in Banbridge ain't no poor devil. S'pose you know we've got a J. P. Morgan right amongst us?"

"Who?" asked the postmaster; and Amidon, directly now the conversation was thoroughly shifted from himself, returned to his former place.

"I know who he means," said he, importantly. "Oh, it's the man what's rented the Ranger place. They say he's a millionaire."

The milkman straightened himself interestedly. "I rather guess he is," said he. "They take two quarts of cream every morning, and three quarts of milk."

"Lord!" said the barber, gaping over his patron's head. "Lord!"

Although very short and slight, the barber had a large face, simple, amiable with a smirk of conceit as to the lower part; his forehead was very large and round, as was his head, and his blue eyes were very placid, even beautiful. The barber never laughed.

"Two quarts of cream!" said the small man. "Whew!"

"He must be rich if he takes all that cream," said the postmaster. "A half a pint a day about breaks me, but my wife must have it for her coffee."

Rosenstein had so far got his freedom of speech, for the barber had never ceased operation to speak, though rather guardedly. "He must be rich," he said. "Any man in Banbridge that buys as much as he does from a store in the place, an' wants his bills regular every Saturday night, has got somethin'."

"Has he paid 'em?" asked the postmaster.

"All except the last one, an' that he didn't pay because I couldn't cash a check for five hundred and give him the balance. 'Lord, sir,' says I, 'ef you want a check of that value cashed, you'll have to go to John Wanamaker. That's as much as I take in Banbridge in a whole year.' 'Well, mebbe you'll do better this year,' says he, laughing, and goes out. He's a fine-spoken man, an' it was a lucky day for Banbridge when he come here."

"He don't buy many postage-stamps," said the postmaster, thoughtfully, "but he asked me if I should be able to let him have as much as ten dollars' worth at a time, ef he wanted 'em, an' I said I should, an' I've just ordered in more. An' he has a big mail."

The barber had been opening his mouth and catching his breath preparatory to speaking and saying more than any of them. Now he spoke: "That man's wuth a mighty lot of money now," said he, "but what he's wuth now ain't nothin' to what he's goin' to be wuth some day."

"What do you mean, John?" asked Amidon, patronizingly.

"Well, now, I'll tell you what I mean. That man, it's Cap. Carroll what's just arraigned to Banbridge that you're all talkin' about, ain't it?"

"Yes. Go ahead."

"Well, now, Cap. Carroll is agoin' to be one of them great clapatalists, ef he ain't now," he said.

"How?"

"Well, he got holt of some stock that's goin' to bust the market and turn Wall Street into a mill-stream in less than a year, ef it keeps on as it has went so fur."

"What is it?" asked the small man.

The milkman sighed wearily. "Oh, slow up yer jaw, and gimme a chance sometime," he growled. "I want to git home an' git my breakfast. I'm hungry."

Flynn began hurriedly finishing off Rosenstein, talking with no less eagerness as he did so. "Well, it's Bonaflora mining-stock, ef you want to know," he said, importantly.

"Where is it?" asked the postmaster, with a peculiar smile.

"Out West somewhere. It ain't but fifty cents a share, an' it's goin' up like a skyrocket, an' there's others. There's a new railroad out there, an' other mines, an' a new invention for makin' fuel out of coal-dust, an' some other things."

"Is Captain Carroll the president of them?" asked the small man, with an impressed air. He was very young, and eager-looking, and very shabby. He grubbed on a tiny ancestral farm, for a living for himself and wife and four children, young as he was. He had never had enough to eat, at least of proper food. He did not come to the "Tonsorial Parlor" to be shaved, for he hacked away at his innocent cheeks at home with his deceased father's old razor, but he loved a little gossip. In fact, John Flynn's barbershop was his one dissipation. Sometimes he looked longingly at a beer-saloon, but he had no money, unless he starved Minna and the children, and for that he was too good and too timid. His Minna was a stout German girl, twice his size, and she ruled him with a rod of iron. She did not approve of the barbershop, and so the pleasure had something of the zest of a forbidden one.

Every Sunday he was at his wit's end, which was easily reached, to invent a suitable excuse for his absence. Today it had been to see if Mrs. Amidon did not want to buy some apples. Some of their last winter's store had been miraculously preserved, and Minna saw the way to a few pennies thereby. He could quite openly say that he had been to the barbershop today, having seen Amidon there, therefore he was quite easy in his mind, and leaned back in his chair with perfect content. One of the children at home cried all the time. A yawning mouth of wrath at existence was about all he ever saw of that particular baby, and Minna almost always scolded, and this was a haven of peace to little Willy Eddy.

Here he felt like a man among men; at home he felt like nothing at all among women. The children were all girls. Sometimes he wondered if a boy-baby might not have been a refuge. He was not very clean; his hands were still stained with picking over potatoes the day before; his shoulders in their rusty coat had a distinct hunch; but he was radiantly happy talking of the rich Captain Carroll. He seemed to taste the honey of the other man's riches and importance in his own mouth. Willy Eddy did not know the meaning of envy. He had such a fund of sympathetic imagination that he possessed the fair possessions of others like a child with fairy tales.

"Is he president of all of them?" asked little Willy Eddy, with gusto, and looked as if he himself held them all in his meagre potato-stained hands.

"No," replied the barber, with importance — "no, he's more than a president. A president is nothin' except a figger-head. I don't care what he's president of, whether it is of this great country or of railroads or what not. They could git along without the president, but they can't without this gentleman. He's the promoter."

"Oh!" said the small man.

The milkman sighed wrathfully again. "Oh, hang it all!" he said. "I've seed promoters. It's mostly their own pockets they promote."

"Well, I don't know," said the postmaster, as one with authority. "I don't know. Captain Carroll was in the office the other day, and we had a little talk, and it struck me that some of the ventures he is interested in were quite promising. And it is different with a man of his wealth. When a poor man takes up anything of the kind, you can suspect, but this is different. He said to me that he had no occasion, so far as the money was concerned, to turn his finger over for any of them or to open his mouth concerning them. He said he would not be afraid to stake every dollar he had in the world on them if it was necessary."

Flynn had daintily anointed Rosenstein's shaven face with witch-hazel and was now dusting it with powder. Tappan was slouching towards the chair.

"Have you bought some of the stock?" the barber asked, abruptly, of the postmaster, who smiled mysteriously and hedged.

"Well, maybe I have, and maybe again I haven't," said he. "Have you, John?"

"Not yet," replied the barber. "I am deflecting upon the matter. It requires considerable loggitation when a man has penuriously saved a circumscribed sum from the sweat of his brow."

"That's so. Don't be rash, John," said Amidon.

It was not especially funny, but since Amidon intended it to be, they all obligingly laughed, except Tappan, who set himself with a grunt in the chair and had the white sheet of which Rosenstein had been denuded tied around his neck.

Rosenstein, who was a lean man, with a much-lined face, cast a glance at himself in the looking-glass, and heaved an odd sigh as he turned away to get his hat.

"You don't seem to be much stuck on your looks, old man," remarked Amidon.

Rosenstein cast a perfectly good-humored but rather melancholy look at Amidon. "No; I never was," he replied, soberly. "Can't remember when I wouldn't have preferred to meet some other fellow in the looking-glass. It's such an awful thing, the intimacy with himself that's forced on a man when he comes into this world."

"That's so," assented Amidon, rather stupidly, but he was not to be abashed with the other man's metaphysics. Rosenstein did credit to his German ancestry at times, and was then in deep waters for his village acquaintances.

"Who would you ruther meet in the lookin'-glass than yerself?" pursued Amidon.

"Not you," replied Rosenstein, with unexpected repartee, and was going out amid a chorus of glee at Amidon's discomfiture when another man darkened the doorway, and the storekeeper fell back as Captain Carroll entered amid a sullen silence.

The postmaster rose, and in a second the small man and Amidon followed his example. Carroll greeted them all with a cordiality which had in it a certain implication of admiring confidence. Not a man there but felt at once that this new-comer had a most flattering recognition of himself in particular, to the exclusion of all the others. It was odd how he contrived to produce this impression, but produce it he did. It was Arthur Carroll's great charm, the great secret of a remarkable influence over his fellow-men. He appealed with consummate skill to the selfish side of every one with whom he came in contact, he exalted him in his own eyes far above the masses with whom he was surrounded, by who could tell what subtle alchemy. Each man preened unconsciously his panoply of spiritual pride under this other man's gentle, courteous eyes. Even Rosenstein straightened himself. And besides, this was the respectful admiration which the man himself excited, by reason of his fine appearance and address, his good looks, his irreproachable clothes, and his reputed wealth.

Arthur Carroll made an entrance into the "Tonsorial Parlor." Moreover, the other men could see out in front of the establishment, the coach, the coachman in livery — the first livery on record as actually resident in Banbridge; liveries had passed through, but never before tarried — the fretting steeds with their glittering equipment. Around the coach had already gathered several small boys, huddled together, and transfixed with awe too deep for impudence.

Carroll, having greeted the men, said good-morning urbanely to the barber, who had ceased lathering Tappan and was looking at him indeterminately. It seemed dreadful to him that this great man should have to wait for the milkman. The barber was a conservative to the core, and would speak of the laboring-classes and tradesmen as if he himself were on the other side of the highway from birth. Tappan himself, who, as said before, was naturally surly, was also a dissenter on principle, and had an enlarged sense of injury, had qualms at keeping waiting a man who patronized him to the extent of two quarts of cream and three quarts of milk daily. It was like quarrelling with his bread-and-butter, as he put it, when alluding to the affair later on.

"I ain't goin' through the world seein' no men as is better 'n I be," he said, "but there's jest this much about it, I ain't a fool, an' I know enough to open the door when a man wants to walk through to pay me some money. Ef Carroll hadn't been takin' that much cream and milk, I'd set there in that barber's-chair ef I'd had a year's beard to shave, an' I'd kept him waitin', and enjoyed it, but, as it was, I did what I did."

What Tappan did was to wave back Flynn's lathering-hand, and to say, rather splutteringly, that he would wait, "ef Captain Carroll was in a hurry."

But Captain Carroll was in no hurry, it seemed, and, moreover, gave the impression that if he had been about to catch a railroad train to keep an important business engagement, he would not have dreamed of thrusting himself in before the milkman with his milk all delivered. He, moreover, gave the impression that he considered the milkman a polished gentleman for his handsome offer, and all this without saying so much. Captain Carroll seated himself, and completed the impression by tendering everybody cigars. Then the "Tonsorial Parlor" and its patrons waiting for a Sunday-morning shave became a truly genteel function. Willy Eddy, who was dreamily imaginative, and read the Sunday papers when his Minna gave him a chance and did not chide him for the waste of money, remembered things he had read about the swagger New York clubs. He smoked away and made-believe he was a clubman, and enjoyed himself artlessly. The sun got farther around and the south window was a sheet of burning radiance. It became rather too warm, and on Carroll making a motion to move his chair into the shade, every other man moved into the sunshine, and sat sweltering and smoking in a fatuous vainglory. The canary bird hopped faster and faster. The goldfishes swam with a larger school of bright reflections. A bumblebee flew in the open window and buzzed dangerously near the hero's head. Willy Eddy rose and, ostentatiously, at his own risk, drove the intruder away, and was gratefully thanked. Truly hero-worship, while it is often foolish and fool-making, is not the worst sentiment of mankind. When the great man made a move to order his coachman to take the wonderful rig away, and drive, because the horses were restive and needed exercise, and he himself — the delicate humor of the thing — also needed exercise and would walk home, Amidon sped in his service as he had never sped in the service of the long-suffering wife, at that moment struggling painfully with the Sunday dinner, and bringing wood from the shed to replenish the fire.

Carroll did not need to lead up to his mining and other interests. The subject was broached at once by the others. The postmaster opened it. He spoke with less humility than the others, as being more on a footing of equality.

"Well, captain, heard lately from the Boniflora?" he asked, knowingly. And Carroll replied that he had received a letter from the manager the night before which gave most encouraging information concerning the prospects.

"Anything of the United Fuel?" continued the postmaster.

"Large block just sold, at an advance of six and three-eighths," replied Carroll, blowing the smoke from his mouth. Carroll inspired confidence by the very quietness and lack of enthusiasm with which he spoke of his enterprises. All his listeners thought privately that he was in no way anxious to sell his stock, after all. Perhaps, moreover, he did not intend to sell any but large blocks. Little Willy Eddy ventured to ask for information on the latter point.

"Mebbe you don't keer nothin' about sellin' of it unless it is in big lumps?" he queried, timidly. He was thinking of a matter of $250 which his father had saved from pension-money, and was still in the savings-bank. Carroll replied (but with the greatest indifference) that they often sold stock in very small blocks, and the confidence of them waxed apace. Amidon thought of a little money which his wife had saved from her boarders, and the barber immediately resolved to invest every cent he had in the United Fuel. Such was Captain Carroll's graciousness and urbanity that he idled away an hour in the barbershop, and the other men melted away, although reluctantly, from an atmosphere of such effulgence. The milkman's hollow stomach drove him home for his breakfast. Little Willy Eddy thought uneasily of his Minna, and took his departure. The postmaster had a Sunday mail to sort. And Amidon went out to get a drink of beer; Carroll's cigar had dried his throat. Carroll was shaven last, and Flynn did his best by him, even unto a new jar of cold cream, double the quantity of witch-hazel, and a waste of powder. Then after he had carefully adjusted his hat, and was at last about to go, Flynn stopped him.

"Beg your pardon, sir," said he, "but —"

"But what?" said Carroll, rather kindly.

The barber's lip was actually quivering. The magnitude and importance of what he was about to propose almost affected his weakly emotional nature to tears.

He finally made out to say, while tears were actually rolling down his cheeks under Carroll's puzzled regard, that he had $1000 which he had saved, and he would like to invest every penny of it in United Fuel. And before Carroll knew what he was at, he had actually produced $1000 in a bulky roll of much-befingered notes, from some hiding-place, and was waving them before Carroll's eyes.

"Here," said he, "here is the money. You may as well take it now. You can get the securities in New York tomorrow, and bring them out on the train. Here is the money. Take it."

Arthur Carroll did not move to take the money. He stood looking at the excited man with a curious expression. In fact, his face seemed to reflect the emotion of the barber's. His voice was a trifle husky.

"Is that all you have saved?" he asked.

"Every dollar," replied the barber, continuing to wave and thrust the bills, but he raised an edge of his apron to his eyes, overflowing with the stupendousness of it. "Every dollar. I might have saved more, but I've been laid up winters considerable with grippe, and folks don't like to be shaved by a grippy barber. Dunno's I blame 'em. I've had to hire, and hirin' comes high. I've had considerable to do for a widder with four children, too — she's my brother's widder — an', take it all together, I ain't been able to save another dollar. But that don't make no odds, as long as I'm going to double it in that stock of yourn. Take it."

Carroll backed away almost sternly. "I don't want your money," he said.

The barber stood aghast. Captain Carroll had actually a look of offence.

"I hope as I hain't done nothin' that ain't reg'lar," he stammered.

Captain Carroll stepped close to him. He laid one white long-fingered hand on the barber's white jacket-sleeve. He whispered with slyest confidence, although no one was within hearing:

"You keep that money a little while longer," he whispered. "I wouldn't say it to every man, but I will to you. There's going to be a lawsuit, and the stock may drop a point or two. It won't drop much, and it will recover more than it loses, but then is the time to buy, especially when you want a big block, and — I'll let you know."

"Thank you, thank you," said the barber, restoring the bills to a greasy old pocket-book. He was faint with gratitude. "All right," he said, and he nodded and winked with intensest comprehension. "All right. You let me know."

"Yes, I'll let you know when it is best to invest," repeated Carroll. He turned on the threshold. "See here," he said, "if I were you, I'd put that money in a bank. I wouldn't keep it here."

"Oh, nobody knows it's here, except you, and you are safe, I ruther guess."

The barber laughed like a child. Carroll went out and passed up the street. He heard from the Episcopal church the sound of singing. Finally he left it behind. He was passing along a short extent where there were no houses. On one side there was a waste tract of land, and on the other a stretch of private grounds. The private grounds were bordered by a budding hedge, the waste lot bristled with strong young weeds. Carroll, as he swung along with his stately carriage of the head and shoulders, took out his pocket-book. It was an important-looking affair, the size of banknotes. He opened it. There was not a vestige of money within. He laughed a little softly to himself, and replaced it. He lived on a street which diverged at right angles from the main street. Just as he was about turning the corner, a runabout in which were seated two men passed him. It stopped, and the men turned and looked back at him. Then before Carroll turned the corner, one hailed him:

"Hullo!" he said.

"Hullo!" returned Carroll, and stood waiting while the man swung his trap round with cautious hisses — he drove a high-stepping mare.

"Are you a man by the name of Carroll?" said he, holding the fretting mare tightly, and seesawing the lines, as she tried to dart first one way, then the other.

Carroll nodded.

"Well, look a-here," said the man, "I heerd you wanted to buy some hosses."

"You heard rightly," said Carroll.

"Wall, I've got a pair that can't be beat. Kentucky bred, four-year-old, sound as a whip. Not an out."

"Are you a trader?"

"Yep. Hed them hosses in last week. New-Yorker jest sent for 'em, then he died sudden, and his heirs threw 'em on the market at a sacrifice."

Carroll looked at the men, and they looked at him. The two men in the runabout resembled each other, and were evidently brothers. Carroll's eyes on the men were sharp, so were theirs on him. Carroll's eyes were looking for knavery, and the men's were looking for suspicion of knavery.

"How much?" asked Carroll, finally.

The men looked at each other. One made a motion with his lips; the other nodded.

"Fifteen hundred," said the first speaker, "and damned cheap."

"Well, you can bring them around, and I'll look at them," said Carroll. "Any night after seven."

Carroll walked on, turning up the road which led to his own house, and the men whirled about again and then drove on, the mare breaking into a gallop.

CHAPTER IV

In Banbridge no one in trade was considered in polite society, with one exception. The exception was Randolph Anderson. Anderson had studied for the law. He had set up his office over the post-office, hung out his innocent and appealing little sign, and sat in his new office-chair beside his new desk, surrounded by the majesty of the lettered law, arranged in shelves in alphabetical order, for several years, during which his affairs were constantly on a descending scale. Then at last came a year when scarcely one client had darkened his doors except Tappan, who wanted to sue a delinquent customer and attach some of his personal property. After ascertaining that the personal property had been cannily transferred to the debtor's wife, he had told Anderson, upon the presentation of a modest bill, that he was a fraud and he could have done better himself. Beside this backward stroke of business, Anderson had that year a will to draw up, for which he was never paid, and had married a couple who had reimbursed him in farm produce. At the expiration of that year the lawyer, having to all intents and purposes been given up by the law, gave it up in his turn. Every cent of the money which he had inherited from his father had been expended. Nothing remained except his mother's small property, which barely sufficed to support her. Anderson then borrowed money from his uncle, who was well-to-do, giving him his note for three years, rented a store on Main Street, purchased a stock of groceries, and went into trade. His course made quite a sensation. He was the first Anderson in the memory of Banbridge, where the name was an old one, to be outside the genteel pale of a profession. His father had been a physician, his grandfather a clergyman.

"If my son had studied medicine instead of law, he could have at least subsisted upon the proceeds of his profession," his mother said, with the gentle and dignified dissent which was her attitude with regard to her son's startling move. "People are simply obliged by the laws of the flesh to go through measles and whooping-coughs and mumps, and they have to be born and die, and when they get in the way of microbes they have to be ill and they have to call in a physician, and some few of them pay him, so he can manage at least to live. Of course law is different. If people haven't any money they can forego quarrels, unless they are forced upon them. Quarrels are luxuries. It really began to seem to me that all the opportunity for a lawyer in Banbridge was in the simple line of suing some one for debt, and there is always that way, which does seem to me rather dishonest, of putting the property out of one's hands."

There was undoubtedly much truth in what Mrs. Sylvia Anderson said. She was a shrewd old woman, with such a softly feminine manner that she misled people into thinking the contrary. Banbridge folk rather pitied Randolph Anderson for having such a sweetly helpless and incapable mother, albeit very pretty and very much of a lady.

Mrs. Anderson was a large woman, but delicately articulated, with small hands, and such tiny feet that she toppled a little when she walked. Her complexion was like a child's, and she fluffed her thick white locks over her ears and swathed her throat high in soft laces, concealing all the aged lines in face and figure with innocent feminine arts.

Randolph adored his mother. He had never cared for any other woman. He had sat at his mother's little feet all his life, although he had at times his own masculine way, as in the matter of the deserting of his profession for trade. He had remained firm, although his mother had said much against it.

"Frankly, I do not approve of it, dear," she said. "I agree, but I do not approve. I do not like it, that you should desert the trodden path of your forebears. It is not so much that I am proud, but I am conservative. I believe there is a certain harmony between the man and the road his race have travelled. I believe he is a very sorry figure on another, especially if it be on a lower level."

"I don't think it is a question of level," said Randolph. "A road is simply a question of progress."

"Well, perhaps," said his mother, "but in that case the state of things is the same. A grocer would cut a sorry figure on your road, even if it ran parallel towards the same goal, and a lawyer would cut a sorry figure on a grocer's. Frankly, dear, I really doubt if you will make a good grocer."

Randolph laughed. "At least I hope I can earn our bread-and-butter," he said. Then he went on seriously. "It is just here," he said — "you and I are not sordid. Neither of us cares about money for itself, but here we are on this earth, with that existence which has its money price, and obligations imposed upon us. We cannot shirk it. We must live, and in order to live we must have a certain amount of money. Now all we have in this world for material goods is this old house and your little pittance. We have not a cent besides. If we were to try living on that, it would not last out your lifetime. If it would, I should not combat your prejudices, but we could lie on our oars and eat up the old place, and later on I would hustle for myself. But it will not. Now, I have demonstrated that I cannot earn anything by my profession. I have tried it faithfully and well. Last year I did not earn enough to pay my office rent. I never shall in Banbridge, and there is no sense whatever in my striking out in a new place with no prestige and no money. You and I simply want enough to live on, enough money to buy the wherewithal to keep the flame of life comfortably burning, and I can think of no other way than this grocery business. People must eat. You are certainly sure of earning something, if you offer people something they want. In my profession there is nothing that they do want."

"But your education," said his mother. She thought of the rows of law-books of whose contents she fondly believed her son a master.

"Oh, that is mine still," said Randolph, "but other people don't want it. There is no use, mother, in evading the question. We live in an age of market values. We must consider them. Butter and cheese have a sure market value, and the knowledge of the law in my head has not. Nobody wants it enough to pay anything for it, to give us a moneyed equivalent wherewith we may buy the things we need. Therefore, if nobody wants that, we must offer them something else. When it comes to the rights of our fellow-men to spend their own money as they choose, that is inalienable. It is about the most firmly established right in the country. No; people cannot be coerced into buying my little store of knowledge, therefore I will try them with my little store of butter and cheese and eggs and molasses."

Randolph Anderson laughed. Aside from regard for his mother's feelings, he had not the slightest scruple against his business venture. On the contrary, it rather amused him. He must have had a latent taste for business, for he quite enjoyed studying the markets and purchasing his stock in trade. He purchased wisely, too. He offered a choice stock of goods, or, rather, his two salesmen did. He himself did not sell much over his own counters, except in the case of a great rush of business. But it was not from the least sensation of superiority. It was merely because of a distrust of his own ability to acquit himself well in such a totally different branch of industry. Anderson was cast on unusually simple and ingenuous lines. Nobody would have believed it, but he was actually somewhat modest and shy before his own clerks, and realized sensitively his own lack of experience. So he had a way of subsiding when customers appeared, and retreating to his office in the rear of the building. He spent most of his time in this office. It was a very pleasant one, overlooking the river, on which steamboats and canal-boats travelled to the city. From Anderson's office the bank of red clay soil sloped to the water's edge. He could see the gleam of the current through the shag of young trees which found root in the unpromising soil. Now and then the tall mast of a sailing-vessel glided by, now the smoke-stack of a steamer. Often the quiet was broken by the panting breath of a tug. Often into his field of vision flapped the wet clothes from the line strung along the deck of a canal-boat. The canal ran along beside the regular current of the river, separated from it by a narrow tow-path. Farther down, the great railroad bridge crossed the stream, and at all hours he could catch the swift glisten of the train-windows as they shot past.

Anderson's office was about twelve by fourteen, and lined with shelves on two sides. On these he had books, not law-books. Those he had relegated to the library at home. He had probably in the depths of his consciousness a sensation of melancholy at the contemplation of those reminders of his balked career. No man, no matter how gracefully he may yield to it, cares to contemplate failures. He had filled these shelves with books of which he was fond, for daily reading. They were most of them old. He had little money with which to purchase new ones. He had been forced to rely upon those which his father and grandfather had accumulated. There were, however, a few recent and quite valuable books which he had acquired since his venture in trade, upon entomology, especially books upon butterflies. Since his retreat from the law he had developed suddenly, perhaps by the force of contrast, or the opposite swing of the pendulum, an overwhelming taste for those airy flowers of animated life. The two walls of the office not occupied with books were hung with framed specimens. He had also under the riverward window a little table equipped with the necessary paraphernalia for mounting them. Many a sunny day in the season he spent in the fields on this gentle hunt. There was a broad sill to the window, and upon it stood a box filled with green plants. When the season was enough advanced and the window always open, the trailing vines rooted in the box hung far down outside, and the women on the passing canal-boats looked up at them. The window-ledge was wide enough, moreover, for an old red cushion upon which slept in the sun when he was not afield for love or war or prey, a great cat striped like a tiger, with fierce green eyes, and a mighty purr of comfort, and a rounding back of affection for Anderson's legs when he talked to him.

Anderson had two comfortable old chairs in his office, and a goodly assortment of pipes, for he was a great smoker. He made tobacco a part of his grocery business, and had a strong sense of comfort in reflecting upon the unlimited supply. He had been forced, in the last days of his law-practice, to stint himself even in this creature comfort. On the whole, he was much happier when fairly established in trade than he had ever been before. He was so absorbed in his business (all the details of which he mastered), in his books, and his butterflies, that he saw very little of the people, and knew very little of what was going on in Banbridge, except through his mother. Mrs. Anderson, in spite of her years, and a certain lack of strength which had always hampered her, was quite prominent in Banbridge society. She was one of the old women whom young girls adore, even when the adoration is not increased by the existence of a marriageable son. Sometimes the old lady would regard an unmarried female-caller with a soft suspicion of ulterior motives, but she never whispered them to her son. Sylvia Anderson had a lovely, fine delicacy where the foibles of her own sex were concerned. She was so essentially feminine herself that she was never quite rid of her maiden sense of alienation even with her son. She would have been much happier with a daughter, although she was very fond of her son.

One afternoon in May, a short time after Mrs. Van Dorn and Mrs. Lee had made their circuit of calls which had included her, some other ladies were making the rounds in the calling-coach, which drew up before her door. There were three ladies, two of them unmarried. They were an elder aunt, her young unmarried niece, and a married lady who had been the girl friend of the aunt. They made a long call, and Mrs. Anderson entertained them with tea in her pink-and-gold china cups, with cream in the little family silver cream-jug, and with slices of pound-cake. It was an old custom of Mrs. Anderson's which she had copied all through her married life from Madam Anderson, Randolph's grandmother, the widow of old Dr. Anderson, the clergyman.

"I always make it a custom, my dear, to keep pound-cake on hand, and have some of the best green tea in the caddy, and then when callers come of an afternoon I can offer them some refreshment," she had said when her son's wife first came to live with her. So Mrs. Anderson had antedated the modern fashion in Banbridge, but she did not keep a little, ornate tea-table in her parlor. The cake and tea were brought in by the one maid on a tray covered with a polka-dotted damask.

This afternoon the callers had their cake and tea, and lingered long afterwards. Now and then Mrs. Anderson glanced imperceptibly at the window, thinking her son might pass. She regarded the unmarried aunt and the young niece with asides of reflection even while she talked to them. The niece was not pretty, but her bloom of youth under the roses of her spring hat was ravishing. The aunt had never been pretty; and, moreover, her bloom had gone, but she was well dressed, and her thin figure was full of grace. She sat in her chair with delicate erectness, the folds of her gray gown was disposed over her supple length of limb with charming effect. She also had a sort of eager, almost appealing amiability. It was as if she said:

"Yes, I know I am no longer young. I am not fair to see, but indeed I mean well by you. I would do much for you. I even love you. Cannot you love me for that?" and that was softly compelling.

Mrs. Anderson reflected that a man might easily admire either of these women. Her manner, in spite of herself, cooled towards them. She did not think of the third woman, who was married, except to ply her with cake and tea and inquire for her husband and children. The woman, after she had finished her cake and tea, sat sunken in her corsets, under her loosely fitting black silk, and looked stupidly amiable. She rose with a slight sigh of relief when at last the others made a motion to go. She thought of her supper at home, and the children long out of school. It was past supper-time for Banbridge. The sun was quite low. An hour ago a little herd of cows had pelted by in a cloud of dust, with great udders swinging perilously, going home to be milked.

"That Flannigan boy always runs those cows home," said the aunt, disapprovingly, as she passed the window.

"I have always heard it was bad for the milk," assented Mrs. Anderson.

Now that her callers were on the move, Mrs. Anderson was exceedingly cordial. She said something further about the quality of the cream obtained from the cows, and the aunt said yes, it was very good, although so dear. The old lady kissed both the aunt and the niece when they at last went out of the door, and said she was so glad that she was at home, and begged them to come again. She stood in the door watching them get into the coach. The young girl's face in the window, with her beflowered hat, a rose crowned with roses, in the dark setting of the window, was beautiful. Even the aunt's face, older and more colorless, except for an unlovely flush of excitement, was pathetically compelling and charmed. Mrs. Anderson, filling up the doorway with her stately bulk, swept around by her soft black draperies, her fair old face rising from a foam of lace, and delicately capped with lace, on which was a knot of palest lavender, stood in a frame of luxuriant Virginia-creeper, and smiled and nodded graciously to her departing guests, while wondering if they would meet her son coming home. After that followed a reflection as to the undesirability of either of them as a possible daughter-in-law.

Just as she was turning to enter the house, after the coach had rolled out of sight, she saw her son coming down the street under the green shade of the maples which bordered it. The mother went toddling on her tiny feet down the steps to the gate to meet her son. The house stood quite close to the road; indeed, only a little bricked-path separated it from the sidewalk. All the ground was at the sides and back. The house was a square old affair with a row of half-windows in the third-story, or attic, and considerable good old panel-work and ornamentation about it. On the right side of the house was a large old flower-garden, now just beginning to assert itself anew; on the left were the stable and some out-buildings, with a grassy oval of lawn in the centre of a sweep of drive; in the rear was a kitchen-garden and a field rising to the railroad, for railroads circled all Banbridge in their vises of iron arms. A station was only a short distance farther up this same street. As Mrs. Anderson stood waiting and her son was advancing down the street a train from the city rumbled past. When Randolph had come up, and they had both entered the house, a carriage passed swiftly and both saw it from the parlor window.

"Do you know who's carriage that is?" asked Mrs. Anderson. "It is something new in Banbridge, isn't it?"

"It belongs to those new people who have moved into the Ranger place," replied Randolph. He wore a light business-suit which suited him, and he looked like a gentleman, as much so as when he had come from a law-office instead of a grocery-store. Indeed, he had been much shabbier in the law-office and had not held his head so high. In the law-office he had constantly been confronted with the possibility of debt. Here he was free from it. He had been smoking, as usual, and there was about his garments an odor of mingled coffee and tobacco. He had been selling coffee, and grinding some. One of his two salesmen was ill, and that was why he was so late. The new carriage rolled silently on its rubber tires along the macadamized road; the high black polish and plate-glass flashed in the sunlight, the coachman in livery sat proudly erect and held his whip stylishly, the sleek horses pranced, seeming scarcely to touch the road with their dainty hoofs.

"Those are fine horses," said Randolph.

"Yes," assented his mother. "They must be very wealthy people, I suppose."

"It looks so," replied Randolph.

His mother, still staring out of the window, started. "Why," she said, "the coachman is turning around!"

"Perhaps he has forgotten something at the station," said Randolph.

"Why, it is stopping here!" cried Mrs. Anderson, wonderingly. The carriage indeed stopped just before the Anderson gate, and remained there perfectly still. The coachman gazed intently at the house, but made no motion to get down. At a window was seen a gentleman's face; past him the fresh face of a girl, also gazing. Randolph looked out, and the gentleman in the carriage made an imperious beckoning motion.

"Why, he is beckoning you!" said Mrs. Anderson, amazedly and indignantly.

Anderson moved towards the door.

"You are not going out when you are beckoned to in that way?" cried his mother.

Anderson laughed. "You forget, mother," he said, "that a grocer is at the beck and call of his patrons."

"I am ashamed of you!" she said, hotly, her fair old face flushing, "to have no more pride —"

Anderson laughed again. "I am too proud to have pride," he said, and went out of the room. He went leisurely down the steps, and crossed the little brick walk to the gate, and then approached the carriage. The gentleman inside, with what seemed an unpremeditated movement, raised his hat. Randolph bowed. Carroll smiled in the gentle, admiring way which he had.

"Perhaps I have made a mistake," he said, "but I was directed here. I was told that Anderson, who keeps the grocery, lives here."

"I am Anderson," replied Randolph, with dignity and a certain high scorn, and purposely leaving off the Mr. from his name.

Arthur Carroll no longer smiled, but his voice had a certain urbanity, although it rang imperiously. "Now, see here," he said. "I want to know why you did not do as I left instructions at your shop?"

"To what do you refer?" inquired Anderson, quietly.

"I want to know why you did not send in your bill last Saturday night, as I ordered." Carroll's voice was so loud that Mrs. Anderson, in the house, heard him distinctly through the open windows.

"I did not know that you had so ordered," replied Anderson, still quietly, with a slight emphasis on the ordered. He looked slightly amused.

"Well, I did. I told your clerk to be sure to send in my bills promptly every Saturday morning. I wish to settle weekly."

"The mistake was doubtless due to the fact that my clerk has been at home ill for the last three days," said Anderson. "This is the first time I have heard of your order."

"Well," said Carroll, "send it in at once now, and don't let it happen again."

Although the tone was harsh and the words were imperious, still they were not insolent. There was even an effect of *camaraderie* about them. At the last he flashed a quick smile at Anderson, which Anderson returned. He was dimly conscious all the time of Charlotte's very pretty face past her father's, peeping around his gray shoulder with a large-eyed, rather puzzled expression. Carroll nodded slightly after the smile, and told the coachman to go on, and the horses sprang forward after a delicate toss of their curving forelegs.

Randolph re-entered the house, and his mother, who was waiting, faced him with soft indignation.

"I must say, my son, that I am surprised that you submit to being addressed in such a fashion as that," she said, her blue eyes darkening at him.

Randolph laughed again. "There was no real insolence about it, after all, mother," he replied.

"It sounded so," said she.

"That was because you could not see his face," said Randolph. "He looked very amiable."

"He was angry because he did not get his bill Saturday?" said Mrs. Anderson, interrogatively.

"Yes. He must have given the order to Sam Riggs the day before he went home ill, I suppose."

"He must be a very wealthy man," said Mrs. Anderson. "It is rather good of him to be so anxious to pay his bill every week."

"Yes, it is a very laudable desire," said Randolph. "I only hope his ability may equal it."

His mother looked at him with quick surprise. "Why, you surely don't think —" she said.

"I think nothing. The man is all right, so far as I know. He seems a gentleman, and if he is well off he is a very desirable acquisition to Banbridge."

"Who was that with him in the coach?" asked Mrs. Anderson.

"One of his daughters, I should judge. I hear he has two."

"Pretty?"

"Well, I hardly know. Have you had any callers?"

"Yes. I suppose you met them. They made a very long call."

"You mean the Egglestons?"

"Yes, Miss Josie and little Agnes Eggleston and Mrs. Monroe. They stayed here over an hour. I thought you would meet them."

"Yes, I met them just as I turned from Main Street," replied Randolph, soberly, but he was inwardly amused. He understood his mother. But there was something which he did not tell her concerning his experience with the new-comers, the Carrolls. Shortly, she went out to give some directions about tea, and Randolph, sitting beside a window in the parlor with an evening paper, drew from his pocket a letter just received in the mail, and examined it again. It was from a city bank, and it contained a repudiated check for ten dollars, made out by Captain Arthur Carroll, and which Anderson had cashed a few days previous at the request of the pretty young girl in the carriage, who tonight had sat there looking at him and did not speak, either because she had forgotten his face as he did her the little favor, or because he was so far away from her social scale that she was innocently unaware of any necessity for it.

CHAPTER V

Randolph Anderson had a large contempt for money used otherwise than for its material ends. A dollar never meant anything to him except its equivalent in the filling of a need. Generosity and the impulse of giving were in his blood, yet it had gone hard several times with people who had tried to overreach him even to a trifling extent. But now he submitted without a word to losing ten dollars through cashing Arthur Carroll's worthless check. He himself was rather bewildered at his tame submission. One thing was certain, although it seemed paradoxical; if he had not had suspicions as to Arthur Carroll's perfect trustworthiness, he would at once have gone to him with the check.

"I dare say he overdrew his account without knowing it, as many an honest man does," he reasoned, when trying to apologize to himself for his unbusiness-like conduct, but always he knew subconsciously that if he had been perfectly sure of that view of it he would not have hesitated to put it to the proof. For some reason, probably unconfessed rather than actually hidden from himself, he shrank from a possible discovery to Arthur Carroll's discredit. When a man of Randolph Anderson's kind replies to a question concerning the beauty of a young girl that he does not know, the assumption is warranted that he has given the matter consideration. A man usually leaps to a decision of that kind, and if he has no ulterior motive for concealment, he would as lief proclaim it to the house-tops.

Usually Randolph Anderson would no more have hesitated about giving his opinion as to a girl's looks than he would have hesitated about giving his candid opinion of the weather. For the most part a woman's face had about as much effect upon his emotional nature as the face of a day. He saw that it was rosy or gray, smiling and sunny, or frowning or rainy, then he looked unmovedly at the retreating backs of both. It was all the same thing. Anderson was a man who dealt mostly with actualities where his emotions were concerned. With some, love-dreams grow and develop with their growth and development; with some not. The latter had been true with Randolph Anderson. Then, too, he was scarcely self-centred and egotistical enough for genuine air-castles of any kind. To build an air-castle, one's own personality must be the central prop and pillar, for even anything as unsubstantial as an air-castle has its building law. One must rear around something, or the structure can never rise above the horizon of the future.

Anderson had stored his mind with the poetic facts of the world rather than projected his poetic fancies into the facts of the world. He saw things largely as they were, with no inflorescence of rainbows where there was none; but there are actual rainbows, and even auroras, so that the man who does not dream has compensations and a less chance of disillusion. Of course Anderson had thought of marriage; he could scarcely have done otherwise; but he had thought of it as an abstract condition pertaining to himself only in a general way as it pertains to all mankind. He had never seen himself plainly enough in his fancy as a lover and husband to have a pang of regret or longing. He had been really contented as he was. He had a powerful mind, and the exercising of that held in restraint the purely physical which might have precipitated matters. Some men advance, the soul pushing the body with more or less effort; some with the soul first, trailing the body; some in unison, and these are they who make the best progress as to the real advancement. Anderson moved, on the whole, in the last way. He was a very healthy man, mind and body, and with rather unusual advantages in point of looks. This last he realized in one way but not in another. He knew it on general principles; he recognized the fact as he recognized the fact of his hands and feet; but what he actually saw in the looking-glass was not so much the physical fact of himself as the spiritual problem with its two known quantities of need and circumstance, and its great unknown third which took hold of eternity. Anderson, although not in a sense religious, had a religious trend of thought. He went every Sunday with his mother to the Presbyterian church where his grandfather had preached to an earlier generation.

On the Sunday after his encounter with Arthur Carroll with reference to the bill, he went to church as usual with his mother.

Mrs. Anderson was a picture of a Sunday, in a rich lavender silk and a magnificent though old-fashioned lace shawl which floated from her shoulder in a fairy net-work of black roses. She would never wear plain black like most women of her age. She was one of the blue-eyed women who looks well in lavender. Her blue eyes, now looking at her son from under the rich purples and lavenders of the velvet pansies on her bonnet, got an indeterminate color like myrtle blossoms. A deeper pink also showed on her cheeks because of the color of her gown.

"Mother, you are just such a mixture of color as that lilac-bush," said her son, irrelevantly, looking from her to a great lilac-bush in the corner of the yard they were passing. It was tipped with rose on the delicate ends of its blooming racemes, which shaded to blue at the bases.

"Did you see those new people in church today?" said she.

"Yes, I think I did," replied Randolph. "They sat just in front of the Egglestons, didn't they?"

"Yes," said his mother, "they did sit there. There is quite a large family. The ladies are all very nice-looking, too, and they all look alike. If they are going to church, such a family as that, and so well off, they will be quite an acquisition to Banbridge."

"Yes," said Randolph. He spoke absently, and he looked absently at a great wistaria which draped with pendulous purple blooms the veranda of a house which they were just passing. It arrested his eyes as with a loud chord of color, but his mind did not grasp it at all. Afterwards he could not have said he had seen it. As is often the case, while his eyes actually saw one thing, his consciousness saw another. Great, purple, pendulous flowers filled his bodily vision, and the head and shoulders of a young girl above a church pew his mental outlook. Had he seen the Carrolls in church — had he, indeed? Had he seen anything besides them, or rather besides one of them? Had he not, the moment she came up the aisle and entered the pew, seen her with a very clutch of vision? He could not have described one article of her dress, and yet it was complete in his thought. She had worn a soft silk of a dull-red shade, with a frill of cream lace about the shoulders, and there were pink roses under the brim of her dull-red hat, and under the roses was her face, shaded softly with a great puff of her dark hair. And her dark eyes under the dark hair had in them the very light of morning dew, which sparkled back both this world and heaven itself into the eyes of the looker, all reflected in tiny crystal spheres. Suddenly the man gazing across the church had seen in this girl's face all there was of earth and the overhang of heaven; he had seen the present and the future. It is through the face of another human being that one gets the furthest reach of human vision, and that furthest reach had now come for the first time to Randolph Anderson. All at once a quiver ran through his entire consciousness from this elongated vision, and he realized sight to its uttermost. Yet it did not dawn on him that he was in love with this girl. He would have laughed at the idea. He had seen her only twice; he had spoken to her only once. He knew nothing of her except that she had given him a worthless check to cash. Love could not come to him in this wise, and it had not, in fact. He had only attained to the comprehension of love. He had gotten faith, he had seen the present world and the world to come in the light of it, but not as yet his own soul. Yet always he saw the girl's head under the pink roses under the brim of the dark-red hat. It was evidently a favorite headgear of hers. She had worn it with a white dress when she had come to the store to get the check cashed. But he had not seen her so fully then. His little doubt and bewilderment over the check had clouded his vision. Now, since he had seen her in the church-pew, his last thrifty scruple as to ignoring the matter of the check left him. He felt that he could not put his doubt of her father to the proof. Suppose that the account had not been carelessly overdrawn — Suppose — He never for one instant suspected the girl. As soon suspect a rosebud of foregoing its own sweet personality, and of being in reality something else, say a stinging nettle. The girl carried her patent royal of youth and innocence on her face. He made up his mind to say nothing about the check, to lose the ten dollars, and, since dollars were so far from plenty with him, to sacrifice some luxury for the luxury of the loss. He made up his mind that he could very well do without the book with colored plates of South American butterflies which he had thought of purchasing. Much better live without that than rub the bloom off a better than butterfly's wing. Better anything than disturb that look of innocent ignorance on that girl's little face.

CHAPTER VI

It was the next day that Randolph Anderson, on his way home at noon, saw ahead of him, just as he turned the corner from Main to Elm street, where his own house was, a knot of boys engaged in what he at first thought was a fight or its preliminaries. There was a great clamor, too. In the boughs of a maple in the near-by yard were two robins wrangling; underneath were the boys. The air was full of the sweet jangle of birds and boyish trebles, for all the boys were young. Anderson, as he came up, glanced indifferently at the turbulent group and saw one boy who seemed to be the centre of contention. He was backed up against the fence, an ornate iron affair backed by a thick hedge, the green leaves of which pricked through the slender iron uprights. In front of this green, iron-grated wall, which was higher than his head, for he was a little fellow, stood a boy, who Anderson saw at a glance was the same one whom he had seen with the Carrolls in church the day before. His hair was rather long and a toss of dark curls. His face was as tenderly pretty as his sister's, whom he strongly resembled, although he was somewhat fairer of complexion. But it was full of the utmost bravado of rage and defiance, and his two small hands were clinched, until the knuckles whitened, in the faces of the little crowd who confronted him. The color had not left his face, for his cheeks burned like roses, but his pretty mouth was hard set and his black eyes blazed. The boys danced and made threatening feints at him. They called out confused taunts and demands whose purport Anderson at first did not comprehend, but the boy never swerved. When one of his tormentors came nearer, out swung the little white fist at him, and the other invariably dodged.

Anderson's curiosity grew. He went closer. Amidon and Ray, the postmaster, on his way home to his dinner, also joined him, and the little barber, smelling strongly of scented soap and witch-hazel. They stood listening interestedly.

"Most too many against one," remarked the postmaster.

"He don't look scared," said Amidon. "He's Southern, and he's got grit. He's backed up there like the whole Confederacy."

A kindly look overspread the sleek, conceited face of the man. His forebears were from Alabama. His father had been a small white slave-owner who had drifted North, in a state of petty ruin after the war, and there Amidon, who had been a child at the time, had grown up and married the thrifty woman who supported him. The wrangle increased, the boys danced more energetically, the small fists of the boy at bay were on closer guard.

"Hi, there!" sung out Amidon. "Look at here; there's too many of ye. Look out ye don't git into no mischief, now."

"Hullo, boys! what's the trouble?" shouted the postmaster, in a voice of authority. He was used to running these same boys out of his office when they became too boisterous during the distribution of the mails, making precipitate dashes from the inner sanctum of the United States government. They were accustomed to the sound of his important shout, and a few eyes rolled over shoulder at him. But they soon plunged again into their little whirlpool of excitement, for they were quick-witted and not slow to reason that they were now on the king's highway where they had as much right as the postmaster, and could not be coerced under his authority.

"What is it all about?" the postmaster called, loudly, above the hub-bub, to Anderson.

Anderson shook his head. He was listening to the fusillade of taunt-ing, threatening yells, with his forehead knitted. Then all at once he un-derstood. Over and over, with every pitch possible to the boyish threats, the cry intermingling and crossing until all the vowels and consonants overlapped, the boys repeated: "Yerlie — yerlie — yerlie —" They clipped the reproach short; they elongated it into a sliding thrill. From one boy, larger than the others, and whose voice was changing, came at intervals the demand, in a hoarse, cracking treble, with sudden descents into gulfs of bass: "Take it ba-ck! Take it ba-ck!"

Always in response to that demand of the large boy, who was always the one who danced closest to the boy at bay, came the reply, in a voice like a bird's, "Die first — die first."

After a most energetic dash of this large boy, Anderson stepped up and caught him by the shoulder on his retreat from the determined little fist. He knew the large boy; he was a nephew of Henry Lee, whose wife had invaded the Carroll house in the absence of the family.

"See here, Harry," said Anderson, "what is this about, eh?"

The large boy, who, in spite of his size, was a youngster, looked at once terrifiedly and pugnaciously into his face, and beginning with a whimper of excuse to Anderson, ended with a snarl of wrath for the other boy. "He tells lies, he does. He tells lies. Ya-h!" The boy danced at the other even under Anderson's restraining hand on his shoulder. "Yerlie — yerlie! Ya-h!" he yelled, and all the others joined in. The chorus was deaf-ening. Anderson's hand on the boy's shoulder tightened. He shook him violently. The boy's cap fell off, and his shock of fair hair waved. He rolled eyes of terrified wonder at his captor. "What, wha-at? —" he stammered. "You lemme be. You — Wha-at?"

"I'll tell you what, you big bully, you," said Anderson, sternly. "That boy there is one to a dozen, and he's the smallest of the lot — he's half your size. Now, what in thunder are you all about, badgering that little chap so?"

A sudden silence prevailed. They all stood looking from under low-ered eyebrows at the group of watching men; their small shoulders under their little school-jackets were seen to droop; scarcely a boy but shuffled his right leg, while their hands, which had been gyrating fists, unclinched and twitched at their sides. But the boy did not relax for a second his expression of leaping, bounding rage, of a savage young soul in a feeble body. Now he included Anderson and the other men. He held his head with the haughtiness of a prince. He seemed to question them with silent wrath.

"Who are you who dare to come here and interfere in my quarrel?" he seemed to say. "I was sufficient unto myself. I needed none of your protection. What if I was one to a dozen? Look at *me!*" His little hands did not for a second unclinch. He was really very young, probably no more than ten. He was scarcely past his babyhood, but he was fairly impressive, not the slightest maturity of mind, but of spirit. He could never take a fiercer stand against odds than now if he lived to be a hundred.

Anderson approached him, in spite of himself, with a certain respect. "What is the matter, young man?" he inquired, gravely.

The boy regarded him with silent resentment and scorn; he did not deign an answer. But the big boy replied for him promptly:

"He — he said his father kept a tame elephant when they lived in New York State, and he — he used to ride him —"

He spoke in a tone of aggrieved virtue, and regarded the other with a scowl. The men guffawed, and after a second the boys also. Then a little fellow behind the ringleader offered additional testimony.

"He said he used to get up a private circus once a week, every Saturday, and charge ten cents a head, and made ten dollars a week," he said. Then his voice of angry accusation ended in a chuckle.

Anderson kept his face quite grave, but all the others joined in the chorus of merriment. The little fellow backed against the iron fence gave an incredulous start at the sound of the laughter, then the red roses faded out on his smooth cheeks and he went quite white. The laughter stung his very soul as no recrimination could have done. He suffered tortures of mortified pride. His fists were still clinched, but his proud lip quivered a little. He looked very young — a baby.

Anderson stepped to his aid. He raised his voice. "Now, look here, boys," he said. But he made no headway against the hilarity, which swelled higher and higher. The crowd increased. Several more men and boys were on the outskirts. An ally pressed through the crowd to Anderson's side.

"Now, boys," he proclaimed, and for a moment his thin squeak weighted with importance gained a hearing — "now, boys," said the barber, "this little feller's father is an extinguished new denizen of Banbridge, and you ain't treatin' of him with proper disrespect. Now —" But then his voice was drowned in a wilder outburst than ever. The little crowd of men and boys went fairly mad with hysterical joy of mirth, as an American crowd will when once overcome by the humor of the situation in the midst of their stress of life. They now laughed at the little barber and the boy. The old familiar butt had joined forces with the new ones.

"They have formed a trust," said Amidon, deserting his partisanship, now that it had assumed this phase of harmless jocularity.

But the boy at bay, as the laughter at his expense increased, was fairly frantic. He lost what he had hitherto retained, his self-possession. "I tell you I did!" he suddenly screamed out, in a sweet screech, like an angry bird, which commanded the ears of the crowd from its strangeness. "I tell you I did have an elephant, I did ride him, and I did have a circus every Saturday afternoon, so there!"

The "so there" was tremendous. The words vanished in the sound. The boyish expression denoting triumphant climax became individual, the language of one soul. He fired the words at them all like a charge of shot. There was a pause of a second, then the laughter and mocking were recommencing. But Anderson took advantage of the lull.

"See here, boys," he shouted, "there's been enough of this. What is it to you whether he had a dozen elephants and rode them all at once, and had a circus every day in the week with a dozen tame bears thrown in? Clear out and go home and get your dinners. Clear out! Vamoose! Scatter!" His tone was at once angry and appealing. It implied authority and comradeship.

Anderson had given great promise as a speaker during his college course. He was a man who, if he exerted himself, could gauge the temper of a mob. The men on the outskirts began moving away easily; the boys followed their example. The little barber took the boy familiarly by the arm.

"Now, you look at here," said he. "Don't you hev them chaps a-pesterin' of you no more, an' ef they do, you jest streak right into my parlor an' I'll take care of ye. See?"

The boy twitched his arm away and eyed the barber witheringly. "I don't want anything to do with you nor your old barbershop," said he.

"You had better run along, John," said Anderson to the barber, who was staring amazedly, although the complacent smirk upon his face was undiminished.

"I guess he's a child kinder given to speakin' at tandem," he said, as he complied with Anderson's advice.

The boy turned at once to the man. "What business had that barber telling me to go into his old barbershop?" demanded he. "I ain't afraid of all the boys in this one-horse town."

"Of course not," said Anderson.

"I did have an elephant when I lived in Hillfield, and I did ride him, and I did have circuses every Saturday," said the boy, with challenge.

Anderson said nothing.

"At least —" said the child, in a modified tone. Anderson looked at him with an air of polite waiting. The boy's roses bloomed again. "At least —" he faltered, "at least —" A maid rang a dinner-bell frantically in the doorway of the house near which they were standing. Anderson glanced at her, then back at the boy. "At least —" said the boy, with a blurt of confidence which yielded nothing, but implied the recognition of a friend and understander in the man — "at — least I used to make believe I had an elephant when I lived in Hillfield."

"Yes?" said Anderson. He made a movement to go, and the boy still kept at his side.

"And —" he added, but still with no tone of apology or confession, "I might have had an elephant."

"Yes," said Anderson, "you might have."

"And they did not know but what I might," said the boy, angrily.

Anderson nodded judicially. "That's so, I suppose; only elephants are not very common as setter dogs for a boy to have around these parts."

"It was a setter dog," said the boy, with a burst of innocence and admiration. "How did you know?"

"Oh, I guessed."

"You must be real smart," said the boy. "My father said he thought you were, and somehow had got stranded in a grocery store. Did you?"

"Yes, I did," replied Anderson.

Anderson was now walking quite briskly towards home and dinner, and the boy was trotting by his side, with seemingly no thought of parting. They proceeded in silence for a few steps; then the boy spoke again.

"I began with the setter dog," said he. "His name was Archie, and he used to jump over the roof of a part of our house as high as" — he looked about and pointed conclusively at the ell of a house across the street — "as high as that," he said, with one small pink finger indicating unwaveringly.

"That must have been quite a jump," remarked Anderson, and his voice betrayed nothing.

"That setter was an awful jumper," said the little boy. "He died last winter. My sisters cried, but I didn't." His voice trembled a little.

"He must have been a fine dog," said Anderson.

"Yes, sir, he could jump. I think that piece of our house he used to jump over was higher than that," said the boy, reflectively, with the loving tone of a panegyrist who would heap more and more honors and flowers upon a dear departed.

"A big jump," said Anderson.

"Yes, sir, he was an awful jumper. Those boys they said I lied. First they said he couldn't do it, then they said I didn't have any dog, and then I —"

"And then you said you had the elephant?"

"Yes, sir. Say, you ain't going to tell 'em what I've told you?"

"You better believe I'm not. But I tell you one thing — next time, if you'll take my advice, you had better stick to the setter dog and let elephants alone."

"Maybe it would be better," said the boy. Then he added, with a curious sort of naïve slyness, "But I haven't said I didn't have any elephant."

"That's so," said Anderson.

Suddenly, as the two walked along, the man felt a hard, hot little hand slide into his. "I guess you must be an awful smart man," said the boy.

"What is your name?" said Anderson, in lieu of a disclaimer, which somehow he felt would seem to savor of mock modesty in the face of this youthful enthusiasm.

"Why, don't you know?" asked the boy, in some wonder. "I thought everybody knew who we were. I am Captain Carroll's son. My name is Eddy Carroll."

"I knew you were Captain Carroll's son, but I did not know your first name."

"I knew you," said the boy. "I saw you out in the field catching butterflies."

"Where were you?"

"Oh, I was fishing. I was under those willows by the brook. I kept pretty still, and you didn't see me. Have to lay low while you're fishing, you know."

"Of course," said Anderson.

"I didn't catch anything. I don't believe fish are very thick in the brooks around here. I used to catch great big fellers when I lived in Hillfield. One day —"

"When do you have your dinner at home?" broke in Anderson.

"'Most any time. Say, Mr. Anderson, what are you going to have for dinner?"

Anderson happened to know quite well what he was going to have for dinner, because he had himself ordered it on the way to the store that morning. He answered at once:

"Roast lamb and green pease and new potatoes," said he.

"Oh!" said the boy, with unmistakable emphasis.

"And I am quite sure there is going to be a cherry-dumpling for dessert," said Anderson, reflectively.

"I like all those things," stated the boy, with emphasis that was pathetic.

The man stopped and looked down at the boy. "Now, see here, my friend," said he. "Honest, now, no dodging. Never mind if you do like things. Honest — you can't cheat me, you know —"

The boy looked back at him with eyes of profound simplicity and faith. "I know it," he replied.

"Well, then, now you tell me, honest, if you do stay and have dinner with me won't your folks, your mother and your sisters, worry?"

The boy's face, which had been rather anxious, cleared at once. "Oh no, sir!" he replied. "Amy never worries, and Ina and Charlotte won't."

"Who is Amy?"

"Amy? Why, Amy is my mother, of course."

"And you are sure she won't worry?"

"Oh no, sir." The boy fairly laughed at the idea. His honesty in this at least seemed unmistakable.

"Well, then," said Anderson, "come along and have dinner with me."

The boy fairly leaped with delight as, still clinging to the man's hand, he passed up the little walk to the Anderson house. He could smell the roast lamb and the green pease.

CHAPTER VII

Arthur Carroll went on business to the City every morning. He brought up to the station in the smart trap, the liveried coachman, with the mute majesty of his kind, throned upon the front seat. Sometimes one of Carroll's daughters, as delicately gay as a flower in her light daintiness of summer attire, was with him. Often the boy, with his outlook of innocent impudence, sat beside the coachman. Carroll himself was always irreproachably clad in the very latest of the prevailing style. Had he not been such a masterly figure of a man, he would have been open to the charge of dandyism. He was always gloved; he even wore a flower in the lapel of his gray coat. He carried always, whatever the state of the weather, an eminent umbrella with a carved-ivory handle. He equipped himself with as many newspapers from the stand as would an editor of a daily paper. The other men drew conclusions that it was highly necessary for him to study the state of the market and glean the truth from the various reports.

One morning Henry Lee was also journeying to the City on the eight-o'clock train. He held a $2500 position in a publisher's office, and felt himself as good as any man in Banbridge, with the possible exception of this new-comer, and he accosted him with regard to his sheaf of newspapers.

"Going to have all the news there is?" he inquired, jocularly.

Carroll looked up and smiled and nodded. "Well, yes," he replied. "I find this my only way — read them all and strike an average. There is generally a kernel of truth in each."

"That's so," said Lee.

Carroll glanced speculatively at the ostentatiously squared shoulders of the other man as he passed through the car.

When the train reached Jersey City, Carroll, leaving his newspapers fluttering about the seat he had occupied, passed off the train and walked with his air of careless purpose along the platform.

"This road is a pretty poorly conducted concern," said a voice behind him, and Lee came up hurriedly and joined him.

"Yes," replied Carroll, tentatively. His was not the order of mind which could realize its own aggrandizement by wholesale criticism of a great railroad system for the sake of criticism, and, moreover, he had a certain pride and self-respect about maintaining the majesty of that which he must continue to patronize for his own ends.

"Yes," said Lee, moving, as he spoke, with a sort of accelerated motion like a strut. He was a much shorter man than Carroll, and he made futile hops to get into step with him as they proceeded. "Yes, sir, every train through the twenty-four hours is late on this road."

Carroll laughed. "I confess that rather suits me, on the whole. I am usually late myself."

They walked together to the ferry-slip, and the boat was just going out.

"Always lose this boat," grumbled Lee, importantly.

Carroll looked at his watch, then replaced it silently.

"Going to miss an appointment?" questioned Lee.

"No, think not. These boats sail pretty often."

"I wish the train-service was as good," said Lee.

The two men stood together until the next boat came in, then boarded it, and took seats outside, as it was a fine day. They separated a couple of blocks from the pier. Lee was obliged to take an up-town Elevated.

"I suppose you don't go my way?" he said to Carroll, wistfully.

"No," said Carroll, smiling and shaking the ashes from his cigar. Both men had smoked all the way across — Carroll's cigars.

"And I tell you they were the real thing," Lee told his admiring wife that night. "Cost fifteen cents apiece, if they cost a penny; no cheap cigars for him, I can tell you."

Carroll said good-morning out of his atmosphere of fragrant smoke, and Lee, with a parting wave of the hand, began his climb of the Elevated stairs. He cast a backward look at Carroll's broad, gray shoulders swinging up the street. Even a momentary glimpse was enough to get a strong impression of the superiority of the man among the crowd of ordinary men hastening to their offices.

"I wonder where he is going? I wonder where his office is?" Lee said to himself, accelerating his pace a little as the station began to quiver with an approaching train.

What Lee asked himself many another man in Banbridge asked, but no one knew. No one dared to put the question directly to Carroll himself.

Arthur Carroll had never been a man who opened wide all the doors of his secrets of life to all his friends and acquaintances. Some had one entrance, some another, and it is probable that he always reserved ways of entrance and egress unknown to any except himself. At the very time that he evaded the solicitude of Banbridge with regard to his haunts in the City he was more than open, even ostentatious concerning them to some parties in the City itself, but he was silent regarding Banbridge. It may have been for the reason that he did not for the present wish to mix the City and Banbridge, that he wished to preserve mysteries concerning himself in the regard of both. It is certain that nobody in his office, where he roused considerable speculation even among a more engrossed and less inquisitive class, knew where he lived. The office had not heard of Banbridge; Banbridge had heard of the office, but knew nothing about it. The office, in a way, was not nearly as wise as Banbridge, for it knew nothing whatever of his family affairs. There was therein much speculation and, more than that, heart-burning as to whether Captain Carroll was or was not married. In the inner office, whence issued a mad tick of type-writers all through business hours, were two girls, one quite young and very pretty, the other also young, but not so pretty, both working for very small returns. There was also a book-keeper, a middle-aged man, and vibrating from the inner to the outer office was a young fellow with an innocent, high forehead and an eager, anxious outlook of brown eyes and a fashion of seeming to hang suspended on springs of readiness for motion when an order should come.

This young fellow, who sped in and out with that alacrity at the word of command, who hastened on errands with such impetus that he inspired alarm among the imaginative, had acquired a curious springiness about his hips that almost gave the effect of dislocation. He winked very fast, having gotten a nervous trick. He hurried ceaselessly. He had upon him the profound conviction of not time enough and the need of haste. He was in love with the prettier of the stenographers, and his heart was torn when he heard the surmises as to his employer's married or single estate. He used to watch Carroll when he left the office at night, and satisfied himself that he turned towards Sixth Avenue, and then he satisfied himself no more. Carroll plunged into mystery at night as he did for Banbridge in the morning. It was borne in upon the clerk who had an opulent imagination that Carroll was a great swell and went every night to one of the swellest of the up-town clubs, where he resided in luxury and the most genteel and lordly dissipation. He had, at the same time, a jealousy of and a profound pride in Carroll. Carroll himself had a sort of kindly scorn of him, and treated him very well. He was not of the description of weak character who antagonized him.

As for the girls in the inner office, Carroll only recognized them there. Seen on the street, away from the environment, he would simply not have dreamed he had ever seen them. He knew them only in their frames. As for the middle-aged man at the book-keeper's desk, he disturbed him in a way that he would not admit to himself. He spoke to him rather curtly. If he could avoid speaking to him he did so. He had a way of sending directions to the book-keeper by the young man. The book-keeper, if he also surmised Carroll's private life, gave no sign, although he had ample time. He sat at his desk faithfully from eight o'clock until half-past four, but the work which he had to do was somewhat amazing to a mind which stopped to reason. Sometimes even this man, who understood the world in general as a place to be painfully clambered and tramped and even crawled over, to the accomplishment of the ulterior end of remaining upon it at all, and who paid very little attention to other people's affairs, except as they directly concerned the tragic pettiness of his own, wondered a little at the nature of the accounts which he faithfully kept.

This book-keeper, whose name was William Allbright, lived in Harlem, so far up that it seemed fairly in the country, and on the second floor of a small, ancient building which, indeed, belonged to the period when Harlem was country and which remained between two modern apartment houses. The book-keeper had a half-right in a little green backyard, wherein flourished with considerable energy an aged cherry-tree, from which the tenants always fondly hoped for cherries. The cherries never materialized, but the hope was something. The book-keeper's elder sister, who kept house for him, was fond of gazing at the cherry-tree, with its scanty spread of white blossoms, and dreaming of cherries. She was the fonder because she had almost no dreams left. It is rather sad that even dreams go, as well as actualities. However, the sister seemed not to mind so very much. Very little, except the pleasure which she took in watching the cherry-tree, gave evidence that she lamented anything that she had lost or merely missed in life. In general she had an air of such utter placidity and acquiescence that it almost amounted to numbness. The book-keeper at this time of year scratched away every evening with a hoe and trowel in his half of the backyard, where he was making a tiny garden-patch.

The garden represented to him, as the tree did to his sister, his one ladder by which his earthly dreams might climb higher. One night he came home and there were three green spears of corn piercing the mould, and he fairly chuckled.

"The corn has come up," said he.

"So it has," said his sister.

A widow woman and her son, who worked in one of the great retail stores, lived down-stairs in the building. The young man, rather conse-quential but interested, strolled out in the backyard and surveyed the corn. The widow, who was consumptive, thrust her head and shoulders, muffled in a white shawl, out of her kitchen window into the soft spring air.

"So the corn has come up," said the son, throwing himself back on his heels with a lordly air. The mother smiled dimly at the green spears from between the woolly swaths of her shawl. She coughed, and pulled the white fleece closely over her mouth and nose. Then only her eyes were visible, which looked young as they gazed at the green spears of corn. The book-keeper nodded his elderly, distinctly commonplace, and unimpor-tant head with the motion of a conqueror who marshals armies.

After all, it is something for a man to be able to call into life, even if under the force which includes him also, the new life of the spring. It is a power like that of a child in leading-strings, but still power. After the mother and son had gone away and he and his sister were still out in the cool, and the great evening star had come out and it was too dark to work any longer, for the first time he said something about the queer accounts in his books in Captain Carroll's office.

"I suppose it is all right," he said, leaning a second on his hoe and staring up at the star, "but sometimes my books and the accounts I keep look rather — strange to me."

"He pays you regularly, doesn't he?" inquired the sister. The ques-tion of pay could sting her from her numbness. Once there had been a period, years ago, before Carroll's advent, of no pay.

"Oh yes," replied the brother. "He pays me. He has never been more than a week behind. Captain Carroll seems like a very smart man. I wonder where he lives. I don't believe anybody in the office knows. He went away very early this afternoon. I don't know whether he lives in the City or in the country. I thought maybe if he did live in the country he wanted to get home and go driving or something."

It had been as the book-keeper surmised. Carroll had gone early to his home in the country with the idea of a drive. But when he reached home he found a state of affairs which precluded the drive. It seemed that young Eddy Carroll was given to romancing in more respects than one, and had not told the truth to Anderson when he had been asked if his family would feel anxious at his non-return to dinner. Eddy knew quite well that they would be anxious. In spite of a certain temperamental aver-sion to worry, the boy's mother and sisters were wont to become quite actively agitated if he failed to appear at expected times and seasons. Eddy

Carroll, in the course of a short life, had contrived to find the hard side of many little difficulties. He had gotten into divers forms of mischief; he had met with many accidents. He had been almost drowned; he had broken an arm; he had been hit in the forehead by a stone thrown by another boy.

When Arthur Carroll reached home that afternoon he found his wife in hysterical tears, his sister trying to comfort her, and the two daughters and the maid were scouring the town in search of the boy. School was out, and he had still not come home. Carroll heard the news before he reached home, from the coachman who met him at the station.

"Mr. Eddy did not come home this noon," said the man, with much deference. He was full of awe at his employer, being a simple sort, and this was his second place, his first having been with the salt of the earth who made no such show as Carroll. He reasoned that virtue and appearances must increase according to the same ratio. "Mrs. Carroll sent me to the school this noon," said the man, further, "and the ladies are very much worried. The young ladies and Marie are out trying to find him." Marie was the maid, a Hungarian girl.

"Well, drive home as fast as you can," said Carroll, with a sigh. He reflected that his drive was spoiled; he also reflected that when the boy was found he should be punished. Yet he did not look out of temper, and, in fact, was not. It was in reality almost an impossibility for Arthur Carroll to be out of temper with one of his own family.

When Carroll reached home his wife came running down the stairs in a long, white tea-gown, and flung her arms around his neck. "Oh, Arthur!" she sobbed out. "What do you think has happened? What do you think?"

Carroll raised his wife's lovely face, all flushed and panting with grief and terror like a child's, and kissed it softly. "Nothing, Amy; nothing, dear," he said. "Don't, my darling. You will make yourself ill. Nothing has happened."

His sister Anna's voice, clear and strained, came from the top of the stairs. She stood there, holding an unbuttoned dressing-sack tightly across her bosom. The day was warm and neither of the ladies had dressed. "But, Arthur, he has not been home since morning," said Anna Carroll, "and Martin has been to the school-house, and the master says that Eddy did not return at all after the noon intermission, and he did not come home to dinner, after all."

"Yes, he did not come home to dinner," said Mrs. Carroll; "and the butcher did send the roast of veal, after all. I was afraid he would not, because he had not been paid for so long, and I thought Eddy would come home so hungry. But the butcher did send it, but Eddy did not come. He cannot have had a thing to eat since morning, and all he had for breakfast were rolls and coffee. Thee egg-woman would not leave any more eggs, she said, until she was paid for the last two lots, and —"

Carroll pulled out a wallet and handed a roll of notes, not to his wife, but to his sister Anna, who came half-way down the stairs and reached down a long, slender white arm for it.

"There," said he, "pay up the butcher and the egg-woman tomorrow. At least —"

"I understand," said Anna, nodding.

"What do you care whether the butcher or the egg-woman are paid or not, when all the boy we've got is lost?" asked Mrs. Carroll, looking up into her husband's face with the tears rolling over her cheeks.

"That's so," said Anna, and she gave the roll of notes a toss away from her with a passionate gesture. "Arthur, where do you suppose he is?"

The notes fell over the banisters into the hall below.

Carroll watched them touch the floor as he answered, "My dear sister, I don't know, but boys have played truant before, and survived it; and I have strong hopes of our dear boy." Carroll's voice, though droll, was exceedingly soft and soothing. He put an arm again around his wife, drew her close to him, and pressed her head against his shoulder. "Dear, you will be ill," he said. "The boy is all right."

"I am sure this time he is shot," moaned Mrs. Carroll.

"My dear Amy!"

"Now, Arthur, you can laugh," said his sister, coming down the stairs, the embroidered ruffles of her white cambric skirt fluttering around her slender ankles in pink silk stockings, and her little feet thrust into French-heeled slippers, one of which had an enormous bow and buckle, the other nothing at all. "You may laugh," said Anna Carroll, in a sweet, challenging voice, "but why is it so unlikely? Eddy Carroll has had everything but shooting happen to him."

"Yes, he has been everything except shot," moaned Mrs. Carroll.

"My dearest dear, don't worry over such a thing as that!"

"But, Arthur," pleaded Mrs. Carroll, "what else is there left for us to worry about?"

Carroll's mouth twitched a little, but he looked and spoke quite gravely. "Well," he said, "I am going now, and I shall find the boy and bring him home safe and sound, and — Amy, darling, have you eaten anything?"

"Oh, Arthur," cried his wife, reproachfully, "do you think I could eat when Eddy did not come home to dinner, and always something dreadful has happened other times when he has not come? Eddy has never stayed away just for mischief, and then come home as good as ever. Something has always happened which has been the reason."

"Well, perhaps he has stayed away for mischief alone, and that is what has happened now instead of the shooting," said Carroll.

"Arthur, if — if he has, you surely will not —"

"Arthur, you will not punish that boy if he does come home again safe and sound?" cried his sister.

Carroll laughed. "Have either of you eaten anything?" he asked.

"Of course not," replied his sister, indignantly.

"How could we, dear?" said his wife. "I had thought I was quite hungry, and when the butcher sent the roast, after all —"

"Perhaps I had better wait and not pay him until he does not send anything," murmured Anna Carroll, as if to herself. "And when the roast did come, I was glad, but, after all, I could not touch it."

"Well, you must both eat tonight to make up for it," said Carroll.

"I had thought you would as soon have it cold for dinner tonight," said Mrs. Carroll, in her soft, complaining voice. "We would not have planned it for our noon lunch, but we were afraid to ask the butcher for chops, too, and as long as there were no eggs for breakfast, we felt the need of something substantial; but, of course, when that darling boy did not come, and we had reason to think he was shot, we could not —" Mrs. Carroll leaned weepingly against her husband, but he put her from him gently.

"Now, Amy, dearest," said he, "I am going to find Eddy and bring him home, and — you say Marie has gone to hunt for him?"

"Yes, she went in one direction, and Ina and Charlotte in others," said Anna Carroll.

"Well," said Carroll, "I will send Marie home at once, and I wish you would see that she prepares an early dinner, and then we can go for a drive afterwards."

"Eddy can go, too," said Mrs. Carroll, quite joyously.

"No, Amy," said Carroll, "he will most certainly not go to drive with us. There are times when you girls must leave the boy to me, and this is one of them." He stopped and kissed his wife's appealing face, and went out. Then the carriage rolled swiftly round the curve of drive.

"He will whip him," said Anna to Mrs. Carroll, who looked at her with a certain defiance.

"Well," said she, "if he does, I suppose it will be for his good. A man, of course, knows how to manage a boy better than a woman, because he has been a boy himself. You know you and I never were boys, Anna."

"I know that, Amy," said Anna, quite seriously, "and I am willing to admit that a man may know better how to deal with a boy than a woman does, but I must confess that when I think of Arthur punishing Eddy for the faults he may have —"

"May have what?" demanded Mrs. Carroll, quite sharply for her.

"May have inherited from Arthur," declared Anna, boldly, with soft eyes of challenge upon her sister-in-law.

"Eddy has no faults worth mentioning," responded Mrs. Carroll, seeming to enlarge with a sort of fluffy fury like an angry bird; "and the idea of your saying he inherits them from his father. You know as well as I do, Anna, what Arthur is."

"I knew Arthur before you ever did," said Anna, apologetically. "Don't get excited, dear."

"I am not excited, but I do wonder at your speaking after such a fashion when we don't know what may have happened to the dear boy. Of course Arthur will not punish him if he is shot or anything."

"Of course not."

"And if he is not shot, and Arthur should punish him, of course it will be all right."

"Yes, I suppose it will, Amy," said Anna Carroll.

"Arthur feels so sure that nothing has happened to him that I begin to think so myself," said Mrs. Carroll, beginning to ascend the stairs with a languid grace.

"Yes, he has encouraged me," assented Anna. "I suppose we had better dress now."

"Yes, if we are going to drive directly after dinner. I'll put on my cream foulard, it is so warm. I suppose we have, perhaps, worried a little more than was necessary."

"I dare say," said Anna, trailing her white frills and laces before her sister the length of the upper hall. "I think I'll wear my blue embroidered linen."

"You said the bill for that came yesterday?"

"No, six weeks ago; certainly six weeks ago. You know I had it made very early. Oh yes, the second or third bill did come yesterday. I have had so many, I get mixed over those bills."

"Well, it is a right pretty gown, and I would wear it if I were you," said Mrs. Carroll.

CHAPTER VIII

Shortly after Captain Carroll started upon his search for his missing son, Randolph Anderson, sitting peacefully in his back office, by the riverward window, was rudely interrupted. He was mounting some new specimens. Before him the great tiger cat lay blissfully on his red cushion. He was not asleep, but was purring loudly in what resembled a human day-dream. His claws luxuriously pricked through the velvet of his paws, which were extended in such a way that he might have served as a model for a bas-relief of a cat running a race. Now and then the tip of his tail curled and uncurled with an indescribable effect of sensuousness. The green things in the window-box had grown luxuriantly, and now and then trailing vines tossed up past the window in the infrequent puffs of wind. The afternoon was very warm. The temperature had risen rapidly since noon. Down below the wide window ran the river, unseen except for a subtle, scarcely perceptible glow of the brilliant sunlight upon the water. It was a rather muddy stream, but at certain times it caught the sunlight and tossed it back as from the facets of brown jewels.

The murmur of the river was plainly audible in the room. It was very loud, for the stream's current was still high with the spring rains. The rustle of the trees which grew on the river-bank was also discernible, and might have been the rustle of the garments of nymphs tossed about their supple limbs by the warm breeze. In fact, a like fancy occurred to Anderson as he sat there mounting his butterflies.

"I don't wonder those old Greeks had their tales about nymphs closeted in trees," he thought, for the rustle of the green boughs had suggested the rustle of women's draperies.

Then he remembered how Charlotte Carroll's skirts had rustled as she went out of the store that last afternoon when he had spoken to her. There was a soft crispness of ruffling lawns and laces, a most delicate sound, a maidenly sound which had not been unlike the sound of the young leaves of the willows overfolding and interlacing with one another when the soft breeze swelled high. Now and then all the afternoon came a slow, soft wave of warm wind out of the west, and all sounds deepened before it, even the purring song of the cat seemed to increase, and possibly did, from the unconscious assertion of his own voice in the peaceful and somnolent chorus of nature. It was only spring as yet, but the effect was as of a long summer afternoon. Anderson, who was always keenly sensitive to all phases of nature and all atmospheric conditions, was affected by it. He realized himself sunken in drowsy, unspeculative contentment. Even the strange, emotional unrest and effervescence, which had been more or less over him since he had seen Charlotte Carroll, was in abeyance. After all, he was not a passionate man, and he was not very young. The young girl seemed to become merely a part of the gracious harmony which was lulling his soul and his senses to content and peace. He was conscious of wondering what a man could want more than he had, as if he had suspected himself of guilt in that direction.

Then, suddenly, pell-mell into the office, starling the great cat to that extent that he sprang from his red cushion on the window-ledge, and slunk, flattening his long body against the floor, under the table, came the boy Eddy Carroll. The boy stood staring at him rather shamefacedly, though every muscle in his small body seemed on a twitch with the restrained impulse of flight.

"Well," said Anderson, finally, "what's the trouble, sir?"

Then the boy found his tongue. He came close to the man.

"Say," he said, in a hoarse whisper, "jest let a feller stay in here a minute, will you?"

Anderson nodded readily. He understood, or thought he did. He immediately jumped to the conclusion that the teasing boys were at work again. He felt a little astonished at this headlong flight to cover of the boy who had so manfully stood at bay a few hours before. However, he was a little fellow, and there had been a good many of his opponents. He felt a pleasant thrill of fatherliness and protection. He looked kindly into the little, pink-flushed face. "Very well, my son," said he. "Stay as long as you like. Take a seat." The boy sat down. His legs were too short for his feet to touch the floor, so he swung them. He gazed ingratiatingly at Anderson, and now and then cast an apprehensive glance towards the door of the office. Anderson continued mounting his butterflies, and paid no attention to him, and the boy seemed to respect his silence. Presently the great cat emerged quite boldly from his refuge under the table, crouched, calculated the distance, and leaped softly back to his red cushion. The boy hitched his chair nearer, and began stroking the cat gently and lovingly with his little boy-hand, hardened with climbing and playing. The cat stretched himself luxuriously, pricked his claws in and out, shut his eyes, and purred again quite loudly. Again the little room sang with the song of the river, the wind in the trees, and the cat's somnolent note. The afternoon light rippled full of green reflections through the room. The boy's small head appeared in it like a flower. He smiled tenderly at the cat. Anderson, glancing at him over his butterflies, thought what an angelic aspect he had. He looked a darling of a boy.

The boy, stroking the cat, met the man's kindly approving eyes, and he smiled a smile of utter confidence and trust, which conveyed delicious flattery. Then suddenly the hand stroking the cat desisted and made a dive into a small jacket-pocket and emerged with a treasure. It was a great butterfly, much dilapidated as to its gorgeous wings, but the boy looked gloatingly from it to the man.

"I got it for you," he whispered, with another glance at the office door. Anderson recognized, with the dismay of a collector, a fine specimen, which he had sought in vain, made utterly worthless by ruthless handling, but he controlled himself. "Thank you," he said, and took the poor, despoiled beauty and laid it carefully on the table.

"It got broke a little, somehow," remarked the boy; "it's wings are awful brittle."

"Yes, they are," assented Anderson.

"I had to chase it quite a spell," said the boy, with an evident desire not to have his efforts underestimated.

"Yes, I don't doubt it," replied Anderson, with gratitude well simulated.

"It seemed rather a pity to kill such a pretty butterfly as that," remarked the boy, unexpectedly, "but I thought you'd like it."

"Yes, I like to have a nice collection of butterflies," replied Anderson, with a faint inflection of apology. In reality, the butterflies' side of it had failed to occur to him before, and he felt that an appeal to science in such a case was rather feeble. Then the boy helped him out.

"Well," said he, "I do suppose that a butterfly don't live very long, anyhow; he has to die pretty soon, and it's better for human beings to have him stuck on a pin and put where they can see how handsome he is, rather than have him stay out in the fields, where the rain would soak him into the ground, and that would be the end of him. I suppose it is better to save anything that's pretty, somehow, even if the thing don't like it himself."

"Perhaps you are right," replied Anderson, regarding the boy with some wonder.

"Maybe he didn't mind dying 'cause I caught him any more than just dying himself," said Eddy.

"Maybe not."

"Anyhow, he's dead," said the boy.

He watched Anderson carefully as he manipulated the insect.

"I'm sorry his wing got broken," he said. "I wonder why God makes butterflies' wings so awful brittle that they can't be caught without spoiling 'em. The other wing ain't hurt much, anyhow."

A sudden thought struck Anderson. "Why, when did you get this butterfly?" he asked.

The boy flushed vividly. He gave a sorrowful, obstinate glance at the man, as much as to say, "I am sad that you should force me into such a course, but I must be firm." Then he looked away, staring out of the window at the tree-tops tossing against the brilliant blue of the sky, and made no reply.

Anderson made a swift calculation. He glanced at a clock on the wall. "Where did you get this butterfly?" he inquired, harmlessly, and the boy fell into the net.

"In that field just beyond the oak grove on the road to New Sanderson," he replied, with entire innocence.

Anderson surveyed him sharply.

"When is afternoon school out?" asked Anderson.

"At four o'clock," replied the boy, with such unsuspicion that the man's conscience smote him. It was too easy.

"Well," said Anderson, slowly. He did not look at the boy, but went on straightening the mangled wing of the butterfly which he had offered on his shrine. "Well," he said, "how did you get time to go to that field and catch this butterfly? You say it took a long time, and that field is a good twenty minutes' run from here, and it is a quarter of five now." The boy kicked his feet against the rounds of his chair and made no reply. His forehead was scowling, his mouth set. "How?" repeated Anderson.

Then the boy turned on the man. He slid out of his chair; he spoke loudly. He forgot to glance at the door. "Ain't you smart?" he cried, with scorn, and still with an air of slighted affection which appealed. "Ain't you smart to catch a feller that way? You're mean, if you are a man, after I've got you that big butterfly, too, to turn on a feller that way."

Anderson actually felt ashamed of himself. "Now, see here, my boy," he said, "I'm grateful to you so far as that goes."

"I didn't run away from school," declared Eddy Carroll, looking straight at Anderson, who fairly gasped.

He had seen people lie before, but somehow this was actually dazzling. He was conscious of fairly blinking before the direct gaze of innocence of this lying little boy. And then his elderly and reliable clerk appeared in the office door, glanced at Eddy, whom he did not know, and informed Anderson, in a slightly impressed tone, that Captain Carroll was in the store and would like to speak to him. Anderson glanced again at his young visitor, who had got, in a second, a look of pale consternation. He went out into the store at once, and was greeted by Carroll with the inquiry as to whether or not he had seen his son.

"My boy has not been seen since he started for school this morning," said Carroll. "I came here because another little boy, one of my son's small school-fellows, who has succeeded in treading the paths of virtue and obedience, volunteered the information, without the slightest imputation of any guilty conspiracy on your part, that you had been seen leading my son home to your residence to dinner," said Carroll.

"Your son made friends with me on his way from school this noon," said Anderson, simply, "and upon his evident desire to dine with me I invited him, being assured by him that his so doing would not occasion the slightest uneasiness at home as to his whereabouts."

Anderson was indignant at something in the other man's tone, and was careful not to introduce in his tone the slightest inflection of apology.

He made the statement, and was about to add that the boy was at that moment in his office, when Carroll interrupted. "I regret to say that my son has not the slightest idea of what is meant by telling the truth. He never had," he stated, smilingly, "especially when his own desires lead him to falsehood. In those cases he lies to himself so successfully that he tells in effect the truth to other people. He, in that sense, told the truth to you, but the truth was not as he stated, for the ladies have been in a really pitiable state of anxiety."

"He is in my office now," said Anderson, coldly, pointing to the door and beginning to move towards it.

"I suspected the boy was in there," said Carroll, and his tones changed, as did his face. All the urbanity and the smile vanished. He followed Anderson with a nervous stride. Both men entered the little office, but the boy was gone. Both stood gazing about the little space. It was absolutely impossible for anybody to be concealed there. There was no available hiding-place except under the table, and the cat occupied that, and his eyes shone out of the gloom like green jewels.

"I don't see him," said Carroll.

Then Anderson turned upon him.

"Sir," he said, with a kind of slow heat, "I am at a loss as to what to attribute your tone and manner. If you doubt —"

"Not at all, my dear sir," replied Carroll, with a wave of the hand. "But I am told that my son is in here, and when, on entering, I do not see him, I am naturally somewhat surprised."

"Your son was certainly in this room when I left it a moment ago, and that is all I know about it," said Anderson. "And I will add that your son's visit was entirely unsolicited —"

"My dear sir," interrupted Carroll again, "I assure you that I do not for a moment conceive the possibility of anything else. But the fact remains that I am told he is here —"

"He was here," said Anderson, looking about with an impatient and bewildered scowl.

"He could not have gone out through the store while we were there," said Carroll, in a puzzled tone.

"I do not see how he could have done so unobserved, certainly."

"The window," said Carroll, taking a step towards it.

"Thirty feet from the ground; sheer wall and rocks below. He could not have gone out there without wings."

"He has no wings, and I very much fear he never will have any at this rate," said Carroll, moving out. "Well, Mr. Anderson, I regret that my son should have annoyed you."

"He has not annoyed me in the least," Anderson replied, shortly. "I only regret that his peculiar method of telling the truth should have led me unwittingly to occasion your wife and daughters so much anxiety, and I trust that you will soon trace him."

"Oh yes, he will turn up all right," said Carroll, easily. "If he was in your office a moment ago, he cannot be far off."

There was the faintest suggestion of emphasis upon the "if."

Anderson spoke to the elderly clerk, who had been leaning against the shelves ranged with packages of cereal, surmounted by a flaming row of picture advertisements, regarding them and listening with a curious abstraction, which almost gave the impression of stupidity. This man had lived boy and man in one groove of the grocer business, until he needed prodding to shift him momentarily into any other.

In reality he managed most of the details of the selling. He heard what the two men said, and at the same time was considering that he was to send the wagon round the first thing in the morning with pease to the postmaster's, and a new barrel of sugar to the Amidons, and he was calculating the price of sugar at the slight recent rise.

"Mr. Price," said Anderson to him, "may I ask that you will tell this gentleman if a little boy went into my office a short time ago?"

The clerk looked blankly at Anderson, who patiently repeated his question.

"A little boy," repeated the clerk.

"Yes," said Anderson.

Price gazed reflectively and in something of a troubled fashion at Anderson, then at Carroll. His mind was in the throes of displacing a barrel of sugar and a half-peck of pease by a little boy. Then his face brightened. He spoke quickly and decidedly.

"Yes," said he, "just before this gentleman came in, a little boy, running, yes."

"You did not see him come out while we were talking?" asked Anderson.

"No, oh no."

Carroll asked no further and left, with a good-day to Anderson, who scarcely returned it. He jumped into his carriage, and the swift tap of the horse's feet died away on the macadam.

"Sugar ought to bring about two cents on a pound more," said the clerk to Anderson, returning to the office, and then he stopped short as Anderson started staring at an enormous advertisement picture which was stationed, partly for business reasons, partly for ornament, in a corner near the office door. It was a figure of a gayly dressed damsel, nearly life-size, and was supposed by its blooming appearance to settle finally the merit of a new health food. The other clerk, who was a young fellow, hardly more than a boy, had placed it there. He had reached the first fever-stage of admiration of the other sex, and this gaudy beauty had resembled in his eyes a fair damsel of Banbridge whom he secretly adored.

Therefore he had ensconced it carefully in the corner near the office door, and often glanced at it with reverent and sheepish eyes of delight. Anderson never paid any attention to the thing, but now for some reason he glanced at it in passing, and to his astonishment it moved. He made one stride towards it, and thrust it aside, and behind it stood the boy, with a face of impudent innocence.

Anderson stood looking at him for a second. The boy's eyes did not fall, but his expression changed.

"So you ran away from your father and hid from him?" Anderson observed, with a subtle emphasis of scorn. "So you are afraid?"

The boy's face flashed into red, his eyes blazed.

"You bet I ain't," he declared.

"Looks very much like it," said Anderson, coolly.

"You let me go," shouted the boy, and pushed rudely past Anderson and raced out of the store. Anderson and the old clerk looked at each other across the great advertisement which had fallen face downward on the floor.

"Must have come in from the office whilst our back was turned, and slipped in behind that picture," said the clerk, slowly.

Anderson nodded.

"He is a queer feller," said the clerk, further.

"He certainly is," agreed Anderson.

"As queer as ever I seen. Guess his father'll give it to him when he gits home."

"Well, he deserves it," replied Anderson, and added, in the silence of his mind, "and his father deserves it, too," and imagined vaguely to himself a chastening providence for the eternal good of the father even as the father might be for the eternal good of his son. The man's fancy was always more or less in leash to his early training.

Just then the younger clerk, Sam Riggs, commonly called Sammy, entered, and espying at once with jealous eyes the fallen state of his idol in the corner, took the first opportunity to pick her up and straighten her to her former position.

CHAPTER IX

Little Eddy Carroll, running on his slim legs like a hound, raced down the homeward road, and came in sight of his father's carriage just before it turned the corner. Carroll had stopped once on the way, and so the boy overtook him. When Carroll stopped to make an inquiry, he caught a glimpse of the small, flying figure in the rear; in fact, the man to whom he spoke pointed this out.

"Why, there's your boy, now, Cap'n Carroll," he said, "runnin' as fast after you as you be after him." The man was an old fellow of a facetious turn of mind who had done some work on Carroll's garden.

Carroll, after that one rapid, comprehensive glance, said not another word. He nodded curtly and sprang into the carriage; but the old man, pressing close to the wheel, so that it could not move without throwing him, said something in a half-whisper, as if he were ashamed of it.

"Certainly, certainly, very soon," replied Carroll, with some impatience.

"I need it pooty bad," the old man said, abashedly.

"Very soon, I tell you," repeated Carroll. "I cannot stop now."

The old man fell back, with a pull at his ancient cap. He trembled a little nervously, his face was flushed, but he glanced back with a grin at Eddy racing to catch up.

"Drive on, Martin," Carroll said to the coachman.

The old gardener waited until Eddy came alongside, then he called out to him. "Hi!" he said, "better hurry up. Guess your pa is goin' to have a reckonin' with ye."

"You shut up!" cried the boy, breathlessly, racing past. When finally he reached the carriage, he promptly caught hold of the rear, doubled up his legs, and hung on until it rolled into the grounds of the Carroll place and drew up in the semicircle opposite the front-door. Then he dropped lightly to the ground and ran around to the front of the carriage as his father got out. Eddy without a word stood before his father, who towered over him grandly, confronting him with a really majestic reproach, not untinctured with love. The man's handsome face was quite pale; he did not look so angry as severe and unhappy, but the boy knew well enough what the expression boded. He had seen it before. He looked back at his father, and his small, pink-and-white face never quivered, and his black eyes never fell.

"Well?" said Carroll.

"Where have you been?" asked Carroll.

The anxious faces of the boy's mother and his aunt became visible at a front window, a flutter of white skirts appeared at the entrance of the grounds. The girls were returning from their search.

"Answer me," commanded Carroll.

"Teacher sent me on an errand," he replied then, with a kind of dog-gedness.

"The truth," said Carroll.

"I went out catching butterflies, after I had dined with Mr. Anderson and his mother."

"You dined with Mr. Anderson and his mother?"

"Yes, sir. You needn't think he was to blame. He wasn't. I made him ask me."

"I understand. Then you did not go to school this afternoon, but out in the field?"

"Yes, sir."

Carroll eyed sharply the boy's right-hand pocket, which bulged enormously. The girls had by this time come up and stood behind Eddy, holding to each other, their pretty faces pale and concerned.

"What is that in your pocket?" asked Carroll.

"Marbles."

"Let me see the marbles."

"It ain't marbles, it's candy."

"Where did you get it?"

"Mr. Anderson gave it to me."

Carroll continued to look his son squarely in the eyes.

"I stole it when they wasn't looking," said the boy; "there was a glass jar —"

"Go into the house and up to your own room," said Carroll.

The boy turned as squarely about-face as a soldier at the word of command, and marched before his father into the house. The four women, the two at the window, the two on the lawn, watched them go without a word. Ina, the elder of the two girls, put her handkerchief to her eyes and began to cry softly. Charlotte put her arm around her and drew her towards the door.

"Don't, Ina," she whispered, "don't, darling."

"Papa will whip him very hard," sobbed Ina. "It seems to me I cannot bear it, he is such a little boy."

"Papa ought to whip him," said Charlotte, quite firmly, although she herself was winking back the tears.

"He will whip him so hard," sobbed Ina. "I quite gave up when papa found the candy. Stealing is what he never will forgive him for, you know."

"Yes, I know. Don't let poor Amy see you cry, Ina."

"Wait a minute before we go in. You remember that the time papa whipped me, the only time he ever did, when —"

"Yes, I remember. You never did again, honey."

"Yes, it cured me, but I fear it will not cure Eddy. A boy is different."

"Stop crying, Ina dear, before we go in."

"Yes — I — will. Are my eyes very red?"

"No; Amy will not notice it if you keep your eyes turned away."

But Mrs. Carroll turned sharply upon Ina the moment she saw her. The two elder ladies had left the parlor and retreated to a small apartment on the right of the hall, called the den, and fitted up with some Eastern hangings and a divan. Upon this divan Anna Carroll had thrown herself, and lay quite still upon her back, her slender length extended, staring out of the window directly opposite at the spread of a great oak just lately putting forth its leaves. Mrs. Carroll was standing beside her, and she looked at the two girls entering with a hard expression in her usually soft eyes.

"Why have you been crying?" she asked, directly, of Ina. Her hair was in disorder, as if she had thrust her fingers through it. It was pushed far off from her temples, making her look much older. Red spots blazed on her cheeks, her mouth widened in a curious, tense smile. "Why have you been crying?" she demanded again when Ina did not reply at once to her question.

"Because papa is going to whip Eddy," Ina said then, with directness, "and I know he will whip him very hard, because he has been stealing."

"Well, what is that to cry about?" asked Mrs. Carroll, ruffling with indignation. Don't you think the boy's father knows what is best for his own son? He won't hurt him any more than he ought to be hurt."

"I only hope he will hurt himself as much as he ought to be hurt," muttered Anna Carroll on the divan. Mrs. Carroll gave her sister-in-law one look, then swept out of the room. The tail of her rose-colored silk curled around the door-sill, and she was gone. She passed through the hall, and out of the front-door to the lawn, whence she strolled around the house, keeping on the side farthest from the room occupied by her son.

"Hark!" whispered Ina, a moment after her mother had gone.

They all listened, and a swishing sound was distinctly audible. It was the sound of regular, carefully measured blows.

"Amy went out so she should not hear," whispered Ina. "Oh, Dear!"

"It is harder for her than for anybody else because she has to uphold Arthur for doing what she knows is wrong," said Anna Carroll on the divan. She spoke as if to herself, pressing her hands to her ears.

"Papa is doing just right," cried Charlotte, indignantly. "How dare you speak so about papa, Anna?"

"There is no use in speaking at all," said Anna, wearily. "There never was. I am tired of this life and everything connected with it."

Ina was weeping again convulsively. She also had put her hands to her ears, and her piteous little wet, quivering face was revealed.

"There is no need of either of you stopping up your ears," said Charlotte. "you won't hear anything except the — blows. Eddy never makes a whimper. You know that."

She spoke with a certain pride. She felt in her heart that a whimper from her little brother would be more than she herself could bear, and would also be more culpable than the offence for which he was being chastised. She said that her brother never whimpered, and yet she listened with a little fear that he might. But she need have had no apprehension. Up in his bedroom, standing before his father in his little thin linen blouse, for he had pulled off his jacket without being told, directly when he had first entered the room, the little boy endured the storm of blows, not only without a whimper, but without a quiver.

Eddy stood quite erect. His pretty face was white, his little hands hanging at his sides were clinched tightly, but he made not one sound or motion which betrayed pain or fear. He was counting the blows as they fell. He knew how many to expect. There were so many for running away and playing truant, and so many for lying, more for stealing, so many for all three. This time it was all three. Eddy counted while his father laid on the blows as regularly as a machine. When at last he stopped, Eddy did not move. He spoke without moving his head.

"There are two more, papa," he said. "You have stopped too soon."

Carroll's face contracted, but he gave the two additional blows. "Now undress yourself and go to bed," he told the boy, in an even tone. "I will have some bread and milk sent up for your supper. Tomorrow morning you will take that candy back to the store, and tell the man you stole it, and ask his pardon."

"Yes, sir," said Eddy. He at once began unfastening his little blouse preparatory to retiring.

Carroll went out of the room and closed the door behind him. His sister met him at the head of the stairs and accosted him in a sort of fury.

"Arthur Carroll," said she, tersely, "I wish you would tell me one thing. Did you whip that child for his faults or your own?"

Carroll looked at her. He was very pale, and his face seemed to have lengthened out and aged. "For both, Anna," he replied.

"What right have you to punish him for your faults, I should like to know?"

"The right of the man who gave them to him."

"You have the right to punish him for your faults — *your* faults?"

"I could kill him for my faults, if necessary."

"Who is going to punish you for your faults? Tell me that, Arthur Carroll."

"The Lord Almighty in His own good time," replied Carroll, and passed her and went down-stairs.

CHAPTER X

The next morning, just before nine o'clock, Anderson was sitting in his office, reading the morning paper. The wind had changed in the night and was blowing from the northwest. The atmosphere was full of a wonderful clearness and freshness. Anderson was conscious of exhilaration. Life assumed a new aspect. New ambitions pressed upon his fancy, new joys seemed to crowd upon his straining vision in culminating vistas of the future. Without fairly admitting it to himself, it had seemed to him as if he had already in a great measure exhausted the possibilities of his own life, as if he had begun to see the bare threads of the warp, as if he had worn out the first glory of the pattern design. Now it was suddenly all different. It looked to him as if he had scarcely begun to live, as if he had not had his first taste of existence. He felt himself a youth. His senses were sharpened, and he got a keen delight from them, which stimulated his spirit like wine. He perceived for the first time a perfume from the green plants in his window-box, which seemed to grow before his eyes and give an odor like the breath of a runner. He heard whole flocks of birds in the sky outside. He distinguished quite clearly one bird-song which he had never heard before. His newspaper rustled with astonishing loudness when he turned the pages, his cigar tasted to an extreme which he had never before noticed. The leaves of the plants and the tree-boughs outside cut the air crisply. His window-shade rattled so loudly that he could not believe it was simply that. A great onslaught of the splendid wind filled the room, and everything waved and sprang as if gaining life. Then suddenly, without the slightest warning, came a shower of the confection known as molasses-peppermints through the door of the office. They are a small, hard candy, and being thrown with vicious emphasis, they rattled upon the bare floor like bullets. One even hit Anderson stingingly upon the cheek. He sprang to his feet and looked out. Nothing was to be seen except the young clerk, standing, gaping and half frightened, yet with a lurking grin. Anderson regarded him with amazement. An idea that he had gone mad flashed through his mind.

"What did you do that for, Sam?" he demanded.

"I didn't do it."

"Who did?"

"That kid that was in here last night. That Carroll boy. He run in here and flung that candy, and out again, before I could more 'n' see him. Didn't know what were comin'."

Anderson returned to his office, and as he crossed the threshold heard a duet of laughter from Sam and the older clerk. His feet crushed some of the candy as he resumed his seat. He took up his newspaper, but before he had fairly commenced to read he heard the imperious sound of a girl's voice outside, a quick step, and a dragging one.

"Come right along!" the girl's voice ordered.

"You lemme be!" came a sulky boy's voice in response.

"Not another word!" said the girl's. "Come right along!"

Anderson looked up. Charlotte Carroll was entering, dragging her unwilling little brother after her.

"Come," said she again. She did not seem to regard Anderson at all. She held her brother's arm with a firm grip of her little, nervous white hand. "Now," said she to him, "you pick up every one of those molasses-peppermint drops, every single one."

The boy wriggled defiantly, but she held to him with wonderful strength.

"Right away," she repeated, "every single one."

"Let me go, then," growled the boy, angrily. "How can I pick them up when you are holding me this way?"

The girl with a swift motion swung to the office door in the faces of the two clerks, the grinning roundness of the younger, and the half-abstracted bewilderment of the elder. Then she placed her back against it, and took her hand from her brother's arm. "Now, then, pick them up, every one," said she.

Without another word the boy got down on his hands and knees and began gathering up the scattered sweets. Anderson had risen to his feet, and stood looking on with a dazed and helpless feeling. Now he spoke, and he realized that his voice sounded weak.

"Really, Miss Carroll," he said, "I beg — It is of no consequence —" Then he stopped. He did not know what it was all about; he had only a faint idea of not putting any one to the trouble to pick up the débris on his office floor.

Charlotte regarded him as sternly as she had her brother. "Yes, it is of consequence. Papa told him to bring them back and apologize."

Anderson stared at her, bewildered, while the little boy crawled like a nervous spider around his feet.

"Why bring them back to me?" he queried. For the moment the ex-lawyer forgot that molasses-peppermint balls yielded a part of his revenue, and were offered by him to the public from a glass jar on his shelf. He cast about in his mind as to what he could possibly have to do with those small, hard, brown lollipops rolling about on his office floor.

"You had them in a glass jar," said Charlotte, in an accusing voice, "right in his way, and — when he came home last night he had them in his pocket, and — papa whipped him very hard. He always does when — My brother is never allowed to take anything that does not belong to him, however unimportant," she concluded, proudly.

Anderson continued to look at her in a sort of daze.

"No," she added, severely, "he is not. No matter if he is so young, no more than a child, and a child is very fond of sweets, and — they were left right in his way."

Anderson looked at her with the vague idea floating through his mind that he owed this sweet, reproachful creature an abject pardon for keeping his molasses-peppermint balls in a glass jar on his own shelf and not locking them away from the lustful eyes of small boys.

"Papa told Eddy that he must bring them back this morning and ask your pardon," said Charlotte, "and when he came running out of the store I suspected what he had done; and when I found out, I made him come back. Pick up every one, Eddy."

"Here is one he stepped on his own self and smashed all to nothing," said Eddy, in an aggrieved tone. "I can't pick that up, anyhow."

"Pick up what you can of it, and put it in the paper bag."

"I shouldn't think he could sell this to anybody without cheating them," remarked Eddy, in a lofty tone, in spite of his abject position.

"Never you mind what he does with it. You pick up every single speck," ordered the girl; and the boy scraped the floor with his sharp finger-nails, and crammed the candy and dust into a small paper bag. The girl stood watchfully over him; not the smallest particle escaped her eyes. "There's some more over there," said she, sharply, when the boy was about to rise; and Eddy loped like some small animal on all-fours towards a tiny heap of crushed peppermint-drops.

"He must have stepped on this, too," he muttered, with a reproachful glare at Anderson, who had never in his life felt so at a loss. He was divided between consternation and an almost paralyzing sense of the ridiculous. He was conscious that a laugh would be regarded as an insult by this very angry and earnest young girl. But at last Eddy tendered him the bag with the rescued peppermint-drops.

"I shouldn't think you would ask more than half-price for candy like this, anyway," said Eddy, admonishingly, and that was too much for the man. He shouted with laughter; not even Charlotte's face, which suddenly flushed with wrath, could sober him. She looked at him a moment while he laughed, and her face of severe judgment and anger intensified.

"Very well," said she, "if you see anything funny about this, I am glad, Mr. Anderson."

But the boy, who had viewed with doubt and suspicion this abrupt change of aspect on the part of the man, suddenly grinned in response; his black eyes twinkled charmingly with delight and fun. "Say, *you're* all right," he said to Anderson, with a confidential nod.

"Eddy!" cried Charlotte.

"Now, Charlotte, you don't see how funny it is, because you are a girl," said Eddy, soothingly, and he continued to grin at the man, half-elfishly, half-innocently. He looked very small and young.

The girl caught hold of his arm. "Come away immediately," she said, in a choking voice. "Immediately."

"It's just like a girl to act that way about my going, as if I wanted to come myself at all," said the boy, following his sister's pulling hand, and still grinning understandingly at Anderson over his shoulder.

Charlotte turned in the doorway and looked majestically at Anderson. "I thought, when I obliged my brother to return here and pick up the candy, that I was dealing with a gentleman," said she. "Otherwise I might not have considered it necessary."

Even then Anderson could scarcely restrain his laughter, although he was conscious that he was mortally offending her. He managed to gasp out something about his surprise and the triviality of the whole affair of the candy.

"I regret that you should consider the taking anything without leave, however worthless, as trivial," said she. "I have not been so brought up, and neither has my brother." She said this with an indescribable air of offended rectitude. She regarded him like a small, incarnate truth and honesty. Then she turned, and her brother was following with a reluctant backward pull at her leading hand, when suddenly he burst forth with a shout of malicious glee.

"Say, you are making me go away, when I haven't given him back his old candy, after all! He didn't take it."

Charlotte promptly caught the paper bag from her brother's hand, advanced upon Anderson, and thrust it in his face as if it had been a hostile weapon. Anderson took it perforce.

"Here is your property," said she, proudly, but she seemed almost as childish as her brother.

"I ain't said any apology, either," said Eddy.

"The coming here and returning it is apology enough," said Anderson.

He looked foolishly at the ridiculous paper bag, sticky with lollipops. For the first time he felt distinctly ashamed of his business. It seemed to him, as he realized its concentration upon the petty details of existence, its strenuous dwelling upon the small, inane sweets and absurdities of daily life which ought to be scattered with a free hand, not made subjects of trade and barter, to be entirely below a gentleman. He gave the paper bag an impatient toss out of the open window over the back of the sleeping cat, which started a little, then stretched himself luxuriously and slept again.

"There, he's thrown it out of the window!" proclaimed Eddy. He looked accusingly at Charlotte. "I might just as well have kept it as had it thrown out of the window," said he. "What good is it to anybody now, I'd like to know?"

"Never mind what he has done with it," said Charlotte. "Come at once."

"Papa told me I must apologize. He will ask me if I did."

"Apologize, then. Be quick."

"It is not —" began Anderson, who was sober enough now, and becoming more and more annoyed, but Charlotte interrupted him.

"Eddy!" said she.

"I am very sorry I took your candy," piped Eddy, in a loud, declamatory voice which was not the tone of humble repentance. The boy, as he spoke, eyed the man with defiance. It was as if he blamed him, for some occult reason, for having his own property stolen. The child's face became, under the forced humiliation of the apology, revolutionary, anarchistic, rebellious. He might have been the representative, the walking delegate, of some small cult of rebels against the established order of regard for the property-rights of others. The sinner, the covetous one of another's sweets, became the accuser. Just as he was going out of the door, following the pink flutter of his sister's muslin gown, he turned and spoke his whole mind.

"You had a whole big glass jar of them, anyhow," said he, "and I didn't have a single one. You might have given me some, and then I shouldn't have stolen them. It's your own fault. You ought not to have things that anybody else wants, when they haven't got money to pay for them. It's a good deal wickeder than stealing. It was your own fault."

But Eddy had then to deal with his sister. She towered over him, pinker than her pink muslin. The ruffles seemed agitated all over her slender, girlish figure, like the plumage of an angry bird. She caught her small brother by the shoulders, and shook him violently, until the dark hair which he wore rather long waved and his whole head wagged.

"Eddy Carroll," she cried, "aren't you ashamed of yourself? Oh, aren't you ashamed of yourself? Begging, yes, *begging* for candy! If you want candy, you will buy it. You will not beg it nor take it without permission. If you cannot buy it, you will go without, if you are a brother of mine."

The boy for the first time quailed somewhat. He looked at her, and raised a hand childishly as if to ward off something.

"I didn't ask, Charlotte," he half whimpered. "If he was to offer me any now, I would not take it. I would just fling it in his face. I would, Charlotte; I would, honest."

"I heard you," said Charlotte.

"I didn't ask him. I said if he had given me a little of that candy, I wouldn't have been obliged to take any. I said —"

"I heard what you said. Now you must come at once."

Anderson said good-morning rather feebly. Charlotte made a distant inclination of her head in response, and they were gone, but he heard Eddy cry out, in a tone of reproachful glee:

"There! you've made me late at school, Charlotte. Look at that clock; it's after nine. You've made me late at school with all that fussing over a few old peppermint-drops."

CHAPTER XI

Anderson, after they were gone, sat staring out of the window at the green spray of the spring boughs. His mouth was twitching, but his forehead was contracted. This problem of feminity and childhood which he had confronted was too much for him. The boy did not perplex him quite so much — he did not think so much about him — but the girl, the pure and sweet unreason of her proceedings, was beyond his mental grasp. The attitude of reproach which this delicate and altogether lovely young blossom of a thing had adopted towards him filled him with dismay and a ludicrous sense of guilt. He had a keen sense of the unreason and contrariness of her whole attitude, but he had no contempt towards her on account of it. He felt as if he were facing some new system of things, some higher order of creature for whom unreason was the finest reason. He bowed before the pure, unordered, untempered feminine, and his masculine mind reeled. And all the time, deeper within himself than he had ever reached with the furthest finger of his emotions, whether for pain or joy, he felt this tenderness, which was like the quickening of another soul, so alive was it. He felt the wonder and mystery of the awakening of love in his heart, this reaching out with all the best of him for the protection and happiness of another than himself. He saw before him, with no dimming because of absence, the girl's little, innocent, fair face, and such a tenderness for her was over him that he felt as if he actually clasped her and enfolded her, but only for her protection and good, never for himself.

"The little thing," he thought over and over — "the little, innocent, beautiful thing! What kind of a place is she in, among what kind of people? What does this all mean?"

Suspicions which had been in his mind all the time had developed. He had had proof in divers ways. He said to himself, "That man is a scoundrel, a common swindler, if I know one when I see him." But suspicions as to the girl had never for one minute dwelt in his furthest fancy. He had thought speculatively of the possible complicity of the other women of the household, but never of hers. They were all very constant in their church attendance; indeed, Carroll had given quite a sum towards the Sunday-school library, and he had even heard suggestions as to the advisability of making him superintendent and displacing the present incumbent, who was superannuated. Sometimes in church Anderson had glanced keenly from under the quiet droop of languid lids at the Carrolls sitting in their gay fluff and flutter of silks and muslins and laces, and wondered, especially concerning Mrs. Carroll and her sister-in-law. It seemed almost inconceivable that they were ignorant, and if not, how entirely innocent! And then the expressions of their pretty, childish faces disarmed him as they sat there, their dark, graceful heads drooping before the divine teaching with gentle acquiescence like a row of flowers. But there was something about the fearless lift to Charlotte's head and the clear regard of her dark eyes which separated her from the others. She bloomed by herself, individual, marked by her own characteristics. He thought of her passionate assertion of the principles of her home training with pity and worshipful admiration. It was innocence incarnate pleading for guilt which she believed like herself, because of the blinding power of her own light. "She thinks them all like herself," he said to himself. "She reasons from her knowledge of herself." Then reflecting how Carroll had undoubtedly sent his son to return his pilfered sweets, he began to wonder if he could possibly have been mistaken in his estimate of the man's character, if he had reasoned from wrong premises, and from that circumstantial evidence which his experience as a lawyer should have led him to distrust.

Suddenly a shadow flung out across the office floor and a man stood in the doorway. He was tall and elderly, with a shag of gray beard and a shining dome of forehead over a nervous, blue-eyed face. He was the druggist, Andrew Drew, who had his little pharmacy on the opposite side of the street, a little below Anderson's grocery. He united with his drug business a local and long-distance telephone and the Western Union telegraph-office, and he rented and sold commutation-books of railroad tickets to the City.

"Good-day," he said. Then, before Anderson could respond, he plunged at once into the subject on his mind, a subject that was wrinkling his forehead. However, he first closed the office door and glanced around furtively. "See here," he whispered, mysteriously; "you know those new folks, the Carrolls?" With a motion of his lank shoulder he indicated the direction of the Carroll house.

Anderson's expression changed subtly. He nodded.

"Well, what I want to know is — what do you think of him?"

"I don't quite understand what you mean," Anderson replied, stiffly.

"Well, I mean — Well, what I mean is just this" — the druggist made a nervous, imperative gesture with a long forefinger — "this, if you want to know — is he *good*?"

"You mean?"

"Yes, is he good?"

"He has paid his bills here," Anderson said. He offered the other man a chair, which was declined with a shake of the head.

"No, thank you, can't stop. I've left my little boy in the store all alone. So he has paid you?"

"Yes, he has paid his bills here," Anderson replied, with a guilty sense of evasion, remembering the check.

"Well, maybe he is all right. I'll tell you, if you won't speak of it. Of course he may be all right; and I don't want to quarrel with a good customer. All there is — he came rushing in three weeks ago today and said he was late for the train, and he had used up his commutation and had come off without his pocket-book, and of course could not get credit at the station office, and if I had a book he would take it and write me a check. While he was talking he was scratching a check on a New York bank like lightning. He made a mistake and drew it for ten dollars too much; and I hadn't a full book anyway, only one with thirty-five tickets in it, and I let him have that and gave him the difference in cash — fifteen dollars and forty-two cents. And — well — the long and short of it is, the check came back from the bank, no good."

"Did you tell him?"

"Haven't seen him since. I went to his house twice, but he wasn't home. I tried to catch him at the station, but he has been going on different trains lately; and once when I got a glimpse of him the train was in and he had just time to swing on and I couldn't stop him then, of course. Then I dropped him a line, and got a mighty smooth note back. He said there was a mistake; he was very sorry; he would explain at once and settle; and that's over a week ago, and —"

"Probably he will settle it, if he said so," said Anderson, with the memory of the little boy who had been sent to return the stolen candy in his mind.

"Well, I hope he will, but —" The druggist hesitated. Then he went on: "There is something else, to tell the truth. One of his girls came in just now and asked me to cash a check for twenty-five dollars — her father's check, but on another bank — and — I refused."

Anderson flushed. A great gust of wind made the window rattle, and he pulled it down with an irritated jerk.

"Do you think I did right?" asked the druggist, who had a nervous appeal of manner. "Maybe the check was good. I hated to refuse, of course. I said I was short of ready money. I don't think she suspected anything. She is a nice-spoken girl. I don't suppose she knew if the check wasn't good."

"Any man who thinks so ought to be kicked," declared Anderson, with sudden fury, and the other man started.

"I told you I didn't think so," he retorted, eying him with some wonder and a little timidity. "But I declare I didn't know what to do. There was that other check not accounted for yet; and I can't afford to lose any more, and that's a fact. Then you think I ought to have cashed it?"

Anderson's face twitched a little. Then he said, as if it were wrung out of him, "On general principles, I should not call it good business to repeat a transaction of that kind until the first was made right."

The druggist looked relieved. "Well, I am glad to hear you say so. I hated to —"

"But Captain Carroll may be as good pay in the end as I am," interrupted Anderson. "He seems to me to have good principles about things of that kind."

"Well, I'll cash the next check," said Drew, with a laugh. "I must go back, for I left my little boy alone in the store."

The druggist had scarcely gone before the old clerk came to the office door. "That young lady who was here a little while ago wants to speak to you, Mr. Anderson," he said, with an odd look.

"I will come out directly," replied Anderson, and passed out into the store, where Charlotte Carroll stood waiting with a heightened color on her cheeks and a look of mingled appeal and annoyance in her eyes.

"I beg your pardon," she said, "but can you cash a check for me for twenty-five dollars? It will be a great favor."

"Certainly," replied Anderson, without the slightest hesitation. He was conscious that both clerks, the man and the boy, were watching him with furtive curiosity, and he was aware that Carroll's unreliability in the matter of his drafts had become widely known. He passed around the counter to the money-drawer.

"Money seems to be very scarce in Banbridge this morning," remarked Charlotte, in a sweet, slightly petulant voice. She was both angry and ashamed that she had been forced to apply to Anderson to cash the check. "I have been everywhere, and nobody had as much as twenty-five dollars," she added.

Anderson heard a very faint chuckle, immediately covered by a cough, from Sam Riggs. He began counting out the notes, being conscious that the man and the boy were regarding each other with meaning, that the boy's elbow dug the man's ribs. He handed the money to Charlotte with a courteous bow, and she gave him in return the check, which was payable to her mother, and which had been indorsed by her.

"Thank you very much indeed," she said, but still in a piqued rather than very grateful voice. She really had no suspicion that any particular gratitude was called for towards any one who cashed one of her father's checks.

"You are quite welcome," Anderson replied.

"It is a great inconvenience not having a bank in Banbridge," she remarked, accusingly, as she went out of the door with a slight nod of her pretty head. Then suddenly she turned and looked back. "I am very much obliged," she said, in an entirely different voice. Her natural gentleness and courtesy had all at once reasserted themselves. "I trust I have not inconvenienced you," she added, very sweetly. "I would have waited until papa came home tonight and got him to cash the check. He was a little short this morning, and had to use some money before he could go to the bank, but my sister and I are very anxious to take the eleven-thirty train to New York, and we had only a dollar and six cents between us." She laughed as she said the last, and Anderson echoed her.

"That is not a very large amount, certainly, to equip two ladies to visit the shopping district," he said.

"I am very glad to accommodate you, and it is not the slightest inconvenience, I assure you."

"Well, I am very much obliged, very much," she repeated, with a pretty smile and nod, and she was gone with a little fluttering hop like a bird down the steps.

"He's got stuck," the boy motioned with his lips to the old clerk as Anderson re-entered the office, and the man nodded in assent. Neither of them ventured to express the opinion to Anderson. Both stood in a certain awe of him. The former lawyer still held familiarity somewhat at bay.

However, there followed a whispered consultation between the two clerks, and both chuckled, and finally Sam Riggs advanced with bravado to the office door.

"Mr. Anderson," he said, with mischief in his tone, and Anderson turned and looked at him inquiringly. "Oh, it is nothing, not worth speaking of, I suppose," said Sammy Riggs, "but that kid, the Carroll boy, swiped an apple off that basket beside the door when he went out with his sister. I saw him."

CHAPTER XII

Anderson was in the state of mind of a man who dreams and is quite aware all the time that he is dreaming. He deliberately indulged himself in this habit of mind. "When I am ready, I shall put all this away," he continually assured his inner consciousness. Then into the delicious charm of his air-castle he leaped again, mind and body. In those days he grew perceptibly younger. The fire of youth lit his eyes. He fed on the stimulants of sweet dreams, and for the time they nourished as well as exhilarated. Everybody whom he met told him how well he looked and that he was growing younger every day. He was shrewd enough to understand fully the fact that they considered him far from youth, or they would not have thus expressed themselves, but the triumph which he felt when he saw himself in his looking-glass, and in his own realization of himself, caused him to laugh at the innuendo. He felt that he *was* young, as young as man could wish to be. He, as before said, had never been vain, but mortal man could not have helped exultation at the sight of that victorious visage of himself looking back at him. He did not admit it to himself, but he took more pains with his dress, although he had always been rather punctilious in that direction. All unknown to himself, and, had he known it, the knowledge would have aroused in him rebellion and shame, he was carrying out the instinct of the love-smitten male of all species. In lieu of the gorgeous feathers he put on a new coat and tie, he trimmed his mustache carefully. He smoothed and lighted his face with the beauty of joy and hope and of pleasant dreams. But there was, since he was a man at the head of creation, something more subtle and noble in his preening. In those days he became curiously careful — although, being naturally clean-hearted, he had little need for care — of his very thoughts. Naturally fastidious in his soul habits, he became even more so. The very books he read were, although he was unconscious of it, such as contributed to his spiritual adornment, to fit himself for his constant dwelling in his country of dreams. Certain people he avoided, certain he courted. One woman, who was innately coarse, although her life had hedged her in safely from impropriety, was calling upon his mother one afternoon about this time. She was the wife of the old Presbyterian clergyman, Dr. Gregg. She was a small, solidly built woman, in late middle life, tightly hooked up in black silk as to her body, and as to her soul by the prescribed boundaries of her position in life. Anderson, returning rather earlier than usual, found her with his mother, and retreated with actual rudeness, the woman became all at once so repellent to him.

"My son gets very tired," Mrs. Anderson said, softly, as she passed the pound-cake again to her caller. "Quite often, when he comes in, he goes by himself and has a quiet smoke before he says much even to me."

Mrs. Gregg was eating the pound-cake with such extreme relish that Mrs. Anderson, who was herself fastidious, looked away, and as she did so heard distinctly a smack of the other woman's lips.

"He grows handsomer and younger every time I see him," remarked Mrs. Gregg when she had swallowed her mouthful of cake and before she took another.

Mrs. Anderson repeated the caller's compliment to her son later on when the two were at the supper-table. "Yes, she paid you a great compliment," said she; "but, dear, why did you run out in that way? It was almost rude, and she the minister's wife, too."

"I don't see how Dr. Gregg keeps up his necessary quota of saving grace, living with her," said Anderson.

"Why, my dear, I think she is a good woman."

"She is a bottled-up vessel of wrath," said Anderson.

"My son, I never heard you speak so before, and about a lady, too."

Anderson fairly blushed before his mother's mild eyes of surprise. "Mother, you are right," he said, penitently. "I ought to be ashamed of myself, and I am. I know I was rude, but I did not feel like seeing her today. Of course she is a good woman."

Mrs. Anderson looked a little reflective. Now that her son had taken a proper attitude with regard to her sister-woman, she began to feel a little critical license herself. "I will admit that she has little mannerisms which are not exactly agreeable and must grate on Dr. Gregg," said she. As she spoke she seemed to hear again the smacking of the lips over the pound-cake. Then she looked scrutinizingly at her son. "But," she said, "I do believe she was right, Randolph, about your looks."

"Nonsense," said Randolph, laughing.

It was a warm night. After supper they both went out on the front porch. Mrs. Anderson sat gazing at her son from between the folds of a little, white lace kerchief which she wore over her head, to guard against possible dampness.

"Randolph," said she, after a while.

"What is it, mother, dear?"

"Do you feel well?"

"Of course I feel well. Why?"

"You look too well to be natural," said she, slowly.

"Mother, what an absurdity!"

"It is so," said she. "I had not noticed it until Mrs. Gregg spoke, but I see it now. I don't know where my eyes have been. You look too well."

Randolph laughed. "Now, mother, don't you think that sounds foolish?"

Mrs. Anderson continued to regard him with an expression of maternal love and severity, which pierced externals more keenly than an X-ray. "No," said she, "I do not think it is foolish. You look too well to be natural. You look this minute as young in your face as you did when I had you in petticoats."

Randolph laughed loudly at that, but his mother was quite earnest.

She was not satisfied, and continued arguing the matter until she became afraid of the increasing dampness and went into the house, and the son drew a breath of relief. The mother little dreamed, with all her astuteness, of what was really transpiring. She did not know that when she had seated herself beside her son on the porch she had displaced with her gentle, elderly materiality the sweetest phantom of a beloved young girl. She did not know that when she entered the house the delicate, evanescent thing returned swifter than thought itself, and filled with the sweet presence that vacuum in her son's heart which she herself had never filled, and nestled there through a delicious hour of the summer night. She did not dream, as she sat by the window, staring out drowsily into the soft shadows and heard no murmur from her son on the porch, that in reality the silence of his soul was broken by words and tones which she had never heard from his lips, although she had brought him into the world.

Anderson never admitted to himself the possibility of his dreams coming true. While his self-respect never wavered, while he viewed himself with no unworthy disparagement, he still saw himself as he was: verging towards middle age, unsuccessful according to the standard of the world. He was one of those inglorious failures, a man who has failed to follow out his chosen course of life. He was one who had turned back, overcome confessedly by odds. He told himself proudly and simply that his earning of money was, to one simple and honest end — the prolonging of existence on the earth for the good of one's fellow-beings, and one's own growth; that he was attaining that end more completely in his little grocery store than he had ever done in his law-office. Yet always he saw himself, in a measure, as others saw him, and the humility of his position in the eyes of the world asserted itself. While he felt not the slightest bend in the erectness of his own soul because of it, while it even amused him, he never forgot the supercilious courtesy of the girls' father towards him. He recognized, even while feeling himself on superior heights, the downward vision of the man who robbed him. It was true that he paid scorn for scorn, but he was forced to take as well as give.

He also was not in the slightest doubt as to Charlotte's own attitude towards him. He understood to the full the signification of the word grocer for her. He was, to her mind, hardly a man at all, rather a mechanical dispenser of butter and eggs for the needs of a superior race. But he understood also the childish innocence and involuntariness of this view of hers. He recognized even the ludicrousness of the situation which perverted tragedy to comedy, almost Cyrano fashion. He compared himself to Cyrano.

"As well consider the possibility of marriage with a girl of her training, even although it is on a false basis, with a monstrosity of nose on my face, as with the legend of retail grocery across my scutcheon," he told himself. He even laughed over it.

Therefore, being of a turn of mind which can rear for itself airy towers of delight over the values of insufficiency of life, and having an access of spirituality which enabled him to get a certain reality from them, he dreamed on, and let his new love irradiate his own life, like a man carrying a lantern on a dark path. There are those that are born to sunlit paths, and there are those whom a beneficient Providence has supplied with lanterns of compensation, and the latter are not always the unhappier nor the less progressive. Never admitting to himself the possibility of the actual presence of the girl in the house as his wife, he yet peopled the rooms with her. He rose up in spirit before her entering a door. There were especial nooks wherein his fancy could project her with such illusion that his heart would leap as if at the actual sight of her. In particular was there one window in the sitting-room which, being in a little projection of the house, overlooked a special little view of its own. From this window between the folds of the muslin curtains could be seen a file of blooming hollyhocks. Behind them a grassy expanse arose with a long ascent, and the rosette — like blossoms of pink and pale-gold, with gray-green bosses of leaves, lay against the green field like the design on a shield.

In this window was an old-fashioned rocking-chair cushioned softly with faded, rose-patterned chintz, and before it stood always a small foot-stool covered with dim-brown canvas on which was a wreath of roses done in cross-stitch by his mother in her girlhood. Anderson loved to see Charlotte sitting in this chair with her feet on the footstool, her pretty head leaning back against the faded roses of the chintz, the delicate curve of her cheek towards him, as she swayed gently back and forth and seemed to gaze peacefully out of the window at the hollyhocks blooming against the green hill. It was characteristic of the man's dreams that the girl's face in them was turned a little from him. She never saw him when he entered, she never broke the sweet silence of her own dreams within dreams, for him, and he never, even in dreams, touched the soft curve of that averted cheek, or even one of the little hands lying as lightly as flowers in her muslin lap. Anderson, the commonplace man in the gro-cery business, in the commonplace present, dreamed as reverently and spiritually of the lady of his love as Dante of his Beatrice, or Petrarch of his Laura. He would go down to the grave with his songs all unsung; but the man was a poet, as are all who worship the god, and not the likeness of themselves in him. As Anderson sat on the porch that summer night, to his fancy Charlotte Carroll sat on the step above him. Without fairly looking he could see the sweep of her white draperies and the mild fair-ness, producing the effect of luminosity, of her face in the dusk.

Then suddenly Charlotte herself dispelled the illusion. She passed by with her sister Ina and a young man. Anderson heard the low, sweet babble of girls' tongues and a hearty, boyish laugh before they came opposite the porch. He knew at once that Charlotte was one of the girls. He could not see them very plainly when they passed, for the moon had not yet risen and the shadows of the trees were dense. He had glimpses of pale contours and ruffling white draperies floating around the young man, who walked on the outside. He towered above them both with stately tenderness. He was smoking, and Anderson noted that with a throb of anger. He had an old-fashioned conviction that a man should not smoke when walking with ladies. He was sitting perfectly motionless when they came alongside, and all at once one of the girls, Ina, the eldest, perceived him, and started violently with an exclamation. All three laughed, and the young man said, raising his hat, "Good-evening, Mr. Anderson."

Anderson returned the salutation. He thought, but was not quite sure, that Charlotte nodded. He heard, quite distinctly, Ina remark, when they were scarcely past, in a voice of girlish scorn and merry ridicule:

"Is the grocer a friend of yours, Mr. Eastman?"

Anderson was sure that he heard a "Hush! he will hear you!" from Charlotte, before young Frank Eastman replied, like a man:

"Yes, every time, Miss Carroll, if he will do me the honor to let me call him one. Mr. Anderson is a mighty fine gentleman."

The girl's voice said something in response with a slightly abashed but still jibing inflection, but Anderson could not catch it. They passed out of sight, the cigar-smoke lingering in their wake. Anderson inhaled it with no longer any feeling of disapproval. He slowly lit a cigar himself, and smoked and meditated. The presence on the step above him was for the time dispelled by her own materiality. The dream eluded the substance. Anderson thought of the young man who had walked past with a curious feeling of something akin to gratitude. "Frank Eastman is a fine young fellow," he thought. He had known him ever since he had been a child. He had been one of the boys whom everybody knew and liked. He had grown up a village favorite. The thought flashed through Anderson's mind that here was a possible husband for Charlotte, and probably a good husband.

"He is an only son," he told himself; "he will have a little money. He is as good as and better than young men average, and he is charming, a man to attract any girl."

Anderson, when he had finished his cigar and one more, and had gone into the house to read a little before going to bed, quite decided that Charlotte Carroll was to marry young Frank Eastman. He walked remorselessly over the step where his fancy had placed her, and when he glanced at her pretty little nook in the sitting-room, as he passed through with his lamp and his book, it was vacant. Anderson felt a rigid acquiescence, and read his book with interest until after midnight.

In the mean time Charlotte, her sister Ina, and young Eastman sauntered slowly along through the shadowy streets of Banbridge. The girls held up their white gowns over their lace petticoats. They wore no hats, and their pretty, soft, dark locks floated like mist around their faces. The young man pressed Ina's arm as closely and lovingly as he dared. He was yet young enough and innocent enough to be in his heart of hearts as afraid of a girl as, when a child, he had been afraid of his mother. He thought Ina Carroll something wonderful; Charlotte he scarcely thought of at all except with vague approbation because she was Ina's sister. He took the girls into Andrew Drew's drug store for ice-cream soda. He watched, with happy proprietorship, the girls dally daintily with the long spoons in the sweet, cold mixture. Seen in the electric light of the store, they had a bewildering and fairly dazzling splendor of youth and bloom. Their faces, freshened to exquisite tints by the damp night air, shone forth from the floating film of dark hair with the unquestioning delight of the passing moment. There was in these young faces at the moment no shadow of the past or future. They were pure light. Young Eastman, eating his ice-cream, looked over his glass at Ina Carroll and realized the dazzle of her in his soul. She felt his look and smiled at him pleasantly, yet with a certain gay defiance. Charlotte caught both looks. She stirred her ice-cream briskly into the liquid and drank it.

"Come, honey," she said to Ina. "It is time to go home."

A man stood near the door as they passed and raised his hat eagerly.

"Who is that man?" Ina said to young Eastman when they were on the sidewalk.

"His name is Lee."

When the party had gone out, Lee turned with his self-conscious, consequential air. Ray, the postmaster, was standing at the counter. Little Willy Eddy also was there. He lingered about the soda-fountain. Nobody knew how badly he wanted a drink of soda. He was like a child about it, but he was afraid lest his Minna should call him to account for the five cents.

"Pretty fine-looking girls," observed Lee to Ray and Drew.

"Yes," assented Ray. "You know them?"

"Well, no, not directly, but Captain Carroll and I are quite intimate in a business way."

The druggist looked up eagerly. "You think he is good?" he asked.

"I have heard some queer things lately," said the postmaster.

Lee faced them both. "Good?" he cried. "Good? Arthur Carroll good? Why, I'd be willing to risk every dollar I have in the world, or ever hope to have. He's the smartest business man I ever saw in my life. I tell you he's A No. 1. He's got a business head equal to any on the Street, I don't care who it is. Well, all I have to say, *I* am not afraid of him! No, sir!"

"I heard he had some pretty promising stock to sell," said the postmaster.

"Promising? No, it is not promising! Promising is not the word for it. It is sure, dead sure."

Little Willy Eddy drew very near.

"What is it selling at?" asked Ray.

"One dollar and sixty cents," replied Lee, with an intonation of pride and triumph.

"Cheap enough," said Ray.

"Yes, sir, one dollar and sixty cents, and it will be up to five in six months and paying dividends, and up to fifty, with ten-per-cent. dividends, in a year and a half."

Little Willy Eddy had in the savings-bank a little money. Before he left he had arranged with Henry Lee to invest it through his influence with the great man, Carroll, and say nothing about it to any one outside. Willy hoped fondly that his Minna might know nothing about it until he should surprise her with the proceeds of his great venture. Then Willy Eddy marched boldly upon the soda-fountain.

"Give me a chocolate ice-cream soda," he said, like a man.

CHAPTER XIII

Three days later, at dinner, Charlotte Carroll said something about the difficulty she had had about getting the check cashed.

"It is the queerest thing," said she, in a lull of the conversation, pausing with her soup-spoon lifted, "how very difficult it is to get a check for even a small amount cashed in Banbridge."

Carroll's spoon clattered against his plate. "What do you mean?" he asked, sharply.

Charlotte looked at him surprised. "Why, nothing," said she, "only I went to every store in town to get your check for twenty-five dollars cashed, and then I had to go to Anderson's finally. I should think they must be very poor here. Are they, papa?"

Carroll went on with his soup. "Who gave you the check to cash?" he said, in a low voice.

"Aunt Anna," replied Charlotte. "Why?"

Anna spoke quite eagerly, and it seemed apologetically. "Arthur," said she, "the girls were very anxious to go to the City."

"Yes," said Ina, "I really had to go that day. I wanted to get that silk. I had that charged; there wasn't money enough; but it has not come yet. I don't see where it is."

"I let Charlotte take the check," Anna Carroll said again, still with an air of nervous apology, "but I saw no reason why — I thought —"

"You thought what?" said Carroll. His voice was exceedingly low and gentle, but Anna Carroll started.

"Nothing," said she, hastily. "Nothing, Arthur."

"Well, I just went everywhere with it," Charlotte said again; "then I had to go to Anderson, after all. I just hated to. I don't like him. He laughed when Eddy and I went there to take back the candy."

"He laughed because we took it back — a little thing like that," said Eddy.

Carroll looked at him, and the boy cast his eyes down and took a spoonful of soup with an abashed air.

"He was the only one in Banbridge that seemed to have as much as twenty-five dollars in his money-drawer," said Charlotte. "I began to think that Ina and I should have to give up going to New York."

"Don't take any more checks around the shops here to cash, honey," said Carroll. "Come to me; I'll fix it up some way. Amy, dear, are you all ready for the drive?"

"Yes, dear," said Mrs. Carroll. She looked unusually pretty that night in a mauve gown of some thin, soft, wool material, with her old amethysts. Even her dark hair seemed to get amethystine shadows, and her eyes, too.

Carroll regarded her admiringly.

"Amy, darling, you do get lovelier every day," he said.

The others laughed and echoed him with fond merriment.

"Doesn't she?" said Ina.

"Amy's the prettiest girl in this old town," said Eddy, and all the Carrolls laughed like children.

"Well, I'm glad you all admire me so much," Mrs. Carroll said, in her sweet drawl, "because —"

"Because what, honey?" said Carroll. The boy and the two girls looked inquiringly, but Anna Carroll smiled with slightly vexed knowledge.

"Well," said Mrs. Carroll, "you must all look at me in my purple gown and get all the comfort you can out of it; you must nourish yourselves through your æsthetic sense, because this soup is all you will get for dinner, except dessert. There is a little dessert."

Poor little Eddy Carroll made a slight, half-smothered exclamation. "Oh, shucks!" he said, then he laughed with the others. None of them looked surprised. They all laughed, though somewhat ruefully.

"Anna came this forenoon and asked me what she should do," Mrs. Carroll said, in her soft tone of childlike glee, as if she really enjoyed the situation. "Poor Anna looked annoyed. This country air makes Anna hungry. Now, as for me, I am not hungry at all. If I can have fruit and salad I am quite satisfied. It is so fortunate that we have those raspberries and those early pears. Those little pears are quite delicious, and they are nourishing, I am sure. And then it is providential that we have lettuce in our own garden. And the grocer did not object in the least to letting last week's bill run and letting us have olive-oil and vinegar. I have plenty, so I can regard it all quite cheerfully; but Anna, poor darling, is hungry like a pussy-cat for real, solid meat. Well, Anna comes, face so long" — Mrs. Carroll drew down her lovely face, to a chorus of admiring laughter, Anna Carroll herself joining. Mrs. Carroll continued. "Yes, so long," and made her face long again by way of encore. "And I said, 'Why, Anna, honey, what is the matter?' 'Amy,' said she, 'this is serious, very serious. Why, neither the butcher nor the egg-man will trust us. We have only money enough to part pay one of them, just to keep them going,' says she, 'and what shall I do, Amy?' 'It's either to go without meat or eggs,' says I. 'Yes, Amy, honey,' says she. 'And you can't pay them each a little?' says I, 'for I am real wise about that way of doing, you know.'" Mrs. Carroll said the last with the air of a precocious child; she looked askance for admiration as she said it, and laughed herself with the others. "'No,' says poor Anna — 'no, Amy, there is not enough money for two littles, only enough for one little. What shall we do, Amy?' 'Well,' says Amy, 'we had chops for lunch.' 'Those aren't paid for, and that is the reason we can't have beef for dinner,' says Anna. 'Well,' says Amy, 'we had those chops, didn't we? And the butcher can't alter that, anyway; and we are all nourished by those chops, and dear Arthur has had his good luncheon in the City, and there is soup-stock in the house, and things to make one of those delicious raspberry-puddings, and we cannot starve, we poor but honest Carrolls, on those things; and eggs are cheaper, are they not, honey, dear?' 'Yes,' says Anna, with that sort of groan she has when her mind is on economy — 'yes, Amy, dear.' 'And,' says I, 'Arthur always wants his eggs for breakfast, and he does not like cold meat in the morning, and if he went to business without his eggs, and there was an accident on his empty stomach, only think how we would feel, Anna. So we will have,' says Amy, 'soup and pudding for dinner, and eggs for breakfast, and we will part pay the egg-man and not the butcher.' And then Amy puts on her new gown and does all she can for her family, to make up for the lack of the roast."

"Did you say it was raspberry-pudding, Amy?" asked Eddy, anxiously.

"Yes, honey, with plenty of sauce, and you may have some twice if you want it."

"Ring the bell, dear," said Carroll.

"You don't mind, Arthur, do you?" Mrs. Carroll asked, with a confident look at him.

Carroll smiled. "No, darling, only I hope none of you are really going hungry."

They all laughed at him. "Soup and pudding are all one ought to eat in such hot weather," Charlotte said, conclusively.

She even jumped up, ran to her father, and threw her arms around his neck and kissed him, to reassure him. "You darling papa," she whispered in his ear, and when he looked at her tears shone in her beautiful eyes.

Carroll's own face turned strangely sober for a second, then he laughed. "Run back to your seat and get your pudding, sweetheart," he said, with a loving push, as the maid entered.

People thought it rather singular that the Carrolls should have but one maid, but there were reasons. Carroll himself, when he first organized his Banbridge establishment, had expressed some dissent as to the solitary servant.

"Why not have more?" he asked, but Anna Carroll was unusually decided in her response.

"Amy and I have been talking it over, Arthur," said she, "and we have decided that we would prefer only Marie."

"Why, Anna?" Carroll had asked, with a frown.

"Now, Arthur, dear, don't look cross," his wife had cried. "It is only that when the truce is over with the butcher and baker — and after a while the truce always is over, you know, you poor, dear boy, ever since you — ever since you were so badly treated about your business, you know, and when the butcher and the baker turn on us, Anna and I have decided it would be better not to have a trust in the kitchen. You know there has always been a trust in the kitchen, and two or even three maids saying they will not make bread and roast and wash the dishes, and having a council of war on the back stoop with the baker and grocer, are so much worse than one maid, don't you know, precious?"

"The long and the short of it is, Arthur," Anna Carroll said, quite bluntly, "it is much less wearing to get on with one maid who has not had her wages, and much easier to induce her to remain or forfeit all hope of ever receiving them, than with more than one."

Only the one maid was engaged, and now Anna's prophecy had come to pass, and she was remaining for the sake of her unpaid wages. She was a young girl, and pretty for one of her sisterhood, who perpetuate, as a rule, the hard and strenuous lineaments and forms held to hard labor, until they have attained a squat solidity of ungraceful muscle. This little Hungarian Marie was still not overdeveloped muscularly, although one saw her hands with a certain shock after her little, smiling face, which still smiled, despite her wrongs. Nothing could exceed the sweetness of the girl's disposition, although she came of a fierce peasant line, quick to resort to the knife as a redresser of injuries, and quick to perceive injuries.

Marie still danced assiduously about her tasks, which were manifold, for not one of the Carroll women had the slightest idea of any accountability in the matter of household labor. It never occurred to one of them to make her bed, or even hang up her dress, but, instead, to wonder why Marie did not do it. However, if Marie really had an ill day, or, as sometimes happened, was up all night at a ball, they never rebelled or spoke an impatient word. The beds simply remained unmade and the dresses where they had fallen. The ladies always had a kindly, ever-caressing smile or word for little Marie. They were actually, in a way, fond of her, as people are fond of a pretty little domestic beast of burden, and Marie herself adored them. She loved them from afar, and one of her great reasons for wishing to stay for her wages was to buy some finery after the fashion of Charlotte's and Ina's. Marie had not asked for her wages many times, and never of Captain Carroll, but tonight she took courage. There was a ball that week, Thursday, and her poor, little, cheap muslin of last season was bedraggled and faded until it was no longer wearable. Marie waylaid Captain Carroll as he was returning from the stable, whither he had been to see a lame foot of one of the horses. Marie stood in her kitchen door, around which was growing lustily a wild cucumber-vine. She put her two coarse hands on her hips, which were large with the full gathers of her cotton skirt. Around her neck was one of the garish-colored kerchiefs which had come with her from her own country. It was an ugly thing, but gave a picturesque bit of color to her otherwise dingy garb.

"Mr. Captain," said Marie, in a very small, sweet, almost infantile voice. It was frightened, yet with a certain coquetry in it. This small Hungarian girl had met with very few looks and words in her whole life which were not admiring. In spite of her poor estate she had the power of the eternal feminine, and she used it knowingly, but quite artlessly. She knew exactly how to speak to her "Mr. Captain," in such a way that a smile in response would be inevitable.

Carroll stopped. "Well, Marie?" he said, and he smiled down into the little face precisely after the manner of her calculation.

"Mr. Captain," said she again, and again came the feeler after a smile, the expression of droll sweetness and appeal which forced it.

"Well, Marie," said Carroll, "what is it? What do you want?"

Marie went straight to the point. "Mine vages," said she, and a bit of the coquetry faded, and her small smile waxed rather piteous. She wanted that new dress for the ball sadly.

Carroll's face changed; he compressed his mouth. Marie shrank a little with frightened eyes on his face.

"How much is it, Marie?" asked Carroll.

"Tree mont vage, Mr. Captain," answered Marie, eagerly, "I haf not had."

Carroll took out his pocket-book and gave her a ten-dollar note.

Marie reached out for it eagerly, but her face fell a little. "It is tree mont, Mr. Captain," she ventured.

"That is all I can spare tonight, Marie," said Carroll, quite sternly. "That will have to answer tonight."

Marie smiled again, eying him timidly. "Yes, it will my dress get for the ball, Mr. Captain."

Marie stood framed in her wild cucumber-vine, regarding the captain with her pretty ingratiation, but not another smile she got. Carroll strolled around to the front of the house, and in a second the carriage rolled around from the stable. Marie nodded to the coachman; there was never a man of her acquaintance but she had a pretty, artless salutation always ready for him. She shook her ten-dollar note triumphantly at him, and laughed with delight.

"Got money," said she. Marie had a way of ending up her words, especially those ending in y, as if she finished them up with a kiss. She pursed up her lips, and gave a most fascinating little nip to her vowels, which, as a rule, she sounded short. "Money," said she again, and the ten-dollar note fluttered like a green leaf from between the large thumb and forefinger of her coarse right hand.

The coachman laughed back in sympathy. He was still smiling when he drove up beside his employer at the front-door. He leaned from his seat just as the flutter of the ladies' dresses appeared at the front-door, and said something to Carroll, with a look of pleased expectation. That money in Marie's hand had cheered him on his own account.

Carroll looked at him gently imperturbable. "I am sorry, Martin. I shall be obliged to ask you to wait a few days," he said, with the utmost courtesy.

The man's honest, confident face fell. "You said —" he began.

"What did I say?" Carroll asked, calmly.

"You said you would let me have some tonight."

"Yes, I remember," Carroll said, "but I have had an unexpected demand since I returned from the City, and it has taken every cent of ready money. I must ask you to wait a few days longer. You are not in serious need of anything, Martin?"

"No, sir," said the man, hesitatingly.

"I was going to say that if you were needing any little thing you might make use of my credit," said Carroll. As the ladies, Mrs. Carroll and Miss Carroll, came up to the carriage, Carroll thrust his hand in his pocket and drew forth a couple of cigars, which he handed to the coachman with a winning expression. "Here are a couple of cigars for you, Martin," he said.

"Thank you, sir," replied the coachman.

He put the cigars in his pocket and took up the lines. As he drove down the drive and along the shady Banbridge road he was wondering hard if Marie had got the money which Carroll had intended to pay him. He did not mind so much if she had it. Marie was Hungarian, and Martin had not much use for outlandish folk on general principles, but he had a sneaking admiration for little Marie. "Now she can go to her ball," thought he. Marie said the word as if it had one l and a short a — bal. Martin smiled inwardly at the recollection, though he did not allow his face of important dignity to relax.

He thought, further, that, after all, he need not worry about his own pay. Carroll had paid Marie and would pay him. He thought comfortably of the cigars, which were sure to be good. His original respect and admiration for his employer swelled high in his heart. He felt quite happy driving his high-stepping horses over the good road. The conversation of the ladies at his back, and of Carroll at his side, passed his ears, trained not to hear, as unintelligibly as the babble of the birds. Martin had no curiosity.

While their elders were driving, the Carroll sisters and the brother were all out on the front porch. Ina was rocking in a rattan chair, Charlotte sat on the highest step of the porch leaning against a fluted white pillar, the boy sprawled miserably on the lowest step.

"It's awful dull," he complained.

Charlotte looked down at him commiseratingly from her semicircle of white muslin flounces. "I'll play ball with you awhile, Eddy, dear," said she.

The boy sniffed. "Don't want to play ball with a girl," he replied.

Charlotte said nothing.

Eddy twitched with his face averted. Then suddenly he looked up at his sister. "Charlotte, I love to play ball with you," said he, sweetly, "only, you see, I can't pitch hard enough, your hands are so awful soft, and I feel like I could pitch awful hard tonight."

"Well, I tell you what you may do, dear," said Ina.

"What?"

"Go down to the post-office and get the last mail."

Eddy started up with alacrity. "All right," said he.

"And you may run up-stairs to my room," said Charlotte, "and hunt round till you find my purse, and get out ten cents and buy yourself an ice-cream."

Eddy was up and out with a whoop.

"Are you expecting a letter, honey?" asked Charlotte of her sister.

Ina laughed evasively. "I thought Eddy would like to go," said she.

"Now, Ina, I know whom you are expecting a letter from; you can't cheat me."

Ina laughed rather foolishly; her face was pink.

Charlotte continued to regard her with a curious expression. It was at once sad, awed, and withal confused, in sympathy with the other girl. "Ina," said she.

"Well, honey?"

"I think you ought to tell me, your own sister, if you are —"

"What —"

"Ina, I really think —"

"Oh, hush, dear!" Ina whispered. "Here comes Mr. Eastman."

Young Frank Eastman, in his light summer clothes, came jauntily around the curve of the drive, his straw hat in hand, and the sisters fluttered to their feet to greet him. Then Eddy reappeared with the dime securely clutched, and inquired anxiously of Charlotte if she cared whether he bought soda or candy with it. Young Eastman ran after him down the walk and had a whispered conference. When the boy returned, which was speedily, he had a letter for his sister Ina and a box of the most extravagant candy which Banbridge afforded. The young people sat chatting and laughing and nibbling sweets until nearly ten o'clock. Then young Eastman took his leave.

He was rather desirous to be gone before Captain Carroll returned. Although Carroll always treated him with the most punctilious courtesy, even going out of his way to speak to him, the young man always felt a curious discomfort, as if he realized some covert disapprobation on the elder's part.

"They are late," Ina said, after the caller's light coat had disappeared behind the shrubbery.

"I suppose they waited for the moon to rise," Charlotte replied. "You know Amy dearly loves to drive by moonlight."

"Well, let's go to bed, and not wait," Ina said, with a yawn. "I'm so sleepy." She had sat with her letter unopened in her lap all evening.

"All right," assented Charlotte.

"I'm going to sit here till they come," said Eddy.

"Very well," said Charlotte, "but mind you don't stir off the porch."

The two girls went up to their own rooms. They occupied adjoining ones. Charlotte slept in a small room out of the larger one which was Ina's.

Charlotte came in from her room brushing out her hair, and Ina was reading her letter. She looked up with a blushing confusion and crumpled the paper involuntarily.

"Oh, you needn't start so," said Charlotte. "I know whom the letter is from. It's that old Major Arms."

"He is not old. He is no older than papa, and you don't call him old," Ina retorted, resentfully.

"I don't call him old for a father, but I would for —"

"Well, he isn't a — yet."

"Ina, you ought to tell me."

"Well, I'm going to marry Major Arms, so there!"

"Oh, Ina!"

The two girls stood staring at each other for a moment, then they ran to each other. "Oh, Charlotte! oh, Charlotte!" sobbed Ina, convulsively.

"Oh, Ina! oh, honey!"

"I'm going to, Charlotte. Oh, I am going to!"

"Ina, do you, do you —"

"What?"

"Love that old Major Arms?" Charlotte spoke out, in a tone of almost horror.

"I don't know. Oh, I don't know," sobbed Ina.

"Ina, you don't love — Mr. Eastman better?"

"No, I don't," replied Ina, in a tone of utter conviction. "Charlotte, do you know what would happen if I married Mr. Eastman? Do you?"

"No, I don't."

"All my life long I would be at war with the butcher and baker, just as — just as we always are."

"Ina Carroll, you aren't getting married just for that? Oh, that is dreadful!"

"No, I am not," said Ina. "You call Major Arms old, and you don't see — you don't see how a girl can ever fall in love with him, but — I think he's splendid. Yes, I do. You can laugh, Charlotte, but I do. And it is a good deal to marry a man you can honestly say you think is splendid! But you can do a thing, for a very good, even a noble reason, and all the time know there is another reason not quite so noble, that you can't help but take some comfort in. And that is the way I do with this. Charlotte, poor papa does just the best he can, and there never was a man like him; Major Arms isn't anything in comparison with papa. I never thought he was, but there is one thing I am very tired of in this world, and I can't help thinking with a good deal of pleasure that when I am married I will be free from it."

"What is that, honey?" The two girls had sat down on Ina's window-seat, and were nestling close together, with their arms around each other's waist, and the two streams of dark hair intermingling.

"I am heartily tired," said Ina, in a tone of impatient scorn, "of this everlasting annoyance to which we are subjected from the people who want us to pay them money for the necessaries of life. We must have a certain amount of things in order to live at all, and if people must have the money for them, I want them to have it, and not have to endure such continual persecution."

"Ina," said Charlotte, in a piteous, low voice, "do you think papa is very poor?"

"Yes, honey, I am afraid he is very poor."

Charlotte began to weep softly against her sister's shoulder.

"Don't cry, honey," soothed Ina. "You can come and stay with me a great deal, you know."

"Ina Carroll, do you think I would leave papa?" demanded Charlotte, suddenly erect. "Do you think — I would? You can, if you want to, but I will not."

"It costs something to support us, dear," said Ina. "Don't be angry, precious."

"I will never have another new dress in all my life," said Charlotte. "I won't eat anything. I tell you I never will leave papa, Ina Carroll."

CHAPTER XIV

It was about a week later when Anderson, going into the drug store one evening, found young Eastman in the line in front of the soda-fountain. A girl in white was with him, and Anderson thought at first glance that she was Charlotte Carroll, as a matter of course — he had so accustomed himself to think of the two in union by this time. Then he looked again and saw that the girl was much larger and fair-haired, and recognized her as Bessy Van Dorn, William Van Dorn's daughter. The girl's semi-German parentage showed in her complexion and high-bosomed, matronly figure, although she was so young. She had a large but charming face, full of the sweetest placidity; her eyes, as blue as the sky, looked out upon the world with amiable assent to all its conditions. It required no acuteness to predict this as an ideal spouse for a man of a nervous and irritable temperament; that there was in her nature that which could supply cushioned fulnesses to all the exactions of his. She sat on a high stool and sipped her ice-cream soda with simple absorption in the pleasant sensation. She paid no attention whatever to her escort beside her, who took his soda with his eyes fixed on her. Her chin overlapping in pink curves like a rose, was sunken in the lace at her neck as she sipped. She did not sit straight, but rested in her corsets with an awkward lassitude of enjoyment. It was a very warm night, but she paid no attention to that. She was without a hat, and the beads of perspiration stood all over her pink forehead, and her thin white muslin clung to her plump neck and arms. There was something almost indecent about the girl's enjoyment of her soda. Hardly a man in the shop but was watching her. Anderson gazed at her also, but with covert disgust and a resentment which was absurd. He scowled at the young fellow with her. He felt like a father whose daughter has been flouted by the man of her choice. "What the devil does the boy mean, taking soda here with that Van Dorn girl?" he asked himself. He felt like a reckoning with him, and chafed at the impossibility of it. When the couple rose to go Anderson met the young man's salutation with such a surly response and such a stern glance that he fairly started. The men stared as the two went out, their shoulders touching as they passed through the door. The girl was round-shouldered from careless standing, but she moved with a palpitating grace of yielding, and the smooth, fair braids which bound her head shone like silver.

"Guess that's a go," a man said, with a chuckle; "a narrower door would have suited them just as well."

"Mighty good-looking girl," said Amidon.

"Healthy girl," said another. "If more young fellows had the horse-sense to marry girls like that, I'd give up medicine and go on a ranch." The Banbridge doctor said that. He was rather young, and had been in the village about five years. He had taken the practice of an old physician, a distant relative who had died six months before. Dr. Wilson was called a remarkably able man in his profession. He had been having several prescriptions filled, and kept several waiting. He was a large man with a coarsely handsome physique and a brutal humor with women. He was not liked personally, but the people rather bragged about their great physician and were proud when he was called to the towns round about.

"There's no getting Dr. Wilson, for a certainty, he has such an enormous practice!" they said, with pride.

"That girl is as handsome and healthy as an Alderney cow," he added, now, and the men laughed.

"She's a stunner," said Amidon.

Anderson went out abruptly without waiting to make his purchase. He felt as repelled as only a man of his temperament can feel. No woman could equal his sense of utter disgust, first with the quite innocent girl herself, next with the young physician for his insistence upon the subject. His wrath against young Eastman, his unreasoning and ridiculous wrath, swelled high as he dwelt upon the outrage of his desertion of a girl like his little Charlotte, that little creature of fire and dew, for this full-blown rose of a woman — the outrage to her and to himself. When he got home, his mother inquired anxiously what the matter was.

"Nothing, dear," he replied, brusquely.

"You look as if something worried you," said she. She had been taking a little evening toddle on her tiny, slippered feet out in the old-fashioned flower-garden beside the house, and she had a little bunch of sweet herbs, which she dearly loved, in her hand. She fastened a sprig of thyme in his coat as she stood talking to him, and the insistent odor seemed as real as a presence when he breathed. "nothing has gone wrong with your business, has there?" she inquired, lovingly.

"No, mother," he replied, and moved away from her gently, with the fragrance of the thyme strong in his consciousness.

His mother put her sweet nosegay in water. Then she went to bed, and Anderson sat on the stoop. Young Eastman and the Van Dorn girl passed after he sat there, and he thought with a loving passion of protection of poor little Charlotte alone at home. "I'll warrant the poor child is watching for that good-for-nothing scoundrel this minute," he told himself. He would have liked to knock young Eastman down; it would have delighted his soul to kick him; he would have given a good deal to have had him at the top of the steps.

The weather was intensely warm. He heard his mother fling her bedroom blinds wide open to catch all the air. The sky was clear, but all along the northwest horizon was a play of lightning from a far-distant storm.

Anderson lit another cigar. The night seemed to grow more and more oppressive. When a breath of wind came, it was like a hot breath of some fierce sentiency. A disagreeable odor from something was also borne upon it. The odors of the flowers seemed in abeyance. The play of blue-and-rosy light along the northwest horizon continued. Anderson got a certain pleasure from watching it. Nature's spectacularity diverted him, as if he had been a child, from his own affairs, which seemed to give him a dull pain. Between the flashes he asked himself why.

"It is just right," he told himself; "just what I desired. Why do I feel this way?"

Presently he decided with self-deception that it was because of the recent scene in the drug store. He remembered quite distinctly the young man's gaze at the stout, blue-eyed girl. "What right had the fellow to look at another girl after that fashion?" he said to himself. Then it struck him suddenly as being perhaps impossible for him ever to look at Charlotte in just that fashion. He thought with a thrill of indignant pride that there was a maiden who would have the best of love as her right. Then sitting there he heard a quick tread and a trill of whistle as meaningless as that of a robin, and young Eastman himself came alongside. He stopped before the gate.

"Hullo!" he said, suddenly.

"Hullo!" responded Anderson.

"Got a match?" said Eastman.

"Sure."

Eastman sprang up the steps until he came in reach of Anderson's proffered handful of matches. "Hotter 'n blazes," he remarked, as he scratched a match on his trousers leg.

"Hottest night of the season so far, I think," responded Anderson.

"I'm about beat out with it," said Eastman, lighting his cigar with no difficulty in the dead atmosphere. He threw himself sprawling on the step at Anderson's feet, without any invitation. "Whew!" he sighed.

"It'll be hotter than hades in the City tomorrow," he remarked, after a moment's silence.

Anderson muttered an assent. He was considering as nervously as a woman whether he should say anything to this boy. While he was hesitating, young Eastman himself led up to it.

"Saw you in the drug store just now," he remarked.

"Yes; you were with —"

"Bessy Van Dorn — yes. Pretty girl?" Eastman spoke with the insufferable air of patronizing criticism of extreme masculine youth towards the opposite sex.

"Very," replied Anderson, dryly.

The young fellow gave a furious puff at his cigar. The smoke came full in Anderson's face. "Passed here the other evening with two other young ladies while you were sitting here," young Eastman remarked, in a curious tone. It was full of pain, but it had a reckless, devil-may-care defiance in it also.

"Yes," said Anderson, "I think you did. About a week ago, wasn't it?"

"Week ago yesterday. Well, I suppose you've heard the news. It's all over town."

"You mean —"

"She's engaged."

Anderson felt bewildered. "Yes?" he replied, questioningly.

"She's engaged," the young fellow repeated, with a sobbing sigh, which he ended in a laugh. "They all do it, sir."

Anderson was too puzzled to say anything.

"Suppose you've heard about the man?" said Eastman, in a nonchalant voice. He inhaled the smoke from his cigar with an air of abstract enjoyment.

Anderson unassumedly stared at him. "Why, I thought it was —"

"Who?" asked the young fellow, eagerly.

Anderson hesitated.

"Who did you think it was?" Eastman persisted. He had a pitiful wistfulness in his face upturned to the older man. It became quite evident that he had a desire to hear himself named as the accepted suitor.

"Why, I thought that you were the man!" Anderson answered.

"Everybody thought so, I guess," the young fellow said, with an absurd and childlike pride in the semblance in the midst of his grief over the reality. "But —" He hesitated, and Anderson waited, looking above at the play of lightning in the sky and smoking. "She's gone and got engaged to a man old enough to be her father. Lord! I guess he's older than her father — old enough to be her grandfather!" cried the young fellow, with a burst of grief and rage and shame. "Yes, sir, old enough to be her grandfather," he repeated. His voice shook. His cigar had gone out. He struck a match and the head flew off. He swore softly and struck another. Sometimes a match refusing to ignite changes mourning to wrath and rebellion. The third match broke short in two and the burning head flew down on the sidewalk. "Wish I had hold of the man that made 'em," young Eastman said, viciously; and in the same breath: "What can the girl be thinking of, that she flings herself away like that? Hang it all, is a woman a devil or a fool?"

Anderson removed his cigar long enough to ask a question, then replaced it. "Who is the man?" he inquired, in a slow, odd voice.

"Oh, he is an old army officer, a major — Major Arms, I believe his name is. He's somebody they've known a long time. He lives in Kentucky, I believe, in the same place where the Carrolls used to live and where she went to school. Oh, it's a good match. They're just tickled to death over it. Her sister feels rather bad, I guess, but, Lord! she'd do the same thing herself, if she got the chance. They're all alike." The boy said the last with a cynical bitterness beyond his years. He sneered effectively. He crossed one leg over the other and puffed his relighted cigar. The last match had ignited. Anderson said nothing. He was accommodating his ideas to the change of situation. Presently young Eastman spoke again. "Well," he said, in a tone of wretched conceit, "girls are as thick as flowers, after all, and a lot alike. Bessy Van Dorn is a beauty, isn't she?"

"I don't think she's much like the other," said Anderson, shortly.

"She's full as pretty."

Anderson made no reply.

"I don't believe Bessy would go and marry a man old enough to be her grandfather," said the boy, with a burst of piteous challenge. Then suddenly he tossed his cigar into the street and flung up his hands to his head with a despairing gesture. "Oh, my God!" he groaned.

"Be a man," Anderson said, in a kind voice.

"I am a man, ain't I? What do you suppose I care about it? I don't want to marry and settle down yet, anyway. I like to fool with the girls, but as for anything else — I am a — man. If you think I am broken up over this, if anybody thinks I am — Lord —" The young fellow rose and squared his shoulders. He looked down at Anderson. "There's one thing I want to say," he added. "I don't want you to think — I don't want to give the impression that she — that she has been flirting, or anything like that. She hasn't. Of course she might have been a little franker, I will admit that, for I have been there a good deal, but I don't suppose she thought it was anything serious, and it wasn't. She was right. But she did not flirt.

Those girls are not that sort. Great Scott! I should like to see a man venture on any little familiarities with them — holding hands, or a kiss, or anything. They respect themselves, those girls do. They have been brought up better than the Banbridge girls. Oh no, she hasn't treated me badly or anything, and of course I don't care a damn about her getting married, only I'll be hanged if I like, on general principles, to see a pretty young girl throwing herself away on a man old enough to be her father. It's wrong — it's indecent, you know." Again the boy's voice seemed bursting with wrath and grief and shame.

Anderson rose, went into the house, and was out again in a few seconds. He had a cigar-box in his hand. "Try one of these," he said. "It's a brand new to me, and I think it fine. I think you'll agree with me."

"Thanks," said Eastman, with a sound in his voice like a heart-broken child's. He almost sobbed, but he took the cigar gratefully. "Well, I must be going," he said. "Mother'll wonder where I am. It was too deuced hot to go to bed, so I've been strolling around. But I've got to turn in sometime. These nights are too hot to sleep, anyhow."

"Yes, they are pretty tough," said Anderson. "Wish we could have a shower."

"So do I. Say, this cigar is a dandy."

"I thought you'd like it. Of course it isn't a cigar that everybody would like. It requires some taste, perhaps a cultivated taste."

"Yes, that's so," replied the boy, with a pleased air. "I guess it does. I shouldn't say every man would appreciate this."

"Have another," said Anderson, and he pressed a couple into the hot young hand, which was greedily reached out for a little solace for its owner's wounded heart and self-love.

"Thanks. I suppose I have quite a good taste for a good cigar. I don't believe it would be very easy to palm off a cheap grade on me. Good-night, Mr. Anderson."

"Good-night," said Anderson, and was conscious of pity and amusement as the boy went away and his footsteps died out of hearing. As for himself, he was in much the same case as before, only the time had evidently arrived for him to dismiss his dreams and the lady of them. He did not think so hardly of her for being willing to marry the older man as the disappointed young man did. He considered himself as comparatively old, and he had a feeling of sympathy for the other old fellow who doubtless loved her. He was prepared to think that she had done a wiser thing than to engage herself to young Eastman, especially if the man was rich enough to take care of her. The position would be good, too. He thought generously of that consideration, although it touched him in his tenderest spot of vanity. "She will do well to marry an ex-army officer," he thought. "She will have the entrée to any society." Presently he arose and went upstairs to bed. He passed roughly by the nook where he had so often fancied her sitting, and closed, as it were, the door of his fancy against her with a bang. He set a lamp on a table at the head of his bed and read his political economy until dawn. It was, in fact, too hot for any nervous person to sleep. Now and then his thoughts wandered, the incessant drone of the night insects outside seemed to distract his attention from his book like some persistent clamor of nature recalling him to his leading-strings in which she had held him from the first. But resolutely he turned again to his book. At dawn he fell asleep, and woke an hour later to another steaming day.

CHAPTER XV

"I think we shall have thunder-showers today," Mrs. Anderson remarked, as she poured the coffee at the breakfast-table. Even this old gentlewoman, carefully attired in her dainty white lawn wrapper, had that slightly dissipated, bewildered, and rancorous air that extreme heat is apt to impart to the finest-grained of us. Her fair old face had a glossy flush, her white hair, which usually puffed with a soft wave over her temples, was stringy. She allowed her wrapper to remain open at the neck, exposing her old throat, and dispensed with her usual swathing of lace. She confessed that she had not been able to sleep at all; still she kept her trust in Providence, and would scarcely admit to discomfort. "I am sure there will be showers, and cool the air," she said, with her sweet optimism. As she spoke she fanned herself with the great palm-leaf fan with a green bow on the stem, which she was never without during this weather. "It is certainly very warm so early in the season. One must feel it a little, but it is always so delightful after a shower that it compensates."

"You are showing a lovely Christian spirit, mother," Anderson returned, smiling at her with fond amusement, "but don't be hypocritical."

"My son, what do you mean?"

"Mother, dear, you don't really like this weather. You only pretend to because man did not make it."

"Randolph!"

"Only think how you would growl if the mayor and aldermen, or even the president, made this weather!"

"My son, they did not," Mrs. Anderson responded, solemnly.

"No, and that settles it, I suppose. If they did, you would say at once they ought to be forced to resign from their offices. Now, mother, be resigned all you like, but don't be pleased, for you can't cheat the Providence that made this beastly heat, and must know perfectly well how beastly it is, better than you or I do, and won't think any more of us for any pretence in the matter."

"You shock me, dear. And, besides, I did not say that I liked it. I said I liked the weather after a shower. You look pale this morning, dear, and you don't talk quite like yourself. I do wish you would take an umbrella when you go to the office today. It is so very warm." Mrs. Anderson had a chronic fear of sunstroke.

When Randolph went away without his umbrella, as he usually did, being, dearly as he loved his mother, impervious to some of her feminine demands, she watched him, standing in the doorway and shaking her head with a dubious air.

That noon she was quite contented, for he did actually carry his umbrella. The sky in the northwest was threatening, although the sun still shone fiercely in the south. She herself sat on the doorstep in the shade, and fairly panted like a corpulent old dog. Her mouth was open and her tongue even lolled a little. She was, in reality, suffering frightfully. She had both flesh and nerves, and, given these two adverse conditions to endurance, and the mercury ninety in the shade, there is torture although the spirit is strong.

Although the sky was threatening all the afternoon, it was not until four o'clock that the northwest sky grew distinctly ominous and the rumble of the thunder was audible. Then Mrs. Anderson called her maid, and they proceeded to close tightly all the windows against the rising wind.

"It is very dangerous indeed to have a draught in the house in a thunder-shower," Mrs. Anderson always said while closing them.

Then she hurriedly divested herself of the white lawn wrapper which she had worn all day, and put on her black summer silk gown, with a wrap and a bonnet and an umbrella at hand. Mrs. Anderson was not afraid of a thunder-shower in the ordinary sense, but her imagination never failed her. Therefore she was always dressed, in case the worst should happen and she be forced to flee from a stricken house. She also had her small and portable treasures ready at hand. Then she sat down in the middle of the sitting-room well out of range of the chimney, and prayed for her own and her son's safety, and incidentally for the safety of the maid, who was in the adjoining room with the door open, and for the house and her son's store. She always did thus in a thunder-shower, but she never told any one this innocent childish secret of an innocent old soul.

She thought with a sort of undercurrent of faithlessness of the great draught in her son's store if the large front doors and the office door were both open, as there was a strong probability of their being. She thought uneasily that her son might be that very moment in that draught, as indeed he was. He stood in the strong current of fresh storm-air, with its pungent odors, more like revelations than odors, of things which had been in abeyance for some time past in the drought. The smell of the wet green things was like a pæan of joy. It was a call of renewed life out of concealed places of fainting and hiding. There were scents of flowers and fruits, and another strange odor, like the smell of battle, from all the ferment on the earth which had precipitated the storm. It was quite a severe thunder-shower. The rain had held off for a fierce prelude, then it came in solid cataracts. Then it was that Charlotte Carroll rushed into the store. She was dripping, beaten like a flower, by the force of the liquid flail of the storm. She had pulled off the rose-wreathed hat which was dear to her heart, and she had it under her dress skirt, which she held up over her lace-trimmed petticoat modestly, with as little revelation as might be. Her dark head glistened with the rain.

Anderson stepped forward quickly. "Pray come into the office, Miss Carroll," he said.

But she remained standing in front of the door, having removed her hat furtively from its shelter. "No, thank you," said she, "I would rather stay here. I like to watch it."

Anderson fetched a chair from his office, but she thanked him and said that she preferred standing.

"I thought I had time to get to Madame Griggs's on the other side of the street," said she, "but all at once it came down."

Anderson felt her ungraciousness, but she herself did not seem to realize it at all. Presently she gave a little sidewise smile at him, and comprehended in the smile the old clerk and the boy who hovered near.

"It is a fine shower," said she, with a kind of confidential glee. As she spoke she looked out at the snarl of rain shot with lances of electric fire, and there was a curious elation, almost like intoxication, in her expression. She was in a fine spiritual excitement.

"Yes," said Anderson. "We needed rain."

Just then the world seemed swimming in blue light and there was a terrific crash. Anderson, who never thought of any personal fear in a tempest, looked rather apprehensively at the girl. He recalled his mother's fear of draughts.

"Perhaps you had better move back a little; that was quite near," he said. Somehow the little fears and precautions which he scorned for himself seemed to apply quite reasonably to this little, tender, pretty creature with the lightning playing around her and the thunder breaking over her defenceless head.

Charlotte laughed. "Oh, I am not afraid," said she. Then she added, quite innocently, with more of personal appeal than she had ever used towards him, "Are you?"

"No," said Anderson.

"I like it," said she, staring out at the swaying, brandishing maples, and the street which ran like a river, with now and then a boiling pool.

"I am afraid you are wet," said Anderson.

"Yes," said she, "but that is nothing. My dress won't hurt. It is just white lawn, you know. All that would be hurt is my hat, and that is hardly damp. I took it off." She held it up carefully on one hand, and gazed solicitously at it. "It is my best hat," said she, simply. "No, I don't think it is hurt at all." She looked sharply towards the counter. "The counter is clean, isn't it?" said she. "I might lay my hat there. I don't want to put it on until my hair gets dry."

The old clerk smiled covertly, the boy grinned at her in a fascinated way. Anderson regarded her with worshipful amazement. This little, artless revelation of the innermost vanity of a woman's heart touched him. It was to him inconceivable that she should so care for the welfare of that flower-bedecked oval of straw, and yet he thought it adorable of her to care. He stared at the hat as if it had been a halo, then he turned and looked anxiously at the counter.

"Get a sheet of clean paper," he ordered the boy, and frowned at him for his grin.

The boy obeyed solemnly.

"I think that will not soil your hat," Anderson said, when the preparations were complete.

"Oh, thank you," she said, and handed him the hat.

Anderson touched it gingerly as if it were alive, and placed it upside down on the clean sheet of paper.

"The other way up, please," said she, and Anderson changed it in alarm.

"I hope I have not injured it," he said.

She was laughing openly at him. "No," she replied, "but you put it right on the roses. Men don't know how to handle girls' hats, do they?"

"No; I fear they don't," replied Anderson.

He remained leaning against the counter near the door; the old clerk lounged against the next one, on the end of which Sam Riggs was perched. Charlotte remained standing in the doorway, leaning slightly against the post, and they all watched the storm, which was fast reaching its height. The flashes of lightning were more frequent, the crashes of thunder followed fast, sound overlapping sight. The rain became a flood. The girl watched, with the intense, self-forgetful delight of a child, the plash of the great blobs of rain on the macadamized road outside. They came to look to her exactly like little figures chasing one another in an unintermittent race of annihilation. She smiled, watching them. Anderson, looking from the rain to her, saw the smile, and thought with a little pang that she was probably thinking of her own happiness when she smiled to herself like that. He kept his eyes fixed upon her for a moment, her glistening dark head, her smooth cheek, her smiling mouth, her shoulders faintly pink through her thin white gown, which, being wet, clung to them. Charlotte's shoulders were thin, but the hollowing curve from the throat to the arm was ravishing. Anderson's face hardened a little. He looked away again at the rain.

All at once Charlotte glanced up from the dancing flight of the rain-drops on the road, and laughed. "Why," she cried, "there is Ina! There is my sister!"

Anderson looked, and in a second-story window opposite was a girl's head in a violet-trimmed hat. She was smiling and nodding. Charlotte waved her hand to her.

"I'll be over as soon as it holds up a little," she cried out. "Did you get wet?"

The girl in the window hollowed a slim hand over an ear.

"Did you get caught in the shower? Did you get wet?" called Charlotte.

The girl in the window shook her head gayly.

"She didn't," Charlotte said, with an absurd but charming confidence to Anderson; "but, anyway, she didn't have on her very best hat."

"I am very glad," Anderson replied, politely. He read a sign fastened beneath the window which framed the girl's head — "Madame Estelle Griggs, Modiste." He reflected that she was the Banbridge dressmaker, and that Charlotte was probably having her trousseau made there, which was a deduction that only a masculine mind of vivid imagination could have evolved.

Charlotte was gazing eagerly across at her sister. "It does not rain nearly so hard now," said she. "I think I might venture." She looked irresolutely at her hat on the counter.

"I can let you have an umbrella," said Anderson.

"Thank you," said Charlotte, "but my hair is still so wet, and my hat is lined with pink chiffon, you know."

"Yes," said Anderson, respectfully. He did not know what pink chiffon was, but he understood that water would injure it.

"If I might leave my hat here," said Charlotte, "until I come back —"

"Certainly," replied Anderson.

"Then I think I can go now. No, thank you; I won't take the umbrella. I am about as wet as I can be now, and, besides, I like to feel the rain on my shoulders."

With a careful but wary gathering up of her white skirts, with chary disclosures of lace and embroidery and little skipping shoes, she was gone in a snowy whirl through the mist across the street. She seemed to fly over the puddles. The girl's head disappeared from the opposite window and Anderson heard quite distinctly the outburst of laughter and explanation.

"You had better get a sheet of tissue-paper and put it over that," he said to Sam Riggs, and he pointed at Charlotte's hat on the counter. Then he went back to his office and wrote some letters. He resolved that he would not see Charlotte when she returned for her hat.

Presently the sun shone into the office, and a new light seemed to come from the rain-drenched branches outside the window. Anderson continued to write, feeling all the time unhappiness heavy in his heart. He also had a sense of injury which was foreign to him. He was distinctly aware that he had an unfair allotment of the good things of life. Yet there was a question dinning through his consciousness: "Why should I have so little?" Then the world-old query considering personal responsibility for misery swept over him. "What have I done?" he asked himself, and answered himself, with a fierce challenge of truth, that he had done nothing. Then the habit of his life of patience, which was at the same time a habit of bravery, asserted itself. He wrote his letters carefully and closed his ears to the questions.

It was about half an hour later, and he was thinking about going home, when Sam Riggs came to the office door and informed him that Mrs. Griggs wanted to see him.

Mrs. Griggs was Madame nowhere except on her sign and in the mouths of a few genteel patrons who considered that Madame had a more fashionable sound than Mrs.

"Ask her to come in here," Anderson said, and directly the dress-maker appeared. She was a tiny, thin, nervous creature with restless, veinous little hands, and a long, thin neck upon which her small frizzled head vibrated constantly like the head of a bird. Anderson knew her very well. Back in his childhood they had been schoolmates. He remembered distinctly little Stella Mixter. She had been a sharp, meagre, but rather pretty little girl, with light curls, and was always dressed in blue. She wore blue now, for that matter — blue muslin, ornate with lace and ribbons. She had had a sad and hard life, but her spirit still asserted itself. Her husband had deserted her; she had lost her one child; she worked like a galley-slave, but she still frizzed her hair carefully, and never neglected her own costume even in her greatest rush of business, and that in a dressmaker showed deathless ambition and self-respect.

Anderson greeted her and offered her a chair. She seated herself with a conscious elegance, and disposed gracefully around her thin knees her blue muslin flounces. There was a slight coquetry in her manner, although she was evidently anxious about something. She looked around and spoke in a low voice.

"I want to ask you something," she said, in a whisper.

"Certainly," said Anderson.

"You used to be a lawyer, and I don't suppose you have forgotten all your law, if you are in the grocery business now." There was about the woman the very naïveté of commonplacedness and offence.

Anderson smiled. "I trust not, Mrs. Griggs," he replied.

"Well" — she lowered her voice still more — "I wanted to ask you — I've got a big job of work for — that Carroll girl that's going to be married, and I've heard something that made me kind of uneasy. What I want to know is, do you s'pose I'm likely to get my pay?"

"I know nothing whatever about the family's financial standing," Anderson replied, after a slight pause. He spoke constrainedly, and did not look at his questioner.

"You don't know whether I'm likely to get my pay or not?"

Anderson looked at her then, the little, nervous, overworked, almost desperate creature, fighting like a little animal in her bay of life against the odds which would drive her from it, and he felt in a horrible perplexity. He felt also profane. Why could not he be left out of this? he inquired, with concealed emphasis. Finally he said that he would rather not advise in a case about which he knew so little.

"I'm willing to pay," said the dressmaker, with her artless vulgarity.

"It is not that," Anderson said, quickly, with some asperity.

"I don't know," said the dressmaker, innocently deepening the offence, "but what you didn't feel as if you could give law-advice for nothin', even if you had quit the law. I s'pose it cost you a good deal to learn the law, and I know you didn't git your money back." She spoke with the kindest sympathy.

"That has nothing to do with it," Anderson repeated, with an inflection of irritated patience. "I cannot give any advice because I know nothing whatever about the matter."

"Can't you find out?"

"That belongs to the business which I have given up."

"Well, I s'pose it does," admitted Madame Griggs, with a sigh. "I wouldn't have bothered you if I hadn't been at my wit's end."

"I am willing to do anything in my power —" began Anderson, with a softened glance at the absurdly pathetic little figure, "but —"

"Then you think I had better not trust them?"

"No; I said —"

"You think I had better send her word I've changed my mind, and can't do her work?"

Anderson winced. "No; I did not say so," he replied, vehemently. "I merely said that you must settle —"

"Then you think I had better keep on with it?"

"If you think best," said Anderson, emphatically. "Really, Mrs. Griggs, I cannot settle this matter for you. You often trust people in your business. You must decide yourself."

The dressmaker arose. "Well, I guess it's all right," said she. "She's a lovely girl, and so are they all. Her mother seems sort of childish, but she's real sweet-spoken. I guess it's all right, but I'd heard some things, and I thought I would ask you what you thought. I thought it wouldn't do any harm. Now I feel a good deal easier about it. Good-afternoon. What a tempest we've had!"

"Yes," said Anderson. "Good-afternoon." He was conscious of a mental giddiness as he regarded her.

"We needed it, and I do think it has cooled the air a little. I'm very much obliged. I don't suppose there is any use in my offering to pay you, now you're in the grocery business?"

"Certainly not. I have done nothing to admit of any question of payment," replied Anderson, curtly.

"Well, I s'pose you throw it in along with the butter and eggs," said Madame Griggs, with a return of her slight coquetry. "By-the-way, I wish you'd send over five pounds of that best butter. Good-afternoon."

"Good-afternoon."

The dressmaker turned in the doorway and looked back. "I'm so glad to have my mind settled about it," she said, with a pathos which overcame her absurdity and vulgarity. "I do work awful hard, and it doesn't seem as if I could lose my money." She appeared suddenly tragic in her cheap muslin and her frizzes. She looked old and her features sharpened out rigidly.

Anderson, looking after her, felt both bewilderment and compunction. He thought for a moment of going after her and saying something further; then he heard a flutter and a quick sweet voice, and he knew that Charlotte had come for her hat. He heard her say: "Where? Oh, I see; all covered up so nicely. Thank you. I did not come before, because the trees were dripping. Thank you." Then there was a silence.

Anderson got his hat and went out through the store. The old clerk was fussing over some packages on the counter.

"That young lady came for her hat," he remarked.

"Did she?"

"Yes. She's a pretty-spoken girl. Her sister's goin' to git married before long, I hear."

Anderson stopped and stared at him. "No; this is the one."

"No; her sister. I had it straight."

Anderson went out. Everything was wonderful outside. The world was purified of dust and tarnish as a soul of sin. The worn prosaicness of nature was adorned as with jewels. Everything glittered; a thousand rainbows seemed to hang on the drenched trees. New blossoms looked out like new eyes of rapture; every leaf had a high-light of joy. Anderson drew a long breath. The air was alive with the breath of the sea from which the fresh wind blew. He walked home with a quick step like a boy. He was smiling, and fast to his breast, like a beloved child, he clasped his dream again.

CHAPTER XVI

There had been considerable discussion among the ladies of the Carroll family with regard to the necessary finery for Ina's bridal.

"It is all very well to talk about Ina's being married in four weeks," said Anna Carroll to her sister-in-law, one afternoon directly after the affair had been settled. "If a girl gets married, she has to have new clothes, of course — a trousseau."

"Why, yes, of course! How could she be married if she didn't have a trousseau? I had a very pretty trousseau, and so would you if you had been married, Anna, dear."

Anna laughed, a trifle bitterly. "Good Lord," said she, "if I had to think of a trousseau for myself, I should be a maniac! The trousseau would at any time have seemed a much more difficult matter than the bridegroom."

"Yes, I know you have had a great many very good chances," assented Mrs. Carroll, "and it would have seemed most of the time much easier to have just managed the husband part of it than the new clothes, because one doesn't have to pay cash or have good credit for a husband, and one does for clothes."

"Well," said Anna Carroll, "that is the trouble about Ina. It was easy enough for her to get the husband. Major Arms has always had his eye on her ever since she was in short dresses; but what isn't at all easy is the new clothes."

"I don't see why, dear."

"Well, how is it to be managed, if you will be so good as to inform me, Amy?"

"How? Why, just go to the dressmaker's and order them, of course."

"What dressmaker's, dear?"

"Well, I think that last New York dressmaker is the best. She really has imagination like a French dressmaker. She doesn't copy; she creates. She is really quite an artist."

"Madame Potoffsky, you mean?"

"Yes, dear. The dressmaker whose husband they say was a descendant of the Polish patriot. They say she herself is descended from a Russian princess who eloped with the Polish patriot, and I can believe it. There is something very unusual about her. She always makes me a little bit nervous, because one does get to associating Russians, especially those that run away with patriots, with bombs and things of that kind, but she is a wonderful dressmaker. I certainly think it would be wise to patronize her for Ina's trousseau, Anna."

Anna laughed, and rather bitterly, again. "Well, dear, I have my doubts about our ability to patronize her," she said, "and, granting that we could, you might in reality encounter the bomb as penalty."

"Anna, dear, what —"

"Amy, don't you know that Madame Potoffsky simply will not give us any further credit?"

"Oh, Anna, do you think so?"

"I know. Amy, only think of the things we owe her for now — my linen, my pongee, my canvas, your two foulards, Ina's muslin, Charlotte's étamine! It is impossible."

"Oh, dear! Do we owe her for all those?"

"We do."

"Well, then, I fear you are right, Anna," Mrs. Carroll said, ruefully.

The two women continued to look at each other. Mrs. Carroll had a curious round-eyed face of consternation, like a baby; Anna looked, on the contrary, older than usual. Her features seemed quite sharpened out by thought.

"What do you think we can do, Anna?" asked Mrs. Carroll, at length. "Do you suppose if we told Madame Potoffsky just how it was, how dear Ina was going to be married, and how interested we all were in having her look nice and have pretty things that she would —"

"No, I don't think so," Anna said, shortly. "What does Madame Potoffsky care about Ina and her getting married, except for what she makes out of it?"

"But, Anna, she is very rich. Everybody says so. She has a beautiful house, and a country-house, and keeps a carriage to go to her shop in."

"Well, what of that?"

"I thought the Russians believed that rich people ought to do things for people who were not rich, or else be blown up with bombs."

"Don't be silly, Amy, darling."

"I am quite in earnest, Anna, I really thought so."

"Well, you thought wrong then, dear. There is no reason in the world why a dressmaker, if she is as rich as a Vanderbilt, should make Ina's wedding-clothes for nothing, and she won't."

"Well, I suppose you are right, Anna, but what is to be done? How about Miss Sargent? She was very good."

"Miss Sargent, Amy *dear*!"

"Do we own her much, Anna?"

"Owe her much? We owe her everything!"

"Madame Rogers?"

"Madame Rogers! The last time I asked her to do anything she insulted me. She told me to my face she did not work for dead-beats."

"She was a very vulgar woman, Anna. I don't think I would patronize her under any circumstances."

"No, I would not either, dear. But that finishes the New York dressmakers."

"How about the Hillfield one?"

"Amy!"

"Well, I suppose you are right; but what —"

"We shall have to go to a dressmaker in Banbridge. We have never had any work done here, and there can be no difficulty about it."

"But, Anna, how can we have her married with a trousseau made in Banbridge?"

"It is either that or no trousseau at all."

Mrs. Carroll seldom wept, but she actually shed a few tears over the prospect of a shabbily made trousseau for Ina. "And she will go in the best society in Kentucky, too," she said, pitifully. "They'll attribute it all to the lack of taste in the North," Anna said.

Ina herself made no objection whatever to employing the Banbridge dressmaker; in fact, she seemed to have little interest in her clothes at first. After a while she became rather feverishly excited over them.

"I have always wondered why girls cared so much about their wedding-clothes," she told her sister after two weeks, when the preparations were well under way, "but now I know."

"Why?" asked Charlotte. The two were coming home from the dressmaker's, where Ina had been trying on gowns for an hour. It was late in the afternoon and nearly time for Captain Carroll's train.

"Why?" repeated Charlotte, when Ina did not answer at once.

"In order to keep from thinking so much about the marriage itself," said Ina, tersely. She did not look at her sister, but kept her eyes fixed on the road ahead of her.

Charlotte, however, almost stopped. "Ina," said she, in a distressed tone — "Ina, dear, you don't feel like that?"

"Why not?" inquired Ina, defiantly.

"Oh, Ina, you ought not to get married if you feel like that!"

"Why not? All girls feel like that when they are going to be married. They must."

"Oh, Ina, I know they don't!"

"How do you know? You were never going to get married."

That argument was rather too much for Charlotte, but she continued to gaze at her sister with a shocked and doubtful air as they walked along the shady sidewalk towards home. "I am almost sure it isn't right for a girl to feel so, anyhow," she said, persistently.

"Yes, it is, too," Ina said, laughing easily. "Charlotte, honey, I really think my things are going to do very well. I really think so. That tan canvas is a beauty, and so is the red foulard. She is really a very good dressmaker."

"I think so too, dear," Charlotte agreed. "I like the wedding-gown, too."

"Yes, so do I; it is very pretty, though that does not so much matter."

"Why, Ina Carroll!"

Ina laughed mischievously. "Now I have shocked you, dear. Of course it matters in one way, but I shall never wear it again after the ceremony; and you know I don't care much about the Banbridge people, and they will be the only ones to see me in it, and only that once."

"But, Ina, he — your — Major Arms."

Ina laughed again. "Oh, well, he thinks me perfectly beautiful anyway," said she, in the tone of one to whom love was as dross because of the superabundance of it.

"Ina," said Charlotte, with a solemn and timidly reflective air, "I don't believe you think half as much of him as you would if he didn't think so much of you."

"Yes, I do think just as much," said Ina, "but things always seem worth rather more when they are in a showcase and marked more than one can ever pay." Then she started, and exclaimed: "Good gracious, there he is now!" She flushed all over her face and neck; then she turned pale and cast a half-wild look around her as if she wanted to run somewhere.

Indeed, at that moment the Carroll carriage drew up beside them, and on the back seat sat Captain Carroll and a very handsome man apparently about his own age, although at first glance he looked older because of snow-white hair and mustache. He was as tall as Carroll, and thinner, and less punctiliously attired, although he wore his somewhat slouching clothes with a certain careless assurance of being the master of them which Carroll, with all his elegance, did not excel.

"Here we are!" called Carroll. He was smiling, although he had a slightly worried look. The other man's black eyes were fixed with a sort of tender hunger on Ina, who hung back a little as she and Charlotte approached the carriage. It was actually Charlotte who shook hands first with Major Arms, although she tried to give her sister precedence.

Ina blushed a good deal, and smiled rather tremulously when her turn came and her little hand was enveloped in the man's eager one.

"I — didn't know — I didn't —" she stammered.

"No, you didn't, did ye, honey?" said the major, in the broadest of Southern drawls. "No, ye didn't. The old fellow thought he'd surprise ye, honey." The man's face and voice were as frankly expressive of delighted love as a boy's. "Arthur," said he, "over with ye to the front seat and let me have my sweetheart in here with me. I want my arms around her. Not another minute can I wait. Over with ye, boy!"

Carroll threw open the carriage door and sprang out. "Jump in, Ina," he said, and placed a hand under his daughter's arm. She gave a smiling and not altogether unhappy, but still piteous, look at him, and hung back slightly. "Jump in, dear," he said, again; and Ina was in the carriage, and there was a sweep of a long gray-clad arm around her and the sound of kisses.

"Now, Charlotte," said Carroll, "get in the front seat. I will walk the rest of the way."

"No, papa," Charlotte replied, "I will walk with you. I would rather." So the carriage rolled on, and Charlotte and Carroll followed on foot.

"Did you expect him, papa?" asked Charlotte.

"No, honey. The first thing I knew he came up to me on the ferry. He came on this morning; he has been in New York all day. I guess he wanted to buy something for Ina."

"Her ring?" asked Charlotte, in a slightly awed tone.

"Very likely."

"Papa, is Major Arms rich?" asked Charlotte.

"Quite, I think, dear. I don't know how much he has in reality, but he has his pay from the government — he is on the retired list — and he owns considerable property. He has enough and to spare, there is no doubt about that."

"So if Ina has things and people trouble her for payment she can pay them," remarked Charlotte, thoughtfully.

"Yes," said Carroll, shortly. He quickened his pace, and Charlotte made a little run to get into step again.

"That will be very nice," said she. "Do you think he will be good to her, papa?"

"Sure as I am of anything in this world, dear."

"It would be dreadful if he wasn't. Whatever else Ina or any of us haven't had, we've always had that. We've always lived with folks that loved us and were good to us. That would kill Ina and me quickest of anything, papa."

"He will be good to her, dear," said Carroll, pleasantly. He looked down at Charlotte and laughed. "It's all right, baby," he said. "She's got one man in a thousand — one worth a thousand of your old dad."

"No, she hasn't," said Charlotte, with indignation. She caught her father's arm and clung to it lovingly. "There is nobody in the world so good as you," said she, with fervor. "I wouldn't leave you for any man in the world, papa."

"You wait," Carroll said, laughing.

"Papa, you don't wish I were going to be married too? You don't want me to go away like Ina?" Charlotte demanded, with a sudden grieved catch in her voice.

"I never want you to go, darling," Carroll replied, and he looked down with adoration at the little face whose whole meaning seemed one of innocent love for and belief in him. He realized the same terror at the mere fancy of losing this artless and unquestioning devotion as one might feel at the fancy of losing his only prop from the edge of a precipice. The man really had for an instant a glimpse of a sheer descent in his own nature which might be ever before his sickened vision if this one little faith and ignorance were removed. In a curious fashion a man sometimes holds an innocent love between himself and himself, and Carroll so held Charlotte's.

"I will never leave you for any other man. I don't care who he is," Charlotte reiterated, and this time her father let her assertion go unchallenged. He pressed the little, clinging hand on his arm closer.

Charlotte looked at him as she might have looked at a king as he walked along in his stately fashion. She was unutterably proud of him.

The carriage had reached the house some time before they arrived. The man was just driving round to the stable when they came up to the front door. The guest and Ina were nowhere to be seen, but on the porch stood Mrs. Carroll and Anna. They were both laughing, but Anna looked worried in spite of her laugh.

"What do you think, Arthur," whispered Mrs. Carroll, with a cautious glance towards a chamber window. "Here he has come, the son-in-law, and there is no meat again for dinner." Mrs. Carroll burst into a peal of laughter.

"I don't see much to laugh at," said Anna, but she laughed a little.

Carroll made a step to the side of the porch and called to the coachman. "Martin," he called, "don't take the horse out. Come back here. We must send for something," he declared, a little brusquely for him.

"It is all very well to send, Arthur," said Mrs. Carroll, "but the butcher won't let us have it if we do send."

"It is no use, Arthur," Anna Carroll said. "We cannot get a thing for this man's dinner, and not only today, but tomorrow and while he stays, unless we pay cash."

Carroll turned to the coachman, who had just come alongside. "Martin," he said, "you will have to drive to New Sanderson before dinner. We cannot get the meat which Mrs. Carroll wishes, and you will have to drive over there. Go to that large market on Main Street and tell them that I want the best cut of porterhouse with the tenderloin that he has. Tell him it is for Captain Carroll of Banbridge. "And I want you to get also a roast of lamb for tomorrow."

"Yes, sir," said the coachman. He gathered up the lines, but sat looking hesitatingly at his employer.

"What are you waiting for?" asked Carroll. "Drive as fast as you can. We are late as it is."

"Shall I pay, sir?" asked the man, timidly, in a low voice.

Carroll took out his pocket-book, then replaced it. "No, not tonight," he said, easily. "Tell him it is for Captain Carroll of Banbridge."

The man still looked doubtful and a trifle alarmed, but he touched his hat and drove out of the grounds. Carroll turned and saw his wife and sister staring at him.

"Oh, Arthur, dear, do you think the butcher will let him have it?" whispered Mrs. Carroll.

"Yes, honey," said Carroll.

"If he shouldn't —"

"Don't worry; he will."

"It is one of your coups, isn't it, Arthur?" said Anna, sarcastically, but rather admiringly. She and Mrs. Carroll both laughed.

"We have never bought any meat in New Sanderson, so maybe Martin can get it," Mrs. Carroll said, as she seated herself in one of the large willow-rockers on the porch.

Dinner was very late that night at the Carrolls'. Even with a fast horse, driving to New Sanderson and back consumed some time, but Martin finally returned triumphant. When he drove into the yard it was dusk and the family and the guest were all seated on the porch. There was a steady babble of talk and laughter on the part of the ladies, who were nervously intent on concealing, or at least softening, the fact that dinner was so late that Major Arms might well be excused for judging that there was to be no dinner at all.

Once, Ina had whispered to Charlotte, when the conversation among the others swelled high: "What is the matter? Do you know?"

"Hush! Poor papa had to send to New Sanderson for meat," whispered Charlotte.

Ina made a face of consternation; Charlotte looked sadly troubled.

"I'm afraid he is awfully hungry," whispered Ina. "I pity him."

"I pity papa," whispered Charlotte. She kept glancing at her father with loving sympathy and understanding as the time went on. His face was quite undisturbed, but Charlotte saw beneath the calm. When at last she heard the carriage-wheels her heart leaped and she turned pale. Then she dared not look at her father. Suppose Martin should not have been successful. The eyes of all the family except Carroll himself, who was talking about the tariff and politely supporting the government against a hot-headed rebellion on the part of the ex-army officer, were on him. Not an inflection in his voice changed when Martin drove past the porch, but the others, even Eddy, who was seated at his sister's feet on the porch-step, eyed the arrival with undisguised eagerness. A brown-paper parcel was distinctly visible on the seat beside Martin.

"Thank God!" Mrs. Carroll whispered, under her breath to her sister. "He's got it."

Eddy gave vent to a small whoop of delight which he immediately suppressed with a scared glance at his father. However, he could not refrain from sniffing audibly with rapture when the first fragrance of the broiling beefsteak spread through the house to the porch. Mrs. Carroll giggled, and so did Ina, but Charlotte looked severely at her brother.

"After all, though, the excessive tax on articles purchased by travellers abroad and brought to this country serves as a legitimate balance-wheel," said Carroll, coolly. One would not have thought that he was in the least conscious of what was going on around him. "It is mostly the very wealthy who go abroad and purchase articles of foreign manufacture," he added, gently, "and it serves to even up things a little for those who cannot go. It marks a notch higher on the equality of possessions."

"Equality of fiddlesticks!" said the other man. "What the devil do the masses of the poor in this country care about the foreign works of art, anyhow? They don't want 'em. And what is going to compensate this country for not possessing works of art which it will never produce here, and which would tend to the liberal education of its citizens?"

"Not many of its citizens in the broader sense would ever see those works of art when they were here and shrined in the drawing-rooms of the millionaires," said Carroll, smiling; "and as far as that goes, the millionaires have them, anyhow. They are not stopped by the tariff."

"Yes, they are, too, more than you think," declared the major; "and not the millionaires alone are defrauded. Suppose I go over now, as I may do" — he cast a glance at Ina — "as I may do, I say. Now there are things over there that I want in my home — things that are not to be had for love nor money in this country. Nothing of the sort is or ever will be manufactured here. I am doing nothing whatever to injure home industries if I bring them over. On the contrary, I am benefiting the country by bringing to it articles which are, in a way, an education which may serve as a stimulus to the growth of art here. I enable those who can never go abroad, and to whom they will be otherwise forever unknown, an opportunity to become acquainted with them. But I have to leave them over there because I cannot afford to pay this government for the privilege of spending my own money and gratifying my own taste."

Anna Carroll, to cover her absorption in the beefsteak and the dinner, joined in the conversation with feminine daring of conclusion. "I suppose," said she, with a kind of soft sarcasm, "that the government would not need to charge so much for its citizens' privilege of buying little foreign vases and mosaics and breastpins and little Paris frills if it did not conduct so many humanitarian wars."

"The humanitarian wars are all right, all right," said the major, hastily; "so far as that goes, all right."

"I suppose," said Mrs. Carroll, "that it would cost so much to bring home gowns from Paris that no one can do it unless they have a great deal of money. I understand that it costs more than it did."

"Yes," replied the major, "and this government can't see or won't see that even in the matter of women's clothes it would pay in the end to bring over every frill and tuck free of duty until our dressmakers here had caught on to their tricks. Then we could pay them back in their own coin.

But, no; and the consequence is that we shall be dependent on France for our best clothes for generations more."

"It does seem such a pity," said Mrs. Carroll. "It would be so nice to have Ina's things made in Paris if it didn't cost anything to get them over here — wouldn't it?"

"I would just as soon have my dresses made in Banbridge," said Ina. "Madame Griggs is as good as a French dressmaker."

"She is fine," said Charlotte.

Ina blushed as the major looked at her with a look that penetrated the dusk. Very soon Marie appeared in the doorway, and they went into dinner.

"How lucky it is that Anderson does not object to trusting us and we can have canned soup and pease," whispered Mrs. Carroll to Anna.

It was a very good dinner at last, and the guest was evidently hungry, for he did justice to it. There were no apologies for the delay. Carroll did not believe in apologies for such things. There was a salad from their own garden, and a dessert of apple-pudding from an early apple-tree in the grounds. The coffee was good, too. There was no lack of anything which could be purchased at the grocery.

"That grocer must be a very decent sort of man as grocers go," Mrs. Carroll was fond of remarking in those days. "I really don't know what we should do if it were not for him."

After dinner was over it was nearly nine o'clock; Carroll and Major Arms walked up and down the road before the house, smoking, leaving the ladies on the porch. The ex-army officer had something which he wished to discuss with his prospective father-in-law. He opened upon the subject when they had gone a piece down the flagged sidewalk and turned towards the house.

"What kind of arrangements have the ladies planned with regard to" — he hesitated and stammered a bit boyishly, for this was his first matrimonial venture, and he felt embarrassed, veteran in other respects as he was — "to the — ceremony?" he finished up. Ceremony did not have the personal sound that marriage did.

Carroll looked at him, smiling. "It is quite a venture for you, old fellow, isn't it?" he said, laughingly, and yet his voice sounded exceedingly kind and touched.

"Not with that child, Arthur," replied the other man, simply.

"Well, Ina is a good girl," assented Carroll. "Both of them are good girls. She will make you a good wife."

"Nobody knows how sure I am of it, and nobody knows how I have looked forward to this for years," said the other, fervently.

"I could not wish anything better for my girl," said Carroll, gently and soberly.

"What about the matter of the — ceremony?" asked Arms, returning to the first subject.

"I think they have decided that they would prefer the wedding in the church, and a little reception at the house afterwards. Of course we are comparatively strangers in Banbridge, but there are people one can always ask to a function of the sort, and I think Ina —"

"Arthur, there is something I would like to propose."

"What, old fellow?"

Major Arms hesitated. Carroll waited, smoking as he sauntered along. The other man held his cigar, which had gone out, in his mouth; evidently he was nervous about his proposition. Finally he blurted it out with the sharpness of a pistol-shot. "Arthur, I want to defray the expenses of the wedding," he said.

Carroll removed his cigar. "See you damned first," said he, coolly, but with emphasis, and then replaced it.

Major Arms turned furiously towards him, but he restrained himself. "Why?" he said, with forced calm.

"Because if I cannot pay my daughter's bridal expenses she never marries you nor any other man," said Carroll.

Then the Major blazed out. He stopped short and moved before Carroll on the sidewalk. "If," said he — "if — you think I marry your daughter if her father goes in debt for the wedding expenses, you are mistaken."

Carroll said nothing. He stood as if stunned. The other went on with a burst of furious truth: "See here, Arthur Carroll," said he, "I like you, and you know how I feel about your girl. She is the one thing I have wanted for my happiness all my life, and I know I can take care of her and make her happy; and I like you in spite of — in spite of your outs. I'm ashamed of myself for liking you, but I do; but you needn't think I don't see you, that I don't know you, because I do. I knew when you went to the dogs after you failed in your mine, just as well as you did yourself. You went to the dogs, and you've been at the dogs' ever since; you're there now, and you've dragged your family with you so far as they're the sort to be dragged. They aren't, altogether, lucky for them; the girls especially aren't, at least not so far. Lord knows when it would come to them. But I'm going to take Ina away from the dogs, out of sound of a yelp even of 'em; and, as for me, I'll be hanged if you get me there! I know you for just what you are. I know you've prowled and preyed like a coyote ever since you were preyed on yourself. I know you, but I love Ina. But I tell you one thing, Arthur Carroll, now you can take your choice. Either you let me pay the wedding expenses or you give up the wedding."

"Ina," began Carroll, in a curious, helpless fashion, "she has set her heart on the wedding — her — dress and everything."

"I can't help that," said Arms, sternly. "This is of more importance even than her pleasure. Take your choice. Let me pay or let us be married in the quietest manner possible."

"I consent to the latter," Carroll said, still in that beaten tone.

He seemed to shrink in stature, standing before the other man's uprear of imperious will.

"All right," said Major Arms.

The two walked on in silence for a moment. Arms relit his cigar. Suddenly Carroll spoke.

"No, I will not, either," he said, abruptly.

"Will not what?"

"I will not consent to the quiet wedding. Ina shall not be disappointed. This means too much to a girl. Good God! it is the one occasion of a woman's life, and women are children always. It is cruelty to children."

"Then I pay," Arms said.

"No, I pay," said Carroll.

"You pay?"

"I pay," Carroll repeated, doggedly.

"How?"

"Never mind how. I tell you I give you my word of honor I pay every dollar of those expenses the day after the wedding."

"You will rob Peter to pay Paul, then," declared Major Arms, incredulously and wrathfully.

Carroll laughed in a hard fashion. "I would kill Peter, besides robbing him, if it was necessary," he said.

"If you think I'll have that way out of it —"

"I tell you I will pay those expenses, every dollar, the next day, and Ina shall have her little festival. What more do you want?" demanded Carroll. "See here, Arms, you will take care of the girl better than I can. I am at the dogs fast enough, and the dogs' is not a desirable locality in which to see one's family. You can take care of Ina, and God knows I want you to have her, but have her you shall not unless you can show some lingering confidence in her father. Even at the dogs' a man may have a little pride left. Either we have the wedding as it is planned, and you trust me to settle the bills for it, or you can give up my daughter."

Arms stood silent, looking at Carroll. "Very well," he said, finally.

"All right, then," said Carroll.

Arms remained staring at Carroll with a curious, puzzled expression.

"Good God! Arthur, how do you ever stand it living this sort of life?" he cried, suddenly.

"I have to stand it," replied Carroll. "As well ask a shot fired from a cannon how it likes being hurled through the air. I was fired into this."

"You ought to have had some power of resistance, some will of your own."

"There are forces for every living man for which he has no power of resistance. Mine hit me."

"If ever there was a damned, smooth-tongued scoundrel —" said Arms, retrospectively.

"Where is he?" Carroll asked, and his voice sounded strange.

"There."

"How is he?"

"Prospering like the wicked in the psalms. There was one respect in which you showed will and self-control, Arthur — that you didn't shoot him!"

"I was a fool," said Carroll.

"He wasn't worth hanging for," said the major, shortly.

"I'd hang five times over if I could get even with him," said Carroll.

"I don't wonder you feel so."

"Feel so! You asked me just now how I stood this sort of life. I believe my hate for that man keeps me up like a stimulant. I believe it keeps me up when I see other poor devils that I —"

Suddenly Arms reached out his hand and grasped Carroll's. "Good God! old fellow, I'm sorry for you!" he said. "You are too good for the dogs."

"Yes, I know I am," said Carroll, calmly.

The two men returned to the house and sat on the porch with the ladies. About half-past ten Anna Carroll said good-night, then Mrs. Carroll. Then Charlotte rose, and Ina also followed her up-stairs.

"Ina," cried Charlotte, in a sort of angry embarrassment, when they had reached her chamber, "you've got to go back; indeed you have."

"I suppose I ought." Ina was blushing furiously, her lip quivered. She was twisting a ring on her engagement-finger.

"You have even kept the stone side in, so nobody could see that beautiful ring he brought you. You are mean — mean!" said Charlotte.

"You just imagine that," said Ina, feebly. As she spoke she held up her hand, and a great diamond flashed rose and green and white.

"No, I don't imagine it. I have not seen it once like that. You ought to be ashamed of yourself. You must go straight back down-stairs. People when they are engaged always sit up alone together. You are not doing right coming up here with me."

"What are you scolding me for? Who said I was not going back?" returned Ina, with resentful shame.

"You know you were not."

"I was."

"Well, good-night, honey," said Charlotte, in a softer tone.

"Good-night."

Charlotte kissed her sister, and saw her leave the room and go down to her lover with a curious mixture of pity and awe and wrath and wistful affection. It almost seemed to her that Ina was happy, although afraid and ashamed to be, and it made her seem like a stranger to the maiden ignorance of her own heart.

CHAPTER XVII

There was a good deal of talk in Banbridge when Ina Carroll's wedding-invitations were out. There were not many issued. When it came to making out the list, the number of persons who, from what the family considered as a reasonable point of view, were possible, was exceedingly small.

"Of course we cannot ask such and such a one," Mrs. Carroll would say, and the others would acquiesce simply, with no thought of the possibility of anything else.

"There's that young man who goes on the train every morning with papa," said Charlotte. "His name is Veazie — Francis Veazie. He has called here. They live on Elm Street. His father is that nice-looking old gentleman who walks past here every day, on his way to the mail, a little lame."

"Charlotte, dear," said Ina, "don't you remember that somebody told us that that young man was a floor-walker in one of the department stores?"

"Oh, sure enough," said Charlotte, "I do remember, dear."

"There are really very few indeed in a place like Banbridge whom it is possible to invite to a wedding," said Mrs. Carroll.

Banbridge itself shared her opinion. Those who were bidden to the wedding acquiesced in their selectedness and worthiness; those who were not bidden, with a very few exceptions of unduly aspiring souls, acquiesced calmly in their own ineligibility. Banbridge, for a village in the heart of a republic, had a curious rigidity of establishment and content as to its social conditions. For the most part those who were not invited would have been embarrassed and even suspicious at receiving invitations. But they talked. In that they showed their inalienable republican freedom. They moved along as unquestioningly as European peasants, in their grooves, but their tongues soared. In speech, as is the way with an American, they held nothing sacred, not even the institutions which they propped, not even themselves. They might remain unquestioningly, even preferredly, outside the doors of superiority, but out there they raised a clamor of self-assertion. Their tongues wagged with prodigious activity utterly unleashed. In the days before Ina Carroll's wedding all Banbridge seethed and boiled like a pot with gossip, and gossip full of malice and sneer, and a good deal of righteous indignation. Anderson heard much of it. Neither he nor his mother was asked to the wedding. The Carrolls had not even considered the possibility of such a thing. Mrs. Anderson spoke of it one evening at tea.

"I hear they are going to have quite a wedding at those new people's," said she; "a wedding in the church, and reception afterwards at the house. Miss Josie Eggleston and Agnes and Mrs. Monroe were in here this afternoon, and they were speaking about it. They said the young lady was having her trousseau made at Mrs. Griggs's, and everybody thought it rather singular. They are going to the wedding and reception. They inquired if we were going, and I said that we had not been invited, that we had not called. I have been intending to call ever since they came, but now, of course, it is out of the question until after the wedding." Mrs. Anderson spoke with a slight regret. A mild curiosity was a marked trait of hers. "I suppose we could go to the church even if we had no invitation; I suppose many will do that," she said, a little wistfully, after a pause.

"Do you think it wise, without an invitation?" asked Anderson, rather amusedly.

"Why, I don't know, really, dear, that it could do any harm — that is, lower one's dignity at all. Of course it is not as if we had called. If we had called and then received no invitation, the slight would have been marked. But of course we were not invited simply because we had not called —"

"Still, I think I should rather not go, under the circumstances, mother," Anderson said, quietly.

"Well, perhaps you are right, dear," said his mother. "It seems to me that you may be a trifle too punctilious; still, it is best to err on the safe side, and, after all, these are new people; we know very little about them, after all." Nothing was further from Mrs. Anderson than the surmise that, even had she called, no invitation would have come from these unknown new people to the village grocer and his mother. Mrs. Anderson, even with her secret and persistent dissent to her son's giving up his profession and adopting trade, never dreamed of any possible loss of social prestige. She considered herself and her son established in their family traditions beyond possibility of shaking by such minor matters. Anderson did not enlighten her.

"Mrs. Monroe said that she had heard that the Carrolls were owing a good deal," said she, presently. "She said she heard that Blumenfeldt said he must have cash for the flowers for the decorations. They have ordered a great many palms and things. She said she heard that Captain Carroll told him that the money would be forthcoming, and scared him out of his wits, he was so high and mighty, and the florist just gave right in and said he should have all he wanted. She said Mr. Monroe was in there and heard it. I hope Mrs. Griggs will get her pay. They don't owe you, I hope, dear?"

"Don't worry about me, mother?" Randolph replied, smiling. However, she had placed a finger upon a daily perplexity of his. The Carrolls indeed owed him, and every day the debt was increasing. He felt that his old clerk regarded him with wonder at every fresh entry on the books. That very day he had come into the office to inform him, in a hushed voice, that the Carrolls had sent for a pail of lard and a box of butter, besides a bag of flour, and to inquire what he should do about supplying them.

"The girl hasn't brought any money," said he, further, in an ominous whisper.

Anderson, glancing out, saw the small, sturdy, and smiling face of the Hungarian girl employed by the Carrolls. She was gazing straight through at him in the office with a shrewd expression in her untutored black eyes. "Send the order," Anderson replied, in a low voice.

"But," began the clerk.

"It's all right," said Anderson. He dipped his pen in the ink and went on with the letter he was writing. The clerk retreated with a long, anxious, wondering look, which the other man felt.

The Hungarian girl plodded smiling forth with the promise to have the groceries sent at once. Stepping flat-footedly and heavily through the door, she caught her cotton skirt on a nail, and, lo! a rent. The boy, who was a gallant soul for all femininity in need, hurried to her aid with some pins gathered from the lapel of his gingham coat. Little Marie, with a coquettish shake of her head and a blush and smile began repairing the damage.

"It is the cloth that is easy broke," explained she, when she lifted her suffused but still smiling face, "and I a new one will have when I haf my money, my vage." With that Marie was gone, her poor gown scalloping around her heavy, backward heels, her smiling glance of artless coquetry over her shoulder to the last, and the boy and the old clerk looked at each other. The boy whistled.

Just then the delivery-wagon drove up in front of the store. The driver, who was a young fellow in the first stages of pulmonary consumption, got down with weakly alacrity from the seat and came in to get the new orders. He coughed as he entered, but he looked radiant. He was driving the delivery-wagon in the hope of recovering his health by out-of-door life, and he was, or flattered himself that he was, perceptibly gaining.

"Where's the next delivery?" he inquired, hoarsely.

"Wait a minute," said the old clerk, and again invaded the office.

"They ain't paid their hired girl," he said, in a whisper. "Had we better —"

"Better what?" said Anderson, impatiently, though he looked confused.

"Better send them things to the Carrolls'?"

"Didn't I tell you? What —"

"Oh, all right, sir," said the clerk, and retreated hastily. At times he had an awe of his employer.

"Goin' to take all that truck to the Carrolls'?" inquired the consumptive deliverer.

"Yep," replied the boy, lugging out the flour-bag.

"Credit," whispered the man.

The boy nodded.

The man essayed a whistle, but he coughed. "Well, it's none of my funeral," he declared, when he got his breath, "but I hear he's a dead-beat. I s'pose he knows what he is about."

"If he don't, nobody is goin' to tell him, you bet," said the boy, succinctly.

"Well, it's none of my funeral," said the man, and he coughed again, and gathered up the reins, and drove away in a cloud of dust down the street. It had not rained for two weeks and the roads gave evidence of it.

Anderson, back in his office, heard the sound of the retreating wheels with a feeling of annoyance, even scorn of himself for his gullibility, and his stress upon the financial part of the affair.

He was losing a good deal of money, and he did not wish to do so. "I am a fool," he told himself, with that voice of mentality which sounds loudest, to the consciousness, of any voice on earth. He frowned, then he laughed a little, and began mounting a fine new butterfly specimen.

"Other men marry and spend their hard earnings in that way, on love," said he. "Why should I not spend mine after this fashion if I choose?"

That noon, as he passed out of the store on his way home to dinner, Ina and Charlotte came out of the dressmaker's opposite. They looked flushed and happily excited. Charlotte carried a large parcel. They rushed past without seeing him at all, as he gained the opposite sidewalk. He walked along, grave and self-possessed. Nobody seeing him would have dreamed of his inward perturbation, that spiritual alienation as secret as the processes of the body.

Nobody could have suspected how his fond thought and yearning followed one of those small, hurrying, girlish figures. In a way the man, even with his frustrated aims in the progress of life, was so superior to the little, unconscious feminine thing whose chief assets of life were her youth and innocence, and even those of slight weight against the man's age and innocence, that it seemed a pity.

It was not a case of pearls before swine, but seemingly rather of pearls before canary-birds or butterflies, which would not defile them, but flutter over them unheedingly.

However, it may be better to cast away one's pearls of love before anything, rather than keep them. Anderson, walking along home to his dinner in the summer noon, loving foolishly and unreasonably this young girl who would never, probably, place the slightest value on his love, was not actively unhappy. After he had turned the corner of the street on which his house stood he heard the whistle of the noon-train, and soon the carriages from the station came whirling in sight.

Samson Rawdy came first, driving a victoria in which sat the gentleman who had been pointed out to him as Ina Carroll's *fiancé*. He glanced at him approvingly, and the thought even was in his mind that had this stranger been going to marry Charlotte, instead of her sister, he could have had nothing to say against his appearance. Suddenly, Major Arms in the victoria looked full at him and bowed, raising his hat in his soldierly fashion. Anderson was surprised, but returned the salutation promptly.

"Who was that gentleman bowing to you?" his mother asked, as he went up the front steps. She was standing on the porch in her muslin morning panoply.

"He is the gentleman who is to marry the eldest daughter of Captain Carroll," replied Anderson.

"Do you know him?"

"No."

"He bowed."

"I suppose he thought he recognized me."

"He looks old enough to be her grandfather, but he looks like a fine man. I hope she will make him a good wife. It is a risk for a man of his age, marrying a little young thing. I wonder why Samson Rawdy was bringing him from the station. Strange the Carroll carriage didn't meet him, wasn't it?"

"Perhaps they were not expecting him," replied Randolph, which was true.

The carriage occupied by Major Arms and Samson Rawdy overtook

Ina and Charlotte before they had walked far, in front of Drake's drug-store. They had stopped in there for soda, in fact, and were just coming out.

"Why, there's Major Arms!" cried Charlotte, so loudly that some lounging men in the drug-store heard her. Drake, Amidon, and the post-master, who had just stopped, stood in the doorway, with no attempt to disguise their interest, and watched Major Arms spring out of the car-riage like a boy, kiss his sweetheart, utterly unmindful of their obser-vance, then assist the sisters to the back seat, and spring to the front himself.

"Pretty spry for an old boy," remarked the postmaster as the carriage rolled away.

"Oh, he's Southern," returned Amidon, easily. "That is why. Catch a Yankee his age with joints as limber. The cold winters here stiffen folk up quick after they get middle-aged."

"You don't seem very stiff in the joints," said Drake, jocularly. "Guess you are near as old as that man."

"I'm a right smart stiffer than I'd been ef I'd stayed South," replied Amidon.

Then the postmaster wondered, as Mrs. Anderson had done, why Major Arms was driving up with Samson Rawdy rather than in the Carroll carriage, and the others opined, as Randolph had done, that they had not expected him.

"I don't see, for my part, what they get to feed him on when he comes," said Amidon, wisely.

The postmaster and Drake looked at him with expressions like hunting-dogs, although a certain wisdom as to his meaning was evident in both faces.

"I suppose it's getting harder and harder for them to get credit," said Drake.

"Harder," returned Amidon. "I guess it is. I had it from Strauss this morning, that he wouldn't let them have a pound of beef without cash, and I know that Abbot stopped giving them anything some time ago."

"How do they manage, then?" asked the postmaster.

"Strauss says sometimes they send a little money and get a little, the rest of the time he guesses they go without; live on garden-sauce — they've got a little garden, you know, or grocery stuff."

"Can they get trusted at the grocer's?"

"Ingram won't trust 'em, but Anderson lets 'em have all they want, they say."

"S'pose he knows what he's about."

"Lawyers generally do," said Drake.

"He wasn't much of a lawyer, anyhow," said Amidon.

"That's so. He didn't set the river afire," remarked the postmaster.

"I don't believe, if Anderson trusts him, but he knows what he is about," said the druggist. "I guess he knows he's goin' to get his pay."

"Mebbe some of those fine securities of his will come up sometime," Amidon said. "I heard they'd been slumpin' lately. Guess there's some Banbridge folks got hit pretty bad, too."

"Who?" asked Drake, eagerly.

"I heard Lee was in it, for one, and I guess there's others. I must light out of this. It's dinner-time. Where's that arrow-root? My wife's got to make arrow-root gruel for old Mrs. Joy. She's dreadful poorly. Oh, there it is!"

Amidon started, and the postmaster also. In the doorway Amidon paused. "Suppose you knew Carroll was away?" he said.

"No," said Drake.

"Yes, he's been gone a week; ain't coming home till the day before the wedding. Their girl told ours. We've got a Hungarian, too, you know. Carroll's girl can't get any pay. It's a dam'ed shame."

"Why don't she leave?"

"Afraid she'll lose it all, if she does. Same way with the coachman."

"Where's Carroll gone?" asked the postmaster.

"Don't know. The girl said he'd gone to Chicago on business."

"Guess he'll want to go farther than Chicago on business if he don't look out, before long. I don't see how he's goin' to have the weddin', anyway. I don't believe anybody'll trust him here, and, unless I miss my guess, he won't find it very easy anywhere else."

"They say the man the girl's goin' to marry is rich. Maybe he'll foot the bills," said Drake.

"Mebbe he is," assented Amidon. Then he went out in earnest, and the postmaster with him.

"Look at here," said Amidon, mysteriously, as the two men separated on the next corner. "I'll tell you something, if you want to know."

"What?"

"I believe Drake trusts those Carrolls a little."

CHAPTER XVIII

There was in Banbridge, at this date, almost universal distrust of Carroll, but very little of it was expressed, for the reason, common to the greater proportion of humanity: the victims in proclaiming their distrust would have proclaimed at the same time their victimization. It was quite safe to assume that the open detractors of Carroll had not been duped by him; it was also quite safe to assume that many of those who either remained silent or declared their belief in him had suffered more or less. The latter were those who made it possible for the Carrolls to remain in Banbridge at all. There were many who had a lingering hope of securing something in the end, who did not wish Carroll to depart, and who were even uneasy at his absence, although the fact of his family remaining and of the wedding preparations for his daughter going on seemed sufficient to allay suspicions. It is generally true that partisanship, even of the few, counts for more than disparagement of the many, with all right-intentioned people who have a reasonable amount of love for their fellow-men. Somehow partisanship, up to a certain limit, beyond which the partisan appears a fool to all who listen to him, seems to give credit to the believer in it. At all events, while the number of Arthur Carroll's detractors was greatly in advance of his adherents, the moral atmosphere of Banbridge, while lowering, was still very far from cyclonic for him. He got little credit, yet still friendly, admiring, and even obsequious recognition.

The invitations to his daughter's wedding had been eagerly accepted. The speculations as to whether the bills would be paid or not added to the interest. In those days the florist and the dressmaker were quite local celebrities. They looked anxious, yet rather pleasantly self-conscious. The dressmaker bragged by day and lay awake by night. Every time the florist felt uneasy, he slipped across to the nearest saloon and got a drink of beer. After that, when asked if he did not feel afraid he would lose money through the Carroll wedding, he said something about the general esteem in which people should be held who patronized local industries, in his thick German-English, grinned, and shambled back, his fat hips shaking like a woman's, to his hot-houses, and pottered around his geraniums and decorative palms.

On the Sunday morning before the wedding there were an unusual number of men in the barbershop — old Eastman, Frank's father, who generally shaved himself, besides Amidon, Drake, the postmaster, Tappan the milkman, and a number of others. Amidon was in the chair, and spoke whenever it did not seem too hazardous. He had just had his hair cut also, as a delicate concession to the barber on the part of a free customer on a busy morning, and his rather large head glistened like a silver ball.

"Reckon Carroll must have gone out West promotin' to raise a little wind for the weddin'," he said.

"I haven't seed him, and I atropined he had not come back yet," remarked the barber.

Lee looked up from his Sunday paper — all the men except young Willy Eddy were provided with Sunday papers; he waited patiently for a spare page finished and thrown aside by another. Besides the odors of soap and perfumed oils and bay-rum and tobacco-smoke, that filled the little place, was the redolence of fresh newspapers, staring with violent head-lines, and as full of rustle as a forest.

Lee looked up from his paper, and gave his head a curious, consequential toss. He had been shaved himself, and his little tuft of yellow beard was trimmed to a nicety. He looked sleek and well-dressed, and he had always his indefinable air of straining himself furtively upon tiptoe to reach some unattainable height. Lee's consequentiality had something painful about it at times.

"I guess Captain Carroll hadn't any need to go out West promoting. I rather think he can find all the business he wants right here," he said.

Tappan the milkman, bearded and grim, looked up from an article on the coal strike. "Guess he *can* find about fools enough right here to work on, that's right," said he, and there was a laugh.

Lee's small blond face colored furiously; his voice was shrill in response. "Perhaps those he doesn't work, as you call it, are bigger fools than those he does," said he.

"Say," said the milkman, with a snarling sort of humor. He fastened brutally twinkling eyes on Lee. Everybody waited; the little barber held the razor poised over Amidon's chin. "When do your next dividends come in?" he inquired.

Lee gave an angry sniff, and flirted up his paper before his face.

"Why don't ye say?" pressed Tappan, with a hard wink at the others.

"I don't know that it is any of your business," replied Lee.

"Ask when the millennium's comin'," said Amidon, in the chair.

"I wish I was as sure of the millennium as I am of those dividends," declared Lee, brought to bay.

"Glad you've got faith in that dead-beat. He's owin' me for fifteen dollars' worth of milk-tickets, and I can't get a dam'ed penny of it," said Tappan. He gave the sheet of paper he held a vicious crumple and flung it to the floor, whence little Willy Eddy timidly and softly gathered it up. "Gettin' up at four o'clock in the mornin'," continued the milkman, in a cursing voice, "an' milkin' a lot of dam'ed old kickin' cows, and gittin' on the road half-dead with sleep, to make a present to whelps like him, goin' to the City dressed up like Morgan hisself, ridin' to the station in a carriage he ain't paid for, with a man drivin' that can't git a cent out of him. Talk about coal strikes! Lord! I could give them miners points. Strikin' for eight hours a day! Lord! what's that? Here I've got to go home an' hay, if it *is* Sunday, to git enough for them dam'ed cows to eat in the winter! Eight hours! Hm! I work eighteen an' I ain't got anybody over me to strike again', 'cept the Almighty, an' I ruther guess He wouldn't make much account of it. Guess he'd starve me out ef I quit work, and not make much bones of it. I *can* stop peddlin' milk to sech as Carroll, but the milk sours, an' hanged if I know who suffers most. Here's my wife been makin' dam'ed little pot-cheeses out of the sour milk as 'tis, and sellin' 'em for two cents apiece. They're hangin' all over the bushes tied up in little rags. She's got to work all day today makin' butter to save the cream, and then I s'pose I've got to hustle round and find somebody to give the butter to. Carroll ain't the only one. I wish they all had to work as hard as I do one day for the things they git for nothin', the whole bilin' lot of 'em. He's the worst, though. What business did he have settlin' down on us here in Banbridge, I'd like to know? If he'd got to steal to feather his nest, why didn't he go to some other place, confound him?" The milkman's voice and manner were malignant.

The barber looked at him with some apprehension, but he spoke, still holding his razor aloft. "Now I rather guess you are jumpin' at exclusions too hasty, Mr. Tappan," said he, in an anxiously pacific voice. "I don't know about them dividends Mr. Lee's talkin' about. Captain Carroll, he gave me a little dip." The barber winked about mysteriously. "He told me he'd tell me when to come in, and he ain't told me yet, but I ain't no disprehension, but he's all right. Captain Carroll is a gentleman, he is." Flynn's voice fairly quivered with affectionate championship. There were tears in his foolish eyes. He bent over Amidon's face, which grinned up at him cautiously through the lather.

"Let him pay me them milk-tickets, then, if he's all right," Tappan said, viciously.

"He will when he's disembarrassed and his adventures are on a dividend-paying adipoise," said the barber, in a tearful voice.

"I think he is all right," said the druggist.

Then little Willy Eddy added his pipe. He had been covertly smoothing out Tappan's crumpled newspaper. "He's real nice-spoken," said he. "I guess he will come right in time."

Tappan turned on him and snatched back his newspaper. "Here, I ain't done with that," he said; "I've got to take it home to my wife." Then he added, "For God's sake, you little fool, he ain't been swipin' anything from you, has he?"

Then the barber arose to the situation. He advanced, razor in hand. He strode up to the milkman and stood dramatically before him, arm raised and head thrown back. "Now, look at here," he proclaimed, in a high falsetto, "I ain't agoin' to hear no asparagusment of my friends, not here in this tonsorial parlor. No, sir!" There was something at once touching, noble, and absurd about the demonstration. The others chuckled, then sobered, and watched.

Tappan stared at him a second incredulously. Then he grinned, showing his teeth like a dog.

"Lord! then that jailbird is one of your friends, is he?" he said. He had just lit his pipe. He puffed at it, and deliberately blew the smoke into the little barber's face.

Flynn bent over towards him with a sudden motion, and his mild, consequential face in the cloud of smoke changed into something terrible, from its very absurdity. His blue eyes glittered greenly; he lifted the razor and cut the air with it close to the other man's face. Tappan heard the hiss of it, and drew back involuntarily, his expression changing.

"What the devil are you up to?" he growled, with wary eyes on the other's face.

The barber continued to hold the razor like a bayonet in rest, fixed within an inch of the other's nose. "I'm up to kickin' you out of my parlor if you don't stop speakin' individuously disregardin' my friends," said he, with an emphasis which was ridiculous and yet impressive. The other men chuckled again, then grew grave.

"Come back here and finish up my job, John," Amidon called out; yet he watched him warily.

"Here, put up that razor!" the postmaster called out.

"I'll put it up when you stop speakin' mellifluously of my friends," declared the barber. "There ain't nobody in this parlor goin' to speak a word against Captain Carroll if I'm in hearin'; there ain't an honester man in this town."

The barber's back was towards the door. Suddenly Tappan's eyes stared past him, his grin widened inexplicably. Flynn became aware of a pregnant silence throughout the shop. He turned, following Tappan's gaze, and Arthur Carroll stood there. He had entered silently and had heard all the last of the discussion. Every face in the shop was turned towards him; he stood looking at them with the curious expression of a man taken completely off guard. All the serene force and courtesy which usually masked his innermost emotions had, as it were, slipped off; for a flash he stood revealed, soul-naked, for any one who could see. None there could fully see, although every man looked, sharpened with curiosity and suspicion. Carroll was white and haggard, unsmiling, despairing, even pathetic; his eyes actually looked suffused. Then in a flash it was over, and Arthur Carroll in his usual guise stood before them — it was like one of those metamorphoses of which one reads in fairy tales. Carroll stood there smiling, stately, gracefully, even confidentially condescending. It was as if he appealed to their sense of humor, that he, Carroll, stood among them addressing them as their equals.

"Good-day, gentleman," he said, and came forward.

Little Willy Eddy sprang up with a frightened look and gave him his chair, murmuring in response to Carroll's deprecating thanks that he was just going; but he did not go. He remained in the doorway staring. He had a vague idea of some judgment descending upon them all from this great man whom they had been slandering.

"Well, how are you, captain?" said Lee, speaking with an air of defiant importance. It became evident that what had gone before was to be ignored by everybody except Tappan, who suddenly rose and went out, muttering something which nobody heard. Then the lash of a whip was heard outside, a "g'lang," with the impetus of an oath, and a milk wagon clattered down the street.

Carroll replied to Lee, urbanely: "Fine," he said, "fine. How are you, Mr. Lee?"

"Seems to me you are not looking quite up to the mark," Lee remarked, surveying him with friendly solicitude.

The little barber had returned to Amidon in the chair, and was carefully scraping his cheek with the razor.

"Then my looks belie me," Carroll replied, smiling. He offered a cigar to Lee and to the druggist, who sat next on the other side.

"Been out of town?" asked the druggist.

"Yes," replied Carroll.

Drake looked at him hesitatingly, but Amidon, speaking stiffly and cautiously, put the question directly: "Where you been, cap'n?"

"A little journey on business," Carroll answered, easily, lighting his cigar.

"When did you get home?" asked Amidon.

"This morning."

"You certainly look as if you had lost flesh," said Lee, with obsequious solicitude.

"Well, it is a hard journey to Chicago — quite a hard journey," remarked the druggist, with cunning.

"Not on the fast train," said Carroll.

"So you went on the flyer?" said the postmaster.

Carroll was having some difficulty in lighting his cigar, and did not reply.

"Did you go on the flyer?" persisted the postmaster.

"No, I did not," replied Carroll, with unmistakable curtness.

The postmaster hemmed to conceal embarrassment. He had been shaved and had only lingered for a bit of gossip, and now the church-bells began to ring, and he was going to church, as were also Lee, the druggist, and most of the others. They rose and lounged out, one after another; little Willy Eddy followed them. Flynn finished shaving Amidon, who also left, and finally he was left alone in the shop with Carroll, who arose and approached the chair.

"Sorry to keep you waitin', Captain Carroll," said Flynn, preparing a lather with enthusiasm.

"The day is before me," said Carroll, as he seated himself.

"I hope," said Flynn, beating away his hand in a bowl of mounting rainbow bubbles — "I hope that — that — your feelings were not hurt at — at — our eavesdropping."

"At what?" asked Carroll, kindly and soberly.

"At our eavesdropping," reported the barber, with a worshipful and agitated glance at him.

"Oh!" answered Carroll, but he did not smile. "No," he said, "my feelings were not hurt." He looked at the small man who was the butt of the town, and his expression was almost caressing.

Flynn continued to beat away at the lather, and the rainbow bubbles curled over the edge of the bowl. "You said that you would devise me when the time had come for me to invest that money," he said, diffidently, and yet with a noble air of confidence and loyalty.

"It hasn't come yet," Carroll replied.

CHAPTER XIX

As Ina Carroll's wedding-day drew nearer, the excitement in Banbridge increased. It was known that the services of a New York caterer had been engaged. Blumenfeldt was decorating the church, Samson Rawdy was furbishing up all his vehicles and had hired supplementary ones from New Sanderson.

"No girl has ever went from this town as that Carroll girl will," he told his wife, who assisted him to clean the carriage cushions.

"I s'pose the folks will dress a good deal," said she, brushing assiduously.

"You bet," said her husband.

"Well, they won't get no dirt on their fine duds off *your* carriage-seats," said she. She was large and perspiring, but full of the content of righteous zeal. She and Samson Rawdy thoroughly enjoyed the occasion, and he was, moreover, quite free from any money anxiety regarding it. At first he had been considerably exercised. He had come home and conferred with his wife, who was the business balance-wheel of the family.

"Carroll has been speakin' to me about providin' carriages for his daughter's weddin', an' I dunno about it," said he.

"How many does he want?" inquired his wife. He had sunk on his doorstep on coming home at dusk, and sat with speculative eyes on the pale western sky, while his wife sat judicially, quite filling with her heated bulk a large rocking-chair, placed for greater coolness in front of the step, in the middle of the slate walk.

"He wants all mine and all I can hire in New Sanderson," replied Rawdy.

"Lord!" ejaculated his wife. "All them?"

"All them," replied Rawdy, moodily triumphant.

"Well," said his wife, "that ain't the point."

"No, it ain't," agreed Rawdy.

"The point is," said she, "is he agoin' to or ain't he agoin' to pay."

"That's so," said Rawdy.

"He's a-owin' everybody, ain't he?" said the wife.

"Pooty near, I guess."

"Well, you ain't goin' to let one of your cerridges go, let alone hirin', unless he pays ahead."

"Lord! Dilly, how'm I goin' to ask him?" protested Rawdy.

"How? Why, the way anybody would ask him. Ain't you got a tongue in your head?" demanded she.

"You dunno what a man he is. I asked him the other night when I drove him up, and it wa'n't a job I liked, I can tell you."

"Did he pay you?"

"Paid me some of it."

"He's owin' you now, ain't he?"

"Well, he ain't owin' much, only the few times their cerridge ain't been down. It ain't much, Dilly."

"But it's something."

"Yes; everythin' that ain't nothin' is somethin', I s'pose."

"And now you're goin' right on an' lettin' him have all your cer-ridges, and you'll be wantin' me to help clean the seats, too, I'll warrant, and you're agoin' to hire into the bargain, with him owin' you and owin' everybody else in town."

"Now, Dilly, I didn't say I was agoin' to," protested Rawdy.

"An' me needin' a new dress, and ain't had one to my back for two years, and them Carroll women in a different one every time they appear out, and the girl having enough clothes for a Vanderbilt. I guess Stella Griggs will rue the day. She's a fool, and always was. If you can afford to give that man money you can afford to get me a new dress. I'd go to the weddin' — it's free, in the church — if I had anything decent to wear."

"Now, Dilly, what can I do? I leave it to you," asked Samson Rawdy, with confessed helplessness.

"Do?" said she. "Why, tell him he's got to pay ahead or he can't have the cerridges. If you're afraid to, I'll ask him. I ain't afraid."

"Lord! I ain't afraid, Dilly," said Rawdy.

"You'd better clean up, after supper, an' go up there and tell him," said Dilly Rawdy, mercilessly.

In the end Rawdy obeyed, having shaved and washed, and set forth. When he returned he was jubilant.

"He's a gentleman, I don't care what they say," said he, "and he treated me like a gentleman. Gave me a cigar, and asked me to sit down. He was smokin', himself, out on the porch. The women folks were in the house.

"Did he pay you?" asked Mrs. Rawdy.

Then Rawdy shook a fat roll of bills in her face. "Look at here," said he.

"The whole of it?"

"Every darned mill; my cerridges and the New Sanderson ones, too."

"Well, now, ain't you glad you did the way I told you to?"

"Lord! he'd paid me, anyway," declared Rawdy. He's a gentleman. Women are always dreadful scart."

"It's a pity men wasn't a little scarter sometimes," said his wife.

Rawdy, grinning, tossed a bill to her. "Wa'n't you sayin' you wanted a dress?" said he.

"I ruther guess I do. I ain't had one for two years."

"I guess I'd better git a silk hat to wear. I suppose I shall have to drive some of the Carrolls' folks," said Rawdy, with a timid look at his wife. A silk hat had always been his ambition, but she had always frowned upon it.

"Well, I would," said she, cordially.

Samson Rawdy told everybody how Carroll had paid him in advance — "every cent, sir; and he didn't believe, for his part, half the stories that were told about him. He guessed that he paid, in the long run, as well as anybody in Banbridge. Carroll wa'n't the only one that hadn't paid him, not by a long-shot. He guessed some of them that talked about Carroll had better look to home. He called Carroll a gentleman, and any time when anything happened that his carriage wa'n't on hand when the train come in, he was ready an' willin' to drive him up, or any of his folks, an' if they didn't have a quarter handy right on the spot, he wa'n't goin' to lay awake sweatin' over it."

Rawdy's testimony prevented Blumenfeldt, the florist, from asking for his pay in advance, as he had intended. He and his son and daughter, who assisted him in his business, decorated the church and the Carroll house, and wagons laden with palms and flowers were constantly on the road. Tuesday, the day before the wedding, was unusually warm. Banbridge had an air of festive weariness. Everybody who passed the church stopped and stared at the open doors and the wilting grass leaves strewn about.

Elsa Blumenfeldt, in a blue shirt-waist and black skirt, with the tightest of fair braids packed above a round, pink face, with eyes so blue they looked opaque, tied and wove garlands with the stolid radiance of her kind. Her brother Franz worked as she did. Only the father Blumenfeldt, who was of a more nervous strain, flew about in excitement, his fat form full of vibrations, his fat face blazing, contorting with frantic energy.

"It iss ein goot yob," he repeated, constantly — "ein goot yob." Not a doubt was left. When he came in contact with Carroll he bowed to the ground; he was full of eager protestations, of almost hysterical assertions. All day long he was in incessant and fruitless motion, buzzing, as it were, over his task, conserving force only in the heat of his own spirit, not in the performance of the work. Meanwhile the son and daughter, dogged, undiverted, wrought with good results, weaving many a pretty floral fancy with their fat fingers. Eddy Carroll had taken it upon himself to guard the church doors and prevent people from viewing the splendors before the appointed time. All the morning he had waged war with sundry of his small associates, who were restrained from forcible entry only by the fear of the Blumenfeldt family.

"Mr. Blumenfeldt says he'll run anybody out who goes in, and kick 'em head over heels all the way down the aisle and down the steps," Eddy declared, mendaciously, to everybody, even his elders.

"I think you are telling a lie, little boy," said Mrs. Samson Rawdy, who had come with a timid female friend on a tour of inspection. Mrs. Rawdy, in virtue of her husband's employment, felt a sort of proprietorship in the occasion.

"There won't be a mite of trouble about our goin' in to see the church," she told the friend, who was a humble soul.

But Mrs. Rawdy reckoned without Eddy Carroll. When she told him that he was telling a lie, he smiled sweetly at her.

"You're telling a lie yourself, missis," said he.

Mrs. Rawdy essayed to push past him, but as he stood directly in the door, and she was unable, on account of her stout habit of body, to pass him, and hardly ventured to forcibly remove him, she desisted. "You are a sassy little boy," said she, "and if your sister is as sassy as her brother, I pity the man that's goin' to marry her."

In reply Eddy made up an impish face at her as she retreated. Then he entered the church himself to inspect progress, returning immediately to take up his position of sentry again. About noon Anderson passed on his way to the post-office, and nodded.

"You can't come in," the boy called out.

"All right," Anderson responded. But then Eddy made a flying leap from the church door and caught hold of his arm.

"Say, you can, if you won't tell anybody about it," he whispered, as if the curious village was within ear-shot.

"I am afraid I cannot stop now, thank you," Anderson replied, smiling.

"You ain't mad, are you?"

Anderson assured him that he was not.

"They didn't tell me to keep folks out," Eddy explained, "but I made up my mind I didn't want everybody seeing it till it was done. It's going to be a stunner, I can tell you. There's palms and pots of flowers, and yards and yards of white and green ribbon tied in bows, and the pews are all tied round with evergreen boughs, and tomorrow the smilax is going up. I tell you, it's fine."

"It must be," said Anderson. He strove to move on, but could not break free from the boy's little, clinging hand. "Just come up the steps and peek in," pleaded Eddy. So Anderson yielded weakly and let himself be pulled up the steps to the entrance of the church.

"Ain't it handsome?" asked Eddy, triumphantly.

"Very," replied Anderson.

"Say," said Eddy, "was it as handsome when you were married yourself?"

"I never was married," replied Anderson, laughing.

"You weren't?" said Eddy, staring at him. "Why, I thought you were a widow man."

"No," said Anderson.

"Well, why were you never married?" asked Eddy, sharply.

"Oh, for a good many reasons which I have never formulated sufficiently to give," replied Anderson.

"I hate big words," said Eddy, "and I didn't think you would do it. It's mean."

"So it is," said Anderson, with a kindly look at him. "Well, all I meant was I couldn't give my reasons without thinking it over."

"Perhaps you'll tell me when you get them thought over," said Eddy, accepting the apology generously.

"Perhaps."

Anderson turned to go, after saying again that the church was very handsomely decorated, and Eddy still kept at his side.

"You didn't stay not married because you couldn't get a girl to marry you, anyhow, I know that," said he, "because you are an awful handsome man. You are better-looking than major Arms. I should think Ina would a heap rather have married you."

"Thank you," said Anderson.

"You are going to the wedding, aren't you?" asked Eddy.

"No, I think not."

"Why not?"

"I am very busy."

"Why, you don't keep your store open Wednesday evening?" asked Eddy, regarding him sharply.

"I have letters to write," replied Anderson.

"Oh, shucks! let the letters go!" cried the boy. "There's going to be stacks of fun, and lots of things to eat. There's chicken salad and lobster, and sandwiches, and ice-cream and cake, and coffee and cake, and —" The boy hesitated; then he spoke again in a whisper of triumph that had its meaning of pathos: "They are all paid for. I know, for I heard papa tell Major Arms. The carriages are paid for, too, and the florist is going to be paid."

"That's good," said Anderson.

"Yes, sir, so the things are sure to be there. They won't back out at the last minute, as they do sometimes. Awful mean, too. Say, you'd better come. Your mother can come, too. She likes ice-cream, don't she?"

Anderson said that he believed she did.

"Well, she'll be sure to get all she can eat," said Eddy. "Tell her to come. I like your mother." He clung closely to the man's arm and walked along the street with him, forgetting his post as guardian of the church. "You'll come, won't you?" he said.

"No. I shall be too busy, my son," said Anderson, smiling; and finally Eddy retreated dissatisfied. When he went home an hour later he burst into the house with a question.

"Say," he asked Charlotte, "I want to know if Mr. Anderson and his mother were asked to the wedding."

Charlotte was hurrying through the hall with white and green ribbons flying around her, en route to trim the bay-window where the bridal couple were to stand to receive the guests. "Oh, Eddy, dear," she cried, "I can't stop now; indeed I can't. I don't know who was invited and who not."

"But, Charlotte," Eddy persisted, "I want to know particularly. Please tell me, honey."

Then Charlotte stopped and looked back over her great snarl of white and green ribbon. "Who did you say, dear?" she asked. "Hurry! I can't stop."

"Mr. Anderson," repeated Eddy. "Mr. Anderson and his mother."

"Mr. Anderson and his mother?" repeated Charlotte, vaguely, and just then Anna Carroll came with a little table which was to support a bowl of roses in the bay-window.

"Mr. Anderson," said Eddy again.

"I don't know who you mean, Eddy, dear," said Charlotte.

"Why, yes, you do, Charlotte, Mr. Anderson and his mother."

"What is it?" asked Anna Carroll. "Eddy, you must not stop us for anything. We are too busy."

"You might just tell me if they are asked to the wedding," said Eddy, in an aggrieved tone. "That won't take a minute. Mr. Anderson. He keeps store."

"Gracious!" cried Anna Carroll. "The child means the grocer! No, dear, he isn't asked."

"Why, I never thought!" said Charlotte. "No, dear, he isn't asked."

"Why not?" asked Eddy.

"We couldn't ask everybody, honey," replied Anna. "Now you must not hinder us another minute."

But Eddy danced persistently before them, barring their progress.

"He isn't everybody," he said. "He's the nicest man in this town. Why didn't you ask him? Didn't you think he was nice enough, I'd like to know?"

"Of course he is nice, dear," said Charlotte; "very nice." She flushed a little.

"Why didn't you ask him, then?" demanded Eddy. "I call it mean."

Anna took Eddy by his small shoulders and set him aside.

"Eddy," she said, sternly, "not another word. We could not ask the grocer to your sister's wedding. Now, don't say another word about it. Your sister and I are too busy to bother with you."

"I don't see why you won't ask him because he's a grocer," Eddy called, indignantly, after her. "He's the nicest man here, and he always lets us have things, whether we pay him or not. I have heard you say so. I think you are awful mean to take his groceries, and eat 'em, and use them for Ina's wedding, and then not ask him, just because he is a grocer."

Anna's laughter floated back, and the boy wondered angrily what she was laughing at. Then he went by himself about righting wrongs. He hunted about until he found on his mother's desk some left-over wedding-cards, and he sent invitations to both the wedding and reception to Randolph Anderson and his mother, which were received that night.

Randolph carried them home, and his mother examined them with considerable satisfaction.

"We might go to the ceremony," said she, with doubtful eyes on her son's face.

"I really think we had better not, mother."

"You think we had better not, simply to the ceremony? Of course I admit that we could not go to the reception at the house, since we have not called, but the ceremony?"

"I think we had better not; this very late invitation —"

"Oh, Randolph, that is easily accounted for. It is so easy to overlook an invitation."

But Randolph persisted in his dissent to the proposition to attend. He was quite sure how the invitation had happened to come at all, and later on in the day he was confirmed in his opinion when Eddy Carroll made a rush into his office and inquired, breathlessly, if he had received his invitation and if he was coming.

"Because I found out you hadn't been asked, and I told them it was mean, and I sent you one myself," said he, with generous indignation.

Anderson finally compromised by going with him to the church and viewing the completed decorations. He also presented him with a package of candy from his glass jars when he followed him back to the store.

"Say, you are a brick," Eddy assured him. "When I am a man I am going to keep a grocery store. I'd a great deal rather do that than have a business like papa's. If you have the things yourself in your own store, you don't have to owe anybody for them. Good-bye. If you should get those letters done, you come, and your mother, and I'll look out you have everything you want; and I'll save seats in the pew where I sit, too."

"Thank you," said Anderson, and was conscious of an exceedingly warm feeling for the child flying out of the store with his package of sweets under his arm.

CHAPTER XX

Carroll had arrived home very unexpectedly that Sunday morning. The family were at the breakfast-table. As a usual thing, Sunday-morning breakfast at the Carrolls' was a desultory and uncertain ceremony, but when Major Arms was there it was promptly on the table at eight o'clock. He had not yet, in the relaxation of civilian life, gotten over the regular habits acquired in the army.

"It isn't hard you'll find the old man on you, sweetheart," he told Ina, "but there's one thing he's got to have, and that is his breakfast, and a good old Southern one, with plenty to eat, at eight o'clock, or you'll find him as cross as a bear all day to pay for it."

Ina laughed and blushed, and sprinkled the sugar on her cereal.

"Ina will not mind," said Mrs. Carroll. "She and Charlotte have never been sleepy-heads."

Eddy glanced resentfully at his mother. He was a little jealous in these days. He had never felt himself so distinctly in the background as during these preparations for his sister's wedding.

"I am not a sleepy-head, either, Amy," said he.

"It is a pity you are not," said she, and everybody laughed.

"Eddy is always awake before anybody in the house," said Ina, "and prowling around and sniffing for breakfast."

"And you bet there is precious little breakfast to sniff lately, unless we have company," said Eddy, still in his resentful little pipe; and for a second there was silence.

Then Mrs. Carroll laughed, not a laugh of embarrassment, but a delightful, spontaneous peal, and the others, even Major Arms, who had looked solemnly nonplussed, joined her.

Eddy ate his cereal with a sly eye of delight upon the mirthful faces. "Yes," said he, further. "I wish you'd stay here all the time, Major Arms, and stay engaged to Ina instead of marrying her; then all the rest of us would have enough to eat. We always have plenty when you are here."

He looked around for further applause, but he did not get it. Charlotte gave him a sharp poke in the side to institute silence.

"What are you poking me for, Charlotte?" he asked, aggrievedly. She paid no attention to him.

"Don't you think it is strange we don't hear from papa?" said Charlotte.

Major Arms stared at her. "Do you mean to say you have not heard from him since he went away?" he asked.

"Not a word," replied Mrs. Carroll, cheerfully.

"I am a little uneasy about papa," said Ina, but she went on eating her breakfast quite composedly.

"I should be if I had ever known him to fail to take care of himself," said Mrs. Carroll.

"It's the other folks that had better look out," remarked Eddy, with perfect innocence, though would-be wit. He looked about for applause.

Arms's eyes twinkled, but he bent over his plate solemnly.

"Eddy, you are talking altogether too much," Anna Carroll said.

"You are unusually silly this morning, Eddy," said Charlotte. "There is no point in such a remark as that."

"You said Arthur had gone to Chicago?" Arms said to Mrs. Carroll.

"Well, the funny part of it is, we don't exactly know whether he has or not," replied Mrs. Carroll, "but we judge so. Arthur had been talking about going to Chicago. He had spoken about the possibility of his having to go for some time, and all of a sudden that morning came a telegram from New York saying that he was called away on business."

"Amy, of course he went to Chicago," Anna Carroll said, quickly. "You know there is no doubt of it. He said he might have to go there on business, and he had carried a dress-suit case in to the office, to have it ready, and he had given you the Chicago hotel address."

"Yes, so he did, Anna," assented Mrs. Carroll. "I suppose he must have gone to Chicago."

"You have written him there, I suppose?" said Arms, who was evidently perturbed.

"Oh yes," replied Mrs. Carroll, easily, "I have written three times."

"Did you put a return address on the corner of the envelope in case he was not there?"

"Oh no! I never do. I thought only business men did that."

"Amy doesn't even date her letters," said Ina.

"I never can remember the date," said Mrs. Carroll, "and I never can remember whether it is Banbridge or Banridge, so I never write the name of the place, either."

"And she always signs her name just Amy," said Charlotte.

"Yes, I do, of course," said Mrs. Carroll, smiling.

Arms turned to Anna Carroll. "You have not felt concerned?" said he to her.

"Not in the least," she replied, calmly. "I have no doubt that he has gone to Chicago, and possibly his business has taken him farther still. I think nothing whatever of not hearing from him. Arthur, with all of his considerateness in other respects, has always been singularly remiss as to letters."

"Yes, he has, even before we were married," agreed Mrs. Carroll. "Not hearing from Arthur was never anything to worry about."

"And I think with Amy that Arthur Carroll is perfectly well able to take care of himself," said Anna, further, with her slight inflection of sarcasm.

"I understood that he was going to Chicago, from something he said to me some time ago," Arms said, thoughtfully.

"Of course he has gone there," Anna Carroll said again, with a sharp impatience.

And then there was a whirring flash of steel past the window, and the fiercely hitching curve of a boy's back.

"It's Jim Leech on his wheel, and he's got a telegram," proclaimed Eddy, and made a dash for the door.

There was a little ripple of excitement. Charlotte jumped up and followed Eddy, but he re-entered the room dancing aloof with the telegram. In spite of her efforts to reach it, he succeeded in tearing it open. Charlotte was almost crying and quite pale.

"Eddy," she pleaded, "please give it to me — please."

"Eddy, bring that telegram here," commanded his aunt, half rising from her seat.

"It is only from Arthur, saying he is coming, of course," said Mrs. Carroll, calmly sipping her coffee. "Arthur always telegraphs when he has been away anywhere and is coming home."

"Eddy!" said Charlotte.

But Eddy essayed reading the telegram with an effect of being in the air, such was his defensive agility. "He's coming, I guess," he said. "I don't think anything very bad has happened. I don't think it's an accident or anything, but the writing is awful. I should think that telegraph man would be ashamed to write like that."

"Eddy, bring that telegram to me," said Anna; "bring it at once." And the boy finally obeyed.

Anna read the telegram and her nervous forehead relaxed. "It is all right," said she; then she read the message aloud. It was dated New York, the night before:

"Am in New York. Shall take the first train home in the morning."

"He sent it last night at eight o'clock, and we have only just got it," said Ina.

"He is all right," repeated Anna.

"Of course he is all right," said Mrs. Carroll. "Why doesn't Marie bring in the eggs? We have all finished the cereal?"

"Eggs! Golly!" cried Eddy, slipping into his chair.

"Why, it must be time for him now!" Charlotte said, suddenly.

Arms looked at his watch. "Yes, it is," he agreed.

It was not long before Samson Rawdy drove into the grounds, and everybody sprang up at the sound of the wheels.

"There's papa!" cried Eddy, and led the way to the door, slipping out before the others.

Carroll was engaged in a discussion with the driver. He nodded his head in a smiling aside in response to the chorus of welcome from the porch, and went on conferring with the liveryman, who was speaking in a low, inaudible voice, but gesticulating earnestly. Presently Carroll drew out his pocket-book and gave him some money.

"My!" said Eddy, in a tone of awe, "papa's paying him some money."

Still the man, Samson Rawdy, did not seem quite satisfied. Something was quite audible here about the rest of the bill, but finally he smiled in response to Carroll's low, even reply, raised his hat, sprang into his carriage, and turned round in a neat circle while Carroll came up the steps.

"Arthur, dear, where have you been?" asked his wife, folding soft, silken arms around his neck and putting up her smiling face for his kiss. "We have not heard a word from you since you went away."

"You got my telegram?" replied Carroll, interrogatively, kissing her, and passing on to his daughters. Eddy, meantime, was clinging to one of his father's hands and making little leaps upon him like a pet dog.

"Yes," cried everybody together, "the telegram just came — just a minute ago."

Anna had kissed her brother, then stepped quietly into the house. The others moved slowly after her.

"How are you, old man?" Carroll asked Major Arms.

"First rate," replied Arms, grasping the proffered hand, yet in a somewhat constrained fashion.

"Why didn't you write, Arthur dear?" Mrs. Carroll asked, yet not in the least complainingly or reproachfully. On the contrary, she was smiling at him with the sweetest unreserve of welcome as she entered the dining-room by his side.

"Breakfast is getting cold, papa," said Charlotte. "Come right in."

"We have got a bully breakfast. No end to eat," said Eddy, as he danced at his father's heels.

Carroll need not have answered his wife's question then, for her attention was diverted from it, but he did. "I was very busy, dear," he said, rather gravely. "You were no less in mind. In fact, I never had you all any more in mind."

"You must have had a hard night's journey, papa," Charlotte said, as they all sat down at the table, and Marie brought in the eggs.

"Yes, I had a very hard night," Carroll replied, still with a curious gravity.

Charlotte regarded him anxiously. "Why, papa," she said, "aren't you well?"

"Very well indeed, honey," Carroll replied, and he smiled then.

The others looked at him. "Why, papa, you *do* look sick!" cried Ina.

"Arthur, dear, you look as if you had been ill a month, and I never noticed it till now, I was so glad to see you," cried Mrs. Carroll. Suddenly she jumped from her seat and passed behind her husband's chair and drew his head to her shoulder. "Arthur, dearest, are you ill?"

"No, I am not, sweetheart."

"But, Arthur, you have lost twenty pounds!"

"Nonsense, dear!"

"Haven't you had anything to eat, papa?" Eddy asked, with sharp sidewise eyes on his father.

Then Anna Carroll spoke. "Can't you see that Arthur wants his breakfast?" said she, and in her tone was a certain impatience and pity for her brother.

Major Arms, however, was not a man to take a hint. He also was scrutinizing Carroll. "Arthur," he suddenly exclaimed, "what on earth is the matter, lad? You do look pretty well knocked up."

Carroll loosened his wife's arm and gave her an exceedingly gentle push. He laughed constrainedly at the same time. "Anna is about right," he said. "I am starved. Wait until I have eaten my breakfast before you pass judgment on my appearance."

"Haven't you eaten anything since you left Chicago, papa?" asked Ina.

"Never mind, dear," he replied, in an odd, curt tone, and she looked a little grieved.

"Did you come on the flyer, papa?" asked Eddy. "What are you nudging me for, Charlotte?"

"Papa doesn't want any more questions asked. He wants his breakfast," said Charlotte.

"No, I did not come on the flyer," Carroll answered, in the same curt tone. Then for a moment there was silence, and Carroll ate his breakfast.

It was Major Arms who broke the silence. "You got in last night," he said, with scarcely an inflection of interrogation.

But Carroll replied, "I was in the hotel at midnight."

"We have been frightfully busy since you left, Arthur dear," said Mrs. Carroll. "It is a tremendous undertaking to make a wedding."

"How do the preparations go on?" asked Carroll, while Ina bent over her plate with a half-annoyed, half-pleased expression.

"Very well," replied Mrs. Carroll. "Ina's things are lovely, and the dressmaker is so pleased that we gave her the trousseau. It will be a lovely wedding."

"Where have you been all the week?" Carroll asked of Arms, who was gazing with an utter openness of honest delight at Ina.

"Here some of the time, and in New York. I had to run up to Albany on business for two days. I got home Wednesday night too late to come out here, and I went into Proctor's roof-garden to see the vaudeville show."

"Did you?" remarked Carroll, in an even voice. He sugared his cereal more plentifully.

"Yes. I had the time on my hands. It was a warm night and I did not feel like turning in, and I was trailing about and the lights attracted me. And, by Jove! I was glad I went in, for I saw something that carried me back — well, I won't say how many years, for I'm trying to be as much of a boy as I can for this little girl here — but, by Jove! it did carry me back, though."

"What was it?" asked Charlotte.

"Well, dear, it was nothing except a dance by a nigger. Maybe you wouldn't have thought so much of it. I don't know, though; it did bring down the house. He was called back I don't know how many times. It was like a dance an old fellow on my father's plantation used to dance before the war. Arthur, you must have seen old Uncle Noah dance that. Why, now I think of it, you used to dance it yourself when you were a boy, and sing for the music just the way he did. Don't you remember?"

Carroll nodded laughingly, and went on eating.

"Used to — I guess you did! I remember your dancing that at Bud Hamilton's when Bud came of age. Old Noah must have gone then. It was after the war."

"Oh, papa," cried Eddy, in a rapture, "do dance it sometime, won't you?"

"I'll tell you what we will all do," cried Major Arms, with enthusiasm, "we'll all go to the City tomorrow night, and we'll see that dance. I tell you it's worth it. It's a queer thing, utterly unlike anything I have ever seen. It is a sort of cross between a cake-walk and an Indian war-dance. Jove! how it carried me back!" Arms began to hum. "That's it, pretty near, isn't it, Arthur?" he asked.

"Quite near, I should say," replied Carroll.

"Oh, papa, won't you sing and dance it after breakfast?" cried Eddy.

"Now, hush up, my son," said Arms. "Your father has the dignity of his position to support. A gentleman doesn't dance nigger dances when he is grown up and the head of a family. It's all very well when he is a boy. But we'll all go to New York tomorrow night and we'll see that dance."

"There is a great deal to do," Anna Carroll remarked.

"Nonsense!" said the major. "There's time enough. Where are the Sunday papers? I'll see if it is on tomorrow. Have they come yet?"

"I am going down to get shaved, and I will bring them up," Carroll said.

"Don't they bring them to the door in Banbridge?" asked Arms, wonderingly.

"They used when we first came here," said Eddy. "I guess —" Then he stopped in obedience to a look from his aunt.

"I will bring them when I come home," repeated Carroll.

"Well, we'll all go in tomorrow night, and we'll see that dance," said the major.

But when Carroll, on his return from the barber's shop, brought the papers, Major Arms discovered, much to his disappointment, that that particular attraction had been removed from the roof-garden. There was a long and flattering encomium of the song and dance which upheld him in his enthusiasm.

"Yes, it was a big thing; you can understand by what it says here," said he, "I was right. I'm mighty sorry it's off."

CHAPTER XXI

Anderson on Wednesday evening sat on the porch and saw the people stream by to the wedding. Mrs. Anderson, although it was a very pleasant and warm evening, did not come outside, but sat by the parlor window, well-screened by the folds of the old damask curtain. The wedding was at eight, and by quarter-past seven the people began to pass; by half-past seven the street was quite full of them. It seemed as if all Banbridge was gathering. A church wedding was quite an unusual festivity in the town, and, besides, there had always been so much curiosity with regard to the Carrolls that interest was doubled in this case. His mother called to him softly from the parlor. "There are a great many going, aren't they?" said she.

"Yes, mother," replied Anderson. He distinctly heard a soft sigh from the window, and his heart smote him a little. He realized dimly that a matter like this might seem important to a woman. Presently he heard a soft flop of draperies, and his mother stood large and white and mild behind him.

"They are nearly all gone who are going, I think?" said she, interrogatively.

Anderson looked at his watch, holding it towards the light of the moon, which was just coming above the horizon. The daylight had paled with suddenness like a lamp burning low from lack of oil. "Yes; they must be all gone now," said he. "It is eight o'clock."

He rose and placed a chair for his mother, and she settled into it.

"I thought I would not come out here while the people were passing," said she. "I have my *matinée* on, and I am never quite sure that it is dress enough for the porch."

Anderson looked at the lacy, beribboned thing which his mother wore over her black silk skirt, and said it was very pretty.

"Yes, it is," said she, "but I am never sure that it is just the thing to be out of my own room in. I suppose the dresses tonight will be very pretty. Miss Carroll ought to make a lovely bride. She is a very pretty girl, and so is her sister. I dare say their dresses will be prettier than anything of the kind ever seen in Banbridge."

There was an indescribable wistfulness in Mrs. Anderson's voice. Large and rather majestic woman that she was, she spoke like a disappointed child, and her son looked at her with wonder.

"I don't understand how a woman can care so much about seeing pretty dresses," he said, not unkindly, but with a slight inflection of amused scorn.

"No," said his mother, "I don't suppose you can, dear. I don't suppose any man can." And it was as if she regarded him from feminine heights. At that moment the longing, never quite stilled in her breast, for a daughter, a child of her own kind, who would have understood her, who would have gone with her to this wedding, and been to the full as disappointed as she was to have missed it, was strong upon her. She was very fond of her son, but at the moment she saw him with alien eyes. "No, dear, I don't suppose you can understand," she repeated; "you are a man."

"If you had really cared so much, mother — if I had understood," he said, gently, "you might have gone. You could have gone with the Egglestons."

"There was no reason why we could not have gone by ourselves," said she, "and sat with the invited guests, where we could have seen everything nicely, since we had an invitation."

Anderson opened his mouth to tell his mother of the true source of the invitation; then he hesitated. He had a theory that it was foolish, in view of the large alloy of bitterness in the world, to destroy the slightest element of sweet by a word. It was quite evident that his mother, for some occult reason, took pleasure in the invitation. Why destroy it? So he repeated that she might have gone, had she cared so much; and feeling that he was showing a needless humility in his own scruples, he added that he would have gone with her. Then his mother declared that she did not, after all, really care, that it was a warm night and she would have been obliged to dress, and after fanning herself a little while, went in the house and to bed, leaving him marvelling at the ways of women. The problem as to whether his mother had really wished very much to go to the wedding and whether he had been selfish and foolish in opposing her wish or not, rather agitated him for some minutes. Then he gave it up, and relegated women to a place with the fourth dimension on the shelf of his understanding. The moon was now fairly aloft, sailing triumphant in a fleet of pale gold and rosy clouds. The night was very hot, the night insects were shrieking in their persistent dissonances all over the street. Shadows waved and trembled over the field of silver radiance cast by the moon. No one passed. He could not see a window-light in any of the houses. Everybody had gone to the wedding, and the place was like a deserted village. Anderson felt unutterably lonely. He felt outside of all the happy doors and windows of life. Discontent was not his failing, but all at once the evil spirit swept over him. He seemed to realize that instead of moving in the broad highway trod by humanity he was on his own little side-path to the tomb, and injury and anger seized him. He thought of the man who was being married so short a distance away, and envy in a general sense, with no reference even to Charlotte, swept over him. He had never been disturbed in very great measure with longing for the happiness that the other man was laying hold of, but even that fact served to augment his sense of injury and resentment. He felt that it was due to circumstances, in a very large degree to the inevitable decrees of his fate, that he had not had the longing, and not to any inherent lack of his own nature. He felt that he had had a double loss in both the hunger and the satisfaction of it, and now, after all, had come at last this absurd and hopeless affection which had lately possessed him. Tonight the affection, instead of seeming to warm the heart of a nobly patient and reasonable man, seemed to sting it.

Suddenly out of the hot murk of the night came a little puff of cool wind, and borne on it a faint strain of music. Anderson listened. The music came again.

"It cannot be possible that the wedding is just about to begin," he thought, "not at this hour."

But that was quite possible with the Carrolls, who, with the exception of the head of the family, had never been on time in their lives. It was nearly nine o'clock, and the guests had been sitting in a subdued impatience amid the wilting flowers and greens in the church, and the minister had been trying to keep in a benedictory frame of mind in a stuffy little retiring-room, and now the wedding-party were just entering the church. A sudden impulse seized Anderson. He stole inside the house, and looked and listened in the hall. Everything was dark up-stairs, and silent. Mrs. Anderson always fell asleep like a baby immediately upon going to bed.

Anderson got his hat from the hall-tree, and went out, closing the door with its spring-lock very cautiously. Then he slipped around the house and listened. He could hear a soft, cooing murmur of voices from the back stoop. The servant, as usual, was keeping tryst there with her lover. He walked a little farther and came upon their consolidated shadow of love under the wild-cucumber vine which wreathed over the trellis-hood of the door. The girl gave a little shriek and a giggle, the man, partly pushed, partly of his own volition, started away from her and stood up with an incoherent growl of greeting.

"Good-evening," said Anderson. "Jane, I am going out, and my mother has gone up-stairs. If you will be kind enough to have a little attention in case she should ring." Anderson had fixed an electric bell in his mother's room, which communicated with the kitchen.

"Yes, sir," said the girl, with a sound between a gasp and a giggle.

"I have locked the front-door," said Anderson.

"Yes, sir," said the girl, again.

Anderson went around the house, and the sound of an embarrassed and happy laugh floated after him. He felt again the sense of injury and resentment, as if he were shut even out of places where he would not care to be, even out of the humblest joys of life, out of the kitchens as well as the palaces.

Anderson strolled down the deserted street and turned the corner on to Main Street. Then he strolled on until he reached the church. It was brilliantly lighted. Peering people stood in the entrance and the sidewalk before it was crowded. There was a line of carriages in waiting. But everything was still except for the unintermittent voices of the night, which continued like the tick of a clock measuring off eternity, undisturbed by anything around it. From the church itself a silence which could be sensed seemed to roll, eclipsing the diapason of an organ. Not a word of the minister's voice was audible at that distance. Instead was that tremendous silence and hush. Anderson wondered what that pretty, ignorant little girl in there was, to dare to tamper with this ancient force of the earth? Would it not crush her? If the man loved her would he not, after all, have simply tried to see to it that the fair little butterfly of a thing had always her flowers to hang over: the little sweets of existence, the hats and frocks and ribbons which she loved, and then have gone away and left her? A great pity for the bride came over him, and then a flood of yearning tenderness for the other girl, greater than he had ever known.

In his awe and wonder at what was going on all his own rebellion and unhappiness were gone. He felt only that yearning for, and terror for, that little, tender soul that he loved, exposed to all the terrible and ancient solemn might of existence, which the centuries had rolled up until her time came. He longed to shield her not only from sorrow, but from joy. He took off his hat and stood back in the shadow of a door on the opposite sidewalk. It seemed to him that the ceremony would never end. It was, in fact, unusually long, for the Banbridge minister had much to say for the edification of the bridal pair, and for his own aggrandizement. But at last the triumphant peal of the organ burst forth, and the church swarmed like a hive. People began to stir.

All the heads turned. The rustle of silk was quite audible from outside, also a gathering sibilance of whispers and rustling stir of curious humanity, exactly like the swarming impetus of a hive. Fans fluttered like butterflies over all this agitation of heaving shoulders and turning heads in the church. Outside, the people standing about the steps and on the sidewalk separated hurriedly and formed an aisle of gaping curiosity. A carriage streaming with white ribbons rolled up, the others fell into line. Anderson could see Samson Rawdy on the white-ribboned wedding-coach, sitting in majesty. He was paid well in advance; his wife, complacent and beaming in her new silk waist, was in the church. The contemplation of the new marriage had brought a wave of analogous happiness and fresh love for her over his soul. He was as happy with his own measure of happiness as any one there. Every happiness as well as every sorrow is a source of centrifugal attraction.

Anderson, watching, saw presently, the bridal party emerge from the church. To his fancy, which naturally looked for similes to his beloved pursuits of life, he saw the bride like a white moth of the night, her misty veil, pendant from her head to her feet, carrying out the pale, slanting evanescence of the moth's wings. She moved with a slight wavering motion suggestive of the flight of the vague winged thing which flits from darkness to darkness when it does not perish in the candle beams. This moth, to Anderson, was doing the latter, fluttering possibly to her death, in the light of that awful primæval force of love upon which the continuance of creation hangs. Again, a great pity for her overwhelmed him, and a very fierceness of protection seized him at the sight of Charlotte following her sister in her bridesmaid's attire of filmy white over rose, with pink roses in her hair.

Anderson stood where he could see the faces of the bridal party quite plainly in the glare of the electric light. Charlotte, he saw, with emotion, had an awed, intensely sober expression on her charming face, but the bride's, set in the white mist of her thrown-back veil, was smiling lightly. He saw Arms bend over and whisper to her, and she laughed outright with girlish gayety. Anderson wondered what he said. Arms had smiled, yet his face was evidently moved. What he had said was simple enough: "Fighting Indians is nothing to getting married, honey."

Ina laughed, but her husband's lips quivered a little. She herself realized a curious self-possession greater than she had ever realized in her whole life. It is possible that the world is so old and so many women have married in it that a heredity of self-control supports them in the midst of an occasion which has quickened their pulses in anticipation during their whole lives. But the bridegroom was not so supported. He was manifestly agitated and nervous, especially during the reception which followed the ceremony. He stood with forced amiability responding to the stilted congratulations and gazing with wondering admiration at his bride, whose manner was the perfection of grace.

"Lord, old man!" he whispered once to Carroll, "this part of it is a farce for an old fellow like me, standing in a blooming bower, being patted on the head like a little poodle-dog."

Carroll laughed.

"She likes it, now," whispered Arms, with a fond, proud glance at Ina.

"Women all do," responded Carroll.

"Well, I'd stand here a week if she wanted to, bless her," Arms whispered back, and turned with a successful grimace to acknowledge Mrs. Van Dorn's carefully worded congratulations. As she turned away she met Carroll's eyes, and a burning blush overspread her face to her pompadour crest surmounting her large, middle-aged face. She suddenly recalled, with painful acuteness, the only other occasion on which she had been in the house; but Carroll's manner was perfect, there was in his eyes no recollection whatever.

Mrs. Carroll was lovely in pale-mauve crape embroidered with violets, a relic of past splendors, remodelled for the occasion in spite of doubts on her part, and her beautiful old amethysts. Anna had urged it.

"I shall wear my cream lace, which no one here has ever seen, and I think, Amy, you had better wear that embroidered mauve crape," she said.

"But, Anna," said Mrs. Carroll, "doesn't it seem as if Ina's mother ought not to wear an old gown at the dear child's wedding? I would as lief, as far as I am concerned, but is it doing the right thing?"

"Why not?" asked Anna, rather tartly. Lately her temper was growing a little uncertain. Sometimes she felt as if she had been beset all her life by swarms of gnats. "No one here has ever seen the dress," said she. "And what in the world could you have prettier, if you were to get a new one?"

"Oh, this Banbridge dressmaker is really making charming things," said Mrs. Carroll, rather eagerly. She had a childish fondness for new clothes. "She would make me a beautiful dress, so far as that goes, Anna, dear."

"She has all she can do with Ina's things."

"I reckon she could squeeze in one for me, Anna. Don't you think so?"

"Then there is the extra expense," said Anna.

"But she does not hesitate in the least to trust us," said Mrs. Carroll. "But maybe you are right, Anna. That embroidered mauve is lovely, and perfectly fresh, and it is very warm to fuss over another, and then my amethysts look charming with that."

Therefore, Mrs. Carroll wore the mauve and the amethysts, and was by many considered handsomer than either of her daughters. There had been some discussion about giving the amethysts to Ina for a wedding-gift, but finally a set of wonderful carved corals, which she had always loved and never been allowed to wear, were decided upon. Anna had given a pearl brooch, which had come down from her paternal grandmother, and Carroll had presented her with a large and evidently valuable pearl ring which had excited some wonder in the family.

"Why, Arthur, where did you get it?" his wife had cried, involuntarily; and he had laughed and refused to tell her.

Ina herself, while she received the ring with the greatest delight, was secretly a little troubled. "I am afraid poor papa ought not to have given me such a present as this," she said to Charlotte, when the two girls were in their room that night. As she spoke she was holding the pearl to the lamp-light and watching the beautiful pink lights. It was a tinted pearl.

"It is a little different, because you are going away, and papa will never buy you things again," said Charlotte. "I should not worry, dear." For the few days before her marriage, Charlotte had gotten a habit of treating her sister with the most painstaking consideration for her nerves and her feelings, as if she were an invalid. She was herself greatly troubled at the thought that her father had overtasked his resources to purchase such a valuable thing, but she would not for worlds have intimated such a thing to Ina.

"Well, I do worry," said Ina. "I cannot help it. It was too much for poor papa to do." She even shed a few tears over the pearl, and Charlotte kissed and coddled her a good deal for comfort.

"It is such a beauty, dear," she said. "Look at it and take comfort in it, darling."

"Yes, it is a beauty," sobbed Ina. "I never saw such a pearl except that one of poor papa's, the one he has in his scarf-pin that belonged to that friend of his who died, you know."

"Yes, dear," said Charlotte, "I know. It is another just such a beauty. Don't cry any more, honey. Think how happy you are to have it."

But Charlotte herself, after she had gone to bed in her own little room, had sobbed very softly lest her sister should hear her, until Ina was asleep. Her sister's remarks had brought a suspicion to her own mind. "Poor papa!" she kept whispering softly, to herself. "Poor papa!" It seemed to her that her heart was breaking with understanding of and pity for her father.

Charlotte's own gift to Ina had been some pieces of embroidery. She was the only one in the family who excelled in any kind of handicraft. "Ina will like this better than anything," she had told her aunt Anna, "and then it will not tax poor papa, either. It will cost nothing."

Her aunt had looked at her a minute, then suddenly thrown her arms around her and kissed her. "Charlotte, you little honey, you are the best of the lot!" she had said.

Charlotte herself, the night of the wedding, was looking rather pale and serious. Many observed that she was the least good-looking of the family. Several Banbridge young men essayed to make themselves agreeable to her, but she did not know it. She was very busy. Besides their one maid there were the waiters sent by the caterer, and Eddy was exceedingly troublesome. He was a nervous boy, and unless directly under his father's eye, almost beyond restraint when impressed, as he was then, with an exaggerated sense of his own importance. His activities took especially the form of indiscriminate and superfluous helping the guests to refreshments, until the waiters waxed fairly murderous, and one of them even appealed to Anna Carroll, intimating in Eddy's hearing that unless the young gentleman left matters to them the supply of salad would run short.

"Why didn't we have more, then?" inquired Eddy, quite audibly, to the delight of all within ear-shot. "I thought we were going to have plenty for everybody this time."

"Eddy dear," whispered Charlotte, taking his little arm, "come with me into the hall and help me put back some roses that have fallen out of the big vase. I am afraid I shall get some water on my gown if I touch them, and I noticed just now that some one had brushed against them and jostled some out."

"Charlotte, why didn't we have salad enough?" persisted Eddy, as he followed his sister, pulling back a little at her leading hand.

"Hush, dear; we have enough, only you had better leave it to the waiters, you know."

"Everybody has taken it that I have passed it to," said Eddy. "I have given that gentleman over there four plates heaped up."

"Oh, hush, Eddy dear!" whispered Charlotte, in an agony.

By this time they were in the hall, and Eddy, still full of grievances, was picking up the scattered roses. "I suppose there won't be enough salad for my friend and his mother when they come," said he, further.

"Who are your friend and his mother, darling?"

"Mr. Anderson and his mother," declared Eddy, promptly. "He is the best man in this town, and so is his mother."

"Mr. Anderson, dear?"

"Yes. You know who I mean. You ought to know. He always lets us have all we want out of his store. He and his mother are the nicest people in this town except us."

Charlotte looked at her little brother and her face flushed softly. "But, dear," she whispered, "they did not have any invitations to the reception."

"Yes, they did," declared Eddy, triumphantly.

"Why, who sent them?"

"I did," said Eddy.

Charlotte regarded her little brother with a curious expression. It was amused, and yet strangely puzzled, but more as if the puzzle were in her own mind than elsewhere. It was as if she were trying to remember something.

"Don't you think he is a nice man?" asked Eddy, looking sharply at her.

"Yes, dear, I think so. I don't know anything to the contrary."

"Don't you think he is handsome?"

Suddenly Charlotte saw Anderson's face in her thoughts for the first time very plainly. "Yes," she said, "of course. Let us go in the other room, Eddy, and see if Amy doesn't want anything." She led Eddy forcibly into the parlor.

"It is so late, I am afraid he won't come," the little boy said, disappointedly, when the clock on the mantel struck eleven just as they entered.

It was not long after that when the company began to disperse. The bride and groom were to take a midnight-train, and the bride and her sister stole away up-stairs for the changing of the bridal for the travelling costume.

Charlotte unfastened her sister's wedding-gown, and she was striving her best to keep the tears back. Ina, on the contrary, was gayer than usual.

"It is very odd," said she, as Charlotte hooked the collar of her gray travelling-gown, "how a girl looks forward to getting married, all her life, and thinks more of it than anything else, and how, after all, it is nothing at all. You can remember that I said so, Charlotte, when you come to get married. You needn't dread it as if it were some tremendous undertaking. It isn't, you know."

"You speak exactly as if you had died, and were telling me not to dread dying," said Charlotte. She laughed, and the laugh was almost a sob.

"What an idea!" cried Ina, laughing. "Of course I am very sad at leaving home and you all, you darling, but the getting married is not so much, after all. You will find that I am right."

"I shall never get married," said Charlotte.

"Nonsense, honey! 'Deed you will."

"No, I shall not. I shall stay with papa."

"Yes, you will. Say, honey, Robert" — Ina said Robert quite easily and prettily now — "Robert has a stunning cousin, young enough to be his son. His name is Floyd — Floyd Arms. Isn't that a dear name? And his father has just died, and he has the next place to ours."

"Don't be foolish, dear."

"Robert says he is a fine fellow."

"I know all about him. I have seen Floyd Arms," said Charlotte, rather contemptuously.

"Oh, so you have! He was home that last time you were in Acton, wasn't he? You spoke of him when you came home."

"Yes, the last term I was at school," said Charlotte. "Let me pin your veil, sweetheart."

"Don't you think he was handsome?"

"No, I don't, not so very," said Charlotte.

"Oh, Charlotte, where did you ever see a handsomer man, unless it was papa or Robert?"

"I have seen much handsomer men," declared Charlotte, firmly, as she carefully pinned her sister's veil.

"Well, I would like to know where? Not in this town?"

"Yes, in this town."

"Who?"

"Mr. Anderson."

"The grocer?"

"Yes," said Charlotte, defiantly. The veil was pinned, and Ina turned and looked at her, a rosy vision behind a film of gray lace. "You look lovely," said Charlotte, who had a soft pink in her cheeks.

"I think this hat is a beauty," said Ina. "Wasn't it lucky that New Sanderson milliner was so very good, and did not object to giving credit? Why, Mr. Anderson is the grocer! That is the man you mean, isn't it, honey?"

"Yes," replied Charlotte, still with defiance.

"Oh, well, that doesn't count," said Ina, turning for a last view of herself in the glass. "This dress fits beautifully."

"I don't see what that has to do with it," said Charlotte, as they left the room. She felt, even in the midst of parting, and without knowing why, a little indignation with her sister.

On the threshold, Ina paused suddenly and flung her arms around the other girl. "Oh, honey," she said, with a half-sob — "oh, honey, how can we talk of who is handsome and who isn't, whether he is the butcher, the baker, or the candlestick-maker, when, when —" The two clung together for a minute, then Charlotte put her sister gently away.

"You will muss your veil, dearest," said she, "and it is almost time to go, and Amy and papa will want the last of you."

That night, after the bridal pair had departed and everybody else had gone to bed, Anna Carroll and her brother had a little conference in the parlor amid the débris of the wedding splendor. The flowers and greens were drooping, the room and the whole house had that peculiar phase of squalidness which comes alone from the ragged ends of festivities; the floors were strewn with rice and rose leaves and crumbs from the feast; plates and cups and saucers or fragments stood about everywhere; the chairs and the tables were in confusion. Anna, who had been locking up the silver for the night, had come into the parlor, and found her brother standing in a curious, absent-minded fashion in the middle of the floor.

"Why, Arthur!" said she. "I thought you had gone to bed."

"I am going," said he, but he made no move.

Anna looked at him, and her expression was weary and a little bitter. "Well, it is over," said she.

Carroll nodded. "Yes," he said, with a half-suppressed sigh.

Anna glanced around the room. "This house is a sight for one maid to wrestle with," said she; and her brother, beyond a glance of the utmost indifference around the chaotic room, did not seem to notice her remark at all. However, that she did not resent. Indeed, she herself was so far from taking the matter to heart that she laughed a little as she continued to survey the ruins.

"Well, it went off well; it was a pretty wedding," said she, with a certain tone of pleasure.

Carroll turned to her quite eagerly. "You think Ina was pleased?" he said. "It was all as she wished it to be?"

"What could a girl have wished more?" cried Anna. "Everything was charming, just as it should be. All I think about is —"

"What?" asked her brother.

"We have danced," said Anna. "What I want to know is, is the piper to be paid, or shall we have to dance to another tune by way of reprisal."

"The piper is paid," replied Carroll, shortly. He turned to go, but his sister stepped in front of him.

"How?" she said.

Carroll looked down at her.

"Yes, you are quite right, Arthur," said she. "I am afraid. You are, or may reasonably be, rather a desperate man. You have never taken quite kindly to straits. If the piper is paid, I want to know how, for my own peace of mind. By the piper I mean the creditors for all this" — she glanced around the room — "the wedding flowers and feast and carriages."

"I earned enough honestly," replied Carroll. He had a strangely straightforward, almost boyish way of meeting her sharp gaze.

"How?"

"You had better not press the matter, Anna."

"I do. I am afraid." She responded to his look with a certain bitter, sarcastic insistence. "I have reason to be," said she. "You know I have, Arthur Carroll. We are all on the edge of a precipice, but I, for one, do not intend to let you drag me over, and I do not intend that Amy and the children shall go, either, if I can help it. I want to know where you got the money to pay for the wedding expenses, and I want to know where you got that pearl ring you gave Ina. It never cost a cent under three hundred dollars."

Carroll, looking at her, smiled a little sadly.

"It was then," said she, "Hart Lee's pearl that he left you when he died — your scarf-pin."

Carroll smiled. Anna's face changed a little.

"I noticed that you had not worn it lately," said she.

"Sooner or later it would have been the child's. It might as well be sooner," said Carroll, with a slightly annoyed air.

"Eddy should have had it," Anna said, with a jealous air.

"That child?"

"When he was older, of course."

"That is a long way ahead," said Carroll. He moved to go, but again Anna stood before him.

"Arthur," said she, solemnly, I am living with you and doing all I am able. I am giving my strength for you and yours. You know that as well as I do. You know upon whom the brunt here falls. I do not complain. The one who has the best strength should bear the burden, and I have the strength, such as it is. None of us Carrolls need brag of strength, God knows. But I want to know how you came by that money. Yes, I suspect, and I am not ashamed. I have a right to suspect. How did you get that money?"

"I sang and danced for it in a music-hall, blackened up as a negro," said Arthur Carroll.

"Then that was you, Arthur!" gasped Anna.

"Yes. It was the one thing I could do to get that money honestly and pay the bills, and I did it. I would not let Arms pay."

"I should think not," cried Anna. "We have not fallen quite so low as that yet. But you —"

"Yes, I," said Carroll. "Now let us go to bed, Anna."

Anna stood aside, but as her brother turned to pass her she suddenly put up her arms, and as he stooped she kissed him. He felt her cheek wet against his. "Good-night, Arthur," she said, and all the bitterness was gone from her voice.

CHAPTER XXII

It was a week to a day after the wedding, and Anderson had been to the office for the morning mail, and was just returning to the store when a watching face at a window of Madame Griggs's dress-making establishment opposite suddenly disappeared, and when Anderson was mounting the steps of the store piazza he heard a panting breath and rattle of starched petticoats, and turned to see the dress-maker.

"Good-morning," she gasped.

"Good-morning, Mrs. Griggs," returned Anderson.

"Can I see you jest a minute on business? I have been watching for you to come back from the office. I want to buy a melon, if it ain't too dear, before I go, but I want to see you jest a minute in the office first, if you ain't too busy."

"Certainly. Come right in," responded Anderson; but his heart sank, for he divined her errand.

The dress-maker followed him into the office with a nervous teeter and a loud rattle of starched cottons. That morning she was clad in blue gingham trimmed profusely with white lace, and her face looked infinitesimal and meagre in the midst of her puffs of blond frizzes.

"I should think that woman was dressed in paper bags by the noise she makes," Sam Riggs remarked to the old clerk when the office door had closed behind her.

"I should think it would kinder take her mind off things she starts out to do," remarked Price. The rattle of the oscillating petticoats had distracted his own mind from a nice calculation as to the amount of a bill for a fractional amount of citron at a fractional increase in the market-price. The old clerk was about to send a cost slip with some goods to be delivered to a cash customer.

"Yep," responded Sam Riggs. "I should think she'd git rattled with sech a rattlin' of her petticoats." The boy regarded this as so supernaturally smart that he actually blushed with modest appreciation of his own wit, and tears sprang to his eyes when he laughed. But when he glanced at his fellow-clerk, Price was calculating the cost of the citron, and did not seem to have noticed anything unusual in the speech. Riggs, who was easily taken down, felt immediately humiliated, and doubtful of his own humor, and changed the subject. "Say," he whispered, jerking his index-finger towards the office door, "you don't suppose she is settin' her cap at the boss, do you?"

"Well, I guess she'd have to take it out in settin'," replied the old clerk, in scorn. He had now the price of the citron fixed in his head, and he trotted to the standing desk at the end of the counter to enter it.

"I guess so, too," said Riggs. "Guess she'd have to starch her cap stiffer than her petticoats before she'd catch him." Again Riggs thought he must be funny, but, when the other clerk did not laugh, concluded he must have been mistaken.

The conference in the office was short, and Price had hardly gotten the slip made out when Madame Griggs emerged. Indeed, she had not accepted Anderson's proffer of a chair.

"No," said she, "I can't set down. I ain't got but a minute. Two of my girls is went on their vacation, an' I ain't got nobody but Bessie Starley, an' I've promised Mis' Rawdy she should have her new silk skirt before Sunday to wear to Coney Island. Mr. Rawdy has made so much on hiring his carriages for the weddin' that he has bought his wife a new black silk dress, an' now he is goin' to take her to Coney Island Sunday, and hire the Liscom boy to take his place drivin'. Now what I come in here for was —" Madame Griggs lowered her voice; she drew nearer Anderson, and her anxious whisper whistled in his ear. "What I want to know is," said she, "here's Mr. Rawdy, an' I hear the caterer, were paid in advance, an' Blumenfeldt was paid the day after the weddin', an' I ain't, an' I wonder if I'm goin' to be."

"Have you sent in your bill yet?" inquired Anderson.

"No, I ain't, but Captain Carroll asked Blumenfeldt for his bill an' he paid the others in advance, an' he ain't asked for my bill."

"I do not see why you distress yourself until you have sent in your bill," Anderson said, rather coldly.

"Now, don't you think so?"

"I certainly do not."

"Well," said she, "to tell the truth, I kinder hated to send it too quick. I hated to have it look as if I was scart. It's a pretty big bill, too, an' they seem like real ladies, an' the sister, the one that ain't married, is as nice a girl as I ever see — nicer than the other one, accordin' to my way of thinkin'. She ain't stuck up a mite. The rest of them don't mean to be stuck up, but they be without knowin' it. Guess they was brought up so; but Charlotte ain't. Well, I kinder hated, as I say, to send that bill, especially as it is a pretty big one. I made everything as reasonable as I could, but she had a good many things, an' Charlotte had her bridesmaid's dress, too, an' it's mounted up to considerable, an' I hated to have 'em think I was dreadful scart. I ain't never been in the habit of sendin' in a bill to nobody, not for some weeks after the things was did, an' I didn't like to this time. But I says to myself, as long as there had been so much talk round 'mongst folks about the Carrolls not payin' their bills, I'd wait a week an' then I'd send it in. Now it's jest a week ago today since the weddin', an' there ain't a word. I thought mebbe they'd ask for the bill the way they did with Blumenfeldt, an' now I want to know if you think I had better send the bill or wait a little while longer."

Anderson replied that he thought it would do no harm, that he did not like to advise in such a case.

The dress-maker eyed him sharply and with a certain resentment. "Now, I want to know," said she. "I want you to speak right out and tell me, if you think I'm imposin'."

"I don't quite understand what you mean," Anderson replied, in bewilderment. He was horribly annoyed and perplexed, but his manner was kind, for the memory of poor little Stella Mixter with her shower of blond curls was strong upon him, and there was something harrowingly pathetic about the combination of little, veinous hands twitching nervously in the folds of the blue gingham, the painstaking frizzes, the pale, screwed little face, and the illogical feminine brain.

But the dress-maker's next remark almost dispelled the pathos. "I want you to tell me right out," said she, "if it would make any difference if I paid you. Of course I know you've given up law, an' I ain't thought of offerin' you pay for advice. I've traded all I can in your store, though I always think you are a little dearer, and I didn't know but you'd think that made it all right; but —"

"I do think it is all right," Anderson returned, quickly, "I assure you, Mrs. Griggs, and I have never dreamed of such a thing as your paying me. Indeed, I have given you no advice which I should have felt justified in sending in a bill for, if I were practising my profession."

"Well, I didn't think you had told me anything worth much," said Madame Griggs, "but I know how lawyers tuck on for nothin', and I didn't know but you might feel —"

"I certainly do not," said Anderson.

"Well," said Madame Griggs, "I am very much obliged to you. I'll send the bill a week from today, and I feel a great deal better about it. I don't have nobody to ask, and sometimes I feel as if I didn't have a friend or a brother to ask whether I'd better do anything or not, I should give up. I'm very much obliged, Mr. Anderson."

"You are very welcome to anything I have done," replied Anderson, looking at her with a dismay of bewilderment. It was as if he had witnessed some mental inversion which affected his own brain. Anderson always pitied Madame Griggs, but never, after his conferences with her concerning the Carrolls, did he in his heart of hearts blame her husband for running away.

Madame Griggs's coquettish manner developed on the threshold of the office. She smirked until her little, delicate-skinned face was a network mask, and all the muscles quivered to the sight through the transparent covering. She moved her thin, crooked elbows with a flapping motion like wings as she smirked and thanked him again.

"I should think you'd like the grocery business a heap better than law," said she, amiably, as she went out. "Oh, I want to get a melon if they ain't too dear." She evidently expected Anderson himself to wait upon her, and was a little taken aback that he did not follow her. She lingered for a long time haggling with Price, with a watchful eye on the office door, and finally departed without purchasing.

Shortly after she had gone, Sam Riggs came for Anderson to inspect some vegetables which had been brought in by a farmer. "He's got some fine potatoes," said he, "but he wants too much for 'em, Price thinks. He's got cabbages, too, and them's too high. Guess you had better look at 'em yourself, Price says."

So Anderson went out to interview the farmer, sparsely bearded, lank, and long-necked and seamy-skinned, his face ineffectual yet shrewd, a poor white of the South strung on wiry nerves, instead of lax muscles, the outcome of the New Jersey soil. He shuffled determinedly in his great boots, heavy with red shale, standing guard over his fine vegetables. He nodded phlegmatically at Anderson. He never smiled. Occasionally his long facial muscles relaxed, but they never widened. He was indefinably serious by nature, yet not melancholy, and absolutely acquiescent in his life conditions. The farmer of New Jersey is not of the stuff which breeds anarchy. He is rooted fast to his red-clinging native soil, which has taken hold of his spirit. He is tenacious, but not revolutionary. He was as adamant on the prices of his vegetables, and finally Anderson purchased at his terms.

"You got stuck," Price said, after the farmer, in his rusty wagon, drawn by a horse which was rather a fine animal, had disappeared down the street.

"Well, I don't know," Anderson replied. "His vegetables are pretty fine."

"Folks won't pay the prices you ought to ask to make a penny on it."

"Oh, I am not so sure of that. People want a good article, and very few raise potatoes or cabbages or even turnips in their own gardens."

"Ingram is selling potatoes two cents less than you, and I rather think turnips, too."

"Not these turnips."

"No, guess not. He has his from another man, but they look pretty good, and half the folks don't know the dif."

"Well," Anderson replied, "sell them for less, if you have to, rather than keep them. Selling a superfine article for no profit is sometimes the best and cheapest advertisement in the world."

Anderson stood a while observing the display of vegetables and fruit piled on the sidewalk before his store and in the store window. He took a certain honest pleasure of proprietorship, and also an artistic delight in it. He observed the great green cabbages, like enormous roses, the turnips, like ivory carvings veined with purplish rose towards their roots, the smooth russet of the potatoes. There were also baskets of fine grapes, the tender pink bloom of Delawares, and the pale emerald of Niagaras, with the plummy gloss of Concords. There were enormous green spheres of watermelons, baskets of superb peaches, each with a high light of rose like a pearl, and piles of bartlett and seckel pears. There was something about all this magnificent plenty of the fruits of the earth which was impressive. It was to an ardent fancy as if Flora and Pomona had been that way with their horns of plenty. The sordid question of market value, however, was distinctly irritating, and yet it was justly so. Why should not a man sell the fruits of the earth for dollars and cents with artistic and honorable dignity as anything else? All commodities for the needs of mankind are market-able, are the instruments of traffic, whether they be groceries or books, boots and shoes, dishes or furniture, or pictures; whether they be songs or sermons or corn plasters or shaving-soap; whether they be food for the mind or the body. What difference did it make which was dispensed? It was all a question of need and supply. The minister preached his sermons for the welfare of the soul; the Jew hawked his second-hand garments; everything was interwoven. One must eat to live, to hear sermons, to hear songs, to love, to think, to read. One must be clothed to tread the earth among his fellows. There was need, and one supplied one need, one another. All need was dignified by the man who possessed, all supply was dignified if one looked at it in the right way. There was a certain dignity even about his own need of two cents more on those turnips, which were actually as beautiful as an ivory carving. Anderson finally returned to his office, feeling a little impatient with himself that, in spite of his own per-fect contentment with his business, he should now and then essay to justify himself in his contentment, as he undoubtedly did. It was like a violinist screwing his instrument up to concert-pitch, below which it would drop from day to day.

Anderson had not been long in his office before he heard a quick patter of feet outside, the peculiar clapping sound of swift toes, which none but a child's feet can produce, and Eddy Carroll entered. The door was ajar, and he pushed it open and ran in with no ceremony. He was well in the room before he apparently remembered something. He stopped short, ran back to the door, and knocked.

Anderson chuckled. "Come in," he said, in a loud tone, as if the door was closed.

Then Eddy came forward with some dignity. "I remembered after I got in that I ought to have knocked," said he. "I hope you'll excuse me."

"Certainly," said Anderson. "Won't you have a seat?"

Eddy sat down and swung his feet, kicking the round of the chair, with his eyes fastened on Anderson, who was seated in the other chair, smoking. "How old were you when you began to smoke?" the boy inquired, suddenly.

"Very much older than you are," replied Anderson.

Eddy sighed. "Is it very nice to smoke?" said he.

Anderson was conscious that he was distinctly at a loss for a reply, and felt like a defaulting Sunday-school teacher as he cast about for one.

"Is it?" said Eddy again.

"Different people look at it differently," said Anderson, "and the best way is for you to wait until you are a man and decide for yourself."

"Is it nicer to be a man than it was to be a boy?" inquired Eddy.

"That, also, is a matter of opinion," said Anderson.

"You can do lots of things that a boy can't," said Eddy. "You can smoke, and you can keep store, and have all the candy you want." Eddy cast an innocent glance towards the office door as he spoke.

"Sam!" called Anderson; and when the young clerk's grinning face appeared at the door, "Will you bring some of those peppermint-drops here for this young man."

"I'd rather have chocolates, if you can't sell 'em any better than the peppermint-drops," Eddy said, quickly.

When Sam reappeared with chocolates in a little paper bag, Eddy was blissful. He ate and swung his feet. "These are bully," said he. "I should think as long as you can have all the chocolates you want, you'd rather eat those than smoke a pipe."

"It is a matter of taste," replied Anderson.

"I'm always going to eat chocolates instead of smoking," said Eddy. "He gave me a lot. Say, I don't see how a boy can steal candy, do you?"

"No. It is very wrong," said Anderson.

"You bet 'tis. I knew a boy in New York State, where we used to live before we came here, that stole candy 'most every day, and he used to bring it to school and give the other boys. He used to give me much as a pound a day. Some days he used to give me much as five pounds." Then Eddy Carroll, after delivering himself of this statement, could not get his young, black eyes away from the fixed regard of the man's keen, blue ones, and he began to wriggle as to his body, with his eyes held firm by that unswerving gaze. "What you looking at me that way for?" he stammered. "I don't think you're very polite."

"How much candy did that boy give you every day?" asked Anderson.

Eddy wriggled. "Well, maybe he didn't give me more 'n half a pound," he muttered.

"How much?"

"Well, maybe it wasn't more 'n a quarter. I don't know."

"How much?" persisted Anderson.

"Well, maybe it might have been three pieces; it was a good many years ago. A fellow can't remember everything."

"How much?" asked Anderson, pitilessly.

"One piece."

"How much?"

"Well, maybe it wasn't any at all," Eddy burst out, in desperation, "but I don't see what odds it makes. I call it an awful fuss about a little mite of candy, for my part."

"Now about that boy?" inquired Anderson.

"Oh, shucks, there wasn't any boy, I s'pose." Eddy gazed resentfully and admiringly at the man. "Say," he said, without the slightest sarcasm, rather with affection and perfect seriousness, "you are awful smart, ain't you?"

Anderson modestly murmured a disclaimer of any especial smartness.

"Yes, you are awful smart," declared Eddy. "Is it because you used to be a lawyer that you are so smart?"

"The law may make a difference in a man's skill for finding out the truth," admitted Anderson.

"Say," said the boy, "I've been thinking all along that when I was a man I would rather be a grocer than anything else, but I don't know but I'd rather be a lawyer, after all. It would be so nice to be able to find out when folks were not telling the truth, and trying to hide when they had been stealing and doing bad things. 'No, you don't,' I'd say; 'no, you don't, mister. I see right through you.' I rather think I'd like that better. Say?"

"What is it?" asked Anderson.

"Why didn't you come to the wedding? I saved a lot of things for you."

"I told you I thought I should not be able to come. I was very much obliged for the invitation," said Anderson, apologetically.

"I looked for you till eleven o'clock. You ought to have come, after I took all that trouble to get an invitation for you. I don't think you were very polite."

"I am very sorry," murmured Anderson.

"I think you ought to be. You don't know what you missed. Ina looked awful pretty, but Charlotte looked prettier, if she wasn't the bride. Don't you think Charlotte is an awful pretty girl?"

"Very," replied Anderson, smiling.

"You'd better. I heard her say she thought you was an awful handsome man, the handsomest man in this town. Say, I think Charlotte would like to get married, now Ina is married. I guess she feels kind of slighted. Why don't you marry Charlotte?"

"Wouldn't you like some of those molasses-peppermints, now you have finished the chocolates?" asked Anderson.

"No, I guess not, thank you. I don't feel very well this morning. Say, why don't you? She's an awful nice girl — honest. And maybe I would come and live with you. I would part of the time, anyway, and I would help in the store."

"You had better run out and ask Sam to give you some peppermints," repeated Anderson, desperately.

"No, thank you. I'm real obliged, but I guess I don't feel like it now. But I tell you what I had a good deal rather have?"

"What is that?"

"What are you going to have for dinner?"

"Now, see here, my son," said Anderson, laughing. "We are going to have a fine dinner, and I should be exceedingly glad to have you as my guest, but this time there must be no dining with me without your mother's knowledge."

"Oh, Amy won't care."

"Nevertheless, you must go home and obtain permission before I take you home with me," said Anderson, firmly.

"I don't think you are very polite," said Eddy; but it ended in his presently saying that, well, then, he would go home and ask permission; but it was not of the slightest use. "They would all want me to stay, if they thought anything of me. I know Amy would. Amy said this morning I was the worst off of them all, because I had such a misfortunate appetite." The boy's ingenuous eyes met the man's fixed upon him with a mixture of amusement and compassion. "You see," added Eddy, simply, "all the things left over from the wedding, the caterers let us have; papa said not to ask him, and Amy wouldn't, but Aunt Anna did, and there was a lot, though folks ate so much. There was one gentleman ate ten plates of salad — yes, he did. I saw him. He was the doctor, so I suppose he wasn't ill afterwards. But there was a lot left. Of course the ice-cream melted, but it was nice to drink afterwards, and there was a lot of salad and cake and rolls. The cakes and rolls lasted longest. I got pretty tired of them. But now those are all gone, and the butcher won't let us have any more meat, though he trusted us two days after the wedding, because he heard papa paid the florist and the liveryman, but now he has stopped again. Of course we have things from here, but you don't keep meat. Why don't you keep meat?"

The absurd pathos of the whole was almost too much for Anderson. He rose and went to the window and looked out as he replied that it was not unusual for a grocer to include meat in his stock of trade.

"I know it isn't," said Eddy, "but it would be so nice for us if you did, and all the poor people the butcher wouldn't trust. Did you ever get real hungry, and have nothing except crackers and little gingersnaps and such things?"

"No, I don't know that I ever did."

"Well, it is awful," said Eddy, with emphasis. He started up. "Well," he said, "I'm going to run right home and ask Amy. She'll let me come.

What did you say you were going to have for dinner?"

"Roast beef," replied Anderson.

"Goody!" cried the boy, and was off.

Anderson, left alone, sat down and thought disturbedly. The utter futility of any efforts to assist such a family was undeniable. Nothing could be done. For a vivid instant he had an idea of rushing to the market and setting up surreptitiously a term of credit for the Carrolls, by paying their bills himself, but the absurdity of the scheme overcame him. The ridiculousness of his actually feeding this whole family because of his weakness in giving credit when not another merchant in the town would do so struck him forcibly. Yet what else could he do? He had done a foolish thing in allowing his thoughts and imaginations which were not those of a youth, and were susceptible of control had he made the effort, to dwell upon this girl, who had never even thought of him in the same light. It was romance gone mad. He, an older man who had passed beyond the period when dreams are a part of the physical growth, and unrestrainable, had indulged himself in dreams, and now he must pay in foolish realities. He thought uneasily what a laughing-stock he would become if by any means the fact of his continued credit to this non-paying family were to become known, and he saw no earthly reason why it should not become known. However, no one could possibly suspect the reason for his unbusiness-like credulity. It was simply impossible that it should enter into any one's head to suspect him of a passion for that little Carroll girl, as they would express her. If he had been extending senti-mental credit to the Egglestons, people might have been quick to discover the reason in a lurking and extremely suitable affection for one of them, but this was out of the question.

However, Anderson had not a very long time for his reflections, for Eddy Carroll was back, beaming. "Yes, Amy says I can come," he announced.

"That is good," Anderson replied, hospitably, but he eyed him sharply. "You went very quickly," said he.

"Got a ride on the ice wagon," said he. "The ice-man is a good feller. I asked him why he had stopped bringing us ice, and he said if he was run-ning the business, instead of jest carting for the boss, he'd give us all the ice we wanted for nothing. He was going up past our house, and when we got there he gave me a big chunk of ice, and I went and got Marie, and we lugged it into the kitchen together. Lucky Aunt Anna or Charlotte didn't see me."

"Why?" asked Anderson.

"Oh, nothing, only they wouldn't have let me take it. Say, Marie was crying. Her eyes looked as red as a rabbit's. I asked her what the matter was, and she said she hadn't been paid her wages. Say, isn't it too bad everybody makes such a fuss about being paid. It worries Aunt Anna and Charlotte awfully. Women are dreadful worriers, ain't they?"

"Perhaps they are," replied Anderson, and got out a book with col-ored plates of South American butterflies. "I think you will like to look at these pictures," said he. "I have some letters to write."

"All right," said Eddy, and spread his little knees to form a place for the big book. "I am glad I wasn't a girl," he said, in pursuance of his train of thought. "Golly, what a whopper butterfly!"

"Yes, that is a big fellow," said Anderson.

"I caught one once twice as big as that in a place where we used to live."

"Don't talk any more, son," said Anderson.

"All right," returned Eddy, generously, and turned the pages in silence.

It was nearly noon when Sam Riggs came to the office door to announce Charlotte; but she followed closely behind, and saw her brother over the butterfly-book. She was so surprised that she scarcely greeted Anderson.

"Why, Eddy Carroll, you here?" said she.

"Yes, Charlotte," replied Eddy, with a curious meekness.

"How long have you been here, dear?"

"Oh, quite a while, Charlotte. Mr. Anderson has given me this beautiful book to look at. It's full of butterflies."

"That is very kind," said Charlotte. "You must be very careful."

"Yes, I am," replied Eddy. "I ate up the candy before I touched it. Mr. Anderson gave me some bully candy, Charlotte."

"That was kind," Charlotte replied, smiling a little uneasily, Anderson thought.

Then she turned to him. She had been all the time fumbling with a dainty little green purse, and Anderson saw, with a comical dismay, a check appear. She held it fluttering between a rosy thumb and finger in his direction. "Mr. Anderson, I brought in this check," she began, a little hesitatingly, "and —"

"You would like it cashed?" asked Anderson.

"No, not this time," said she. "Papa left it this morning for my mother, and I — Mr. Anderson, I know we are owing you, and this is a check for twenty-five dollars, and I should like to pay it to you for your bill." At the last Charlotte's hesitation vanished. She spoke with pride and dignity. In reality the child felt that she was doing a meritorious and noble thing. She was taking money which had been left to spend, to pay a bill. Moreover, she had not the slightest idea that the twenty-five dollars did not discharge the whole of the indebtedness to Anderson. She had quite a little dispute with her mother to obtain possession of it for that purpose.

"I think you are very foolish, dear," Mrs. Carroll had said. "You might get Mr. Anderson to cash it, and then go to New York and get yourself a new hat. You really need a new hat, Charlotte."

"I would rather pay that bill," Charlotte replied.

"But I don't see why, dear. It would really be much wiser to pay the butcher's bill, and then we could have some meat for dinner. All we have is eggs. Don't you think Charlotte is very foolish, Anna?"

"I have nothing to say," replied Anna Carroll.

"Why not, Anna? You act very singularly lately, dear."

"I want Charlotte to do as she thinks best, and as you think best, Amy," replied Anna Carroll, who was looking unusually worn, in fact ill, that morning.

"I think Charlotte had much better get the check cashed and go to New York and buy herself a new hat," said Mrs. Carroll.

"No, I don't need a new hat," said Charlotte, and it ended in her going with the check to Anderson to pay his bill.

In spite of his annoyance, the utter absurdity of the whole thing was too much for Anderson. He had little doubt that the check was no more valuable than its predecessors, and now in addition this was supposed to liquidate a bill of several times the amount which it was supposed to represent. But his mind was quickly made up. Rather than have brought a cloud over the happy, proud face of that girl, he would have sacrificed much more. He cast a glance around. Luckily Price, the elder clerk, was engaged in the front of the store, and Riggs was assisting the man who delivered the goods to carry some parcels to the wagon. Therefore no one witnessed this folly.

"Thank you, Miss Carroll," he said, pleasantly, and took the check from the hand which trembled a little. Charlotte was pale that morning. It was quite true that she had not sufficient nourishing food for several days. But she was very proud and happy now, and she looked at Anderson as he received the check with a different expression from any which her face had hitherto worn for him. In fact, for the first time, although she was in reality simple and humble enough, she realized him on a footing with herself. And she could not have told what had led to this reversion of her feelings, nor would it have been easy for any one to have told. The forces which stir human emotions to one or another end are as mysterious often as are the sources of the winds which blow as they list. The check was indorsed by Anna Carroll, to whom it had been made payable. She had taken it from her brother that morning with a fierce nip of thumb and finger, as if she were a mind to tear it in two. She had no idea that it was of any value, but, in fact, at the moment of her receiving it the money was in the bank. Before Anderson had sent it in the account was again overdrawn. Arthur Carroll was getting in exceedingly deep waters, to which his previous ventures had been as shallows.

Charlotte smiled at Anderson as he took the check. She did not think of a receipt, and Anderson did not carry the matter to the farcial extent of giving her one. He put the check in his pocket-book and inquired whether she had any orders to give, and she did order some crackers, cheese, and eggs, which he called to Riggs to carry to the delivery wagon.

After that was settled, Charlotte turned again to Eddy. "When are you coming home, dear?" said she.

"Pretty soon," replied Eddy, with an uneasy hitch.

Anderson, who had had his suspicions, spoke. "I have invited your brother to dine with me, and he has been home to ask permission, he tells me," said Anderson, and Eddy cast a bitterly reproachful glance at him, as if he had been betrayed by an accomplice.

"Did you go home to ask permission, Eddy?" asked Charlotte, gravely.

Eddy nodded and hitched.

"Whom did you ask?"

Eddy hesitated. He was casting about in his mind for the lie likely to succeed.

"Whom?" repeated Charlotte.

"Amy."

"Amy just asked me if I knew where you were," said Charlotte, piti-lessly.

Eddy looked intently at his butterfly-book. "This is a whopper," said he.

"Come, Eddy," said Charlotte.

"This is the biggest one of all," said Eddy.

"Eddy," said Charlotte.

Eddy looked up. "I'm going to dinner with Mr. Anderson," said he. "Aunt Anna said I might."

"You said Amy said you might," said Charlotte. "Eddy Carroll, don't you say another word. Come right home with me."

Then suddenly the boy broke down. All his bravado vanished. He looked from her to Anderson and back again with a white, convulsed little face. Eddy was a slight little fellow, and his poor shoulders in their linen blouse heaved. Then he wept like a baby.

"I — want to — go," he wailed. "Charlotte, I want to — g-o. He is going to have — roast beef for dinner, and I — am hungry."

Charlotte turned whiter than Eddy. She marched up to her brother. She did not look at Anderson. "Begging!" said she. "Begging! What if you are hungry? What of it? What is that? Hunger is nothing. And then you have no reason to be hungry. There is plenty in the house to eat — plenty!" She glanced with angry pride at Anderson, as if he were to blame for having heard all this. "Plenty!" she repeated, defiantly.

"Plenty of old cake left over from Ina's wedding, and dry old crackers, and not enough eggs to go round," returned Eddy. "I am hungry. I am, Charlotte. All I have had since yesterday noon is five crackers and three pickles and one egg and a piece of chocolate cake as hard as a brick, besides one little, round, dry cake with one almond on top in the middle. I'm real hungry, Charlotte. Please let me go!"

Anderson quietly went out of the office. He passed through the store door, and stood there when presently Charlotte and Eddy passed him.

"Good-morning," said Charlotte, in a choked voice.

Eddy looked at him and sniffled, then he flung out, angrily, "What you going to take to our house?" he demanded of the consumptive man gathering up the reins of the delivery-wagon.

"Hush!" said Charlotte.

"I won't hush," said Eddy. "I'm hungry. What are you taking up to our house? Say!"

"Some crackers and cheese and eggs," replied the man, wonderingly.

"Crackers and cheese and old store eggs!" cried Eddy, with a howl of woe, and Charlotte dragged him forcibly away.

"What ails that kid?" Riggs asked of the man in the wagon.

"I believe them folks are half starved," replied the man.

Riggs glanced cautiously around, but Anderson had returned to his office. "I don't believe anybody in town but us trusts 'em," said he, in a whisper.

"Well, I'm sorry for his folks, but he'd ought to be strung up," said the man. "Why in thunder don't he go to work. I guess if he was coughin' as bad as I be at night, an' had to work, he might know a little something about it. I ain't in debt, though, not a dollar."

CHAPTER XXIII

When a strong normal character which has consciously made wrong moves, averse to the established order of things, and so become a force of negation, comes into contact with weaker or undeveloped natures, it sometimes produces in them an actual change of moral fibre, and they become abnormal. Instead of a right quantity on the wrong track, they are a wrong quantity, and exactly in accordance with their environments. In the case of the Carroll family, Arthur Carroll, who was in himself of a perfect and unassailable balance as to the right estimate of things, and the weighing of cause and effect, who had never in his whole life taken a step blindfold by any imperfection of spiritual vision, who had never for his own solace lost his own sense of responsibility for his lapses, had made his family, in a great measure, irresponsible for the same faults. Except in the possible case of Charlotte, all of them had a certain measure of perverted moral sense in the direction in which Carroll had consciously and unpervertedly failed. Anna Carroll, it is true, had her eyes more or less open, and she had much strength of character; still it was a feminine strength, and even she did not look at affairs as she might have done had she not been under the influence of her brother for years. While she at times waxed bitter over the state of affairs, it was more because of the constant irritation to her own pride, and her impatience at the restraints of an alien and dishonest existence, than from any moral scruples. Even Charlotte herself was scarcely clear-visioned concerning the family taint. The word debt had not to her its full meaning; the inalienable rights of others faded her comprehension when measured beside her own right of existence and of the comforts and delights of existence. Even to her a new hat or a comfortable meal was something of more importance than the need of the vender thereof for reimbursement. The value to herself was the first value, her birthright, indeed, which if others held they must needs yield up to her without money and without price, if her purse happened to be empty. Her compunction and sudden awakening of responsibility in the case of Randolph Anderson were due to an entirely different influence from any which had hitherto come into her life. Charlotte, although she was past the very first of young girlhood, being twenty, was curiously undeveloped emotionally. She had never had any lovers, and the fault had been her own, from a strange persistence of childhood in her temperament. She had not attracted, from her own utter lack of responsiveness. She was like an instrument which will not respond to the touch on certain notes, and presently the player wearies.

She was a girl of strong and jealous affections, but the electric circuits in her nature were not yet established. Then, also, she had not been a child who had made herself the heroine of her own dreams, and that had hindered her emotional development.

"Charlotte," one of her school-mates, had asked her once, "do you ever amuse yourself by imagining that you have a lover?"

Charlotte had stared at the girl, a beautiful, early matured, innocently shameless creature. "No," said she. "I don't understand what you mean, Rosamond."

"The next moonlight night," said the girl, "Imagine that you have a lover."

"What if I did?"

"It would make you very happy, almost as happy as if you had a real one," said the girl, who was only a child in years, though, on account of her size, she had been put into long dresses. She had far outstripped the boys of her own age, who were rather shy of her.

Charlotte, who was still in short dresses, looked at her, full of scorn and a mysterious shame. "I don't want any lover at all," declared she. "I don't want an imaginary one, or a real one, either. I've got my papa, and that's all I want." At that time Charlotte still clung to her doll, and the doll was in her mind, but she did not say doll to the other girl.

"Well, I don't care," said the other girl, defiantly. "You will some-time."

"I sha'n't, either," declared Charlotte. "I never shall be so silly, Rosamond Lane."

"You will, too."

"I never will. You needn't think because you are so awful silly everybody else is."

"I ain't any sillier than anybody else, and you'll be just as silly yourself, so now," said Rosamond.

After that, when Charlotte saw the child sitting sunken in a reverie with the color deepening on her cheeks, her lips pouting, and her eyes misty, she would pass indignantly. She remembered her in after years with contempt. She spoke of her to Ina as the silliest girl she had ever known.

Now the child's words of prophecy, spoken from the oldest reasoning in the world, that of established sequence and precedent, did not recur to Charlotte, but she was fulfilling them.

Ina's marriage and perhaps the natural principle of growth had brought about a change in her. Charlotte had sat by herself and thought a good deal after Ina had gone, and naturally she thought of the possibility of her own marriage. Ina had married; of course she might. But her emotions were very much in abeyance to her affections, and the conditions came before the dreams were possible.

"I shall never marry anybody who will take me far away from papa!" said Charlotte. "Perhaps I shall be less of a burden to poor papa if I am married, but I shall never go far away."

It followed in Charlotte's reasoning that it must be a man in Banbridge. There had been no talk of their leaving the place. Of course she knew that their stay in one locality was usually short, but here they were now, and it must be a man in Banbridge. She thought of a number of the crudely harmless young men of the village; there were one or two not so crude, but not so harmless, who held her thoughts a little longer, but she decided that she did not want any of them, even if they should want her. Then again the face of Randolph Anderson flashed out before her eyes as it had done before. Charlotte, with her inborn convictions, laughed at herself, but the face remained.

"There isn't another man in this town to compare with him," she said to herself, "and he is a gentleman, too." Then she fell to remembering every word he had ever said to her, and all the expressions his face had ever taken on with regard to her, and she found that she could recall them all. Then she reflected how he had trusted them, and had never failed to fill their orders, when all the other tradesmen in Banbridge had refused, and that they must be owing him.

"I shouldn't wonder if we were owing him nearly twenty-five dollars," Charlotte said to herself, and for the first time a thrill of shame and remorse at the consideration of debt was over her. She had heard his story. "There he had to give up his law practice because he could not make a living, and go into the grocery business, and here we are taking his goods and not paying him," thought she. "It is too bad." A feeling of indignation at herself and her family, and of pity for Anderson came over her. She made up her mind that she would ask her father for money to pay that bill at least. "The butcher can wait, and so can all the others," she thought, "but Mr. Anderson ought to be paid." Besides the pity came a faint realization of the other side of the creditor's point of view. "Mr. Anderson must look down upon us for taking his property and not paying our bills," she thought. She knew that some of the wedding bills had been paid, and that led her to think that her father might have more money than usual, but she overheard some conversation which passed between Carroll and his sister on the morning when he gave her the check.

"Now about that?" Anna had asked, evidently referring to some bill.

"I tell you I can't, Anna," Carroll replied. "I used the money as it came on those bills for the wedding. There is very little left." Then he had hurriedly scrawled the check, which she took in spite of her incredulousness of its worth. Therefore Charlotte, when the check had been offered her for a new hat, for Anna had carelessly passed it over to her sister-in-law, had eagerly taken it to pay Anderson.

"I paid the grocery bill," Charlotte told her aunt when she returned.

Anna was in her own room, engaged in an unusual task. She was setting things to rights, and hanging her clothes regularly in her closet, and packing her bureau drawers. Charlotte looked at her in astonishment after she had made the statement concerning the grocery bill.

"What are you doing, Anna?" said she.

Anna looked up from a snarl of lace and ribbons and gloves in a bureau drawer. "I am putting things in order," said she.

Then Mrs. Carroll crossed the hall from her opposite room, and entered, trailing a soft, pink, China-silk dressing-gown. She sank into a chair with a swirl of lace ruffles and viewed her sister-in-law with a comical air of childish dismay. "Don't you feel well, Anna, dear?" asked she.

"Yes. Why?" replied Anna Carroll, folding a yard of blue ribbon.

"Nothing, only I have always heard that if a person does something she has never done before, something at variance with her character, it is a very bad sign, and I never knew you to put things in order before, Anna, dear."

"Order is not at variance with my character," said Anna. "It is one of my fundamental principles."

"You never carried it out," said Mrs. Carroll. "You know you never did, Anna. Your bureau drawers have always looked like a sort of chaos of civilization, just like mine. You know you never carried out the principle,

Anna, dear."

"A principle ceases to be one when it is carried out," said Anna.

"Then you don't think you are going to die because you are folding that ribbon, honey?"

Anna took up some yellow ribbon. "There is much more need to worry about Charlotte," said she, in the slightly bitter, sarcastic tone which had grown upon her lately.

Mrs. Carroll looked at Charlotte, who had removed her hat and was pinning up her hair at a little glass in a Florentine frame which hung between the windows. The girl's face, reflected in the glass, flushed softly, and was seen like a blushing picture in the fanciful frame, although she did not turn her head, and made no rejoinder to her aunt's remark.

"What has Charlotte been doing?" asked Mrs. Carroll.

"She has been doing the last thing which any Carroll in his or her senses is ever supposed to do," replied Anna, in the same tone, as she folded her yellow ribbon.

"What do you mean, Anna, dear?"

"She has been paying a bill before the credit was exhausted. That is sheer insanity in a Carroll. If there is anything in the old Scotch superstition, she is fey, if ever anybody was."

"What bill?" asked Mrs. Carroll.

"Mr. Anderson's," replied Charlotte, faintly, still without turning from the glass which reflected her charming pink face in its gilt, scrolled frame.

"Mr. Anderson's?"

"The grocer's bill," said Charlotte.

"Oh! I did not know what his name was," said Mrs. Carroll.

"He probably is well acquainted with ours, on his books," said Anna.

Mrs. Carroll looked in a puzzled way from her to Charlotte, who had turned with a little air of defiance. "Had he refused to let us have any more groceries?" said she.

"No," said Charlotte.

"I told you he had not," said Anna, shaking out a lace handkerchief, which diffused an odor of violet through the room.

"Then why did you pay him, honey?" asked Mrs. Carroll, wonderingly, of Charlotte.

"I paid him just because he had trusted us," said she, in a voice which rang out clearly with the brave honesty of youth.

Suddenly she looked from her mother to her aunt with accusing eyes. "I don't believe it is right to go on forever buying things and never paying for them, just because a gentleman is kind enough to let you," said she.

"I thought you said it was the grocer, Charlotte, honey," said Mrs. Carroll, helplessly.

"He is a gentleman, if he is a grocer," said Charlotte, and her cheek blazed.

Anna Carroll looked sharply at her from her drawer, then went on folding the handkerchief.

"He is a lawyer, and as well-educated as papa," Charlotte said, further, in her clear, brave voice, and she returned her aunt's look unflinchingly, although her cheeks continued to blush.

Mrs. Carroll still looked bewildered. "How much did you pay him, Charlotte, dear?" she asked.

"Twenty-five dollars."

"The whole of the check Arthur gave you?"

"Yes, Amy."

"But you might have bought yourself a hat, honey, and you did need one. I can't quite understand why you paid the grocer, when he had not refused to let us have more groceries, and you might have bought a hat."

Anna, packing the drawer, began to laugh, and Charlotte, after frowning a second, laughed also.

"My hat with the roses looks very nice yet, Amy, dear," said she, sweetly and consolingly.

"But it is getting so late for roses," Mrs. Carroll returned.

"The milliner in New York where Ina got her hats has been paid; maybe she will trust Charlotte for a hat. Don't worry, Amy," said Anna, coolly.

Mrs. Carroll brightened up. "Sure enough, Anna," said she. "She was paid because she wouldn't trust us, and maybe now she will be willing to again. I will go in tomorrow, and I think I can get a hat for myself."

"I saw the dress-maker looking out of the window," said Charlotte.

"She did very well," said Mrs. Carroll.

"I suppose there is no money to pay her?" said Charlotte.

"No, honey, I suppose not, but dear Ina has the dresses and you have your new one."

"That makes me think. I think her bill is on the table. It came two or three days ago. I haven't opened it, because it looked like a bill. Eddy brought it in when I was in here. Yes, there it is." Charlotte, near the table, took up the envelope and opened it. "It is only one hundred and fifty-eight dollars," said she.

"That is very cheap for so many pretty dresses," said Mrs. Carroll, "but I suppose it is all clear profit. I should think dress-makers would get rich very easily."

That night Charlotte was the last to go to her room — that is, the last except her father. He was still smoking in the little room on the left of the hall. They had been playing whist in there; then they had had some sherry and crackers and olives. Major Arms had sent out a case of sherry before the wedding, and it was not all gone. Now Carroll was smoking a last cigar before retiring, and the others except Charlotte had gone. She lingered after she had kissed her father good-night.

"Papa," said she, tentatively. She looked very slim and young in her little white muslin frock, with her pretty hair braided in her neck.

"Well, sweetheart, what is it?" asked Carroll, with a tender look of admiration.

Charlotte hesitated. Then she spoke with such desire not to offend that her voice rang harsh. "Papa," said she, "do you think —"

"Think what, honey?"

"Do you think you can pay the dress-maker's bill?"

"Pretty soon, dear," said Carroll, his face changing.

"Tomorrow?"

"I am afraid not tomorrow, Charlotte."

"She worked very hard over those dresses, and she bought the things, and it is quite a while. I think she ought to be paid, papa."

"Pretty soon, dear," said Carroll again.

Charlotte turned without another word and went out of the room. Her silence and her retreat were full of innocent condemnation. Carroll smoked, his face set and tense. Then there was a flutter and Charlotte was back. She did not speak this time, but she ran to her father, threw her slight arms around his neck, and kissed him, and it was the kiss of love which follows the judgment of love. Then she was gone again.

Carroll removed his cigar and sat staring straight ahead for a moment. Then he gave the cigar a fling into a brass bowl and put his head on his arms on the table.

CHAPTER XXIV

Charlotte, before her sister was married, had been in the habit of taking long walks with her. Now she went alone.

The elder women of the family never walked when they could avoid doing so. Mrs. Carroll was, in consequence, putting on a soft roundness of flesh like a baby, and was daily becoming a creature of more curves and dimples. Anna did not gain flesh, but she moved more languidly, and her languor of movement was at curious odds with the subdued eagerness of her eyes. In these days Anna Carroll was not well; her nerves were giving way. She slept little and ate little.

"You are losing your appetite, Anna, dear," Mrs. Carroll said once at the dinner-table.

"A fortunate thing, perhaps," retorted Anna, with her little, veiled sting of manner, and at that Carroll rose abruptly and left the table.

"What is the matter, Arthur?" his wife called after him. "I don't see what ails Arthur lately," she said, with a soft tone of complaint, when the door had closed behind him and he had made no response.

Charlotte adored her Aunt Anna, and seldom took any exception to anything which she said or did, but then she turned upon her.

"Poor papa is hurt by what Aunt Anna said," she declared, severely, "and I don't wonder. Here he cannot afford to buy as much to eat as he would like, and hasn't enough to pay the butcher, and Aunt Anna says things like that. I don't wonder he is hurt. It is cruel." Tears flashed into Charlotte's eyes. She looked accusingly at her aunt, who laughed.

"I think as much of your father as you do," said she, "and I know him better. Don't fret, honey."

"Your aunt is ill, dear," said Mrs. Carroll, who always veered to the side of the attacked party, and who, moreover, seldom grasped sarcasm, "and besides, sweetheart," she added, "I don't see what she said that could have hurt Arthur's feelings." Just then Carroll passed the window towards the stable. "There," she cried, triumphantly, "he is just going around to order the carriage. He had finished his luncheon. He never did care much for that kind of pudding. You are making too much of it, Charlotte, dear."

"No, I am not," said Charlotte, firmly. "Papa did not like the way Anna spoke; he was hurt. It was cruel." She got up and left the table also, and a soft sob was heard as she closed the dining-room door behind her.

"That dear child is so sensitive and nervous, and she thinks so much of Arthur," Mrs. Carroll said. "Give me the pudding sauce, Marie."

Eddy, who had been busily eating his pudding, looked up from his empty plate. "Aunt Anna did mean it was fortunate she had lost her appetite, because there wasn't enough to eat," he declared, in his sweet treble. "You ain't very sharp, Amy. She did mean that, and that was the reason papa went out. But it was true, too. There isn't enough to eat. I haven't had near enough pudding, and it is all gone. The dish is scraped. There is none left for Marie and Martin, either."

"I want no pudding," said Marie, unexpectedly, from behind Mrs. Carroll's chair. She spoke with a certain sullenness, and her eyes were red. She had a large, worn place in the sleeve of her white shirt-waist, and she was given to lifting her arm and surveying it with an air of covert injury and indignation.

"The omelet is all gone, too," said Eddy. "Marie and Martin haven't got anything to eat."

"Oh, hush, dear!" said Mrs. Carroll. "Marie can cook another omelet." The Hungarian girl opened her mouth as if to speak, then she shut it again. An indescribable expression was on her pretty, peasant face, the face of a down-trodden race, who yet retained in spirit a spark of rebellion and resentment. Marie, in her ragged blouse, with her countenance of inscrutable silence, standing behind her mistress's chair, surveying the denuded table, was the embodiment of a folk-lore song. She had been in America only a year and a half, and the Lord only knew what she had expected in that land of promise, and what bright visions had been dispelled, and how roughly she had been forced back upon her old point of view of the world. The girl was actually hungry. She had no money; her clothes were worn. Her naïve coquetry of expression had quite faded from her face. Her cheek-bones showed high, her mouth was wide and set, her eyes fixed with a sort of stolid and despairing acquiescence. The salient points of the Slav were to the surface, the little wings of her hope and youth folded away. She had fallen in love, moreover, and been prevented from attending a wedding-feast where she would have met him that day, on account of a lack of money for a new waist, and car fare. She knew another girl who was gay in a new gown, and at whom the desired one had often looked with wavering eyes. Her heart was broken as she stood there. She was one of the weariest of the wheels within wheels of Arthur Carroll's miserable system of life.

"I don't believe there are any more eggs to make an omelet," said Eddy.

"The grocer still trusts us," said Mrs. Carroll; "besides, he has been paid. Eddy, dear, you must not speak so to your aunt. Run out, if you have finished your luncheon, and ask your father when he is going to drive."

Carroll had not gone, as usual, to the City that day.

Mrs. Carroll and Anna rose from the table and went into the den on the left of the hall.

"You must not mind the children speaking so, Anna, dear," Mrs. Carroll said. "They would fly at me just the same if they thought I had said anything to hurt Arthur."

"I don't mind, Amy," Anna replied, dully. She threw herself upon the divan with its Oriental rug, lying flat on her back, with her hands under her head and her eyes fixed upon a golden maple bough which waved past the window opposite. She looked very ill. She was quite pale, and her eyes had a strange, earnest depth in dark hollows.

Mrs. Carroll looked a little more serious than was her wont as she sat in the willow rocker and swayed slowly back and forth. "I suppose," she said, after a pause, "that it will end in our moving away from Banbridge."

"I suppose so," Anna replied, listlessly.

"You don't mind going, do you, Anna, dear?"

"I mind nothing," Anna Carroll said. "I am past minding."

Mrs. Carroll looked at her with a bewildered sympathy. "Why, Anna, dear, what is the matter?" she said.

"Nothing, Amy."

"You are feeling ill, aren't you?"

"Perhaps so, a little. It is nothing worth talking about."

"Are you troubled about anything, honey?"

Anna did not reply.

"I can't imagine what you have to trouble you, Anna. Everything is as it has been for a long time. When we move away from Banbridge there will be more for a while. I can't see anything to worry about."

"For God's sake, keep your eyes shut, then, Amy, as long as you can," cried Anna, suddenly, with a tone which the other woman had never heard before. She gazed at her sister-in-law a minute, and her expression of childish sweetness and contentment changed. Tears came in her eyes, her mouth quivered.

"I don't know what you mean, Anna," she said, pitifully, like a puzzled child.

Anna sprang up from the divan and went over to her and kissed her and laughed. "I mean nothing, dear," she said. "There is no more to worry about now than there has been all along. People get on somehow. We are in the world, and we have our right here, and if we knock over a few people to keep our footholds, I don't know that we are to blame. It is nothing, Amy. I have felt wretched for a few days, and it has affected my spirits. Don't mind anything I have said. We shall leave Banbridge before long, and, as you say, we shall get on better."

Mrs. Carroll gave two or three little whimpers on her sister-in-law's shoulder, then she smiled up at her. "I guess it is because you don't feel well that you are looking on the dark side of things so," said she. "You will feel better to go out and have a drive."

"Perhaps I shall," replied Anna.

"We shall go for a long drive. There will be plenty of time, it is so early. How lovely it would be if we had our automobile, wouldn't it, Anna? Then we could go any distance. Wouldn't it be lovely?"

"Very," replied Anna.

Then Eddy burst into the room. "Say, Amy," he cried, "there's a great circus out in the stable. Papa and Martin are having a scrap."

"Eddy, dear," cried Mrs. Carroll, "you must not say scrap."

"A shindy, then. What difference does it make? Martin he won't harness, because he hasn't been paid. He just sits on a chair in the door and whittles a stick, and don't say anything, and he won't harness."

"We have simply got to have an automobile," said Mrs. Carroll.

"How do you know it is because he hasn't been paid, Eddy?" asked Anna.

"Because he said so; before he wouldn't say anything, and began whittling. Papa stands there talking to him, but it don't make any difference."

"With an automobile it wouldn't make any difference," said Mrs. Carroll. "An automobile doesn't have to be harnessed. I don't see why Arthur doesn't get one."

Anna Carroll sat down on the nearest chair and laughed hysterically.

Mrs. Carroll stared at her. "What are you laughing at, Anna?" said she, with a little tone of injury. "I don't see anything very funny. It is a lovely day, and I wanted to go to drive, and it would do you good. I don't see why people act so because they are not paid. I didn't think it of Martin."

"I'll go out and see if he has stirred yet," cried Eddy, and was off, with a countenance expressive of the keenest enjoyment of the situation.

Out in the stable, beside the great door through which was a view of the early autumn landscape — a cluster of golden trailing elms, with one rosy maple on a green lawn intersected by the broad sweep of drive — sat the man in a chair, and whittled with a face as imperturbable as fate. Carroll stood beside him, talking in a low tone. He was quite pale. Suddenly, just as the boy arrived, the man spoke.

"Why in thunder, sir," said he, with a certain respect in spite of the insolence of the words — "why in thunder don't you haul in, shut up shop, sell out, pay your debts, and go it small?"

"Perhaps I will," Carroll replied, in a tone of rage. His face flushed, he raised his right arm as if with an impulse to strike the other man, then he let it drop.

"Sell the horses, papa?" cried Eddy, at his elbow, with a tone of dismay.

Carroll turned and saw the boy. "Go into the house; this is nothing that concerns you," he said, sternly.

"Are the horses paid for, papa?" asked Eddy.

"I believe they ain't," said the man in the chair, with a curious ruminating impudence. Carroll towered over him with an expression of ignoble majesty. But Eddy had made a dart into a stall, and the tramp of iron hoofs was suddenly heard.

"I can harness as well as he can," a small voice cried.

Then Martin rose. "I'll harness," he said, sullenly. "You'll get hurt" — to the boy. "She don't like children round her." He took hold of the boy's small shoulders and pushed him away from the restive horse, and grasped the bridle. Carroll strode out of the stable.

"Say," said Eddy, to the man.

"Well, what? I've got to have my pay. I've worked here long enough for nothin'."

"When I'm a man I'll pay you," said Eddy, with dignity and severity. "You must not speak to papa that way again, Martin."

Martin looked from the tall horse to the small boy, and began to laugh.

"I'll pay you with interest," repeated the boy, and the man laughed again.

"Much obleeged," said he.

"I don't see, now, why you need to worry just because papa hasn't paid you," said Eddy, and walked out of the stable with a gait exactly like his father.

The man threw the harness over the horse and whistled.

"He's harnessing," Eddy proclaimed when he went in.

His mother was pinning on her veil before the mirror over the hall settle. Anna was just coming down-stairs in a long, red coat, with a black feather curling against her black hair under her hat.

"Where is Charlotte?" asked Mrs. Carroll.

"She has gone off to walk," said Eddy.

"Well," said Mrs. Carroll, "you must go after her and walk with her, Eddy."

"I don't want to, Amy," said Eddy. "I want to go to drive."

Then Carroll came down-stairs and repeated his wife's orders. "Yes, Eddy, you must go to walk with your sister. I don't wish her to go alone," said he peremptorily. He still looked pale; he had grown thin during the last month.

"I don't see why Charlotte don't get married, too, and have her husband to go with her," said Eddy, as he went out of the door. "Tagging round after a girl all the time! It ain't fair."

"Eddy!" called Carroll, in a stern voice; but the boy had suddenly accelerated his pace with his last words, and was a flying streak at the end of the drive.

"Where 'm I goin' to find her?" he complained to himself. He hung about a little until he saw the carriage emerge from the grounds and turn in the other direction, then he went straight down to the main street. Just as he turned the corner he met a small woman, carefully dressed and frizzed, who stopped him.

"Is your mother at home, little boy?" she asked, in a nervous voice. There were red spots on her thin cheeks; she was manifestly trembling.

The boy eyed her with a supercilious scorn and pity. He characterized her in his own mind of extreme youth and brutal truth as an ugly old woman, and yet he noted the trembling and felt like reassuring her. He took off his little cap. "No, ma'am," said he. "Amy has gone to drive."

"I wanted to see your mother," said the woman, wonderingly.

"Amy is my mother," replied the boy.

"Oh!" said the woman.

"They have all gone," said Eddy.

"Then I shall have to call another time," said the woman, with a mixture of ingratiation and despair.

The boy eyed her sharply. "Say," he said, "are you the dressmaker that made my sister Ina's clothes for her to be married?"

"Yes, I be," replied Madame Griggs.

"Then," said Eddy, "I can tell you one thing, there isn't any use for you to go to my house now to get any money. I suppose you haven't been paid."

"No, I haven't," said Madame Griggs. Then she loosened the floodgates of her grievance upon the boy. "No, I haven't been paid," said she, "and I've worked like a dog, and I'm owing for the things I bought in New York, and I'm owing my girls, and if I don't get paid before long, I'm ruined, and that's all there is to it. I ain't been paid, and it's a month since your sister was married, and they'll send out to collect the bills from the stores, if I don't pay them. It's a cruel thing, and I don't care if I do say it." The woman was flouncing along the street beside the boy, and she spoke in a loud, shrill voice. "It's a cruel thing," she repeated. "If I couldn't pay for my wedding fix I'd never get married, before I'd go and cheat a poor dress-maker. She'd ought to be ashamed of herself, and so had all your folks. I don't care if I do say it. They are nuthin' but a pack of swindlers, that's what they be."

Suddenly the boy danced in front of the furious little woman, and stood there, barring her progress. "They ain't!" said he.

"They be."

"They ain't! You can't pay folks if you ain't got any money."

"You needn't have the things, then," sniffed Madame Griggs.

"My sister had to have the things to get married, didn't she? A girl can't get married without the clothes."

"Let her pay for 'em, then."

"I'll tell you what to do!" cried Eddy, looking at her with a sudden inspiration. "You are in debt, ain't you?"

"Yes, I be," replied Madame Griggs, hopping nervously along by the boy's side, poor little dressmaker, aping French gentility, holding her skirts high, with a disclosure of a papery silk petticoat and a meagre ankle. Even in her distress she felt of her frizzes to see if they were in order after a breeze had struck her in the sharp, eager face. "Yes, I be."

"Well," said the boy, delightedly, "I can tell you just what to do, you know."

"What, I'd like to know?" Madame Griggs said, in a snapping tone.

"Move away from Banbridge," said the boy.

"What for, I'd like to know?"

"Why, then, don't you see," explained Eddy Carroll, "you would get away from the folks that you owe, and other folks that you didn't owe would trust you for things. You'd get along fine. That's the way we always do."

"Well, I never!" said Madame Griggs. Then she turned on him with sudden fury. "So that's what your folks are goin' to do, be they?" said she. "Go off and leave me without payin' my bill! That's the dodge, is it?"

Eddy was immediately on the alert. He was young and innocent, but he had a certain sharpness. He was quite well aware that a knowledge on the part of the creditors of his family's flittings was not desirable. "I ain't heard them say a word about moving away from Banbridge," declared he. "What you getting so mad about, Missis?"

"I guess I've got some reason to be mad, if that's your folks' game. The way I've worked, slavin' all them hot days and nights on your sister's wedding fix. I guess —"

"We ain't going to move away from Banbridge as long as we live, for all I know," said Eddy, looking at the bundle of feminine nerves beside him with a mixture of terror and scorn. "You don't need to holler so, Missis."

"I don't care how loud I holler, I can tell you that."

"We ain't going to move; and if we did, I don't see why you couldn't. I was just telling you what you could do, if you owed folks and didn't have any money to pay em, and you turn on a feller that way. I'm going to tell my sister and mother, and they won't have you make any more dresses for 'em." With that Eddy Carroll made a dart into Anderson's grocery store, which he had reached by that time. The dressmaker remained standing on the sidewalk, staring after him. She looked breathless; red spots were on her thin cheeks.

Eddy went straight through the store to the office. The door stood open, and the little place was empty except for the cat, which cast a lazy glance at him from under a half-closed lid, stretched, displaying his claws, and began to purr loudly. Eddy went over to the cat and took him up in his arms and carried him out into the main store, where William Price stood behind the counter. He was alone in the store.

"Say," said Eddy, "where's Mr. Anderson?"

"He's gone out," replied the clerk, with a kind look at the boy. He had lost one of his own years ago, and Eddy, in spite of his innocent supercil-iousness, appealed to him.

"Where?" asked Eddy. The cat wriggled in his arms and jumped down. Then he rolled over ingratiatingly at his feet. Eddy stooped down and rubbed the shining, furry stomach.

"He took the net he catches butterflies with," replied the old clerk, "and I guess he's gone to walk in the fields somewhere."

"I should think it was pretty late for butterflies," said Eddy. He straightened himself and looked very hard at the glass jar of molasses-balls on the shelf behind the clerk.

"There might be a stray one," said William Price. "It's a warm day."

"Shucks!" said Eddy. "Say, how much are those a pound?"

The clerk glanced around at the jar of molasses-balls. "Twenty-five cents," replied he.

"Guess I'll take a pound," said Eddy. "I ain't got any money with me, but I'll pay you the next time I come in."

The old clerk's common face turned suddenly grave, and acquired thereby a certain distinction. He turned about, took off the cover of the glass jar, and gathered up a handful of the molasses-balls and put them in a little paper bag. Then he came forth from behind the counter and approached the boy. He thrust the paper bag into a little grasping hand, then he took hold of the small shoulders and looked down at him steadily. The blue eyes in the ordinary face of an ordinary man, unfitted for any work in life except that of an underling, were full of affection and reproof. Eddy looked into them, then he hitched uneasily.

"What you doing so for?" said he; then he looked into the eyes again and was still.

"It's jest this," said William Price. "Here's a little bag of them molasses-balls, I'll give 'em to ye; but don't you never, as long as you live, buy anything you ain't either got the money to pay for in your fist, ready, or know jest where it's comin' from. It's stealin', and it's the wust kind of stealin', 'cause it ain't out an' out. I had a boy once about your size."

"Where's he now?" asked Eddy, in a half-resentful, half-wondering fashion.

"He's dead; died years ago of scarlet-fever, and I'd a good deal rather have it so, much as I thought of him — as much as your father thinks of you — than to have him grow up and steal and cheat folks."

"Didn't he ever take anything that didn't belong to him?" asked Eddy.

"Never. I guess he didn't. John wasn't that kind of a boy. I'd have trusted him with anythin'."

"Then he must have gone to heaven, I suppose," said Eddy. He looked soberly into the old clerk's eyes. "Thank you for the molasses-balls," he said. "I meant to pay for 'em, but I don't know just when I'd have the money, so I guess it's better for you to give them to me. Mr. Anderson won't mind, will he?"

"No, he won't, for I shall put fives cents into the cash-drawer for them," replied the old clerk, with dignity.

"I wouldn't want to have you take anything that Mr. Anderson wouldn't like," said Eddy.

"I shouldn't," replied the old clerk, going back to his place behind the counter, as a woman entered the store.

Eddy looked back as he went out, with a very sweet expression. "The first five-cent piece I get I'll pay you," he said. He had popped a molasses-ball into his mouth, and his utterance was somewhat impeded. "I thank you very much, indeed," he said, "and I'm sorry your boy died."

"Have you just lost a boy?" asked the woman at the counter.

"Twenty years ago," replied the clerk.

"Land!" said the woman. She looked at him, then she turned and looked after Eddy, who was visible on the sidewalk talking with Madame Griggs, and her face showed her mind. Madame Griggs had waited on the sidewalk until Eddy came out of the store. Now she seized him by the arm, which he promptly jerked away from her.

"When will your folks be home? That's what I want to know!" said she, sharply.

"They'll be home tonight, I guess," replied Eddy.

"Then I'll be up after supper," said Madame Griggs.

"All right," said Eddy.

"You tell 'em I'm comin'. I've got to see your ma and your pa."

"Yes, ma'am," replied Eddy. He raised his little cap as the dressmaker flirted away, then he started on a run down the street, sucking a molasses-ball, which is a staying sweet, and soon he left the travelled road and was hastening far afield.

CHAPTER XXV

It was September, but a very warm day. Charlotte had walked along the highway for some distance; then when she came to a considerable grove of oak-trees, she hesitated a moment, and finally left the road, entered the grove, and sat down on a rock at only a little distance from the road, yet out of sight of it. She was quite effectually screened by the trees and some undergrowth. Here and there the oaks showed shades of russet-and-gold and deep crimson; the leaves had not fallen. In the sunlit spaces between the trees grew clumps of blue asters. She saw a squirrel sitting quite motionless on a bough over her head, with bright eyes of inquisitive fear upon her. She felt a sense of delight, and withal a slight tinge of loneliness and risk. There was no doubt that it was not altogether wise, perhaps not safe, for a girl to leave the highway, or even to walk upon it if it were not thickly bordered by dwellings, in this state. Charlotte was fearless, yet her imagination was a lively one. She looked about her with keen enjoyment, yet there was a sharp wariness in her glance akin to that of the squirrel. When she heard on the road the rattle of wheels, and caught the flash of revolving spokes in the sun, she had a sensation of relief. There was not a house in sight, except far to the left, where she could just discern the slant of a barn roof through the trees. Everything was very still. While there was no wind, it was cool in the shade, though hot in the sunlight. She pulled her jacket over her shoulders. She leaned against a tree and remained perfectly quiet. She had on a muslin gown of an indeterminate green color, and it shaded perfectly into the coloring of the tree-trunk, which was slightly mossy. Her dark head, too, was almost indistinguishable against the tree, which at that height was nearly black. In fact, she became almost invisible from that most curious system of concealment in the world, that of assimilation with nature. She was gathered so closely into the arms of the great mother that she seemed one with her. And she was not alone in the shelter of those mighty arms; there was the squirrel, as indistinguishable as she. And there was another.

Charlotte with her bright, wary eyes, and the little animal with his, in the tree, became aware of another sentient thing besides themselves. Possibly the squirrel had been aware of it all the time.

Suddenly the girl looked downward at her right and saw within a stone's-throw a man asleep. He was dressed in an ancient, greenish-brown suit, and was practically invisible. His arm was thrown over his weather-beaten face and he was sleeping soundly, lying in a position as grotesquely distorted as some old tree-root. He was, in fact, distorted by the storms of life within and without. He was evidently a tramp, and possibly worse. His sleeping face could be read like a page of evil lore.

When Charlotte perceived him she turned pale and her heart seemed to stop. Her first impulse was to rise and make a mad rush for the road. Then she became afraid to do that. The road was lonely. She heard no sound of wheels thereon. It was true that she had entered the grove and seated herself without awakening the man; he might quite possibly be in a drunken sleep, difficult to disturb, but she might not be so fortunate a second time. Her slightest motion might awaken him now. So she sat perfectly still; she did not move a finger; it seemed to her she did not breathe. When a slight breeze rustled the tree-boughs over her head, and ruffled the skirt of her dress, her terror made her sick. When the breeze struck him, the sleeping tramp made an uneasy motion, and she felt overwhelmed. Soon, however, he began to breathe heavily. Before his breathing had been inaudible. He was evidently quite soundly asleep, yet if a breeze could disturb him, what might not her rise and flight do? It seemed to her that she must remain there forever. But the time would come when that sleeping terror would awake, whether she disturbed him or not, when that distorted caricature of man, as grotesque as a gargoyle on the temple of life, would stretch those twisted legs and arms, and open his eyes and see her; and then? She became sure, the longer she looked, that this was not one of the harmless wanderers over the earth, one of the Ishmaels, whose hand is turned only against himself. The great dark, bloated face had a meaning that could not be mistaken even by eyes for whom its meaning was written in a strange language. Innocence read guilt by a strange insight of heredity which came to her from the old beginning of things. She dared not stir. She felt petrified. She realized that her one hope was in the passing of some one on the road. She made up her mind that if she heard wheels she would risk everything. She would spring up and run for her life and scream. Then she wondered how loudly she could scream. Charlotte was not one of the screaming kind of girls who lifts up her voice of panic at everything. She tried to remember if she had ever screamed, and how loudly. She kept her ears strained for the sound of wheels, her eyes on the sleeping tramp. She dared not look away from him. Even the squirrel remained motionless, with his round eyes of wariness fixed. It was as if he too were afraid to stir. He retained his attitude of alert grace, sitting erect on his little haunches, an acorn in his paws, his bushy tail arching over his back like a plume.

Then slowly the man opened his eyes with a dazed expression, at first a blur of consciousness. Then gradually the recognition of himself, of his surroundings, of his life, came into them, and that self-knowledge was unmistakable. There was no doubt about the man with his twisted limbs and his twisted soul. He lay quite still a while longer, staring. Charlotte, with her eyes upon him, and the squirrel with his eyes upon him, never stirred. Charlotte heard her heart beat, and wished for some way to stifle it, but that she could not do. It seemed to her that the beating of her heart was like a drum, as if it could be heard through all the grove. She realized that she could not hear the sound of passing wheels on the road, because of this terrible beating of her heart. It seemed inevitable that the man would hear it. She felt then that she should take her one little chance, that she should scream on the possibility of some one passing on the road, and run, but she realized the futility of it. Before she could move a step the man would be upon her. She felt, moreover, paralyzed. She remained as perfectly motionless as the tree against which she leaned, with her eyes full of utmost terror and horror upon the waking man. He still looked straight ahead, and his eyes were still retrospective, fixed inward rather than outward. He still saw only himself and his own concerns.

Then he yawned audibly and spoke. "Damn it all!" he said, in a curious voice, of rather passive rage. It was the voice of one at variance with all creation, his hand against every man and every man against him, and yet the zest of rebellion was not in it. In fact, the man had been so long at odds with life that a certain indifference was upon him. He had become sullen. As he lay there he thrust a hand in his pocket, and again he spoke his oath against all outside, against all creation. He had thought absently that he might find a dime for a drink. Now that he had waked, he was thirsty, but there was none. Then he yawned, stretched out his stiff, twisted limbs with a sort of muffled groan, rested his weight upon one elbow, and shambled up as awkwardly as a camel. The girl sat still in the clutch of her awful fear. She no longer heard her heart beat. She was casting about in her mind for a weapon. A great impulse of fight was stirring in her. She felt suddenly that her little fingers were like steel. She felt that she should kill that man if he touched her. The fear never let go its clutch on her heart, but a fierceness as of any wild thing at bay was over her. She realized that in another minute, when he should see her, she would gather herself up, and spring, spring as she had read of a tarantula springing; that she would be first before the man, that she would kill him. Something which was almost insanity was firing her brain.

The man, when he had stood up, it seemed to Charlotte, looked directly at her. She was always sure that he did. But if he did, it was with unseeing eyes. His brain did not compass the image of her sitting there, leaning against the tree, a creature of incarnate terror and insane fury. He seemed to keep his eyes fixed upon her for a full second. Charlotte's nerves and muscles were tense with the restrained impulse to spring. Then he slowly shuffled away. As he passed, the squirrel slid like swiftness itself down the tree, and across an open space to another. The girl sank limply upon herself in a dead faint, and the tramp gained the road and trudged sullenly on towards Ludbury.

When Charlotte came to herself she was still sitting there limply. She could not realize all at once what had happened. Then she remembered. She looked at the place where the tramp had lain, and so forcibly did her terrified fancy project images that it was difficult to convince herself that he was really gone. She seemed to still see that gross thing lying there. Then she remembered distinctly that he had gone.

She got up, but she could scarcely stand. She had never fainted before, and she wondered at her own sensations. "What ails me?" she thought. She strained her eyes around, but there was no sign of the terrible man. She was quite sure that he had gone, and yet how could she be sure? He might have gone out to the road and be sitting beside it. A vivid recollection of tramps sitting beside that very road, as she had been driving past, came over her. She became quite positive that he was out on the road, and a terror of the road was over her. She looked behind her, and the sunny gleam of an open field came through the trees. The field was shaggy with blue asters and golden-rod gone to seed, and white tufts of immortelles. Charlotte stared through the trees at the field, and suddenly a man crossed the little sunny opening. A great joy swept over her; he was Randolph Anderson. Now she was sure that she was safe. She stumbled again to her feet, and ran weakly out of the oak grove. There was a low fence between the grove and the field, and when she reached that she stopped. She felt this to be insurmountable for her trembling limbs. "Oh, dear!" she said, aloud, and although the man was holding his butterfly-net cautiously over the top of a clump of asters so far away that it did not seem possible that he could hear her, he immediately looked up. Then he hastened towards her. As he drew near a look of concern deepened on his face. He had had an inkling at the first glimpse of her that something was wrong. He reached the fence and stood looking at her on the other side.

"I am afraid I can't get over," Charlotte said, faintly. She never knew quite how she was over, lifted in some fashion, and Anderson stood close to her, looking at her with his face as white as hers.

"What is it?" he asked. "Are you ill, Miss Carroll? What is it?"

"I have been frightened," said she. Without quite knowing what she did, she caught hold of his arm and clung to him tightly.

"What frightened you?" asked Anderson, fairly trembling himself and looking down at her.

"There was a man asleep in the grove, in there," explained Charlotte, falteringly — she still felt faint and strange — "and — and — I sat down there, and did not see him, and then he — he woke up and —"

Anderson seized her arm in a fierce clutch. "What?" he cried. "Where is he? What? For God's sake!"

"He went away out in the road and did not seem to see — me. I sat still," said Charlotte. Then she was very faint again, for he, too, frightened her a little.

Anderson caught her, supporting her, while he tore off his coat. Then he half carried her over to a ledge of rocks cropping out of the furzy gold-and-blue undergrowth, and sat down beside her there. Charlotte sat weakly where she was placed. She was deadly white and trembling. Anderson hesitated a moment, then he put an arm around her, removed her hat, and drew her head down on his shoulder.

"Now keep quiet a little while until you are better," he said. "You are perfectly safe now. You say the man did not see you?"

Charlotte shook her head against his shoulder. She closed her eyes; she was really very near a complete swoon, and scarcely knew where she was or what was happening; only a vague sense of another will thrust under her sinking spirit for a support was over her.

As for the man, he looked down at the little, pale face, with the dark lashes sweeping the soft cheeks, at the mouth still trembling to a sob of terror and grief, and a mighty wave of emotion was over him. He realized that he held in his arms not only the girl whom he loved, towards whom his whole being went out in protection and tenderness, but himself, his whole future, even in some subtle sense his past. He was like one on some height of the spirit, from which he overlooked all that was, all that had gone before, and all that would come. He was on the Delectable Mountain. Within himself he comprehended the widest vision of earth, that which is given through love. The man's face, looking at the woman's on his shoulder, became transfigured. It was full of uttermost tenderness, of protection as perfect as that of a father for his child. His heart, as he looked at her, was at once that of a lover and a father. He unconsciously held her closer, and bent his face down over hers softly, as if she had been indeed a child.

"Poor little soul!" he whispered, and his lips almost touched her cheek.

Then a wave of color came over the girl's face. "I am better," she said, and raised herself abruptly. Anderson drew back and removed his arm. He feared she was offended, and perhaps afraid of him. But she looked piteously up in his face, and, to his dismay, began to cry. Her nerves were completely unstrung. She was not a strong girl, and she had, in fact, been through a period of mental torture which might have befitted the Inquisition. She could still see the man's evil face; her brain seemed stamped with the sight; terror had mastered her. She was for the time being scarcely sane. The terrible imagination of ill which had possessed her, as she sat there gazing at the sleeping terror, still held her in sway. She was not naturally hysterical, but now hysterics threatened her.

Anderson put his arm around her again and drew her head to his shoulder. "You must not mind," he said, in a grave, authoritative voice. "You are ill and frightened. You must not mind. Keep your head on my shoulder until you feel better. You are quite safe now." Anderson's voice was rather admonishing than caressing. Charlotte sobbed wildly against his shoulder, and clung to him with her little, nervous hands. Anderson sat looking down at her gravely. "Is your mother at home?" he asked, presently.

"No," sobbed Charlotte; "they have all gone to drive."

"Nobody in the house?"

"Only Marie."

Anderson reflected. He was much nearer his own home than hers, and there was a short-cut across the field; they would not need to strike the road at all. He rose, with a sudden resolution, and raised the weeping girl to her feet.

"Come," said he, in the same authoritative voice, and Charlotte stumbled blindly along, his arm still around her. She had an under-consciousness that she was ashamed of herself for showing so little bravery, that she wondered what this man would think of her, but her self-control was gone, because of the too tense strain which had been put upon it. It was like a spring too tightly compressed, suddenly released; the vibrations of her nerves seemed endless. She tried to hush her sobs as she was hurried along, and succeeded in some measure, but she was still utterly incapable of her usual mental balance. Once she started, and clutched Anderson's arm with a gasp of fear.

"Look, look!" she whispered.

"What is it?" he asked, soothingly.

"The man is there. See him?"

"There is nothing there, child," he said, and hurried her over the place where her distorted vision had seen again the object of her terror, in his twisted sleep in the grass.

Anderson began to be seriously alarmed about the girl. He did not know what consequences might come from such a severe mental strain upon such a nervous temperament. He hurried as fast as he dared, almost carrying her at times, and finally they emerged upon the garden at the right of his own house. The flowers were thinning out fast, but the place was still gay with marigolds and other late blossoms. As he passed the kitchen door he was aware of the maid's gaping face of stupid surprise, and he called out curtly to her: "Is my mother in the house?"

"Yes, sir. She's in the sitting-room," replied the maid, with round eyes of curiosity upon the pair. Charlotte was making a desperate effort to walk by herself, to recover herself, but Anderson was still almost carrying her bodily. She wondered dimly at the strange trembling of her limbs, at the way the bright orange and red of the marigolds and nasturtiums swam before her eyes, and once again she saw quite distinctly the evil face of the man peer out at her from among them; but this time she said nothing, for her subconsciousness of delusion was growing stronger.

Anderson went around to the front of the house, and his mother's wondering face gazed from a window, then quickly disappeared. When he reached the door she was there, filling it up with her large figure in its voluminous white draperies.

"What —" she began, but Randolph interrupted her.

"Mother, this is Miss Carroll," he said. "She is not hurt, but she has had a terrible fright and shock. Her people are all away from home, and I brought her here; it was nearer. I want her to have some wine, and rest, and get over it before she goes home."

Mrs. Anderson hesitated one second. It was a pause for the gathering together of wits suddenly summoned for new and surprising emergencies; then she rose to the occasion. She had her faults and her weaknesses, but she was one of the women in whom the maternal instinct is a power, and this girl appealed to it. She stretched forth her white-clad arms, and she drew her away almost forcibly from her son.

"You poor child!" said she, in a voice which harked back to her son's babyhood. "Come right in. You go and get a glass of that port-wine," said she to Randolph, and she gave him a little push. She enveloped and pervaded the girl in a voluminous embrace.

Charlotte felt the soft panting of a mother's bosom under her head as she was led into the house. "You poor, blessed child," a soft voice cooed in her ear, a soft voice and yet a voice of strength. Charlotte's own mother had never been in the fullest sense a mother to her; a large part of the spiritual element of maternity had been lacking; but here was a woman who could mother a race, if once her heart of maternal love was awakened.

Charlotte was not led; that did not seem to be the action. She felt as if she were borne along by sustaining wings spread under her weakness into a large, cool bedroom opening out of the sitting-room. Then her dress was taken off, in what wise she scarcely knew; she was enrobed in one of Mrs. Anderson's large, white wrappers, and was laid tenderly in a white bed, where presently she was sipping a glass of port-wine, with Mrs. Anderson sitting behind her and supporting her head.

"No, you can't come in, Randolph," she heard her say to her son, and her voice sounded almost angry. After Charlotte had swallowed the wine, she lay back on the pillow, and she heard Mrs. Anderson talking softly to her in a sort of delicious dream, caused partly by the wine, which had mounted at once to her head, and partly by the sense of powerful protection and perfect peace and safety.

"Poor lamb!" Mrs. Anderson said, and her voice sounded like the song of a mother bird. "Poor lamb; poor, blessed child! It was a shame she was so frightened, but she is safe now. Now go to sleep if you can, dear child; it will do you good."

Charlotte smiled helplessly and gratefully, and after a happy stare around the room, with its scroll-work of green on the walls, reflecting green gloom from closed blinds, and another look of childish wonder into the loving eyes bent over her, she closed her own. Presently Mrs. Anderson tiptoed out into the sitting-room, where Randolph was waiting, standing bolt-upright in the middle of the room staring at the bedroom door. She beckoned him across the hall into the opposite room, the parlor. The parlor had a musty smell which was not unpleasant; in fact, slightly aromatic. There were wooden shutters which were tightly closed, all except one, through an opening in which a sunbeam came and transversed the room in a shaft of glittering motes.

"What scared her so?" demanded Mrs. Anderson. She had upon her a new authority. Anderson felt as if he had reverted to his childhood. He explained. "Well," said his mother, "the poor child has had an awful shock, and she is lucky if she isn't down sick with a fever. I don't like to see anybody look the way she did. But I'm thankful the man didn't see her."

"He might have been harmless enough," said Anderson.

Mrs. Anderson sniffed. "I don't see many harmless-looking ones round here," said she. "An awful-looking tramp came to the door this morning. I shouldn't wonder if it was the same one. I guess she will be all right now. She looked quieted down, but she had an awful shock, poor child."

"I wonder when I ought to take her home," said Anderson.

"Not for two hours," said his mother, decidedly. "She is going to stay here till she gets rested and is a little over it."

"Perhaps she had better," said Anderson; "her folks may have gone on a long drive, too."

"Did you know her before?" asked his mother, suddenly, and a sharp expression came into her soft, blue eyes.

"I have seen her in the store," replied Anderson, and he was conscious of coloring.

"She knew you, then?" said his mother.

"Yes. She was in the store this morning."

"It was lucky you were there."

"Oh, as for that, she was in no danger," said Anderson, coolly. "The tramp had gone."

"If you hadn't been there, I believe that poor little thing would have fainted dead away and lain there, nobody knows how long. It doesn't do anybody any good to get such a fright, and she is a thin, delicate little thing."

"Yes, she had quite a fright," said Anderson, walking over to the window with the defective shutter. "This shutter must be fixed," said he.

"I think she is prettier than the one that got married, but it is a pity she belongs to such a family," said Mrs. Anderson. "Mrs. Ferguson was just in here, and she says it is awful, that they are owing everybody."

"That is not the girl's fault," Anderson rejoined, with sudden fire.

"No, I suppose not," said Mrs. Anderson, with an anxious look at him. "Only, if she hasn't been taught to think it doesn't matter if debts are not paid."

"Well, I don't think that poor child is to be blamed," Anderson said.

"Do they owe you?"

"She came in and paid me this morning."

"Oh, I'm glad of that!" said his mother, and Anderson was conscious of intense guilt at his deception. Somehow half a lie had always seemed to him more ignoble than a whole one, and he had told a half one. He turned to leave the room, when there came a loud peal of the door-bell.

"Oh, dear, that will wake her up!" said his mother.

Anderson strode past her to the door, and there stood Eddy Carroll. He was breathless from running, and his pretty face was a uniform rose.

"Say," he panted, "is my sister in here?"

"Hush!" said Anderson. "Yes, she is."

"I chased you all the way," said Eddy, "but I tumbled down and hurt my knee on an old stone, and then I couldn't catch up." Indeed, the left knee of Eddy's little knickerbockers showed a rub and a red stain. "Where's Charlotte?"

"She is lying down. She was frightened, and I brought her here, and she has had some wine and is lying down."

"What frightened her, I'd like to know? First thing I saw you were lugging her off across the field. What frightened her?"

Anderson explained.

Eddy sniffed with utmost scorn. "Just like a girl," said he, "to get scared of a man that was fast asleep, and wouldn't have hurt her, anyway. Just like a girl. Say, you'd better keep her awhile."

"We are going to," said Mrs. Anderson.

"If she stays to supper, I might stay too, and then I could go home with her, and save you the trouble," said Eddy to Anderson.

CHAPTER XXVI

There had been a mutter as of coming storm in Wall Street for several weeks, and this had culminated in a small, and probably a sham, tempest, with more stage thunder and lightning than any real. However, it was on that very account just the sort of cataclysm to overwhelm phantom and illusory ships of fortune like Arthur Carrolls. That week he acknowledged to himself that his career in the City was over, that it was high time for him to shut up his office and to shake the dust of the City from his feet, for fear of worse to come. Arthur Carroll had a certain method in madness, a certain caution in the midst of recklessness, and he had also a considerable knowledge of law, and had essayed to keep within it. However, there were complications and quibbles, and nobody knew what might happen, so he retreated in as good order as possible, and even essayed to guard as well as might be his retreat. He told the pretty stenographers, with more urbanity than usual, and even smiling at the prettier one, as if the fact of her roselike face did not altogether escape him, that he was feeling the need of a vacation and would close the office for a couple of weeks. At the end of that period they might report. Carroll owed both of these girls; both remembered that fact; both reflected on the possibility of their services being no longer required, but such was the unconscious masculine charm of the man over their foolish and irresponsible feminity that they questioned nothing. Their eyes regarded him half-shyly, half-boldly under their crests of blond pompadours. The younger and prettier blushed sweetly, and laughed consciously, as if she saw herself in a mirror; the other's face deepened like a word under a strenuous pencil — the lines in it grew accentuated. Going down-stairs, the pretty girl nudged the other almost painfully in the side.

"Say," she whispered, "did you see him stare at me. Eh?"

The other girl drew away angrily. "I don't know as I did," she replied, in a curt tone.

"He stared like everything. Say, I don't believe he's married."

"I don't see what difference it makes to you whether he's married or not."

"Sho! Guess I wouldn't be seen goin' with a married man. What do you take me for, Sadie Smith?"

"Wait till there's any question of goin' before you worry. I would."

"Maybe I sha'n't have to wait long," giggled the other. When she reached the sidewalk, she stood balancing herself airily, swinging her arms, keeping up a continuous flutter of motion like a bird, to keep warm, for the wind blew cold down Broadway. She was really radiant, vibrant with nerves and young blood, sparkling and dimpling, and bubbling over, as it were, with perfect satisfaction with herself and perfect assurance of what lay before her. The other stood rather soberly beside her. They were both waiting for a car up Broadway. The young man who was in love with the pretty one came clattering down the stairs. There had been something wrong with the elevator, and it was being repaired. He also had to wait for a car, and he joined the girls. He approached the pretty girl and timidly pressed his shoulder against hers in its trim, light jacket. She drew away from him with a sharp thrust of the elbow.

"Go 'long," said she, forcibly. She laughed, but she was evidently in earnest.

The young man was not much abashed. He stood regarding her, winking fast.

"Say," he said, with a cautious glance around at the staircase, "s'pose the boss is goin' to quit?"

Both girls turned and stared at him. The elder turned quite pale.

"What do you mean, talking so?" said she, sharply.

"Nothin', only I thought it was a kind of queer time of year for a man to take a vacation, a man as busy as the boss seems to be. And — it kind of entered my head —"

"If anything entered your head, do, for goodness' sake, hang on to it," said the pretty girl, pertly. Then her car whirred over the crossing and ground to a standstill, and she sprang on it with a laugh at her own wit. "Good-night," she called back.

The other two, waiting for another car, were left together. "You don't think Mr. Carroll means to give up business?" the girl said, in a guarded tone.

"Lord, no! Why, he has so much business he can hardly stagger under it, and he must be making money. I was only joking."

"I suppose he's good pay," the girl said, in a shamed tone.

"Good pay? Of course he is. He don't keep right up to the mark — none of these lordly rich men like him do — but he's sure as Vanderbilt. I should smile if he wasn't."

"I thought so," said the girl. "I didn't mean to say I had any doubt."

"He's sure, only he's a big swell. That's always the way with these big swells. If he hadn't been such a swell, now, he'd have paid us all off before he took his vacation. But, bless you, money means so little to a chap like him that it don't enter into his head it can mean any more to anybody else."

"It must be awful nice to have money enough so you can feel that way," remarked the girl, with a curious sigh.

"That's so." The young man craned his neck forward to look at an approaching car, then he turned again to the girl. "Say," he whispered, pressing close to her in the hurrying throng, and speaking in her ear, "she's dead stuck on him, ain't she?" By two jerks, one of his right shoulder, one of his left, with corresponding jerks of his head, up the stairs and up Broadway, he indicated his employer and the girl who had just left on the car.

"She's a fool," replied the girl, comprehensively.

"Think she ain't got no show?"

The girl sniffed.

The young man laughed happily. "Well," he said, "I rather think he's married, myself, anyhow."

"I don't think he's married," returned the girl, quickly.

"I do. There's our car. Come along."

The girl climbed after the young man on to the crowded platform of the car. She glanced back at the office window as the car rumbled heavily up Broadway, and it was a pathetic glance from a rather pathetic young face with a steady outlook upon a life of toil and petty needs.

William Allbright had lingered behind the rest, and was in the office talking with Carroll, who was owing him a month's salary. Allbright, respectfully and apologetically, but with a considerable degree of firmness, had asked for it.

"It is not quite convenient for me to pay you tonight, Mr. Allbright," Carroll replied, courteously. "I was expecting a considerable sum today, which would have enabled me to square off a number of other debts beside yours. You know that matter of Gates & Ormsbee?"

"Yes, sir," replied Allbright, rather evasively. He had curious misgivings lately about this very Gates & Ormsbee, who figured in considerable transactions on his books.

"Well," continued Carroll, rather impatiently, looking at his watch, "you know they failed to meet their note this morning, and that has shortened me with ready money."

"How long do you expect to keep the office shut, sir?" inquired the clerk, respectfully, but still with a troubled air, and with serious eyes with the unswerving intentness of a child's upon Carroll's face.

"About two weeks," answered Carroll. "I must have that much rest. I am overworked." It was, indeed, true that Carroll looked fagged and fairly ill.

"And then you expect to resume business?" questioned Allbright, with a mild persistence. He still kept those keen, childlike eyes of his upon the other man's face.

"What else would you understand from what I have already said?" said Carroll. He essayed to meet the other man's eyes, then he turned and looked out of the window, and at that minute the girl who had worked at the type-writer in the back office looked up at him from the crowded platform of the car with her small, intense face, whose intensity seemed to make it stand out from the others around her as from a blurred background of humanity. "may I ask you to kindly wait a moment, Mr. Allbright?" Carroll said, and went out hurriedly, leaving Allbright standing staring in amazement. There had been something in his employer's manner which he did not understand. He stood a second, then presently made free to take up a copy of the Wall Street edition of the *Sun*, and sit down to glance over the panic reports. It was not very long, however, before he heard Carroll approaching the door. Carroll entered quite naturally, and the unusual expression which had perplexed the clerk was gone from his face. His mind seemed to be principally disturbed by the trouble about the elevator.

"It is an outrage," he said, in his fine voice, which was courteous even while pronouncing anathema. "The management of this block is not what it should be."

Allbright had risen, and was standing beside the desk on which lay the *Sun*. "It hasn't been acting right for a week past," he said, referring to the elevator.

"I know it hasn't, and there might have been an accident. It is an outrage. And they are taking twice as long to repair it as they should. I doubt if it is in working order by to-morrow." As he spoke, Carroll was taking out his pocket-book, which he opened, disclosing neatly folded banknotes. "By-the-way, Mr. Allbright," he said, "I find I can settle my arrears with you to-night, after all. I happened to think of a party from whom I might procure a certain sum which was due me, and I did so."

Allbright's face brightened. "I am very glad, sir," he said. "I was afraid of getting behind with the rent, and my sister has not been very well lately, and there is the doctor's bill."

"I am very glad also," said Carroll. "I dislike exceedingly to allow these things to remain unpaid." As he spoke he was counting out the amount of Allbright's month's salary. He then closed the pocket-book with a deft motion, but not before the clerk had seen that it was nearly empty. He also saw something else before Carroll brought his light overcoat together over his chest. "It is really cold tonight," he said.

"I am very much obliged to you, sir, for the money," Allbright said, putting the notes in his old pocket-book. Then he replied to Carroll's remark concerning the weather, that it was indeed cold, and he thought there would be a frost.

"Yes, I think so," said Carroll.

Then Allbright put on his own rather shabby, dark overcoat and his hat and took his leave. Much to his surprise, Carroll extended his hand, something which he had never done before.

"Good-bye," he said.

Allbright shook the extended hand, and felt a sudden, unexplained emotion. He returned the good-bye, and wished Mr. Carroll a pleasant vacation and restoration to health.

"I am tired out and ill," Carroll admitted, in a weary voice, and his eyes, as they now met the other man's, were haggard.

"There's two weeks' vacation," Allbright told his sister when he reached home that night, "and I don't know, but I'm afraid business ain't going just to suit Captain Carroll, and that's the reason for it."

"Has he paid you?" asked his sister, quickly, and her placid forehead wrinkled. Her illness had made her irritable.

"Yes," replied her brother. He looked at her meditatively. He was about to tell her something — that he was almost sure that Carroll had gone out and pawned his watch to pay him — then he desisted. He reflected that his sister was a woman, and would in all probability tell the woman down-stairs and her son about it, and that it would be none of their business whether he worked for a man who was honest enough, or hard up enough, to pawn his watch to pay him his month's salary or not. He was conscious of sentiments of loyalty both to himself and to Carroll. During the next two weeks he often strolled in the neighborhood of the office and stood looking up at the familiar windows. One day he saw some men carrying away a desk which looked familiar, but he was not sure. He hesitated about asking them from what office they had removed it until they had driven away and it was too late. He went up on the elevator and surveyed the office door, but it looked just as usual, with the old sign thereon. He tried it softly, but it was locked.

When he reached the sidewalk he encountered Harrison Day, the young clerk. He did not see him at first, but a nervous touch on his arm arrested his attention, and then he saw the young man's face with its fast-winking eyes.

"Say," said Harrison Day, "it's all right, ain't it?"

"What's all right?" demanded Allbright, a trifle shortly, drawing away. He had never liked Harrison Day.

"Oh, nothin', only it's ten days since he went, and I thought I'd look round to see how things were lookin'. You s'pose he's comin' back all right?"

"I haven't any reason to think anything else."

"Well, I thought I'd look around, and when I saw you I thought I'd ask what you thought. The girls are kind of uneasy — that is, Sadie is — May don't seem to fret much. Say!"

"What?"

"Did he pay you?"

"Yes, he did."

"Ain't he owin' you anything?"

"No, he is not."

The young man gave a whistle of relief. "Well, I s'pose he's all right," he said. "He ain't paid the rest of us up yet, but I s'pose it's safe enough."

A faithful, even an affectionate look came into the other man's face. He remembered his suspicions about the watch, and reasoned from premises. "I have no more doubt of him than I have of myself," he replied.

"You s'pose the business is goin' on just the same, then?"

"Of course I do," Allbright replied, almost angrily. And then a man who had just emerged from the street door coming from the elevator accosted him.

"Can you tell me anything about a man by the name of Carroll that's been running a sort of promoting business up in No. 233," he asked, and his face looked reddened unnaturally. The young man thought he had probably been drinking, but Allbright thought he looked angry. The young man replied before Allbright opened his mouth.

"He's gone on a vacation," he said.

"Queer time of year for a vacation," snapped the man, who was long and lean and full of nervous vibrations.

"He was overworked," said Harrison Day.

"Guess he overworked cheating me out of two thousand odd dollars," said the man, and both the others turned and stared at him.

Then Allbright spoke. "That is a statement no man has any right to make about my employer unless he is in a position to prove it," he said.

"That is so," said Harrison Day. He was a very small man, but he danced before the tall, lean one, who looked as if all his flesh might have resolved to muscle.

The man looked contemptuously down at him and spoke to Allbright. "So he is your employer?" he said, in a sarcastic tone.

"Yes, he is."

"This young man's also, I presume."

"Yes, he is," declared Day. But the man only heeded Allbright's response that he was.

"Well," said the man, "may I ask a question?"

"Yes, you may," said Day, pertly, "but it don't follow that we are goin' to answer it."

"May I ask," said the man, addressing Allbright, "if Captain Carroll has paid you your salaries?"

"He has paid me every dollar he owed me," replied Allbright, with emphasis, and his own face flushed.

Then the man turned to Day. "Has he paid you?" he inquired.

And Day, with no hesitation, lied. "Yes, sir, he has, every darned cent," he declared, "and I don't know what business it is of yours whether he has or not."

"When is he coming back?" asked the man, of Allbright, not heeding Day.

"Next Monday," replied Allbright, with confidence.

"Where does he live?" asked the man.

Then for the first time an expression of confusion came over the book-keeper's face, but Day arose to the occasion.

"He lives in Orange," replied Day.

"What street, and number?"

"One hundred and sixty-three Water Street," replied Day. His eyes flashed. He was finding an unwholesome exhilaration in this inspirational lying.

"Well," said the man, "I can tell you one thing, if your precious boss ain't in this office Monday morning by nine o'clock sharp, he'll see me at one hundred an sixty-three Water Street, Orange, New Jersey, and he'll hand over my two thousand odd dollars that he's swindled me out of, or I'll have the law on him." With that the man swung himself aboard a passing car, and Allbright and Day were left looking after him.

"That feller had ought to have been knocked down," said Day.

Allbright turned and looked at him gravely. "So, Captain Carroll lives in Orange?" he said.

"He may, for all I know."

"Then you don't know?"

"Do you?"

"No; I never have known exactly."

"Well, I haven't, but I wasn't goin' to let on to that chap. And he may live jest where I said he did, for all I know. Say!"

"What?"

"You s'pose it is all right?"

Allbright hesitated. His eyes fell on three gold balls suspended in the air over a door a little way down a cross street. "Yes," he said. "I believe that Captain Arthur Carroll will pay every man he owes every dollar he owes."

"Well, I guess it's all right," said Day. "I'm goin' to take the girls to Madison Square Garden tonight. I'm pretty short of cash, but you may as well live while you do live. I wonder if the boss is married."

"I don't know."

"I guess he is," said Day, "and I guess he's all right and above board. Good-bye, Allbright. See you Monday."

But Monday, when the two stenographers, the book-keeper, and the clerk met at the office, they found it still locked, and a sign "To let" upon the door.

"Mr. Carroll gave up his office last Saturday," said the man in the elevator. "The janitor said so, and they have taken his safe out for rent. Guess he bust in the Wall Street shindy last week."

Out on the sidewalk the four looked at one another. The pretty stenographer began to cry in a pocket-handkerchief edged with wide, cheap lace.

"I call it a shame," she said, "and here I am owing for board, and —"

"Don't cry, May," said Day, with a caressing gesture towards her in spite of the place. "I guess it will be all right. He has all our addresses, and we shall hear, and you won't have a mite of trouble getting another place."

"I think I am justified in telling you all not to worry in the least, that you will be paid every dollar," said Allbright; but he looked perplexed and troubled.

"It looks mighty black, his not sending us word he was going to close the office," said Day; and then appeared the tall, lean man who wanted his two thousand odd dollars. He did not notice them at all, but started to enter the office-building.

"Come along quick before he comes back," whispered Day. He seized the astonished girls each by an arm and hustled them up the street, and Allbright, after a second's hesitation, followed them just as the irate man emerged from the door.

CHAPTER XXVII

Arthur Carroll, when he had started on his drive with his wife and sister that afternoon, was in one of those strenuous moods which seem to make one's whole being tick with the clock-work of destiny and cause everything else, all the environment, and the minor happenings of life, to appear utterly idle. Even when he talked, and apparently with earnestness, it was always with that realization of depths, which made his own voice ring empty and strange in his ears. He heard his wife and sister chatter with the sense of aloofness of the inhabitant of another planet; he thought even of the financial difficulties which harassed him, and had caused this very mood, with that same sense of aloofness. When Anna wondered where Charlotte had gone to walk, and Mrs. Carroll remarked on the possibility of their overtaking her, his mind made an actual effort to grasp that simple idea. He was running so deep, and with such awful swiftness, in his own groove of personal tragedy, that the daughter whom he loved, and had seen only a few moments ago, seemed almost left out of sight of his memory. However, all the while the usual trivialities of his life and the lives of those who belonged to him went on with the same regularity and reality as tragedy, and with as certain a trend to a catastrophe of joy or misery.

On that day when Charlotte had her fright from the tramp, she remained at the Anderson's to supper. Eddy had also remained. When Charlotte had waked from her nap, he followed Anderson into the sitting-room, where was Charlotte in Mrs. Anderson's voluminous, white frilly wrapper, a slight young figure scalloped about by soft, white draperies, like a white flower, seated comfortably in the largest, easiest chair in the room. Mrs. Anderson was standing over her with another glass of wine, and a china plate containing two great squares of sponge-cake.

"Do eat this and drink the wine, dear," she urged. "It is nearly an hour before supper now."

"Then I really must go home, if it is so late," Charlotte cried. She made a weak effort to rise. She was still curiously faint when she essayed to move.

"You are going to stay here and have supper, and after supper my son shall take you home. If you are not able to walk, we shall have a carriage."

"I think I must go home, thank you," Charlotte repeated, in a sort of bewildered and grateful dismay.

"If you think your mother will feel anxious, I will send and inform her where you are," said Mrs. Anderson, "but you must stay, my dear." There was about her a soft, but incontrovertible authority. It was all gentleness, like the overlap of feathers, but it was compelling. It was while Mrs. Anderson was insisting and the girl protesting that Anderson, with Eddy at his heels, had entered the room.

"Why, Eddy dear, is that you?" cried Charlotte.

Eddy stood before her and surveyed her with commiseration and a strong sense of personal grievance and reproach. "Yes, it's me," said he. "Papa told me to go to walk with you, and I didn't know which way you went, and I couldn't find out for a long time. Then I saw Mr. Anderson taking you here, and I ran, but I couldn't catch up. He's got awful long legs." Eddy looked accusingly at Anderson's legs.

"It was too bad," said Charlotte.

"You were awful silly to get so scared at nothing," Eddy pursued. "I saw that tramp. He looked to me like a real nice man. Girls are always imagining things. You'd better eat that cake, Charlotte. You look awful. That looks like real nice cake."

"Bless your heart, you shall have some," Mrs. Anderson said, and Eddy accepted with alacrity the golden block of cake which was offered him.

"Why, Eddy!" Charlotte said.

"Now, Charlotte, you know we never have cake like this at home," Eddy said, biting into the cake. "not since the egg-man won't trust us any more. I know this kind of cake takes lots of eggs. I heard Marie say so when Amy asked her to make it."

Charlotte colored pitifully, and made another effort to rise. "Indeed, I think we must go now," said she. "Come, Eddy."

Mrs. Anderson turned to her son for support. "I tell her she must not think of going until after tea," she said. "Then if she is not able to walk, we will get a carriage."

Eddy removed the fast-diminishing square of cake from his mouth and regarded his sister with an expression of the most open ingenuousness. "Now, Charlotte, I'll tell you something," he said.

"What, dear?"

"You might just as well stay, and I'll tell you why. Papa and Amy and Anna won't be home until after seven."

"Until after seven?"

"No. They are going to Addison."

"To Addison?"

Addison was a large town some fifteen miles from Banbridge.

"Yes; and they are going to get dinner there."

"Eddy, are you sure?"

"Yes, of course I am sure," replied Eddy, with the wide-open eyes of virtue upon his sister's face. "Amy told me to tell you."

"Now, Eddy."

Eddy took another bite of his cake. "I think you are pretty mean to speak that way. I never spoke to you so," he said. "When you say a thing is so, I never say 'Now, Charlotte!'" Eddy, having imitated his sister's doubtful tone exactly, took another bite of cake.

"Well, if Amy really said so," Charlotte returned, and still with a faint accent of incredulity. It was very seldom that the Carrolls took the drive to Addison. However, it was an exceedingly pleasant day, and it did seem possible.

"Well, she did," Eddy declared, stoutly; and there was in his declaration a slight trace of truth, for Mrs. Carroll had mentioned, on starting, that it was such a lovely day, that if they had got an earlier start they might have driven to Addison; and Anna had replied that it was too late now, for they would not get home in time for dinner if they went there. The rest Eddy had manufactured to serve his own small ends — which a stay at the Andersons' to tea, for which he had, remembering his dinner there, the pleasantest anticipations. "You had better stay, Charlotte," Eddy urged, furthermore, "for you do look awful pale, and as if you ought to have something nourishing to eat, and you know we won't get much home. The mutton all went this noon, and you know, unless papa got some in Addison, we wouldn't be likely to get any here. I heard Anna talking about the butcher only this morning. Papa hasn't been able to pay him for a very long time, you know, Charlotte."

Then Charlotte raised herself hastily. "We must go home," she said, with a fierce emphasis; but the effort was too much. She sank back, and Mrs. Anderson sent her son for the camphor-bottle.

"Now," said she to Anderson, "you had better take him out and show him the dog. I'll fix it up." She nodded assuringly towards the little pale face against the rose-patterned chintz.

"Come along, son," said Anderson to the boy, and led him out in the garden. "You must not talk quite so much, young man," he said to him, when they were on their way to the dog-kennel, which was backed up against the terrace at the rear of the house, and before which stood chained fast a large dog with a bad reputation. "You had better not touch him," charged Anderson, as they approached. Then he repeated, "No, you must not talk quite so much."

"Why not?" demanded Eddy. "He don't look very cross."

"Because," said the man, "there are certain things in every family which it is better for a member of the family not to repeat outside his home."

"What did I say?" asked Eddy, wonderingly. "He is wagging his tail. He shakes all over. He wouldn't do that unless his tail was wagging. I can't see his tail, but it must be wagging. What did I say?"

"When it comes to the family's household affairs —" Anderson said.

"Oh, you mean what I said about the butcher, huh? Oh, that don't do any harm. Everybody in Banbridge knows about those things. I don't see what difference that makes. Folks have to have things, don't they? I don't believe that dog would bite me. He is wagging just as hard as he can. Don't they?"

"Yes, of course," agreed Anderson, "but —"

"And if they don't have the money to pay for things, what are they going to do? You wouldn't want all us Carrolls to die, would you?"

Anderson smiled, and stood between the boy and the kennel.

"I ain't afraid of him," said Eddy. "You wouldn't, would you?"

"Oh, of course not," replied Anderson.

"I shouldn't think you would, especially Charlotte. Say, I think Charlotte is a real pretty girl, if she is my sister. Say, why can't I pat him?"

"You had better not. He bit a boy about your size once."

"Hm! I ain't afraid he'll bite me. Don't you think she is? I don't think you are very polite not to say right off."

"Very pretty, indeed," replied Anderson, laughing. Then he spoke to the dog, a large mongrel with a masterly air, and an evident strain of good blood under his white and yellow hide.

"How much did you pay for that dog?" inquired Eddy.

"I didn't pay anything," replied Anderson. "Somebody left him in the street in front of my office when he was a puppy, or he strayed there. I never knew which."

"So you took him in?"

"Yes."

"Do you always keep him shut up here?"

"A great part of the time. Sometimes he stays in my store nights. He is a very good watch-dog."

"You keep him shut up because he bit a boy?"

"Most of the time. He is a little uncertain in his temper, I am afraid."

"Didn't he bite any one but that one boy?"

"No, not that I know of. But he has sprang at a good many people and frightened them, and I have either to keep him tied or shoot him."

"He didn't kill the boy?"

Anderson laughed. "Oh no! He was not very badly bitten."

"Well, I know one thing," said Eddy, with conviction. "I would not like a nice dog like that shut up all his life because he had bitten me."

Before Anderson knew what he was about to do, Eddy had made a spring, leaping up sideways in the air like a kitten, and was close to the dog. And the dog, upon whom there was no reliance to be placed, except in the case of Anderson himself, hardly stopping for a premonitory growl, had seized upon the boy's little arm. Having a strain of pure bulldog in him, it was considerable trouble to make him let go, and Anderson had to use a good deal of force at his collar and a thick stick.

Eddy, meanwhile, made not a whimper, but kept his whitening lips close shut. Luckily he had on a thick jacket, although the day was so warm, and when Anderson drew away at last from the furious, straining animal, and examined the injured member, he found only a slight wound. The marks of the dog's teeth were plainly visible, and there were several breaks of the surface and a little blood, but it was certainly not alarming, and the animal's usual temper made it improbable that any ultra consequences need be feared.

Eddy was trembling and very pale, but he still made not a whimper, as Anderson examined his arm.

"Well, my son," said Anderson, who was as white as the boy, "I think there is not much harm done. But it is lucky you had on such a thick sleeve. I can tell you that."

"That was because we have not paid the Chinaman, and he wouldn't send home my blouses this week. It was so warm I wanted to wear a blouse, but they were all at the Chinaman's." Eddy's teeth chattered as he spoke, his childish lips quivered, and tears were in his eyes. He continued to tremble violently, but he did not for a moment give way. He even shook off the protecting arm which Anderson placed around his little shoulders.

"Come, we will go in the house and have this tied up," said Anderson.

But Eddy rebelled. "I don't want a lot of women fussing over a little thing like this," said he, stoutly. "It isn't anything at all."

"No, it is not very serious, but all the same it had better be tied up, and I have something I want to put on it. I tell you what we will do. We will go around the back way. I will take you in the kitchen door and up the backstairs to my room, and doctor it unknown to anybody."

"I don't want Charlotte to know anything about it; she will be just silly enough to faint away again. Girls always do make such an awful fuss over nothing," said Eddy.

"All right," said Anderson. "Come along, my boy."

Anderson started, and the boy followed, but suddenly he stopped and ran back before Anderson dreamed what he was about. He stopped in front of the kennel, and danced on obviously trembling legs a dance of defiance before the frantic dog.

Anderson grabbed him by the shoulders.

"Come at once," he said, quite sternly.

Eddy obeyed at once. "All right," he said. "I just wanted him to see I wasn't afraid of him, that was all."

Eddy and Anderson entered the house through the kitchen door, ascended the backstairs noiselessly, and gained Anderson's room, where the wound was bound up after an application of a stinging remedy which the boy bore without flinching, although it was considerably more painful than the bite itself. He looked soberly down at his arm, now turning black and blue from the bruise of the dog's teeth, beside the inflamed spots where they had actually entered, while Anderson applied the violent remedy.

"Well," he said, "I suppose I was to blame. I ought to have minded you."

"Yes, I suppose you ought, my son," assented Anderson, continuing to handle the wound gently.

"And I suppose that is an exclusive dog. He doesn't like everybody going right up to him. Say, I guess he is a pretty smart dog, but I guess I should rather be his master than anybody else. He never bit you, did he?"

"No."

"I should think he would be an awful nice watch-dog," said Eddy.

Anderson bound the arm tightly and smoothly with a bandage. When the arm was finally dressed the jacket-sleeve could go over it, much to Eddy's satisfaction.

"Say, this jacket ain't paid for," he said. "Isn't it lucky that the man where Amy bought it didn't know we didn't have much money to pay for things lately and trusted us. If I had on my old jacket, the sleeves were so short and tight, because I had outgrown it, you know, I'd been hurt a good deal worse, and it was lucky we hadn't paid the Chinaman, too. It was real — What do you call it?"

"I don't know what you mean?" said Anderson, smiling.

"It was real — Oh, shucks! you know. What is it folks say when they don't go on a railroad train, and there's an accident, and everybody that did go is killed. You know."

"Oh, providential?"

"Yes, it was real providential."

"Suppose we go down."

"All right. Say, you mind you don't say a word about this to your mother or Charlotte."

"Yes, I promise."

"Your mother is an awful nice lady," said Eddy, in a whisper, descending the stairs behind Anderson, "but I don't want her fussing over me as if I was a girl, 'cause I ain't."

When the two entered the sitting-room, Charlotte started and looked at her brother.

"Eddy Carroll, what is the matter?" she cried.

"Nothing," declared the little boy, stoutly, but he manifestly tottered.

"Why, the dear child is ill!" cried Mrs. Anderson. "Randolph, what has happened?"

"Nothing!" cried Eddy, holding on to his consciousness like a hero. "Nothing; and I ain't a dear child."

"It is nothing, mother," said Anderson, quickly coming to his rescue.

Charlotte was eying wisely the knee of Eddy's knickerbockers. "Eddy Carroll," said she, with tender severity, "your knee must be paining you terribly."

Eddy quickly grasped at the lesser evil. "It ain't worth talking about," he responded, stoutly.

"I can see blood on your knee, dear. It must be bad to make you turn so pale as that."

With a soft swoop like a mother hen, Mrs. Anderson descended upon the boy, who did not dare resist that gentle authority. She tenderly rolled up the leg of the little knickerbockers and examined the bruised, childish knee. Then she got some witch-hazel and bound it up. While she was doing so, Eddy gazed over her head at Anderson with the knowing and confidential twinkle which one man gives another when tolerant of womanly delusion. He even indulged in an apparently insane chuckle when Mrs. Anderson finished, and smoothed his little, dark head, and told him that now she was sure it would feel better.

"Eddy," cried Charlotte, "what are you doing so for?"

"Nothing," replied Eddy. "I was thinking how funny I looked when I tumbled down. "But he rolled his eyes, comically around at Anderson. His arm was paining him frightfully, and it struck him as the most altogether exquisite joke that Mrs. Anderson should be treating his knee, which did not pain him at all, so sympathetically.

CHAPTER XXVIII

During the progress of the tea at the Andersons' Eddy kept furtively glancing at his sister with an expression which signified congratulation.

"Ain't you glad you stayed?" the expression said, quite plainly.

"Did you ever have such nice things to eat? And only think what a snippy meal we should have had at home!"

Charlotte met the first of the glances with a covertly chiding look and an imperceptible shake of her head; then she refused to meet them, keeping her eyes away from her exultant brother. She herself was actually hungry, poor child, for the truth was that for the last few days it had been somewhat short commons at the Carrolls', and Charlotte was one of the sort who, under such circumstances, are seized with a sudden loss of appetite. She had really eaten very little for some hours, and now, in spite of a curious embarrassment and agitation, which under ordinary circumstances would have lessened her desire for food, she herself ate eagerly. The meal was both dainty and abundant. Mrs. Anderson had always prided herself upon the meals she set before guests. There was always in the house a store of sweets to be drawn from on such occasions, and while Anderson had been binding up Eddy's wound, the maid had been sent to the market for a chicken to supplement the beefsteak which had been intended for the family supper. So there was fried chicken and celery salad, and the most wonderful cream biscuits, and fruit and pound cake, and quince preserves — quarters of delectable, long-drawn-out flavor in a rosy jelly — and tea and thick cream and loaf-sugar in the old, solid service with its squat pieces finished with beading. Eddy gloated over it all openly. He fairly forgot his manners, for, after all, he was, although in a desultory sort of way, a well-bred boy. The Carrolls, as far as their manners went, were gentlefolk, and came of a long line of gentlefolk. But it happened that the china which had come to them from their forebears had for the most part been broken in the course of their wanderings from place to place, and in its place was an ornate and rather costly, and unpaid-for, set. Eddy now quite openly lifted the saucer of thin, pink-and-gold china, in which his teacup rested, and held it to the light.

"Whew, ain't it thin?" he ejaculated.

"Why, Eddy!" Charlotte cried, flushing with dismay.

"I don't care. It is awful thin," persisted the boy. He held the saucer before his eyes. "I can see you through it; yes, I can," said he.

But Mrs. Anderson, although her old-fashioned ideas of the decorous behavior due from children at table were somewhat offended, and she later told her son that it did seem to her that the boy must have been somewhat neglected, was yet very susceptible to flattery of those teacups, which had descended to her from her own mother, and which she had always regarded as superior to any of the Anderson family china, of which there was quite a store. So she merely smiled and remarked gently that the china was very old, and she believed quite rare, and it was, indeed, unusually thin, yet not a piece of the original set had been broken.

"Why didn't we have china like this instead of that we have?" demanded Eddy of Charlotte.

"Hush, dear," said Charlotte. "This china is so very old and valuable, you know, that not every one could — that we could not — I believe we had some very pretty china in our family, but it all got broken," she added.

"It didn't begin to be so pretty as this," said Eddy. "I remember it. The cups were like bowls, and there were black wreaths around them. There weren't any handles, either. I don't see why we couldn't have got some china as pretty as this. Suppose it was valuable. Why, I don't believe that we have now is paid for. What difference would it make?"

Charlotte blushed so that Mrs. Anderson felt an impulse to draw the poor, little, troubled head upon her shoulder and tell her not to mind.

"Let me give you some more of the quince preserve, dear," she said, in the softest voice; and Charlotte, who did not want it, passed her little glass dish to take advantage of the opportunity afforded her to cover her confusion.

"What difference would it make, say, Charlotte?" persisted Eddy.

"Hush, dear," said Charlotte, painfully.

"Here, son, pass your plate for this chicken," said Anderson; and Eddy, with a shrewd glance of half-comprehension from one to the other, passed his plate and subsided, after a muttered remark that he didn't see why Charlotte minded.

"Wasn't that a bully supper?" he whispered, pressing close to his sister when they entered the sitting-room after the meal was finished.

"Hush, dear," she whispered back.

"Ain't you glad you stayed? You wouldn't, if it hadn't been for me."

Charlotte turned and looked at him sharply. Mrs. Anderson had lingered in the dining-room to give some directions to the maid, and Anderson had stepped out on the porch for a second's puff at a cigar.

"Eddy Carroll," said she, in a whisper, "you didn't?"

Eddy faced her defiantly. "Didn't what?"

"You didn't tell a lie about that?"

Eddy lowered his eyes, frowned, and scraped one foot in a way he had when embarrassed. "Amy did say something about it was such a pleasant day and Addison," he replied, doggedly.

"But did she say they were really going there, and would not be back?"

"Anna said if they went there they could not get back."

"But did she say they were going? Tell me the truth, Eddy Carroll."

Eddy scraped.

"I see they did not," said Charlotte, severely.

"Eddy, I don't know what papa will say."

"I know," said Eddy, simply, with a curious mixture of ruefulness and defiance. Then he added: "If you want to be mean enough to tell on a feller, after he's been the means of your having such a supper as that (and you were hungry, too; you needn't say you wasn't; you ate an awful lot yourself), you can."

"I am not going to tell unless I am asked, when I certainly shall not tell a lie," replied Charlotte; "but papa will find it out himself, I am afraid, Eddy."

"I shouldn't wonder if he did," admitted Eddy.

"And then, you know —"

"Yes, I know; but I don't care. I have had that bully supper, anyhow. He can't alter that. And, say, Charlotte."

"What?" asked Charlotte, severely. "I am ashamed of you, Eddy."

"I don't see why papa don't get a store, like him" — he jerked an expressive shoulder towards the scent of the cigar smoke — "and then we could have things as good as they do."

But then Charlotte turned on him with fierceness none the less intense, although necessarily subdued. "Eddy Carroll," she whispered, with a long-drawn sibilance, "to turn on your father, a man like papa! Eddy Carroll! Poor papa does the best he can, always, always."

"I suppose he does," said Eddy, quite loudly. "My, Charlotte, you needn't act as if you were going to bite a feller. I've had enough of —"

"What?" asked Charlotte.

"Nothing," said Eddy. His arm was paining him quite severely. It had been quite an ordeal for him to manage his knife and fork at supper without betrayal.

"What were you going to say?" persisted Charlotte.

"Nothing," said Eddy, doggedly — "nothing at all. Don't act so fierce, Charlotte. It isn't lady-like. Amy never speaks so awful quick."

Charlotte began putting on her hat, which had been left on the sitting-room table. "I am ashamed of you," she whispered again. "I was ashamed of you all tea-time."

Eddy whistled in a mannish fashion. Charlotte continued adjusting her hat and smoothing her fluff of dark hair. Her face, in the mirror which hung between the two front windows, looked not so angry as sorrowful, and with a dewy softness in the pretty eyes, and a slight quiver about the soft mouth. Eddy glanced several times at this reflected face; then he stole, with a sudden, swift motion, up behind his sister, threw his arms around her neck, although it hurt him cruelly, and laid his boyish cheek against her soft, girlish one.

"No, you need not think that will make up," whispered Charlotte. But she herself pressed her cheek tenderly against his, and then laughed softly. "Try not to do so again, dear," she said. "It mortified me, and it is not being a credit to papa. Think a little and try to remember how you have been brought up."

"Charlotte," whispered Eddy, in the softest, most furtive of whispers, casting a glance over his shoulder.

"What is it, dear?"

"I suppose they" — he indicated by a motion of his shoulder his host and hostess — "are just as nice people as — we are — as the Carrolls."

"Of course they are," replied Charlotte, hastily. She pushed Eddy away softly and began to fuss again with her hat. "We must go home right away," she said, "or they will worry."

"There is no need of his going home with you, as long as I am here," said Eddy.

"Of course not," replied Charlotte.

But it seemed that Anderson himself had other views, and his mother also, for although a sudden and not altogether easy suspicion had come to her, she whispered aside to him that he must certainly accompany the two home.

"It is quite dark already," she said, "and it is not fit for that child to go alone with nobody but that boy, after the fright she has had this afternoon. She is just in the condition now when a shadow might upset her. You really must go with her, Randolph."

"I have no intention of doing anything else, mother," Randolph replied, laughing. He had been, indeed, taking his overcoat from the tree in the hall when his mother had come out to speak to him. Charlotte had said, on rising from the table, that she must go home at once.

Mrs. Anderson enveloped the girl in her large, gentle, lavender-scented embrace, and received with pleasant disclaimers her assurances of obligations and thanks; then she stood in the window and, with a little misgiving, and a ready imagination for future trouble, watched them emerge from the little front yard and disappear down the street under the low-growing maple branches which were turning slowly, and flashed gold over their heads in electric lights. She reflected judicially that while Charlotte was undoubtedly a sweet girl, and very pretty, very pretty, indeed, and, while her own heart was drawn to her, yet she would make no sort of wife for her son. She remembered with a shudder Eddy's remarks at the table.

"He is a pretty little boy, too," she thought, with a maternal thrill, remembering her own son at that age. When she returned to the dining-room to wash the pink-and-gold cups and saucers, in her little bowl of hot water on the end of the table, as was her custom when the best china had been used, the maid, who was clearing the table, and who had been encouraged to conversation from the lack of another woman in the house, and her mistress's habit of gentle garrulity, spoke upon the subject in her mind.

"Them was them Carrolls that lives in the Ranger place, was they not?" said she. The maid was a curious product of the region, having somewhat anomalously graduated at a high-school in New Sanderson before entering service, and gotten a strange load of unassimilated knowledge, which was particularly exemplified in her English. She scorned contractions, but equally scorned possessives and legitimate tenses. She wrote a beautiful hand, using quite ambitious words, but she totally misinterpreted the meaning of these very words in current literature, particularly the cook-book. Her bread was as heavy with undigested facts as is the stomach of a dyspeptic with food, but she was, in a way, a good servant, very faithful, attached to Mrs. Anderson, and a guileless purveyor of gossip, which rendered her exceedingly entertaining. She sniffed meaningly now in response to Mrs. Anderson's affirmative with regard to the identity of the recent guests.

"They did not fail to eat enough," said she, presently, packing up the plates and looking at her mistress, who was drying carefully a pink-and-gold cup on a soft towel.

"Yes, they seemed to relish the food," responded Mrs. Anderson.

The maid sniffed again, and her sniff meant the gratification of the cook who sees her work appreciated, and something else — an indulgent scorn. "Well, I guess there is reason enough for them relishing it," said she.

Mrs. Anderson made a soft, interrogatory noise, all that was consistent with her dignity and her sense of honor as a recent hostess towards departed guests.

The maid went on. "They do say," said she, "them as knows, that them Carrolls do not have enough to eat."

Mrs. Anderson made a little exclamation expressive of horror and pity.

"Yes, they do say so," the maid went on, solemnly. "They do say, them that knows, that them Carrolls be owing everybody in Banbridge, and have cheated folks that have trusted in them awful."

"Well, I am sorry if it is so," said Mrs. Anderson, with a sigh, "but of course this young lady who was here tonight and her little brother can't be to blame in any way, Emma."

The maid sniffed with a deprecating disagreement. "Mebbe they be not," said she. She was rather a pretty girl, in her late girlhood, thin and large-boned, with a bright color on her evident cheek-bones, and with small, sparkling, blue eyes. She was extremely neat and trim, moreover, in her personal habits, and tonight was quite gorgeously arrayed in a light silk waist and a nice black skirt. She was expecting her beau to take her to evening prayer-meeting. She was a very religious girl, and had reclaimed her beau, who had had a liking for the gin-mills previous to keeping company with her.

"Of course they are not," said Mrs. Anderson, with some warmth of partisanship, remembering poor little Charlotte's pretty, anxious face and her tiny, soft, clinging hands. She glanced, as she spoke, at the maid's large, red-knuckled fingers with a mental comparison.

The maid was fixed in her own rendering of English verbs, and had told her beau that her mistress did not speak just right, like most old folks.

"Mebbe they be not," she said, with firm doubt. Then she added, "It would not hurt them Carroll ladies, that young lady, nor her mother, nor her aunt, if they was to take hold, and do the housework them own selves, instead of keeping a girl, who they do not never pay."

"Oh, dear! Do you know that?"

"Indeed I do know that! Ed, he told me. He had it straight from them Hungarians who live in the house back of his married sister's. The Carroll girl, she goes there, and she told them, and them told Ed's sister."

"Perhaps she has had some of her wages. You don't mean she has not been paid at all?" Mrs. Anderson said.

"I mean not at all," the maid said, firmly. "That girl that works for them Carrolls has not been paid, not at all."

"Why does she remain there, then?"

"She would have went a long time ago if she not been afraid, lest, if she had went, it would have come about that she would have lost all she was going to lose as well as that which she had lost before," replied the girl, and Mrs. Anderson, being accustomed to her method of expression, understood.

"It is dreadful," she said.

"They say he has about ruined a great many of the people in Banbridge who have trusted them," said the maid, with a sly, keen glance at her mistress. She had heard that Mr. Anderson was one of the losers, and she wondered.

"They have paid my son promptly, I believe," said Mrs. Anderson, although a little reluctantly. She always disliked alluding to the store to her maid, much more so than towards her equals. But that the maid misunderstood. She often told her beau that Mrs. Anderson was not a bit set up nor proud-feeling, if her son *did* have a store. Therefore, tonight she understood humility instead of pride from her mistress's tone, and looked at her admiringly as she daintily polished the delicate pink-and-gold cups.

"I am very glad, indeed, that Mr. Randolph has not lost nothing through them," she replied.

"No, he has not," Mrs. Anderson repeated. "I dare say it is all exaggerated. The young lady who was here tonight seems like a very sweet girl."

Mrs. Anderson said that from a beautiful sense of loyalty and justice, while in her mind's eye she saw her beloved son walking along through the early night with the young lady on his arm, and perhaps falling desperately in love, even at this date, and beginning to think of matrimony with a member of a family about which such tales were told in Banbridge.

But the harm had been done long before she had dreamed of it, and her son had been very much in love with the girl on his arm before he had scarcely known her by sight. Anderson that night felt in a sort of dream. He was for the first time practically alone with Charlotte, for Eddy accompanied them very much after the fashion of an extremely lively little dog. He ran ahead, he lagged behind, and made dashes ahead with wild whoops. He hid behind trees, and sprang out at them when they passed. He was frequently startlingly obvious, but could not be said to actually be with them. He had wondered frankly, before they started, as to why Anderson wished to accompany them at all.

"I don't see why you want to go 'way up to our house when Charlotte has got me," he said. "Ain't you tired?"

Something in Anderson's persistency seemed to strike him as significant, for he walked behind them quite soberly, with his eye upon their backs in a speculative fashion at first; then he seemed to be seized with wild excitement, and began frantic demonstrations to attract Anderson's attention. In reality the boy was jealous, although nobody dreamed of such a thing.

"A man will never notice a feller when a pretty girl's around; and she ain't so very pretty, either," he said to himself. He regarded Anderson as his find, and was naturally indignant with Charlotte. So all the way home he darted and veered about them, in order to divert the man's mind from the girl to the faithful little boy, but with no avail. Once or twice Charlotte spoke reproachfully to him, and that was all. Anderson never spoke a word to him, and his grief and jealousy grew.

Anderson, walking along the shadowy street with Charlotte's little hand in his arm, would have been oblivious to much more startling demonstrations than poor Eddy's. He was profoundly agitated, stirred to the depths, and for that very reason he acquitted himself with more dignity and quiet calm than usual. He held himself with such a tight rein that his soul ached, but he never relaxed his hold. He told himself that it would be monstrous if by a word or gesture, by a tone of the voice, he betrayed anything to this little, innocent, timid, frightened girl on his arm. He never dreamed of the remotest possibility of dreams on her part. The soul beside him, seemingly separated only by thin walls of flesh, was in reality separated by an abyss of the imagination. But every minute his heart seemed to encompass her more and more tenderly, seemed to enfold her, shielding her from itself with its own love. Now and then he looked down at her, and the sight of the little, pale, flower-like face turned towards his with a serious, guileless scrutiny, like a baby's, caused him to fairly tremble with his passion of protection and adoration. They talked very little. Charlotte, if the truth were told, in spite of the tender nursing she had received, was still feeling rather shaken, and she had also a curious sense of timid and excited happiness, which tied her tongue and wove her thoughts even into an incoherent dazzle. When Anderson spoke, it was very coolly, on quite indifferent topics, and Charlotte answered him in her soft, rather unsteady little voice, and then conversation lagged again. It was on Anderson's tongue to question her closely as to her entire recovery from her fright of the afternoon, but he did not even do that, being afraid to trust his voice.

As they drew near the Carroll house, a doubt and perplexity which had been haunting Charlotte, assumed larger proportions, and Anderson himself had a thought also of the complication. Charlotte was wondering if she should ask him in. She was wondering what her mother and aunt would think. She knew what they would do, of course — that is, so far as their reception of the man who had befriended her, and whose mother had befriended her was concerned. They were gentlewomen. And she knew quite certainly about her father. But she wondered as to their real attitude, their mental attitude, and she wondered still more with regard to Anderson. Would he expect to be invited in? In what fashion did he read his own social status in the village. Anderson also was considering, during the last of the way, if he should enter the Carroll house and present his apologies and his mother's for having urged the fugitive members of the family to remain, and he wondered a good deal as to the desirable course for him to adopt, even supposing he were invited. While he had no consciousness whatever of any loss of prestige among people whom he had always known in the village, while, in fact, he never gave it a thought — yet he knew reasonably that outsiders might possibly look at matters differently, that his own unshaken estimate of himself, the estimate which was the same in a grocery-store as in a lawyer's office, might not be accepted. He recognized the fact with amusement rather than indignation, but he recognized it. He wondered how the girl would look at it all, whether she would ask him in to make the acquaintance of her family, and whether, if she did so he should accept.

But Charlotte came to have no doubt whatever that she should ask him. Suddenly a great wave of loyalty towards this new friend came over her, loyalty and great courage.

"Of course I shall ask him, when he has done all he has for me, he and his mother," she decided. "I shall, and I don't care what they think. I don't care. He is a gentleman, as much a gentleman as papa." Charlotte walked more erect, the pressure of her hand on Anderson's arm tightened a little unconsciously. When they reached the Carroll grounds she spoke very sweetly, and not at all hesitatingly.

"You will come in and let my family thank you for your kindness to me, Mr. Anderson," she said.

Anderson smiled down at her, and hesitated. "I do not require any thanks. What I have done was only a pleasure," he said. In his anxiety to control his voice, he overdid the matter, and made it exceedingly cool.

"He means he would have done just the same for any other girl, and it is silly for me to think he needs to be thanked so much for it," thought Charlotte, like a flash. She was full of the hair-splitting fancies of young girlhood in their estimate of a man. Her heart sank, but she repeated, still sweetly, though now a little more formally: "Then please come in and meet my father and mother and aunt. I should like to have you know them, and I am sure it would be a great pleasure to them."

"Thank you, Miss Carroll," Anderson said, slowly. Then, while he hesitated, came suddenly the sound of a shrill, vituperating voice from the house, a voice raised in a solo-like effect, the burden of which seemed both grief and rage, and contumely.

Eddy, who had given one of his dashes ahead, when they reached the grounds, came flying back. "Say," he said, "there's an awful shindy in the house. The dressmaker is pitching into papa for all she is worth, and there are some other folks, but she's goin' it loudest; but they are all going it! Cracky! Hear 'em!"

Indeed, at that second the solo became a chorus. The house seemed all clamorous with scolding voices. The door stood open, and the hall-light streamed out in the hall.

"Marie, she's in there, too," said Eddy, in an odd sort of glee, "and Martin. They are all pitching into papa for their money, but he's enough for them." It became evident why the boy's voice was gleeful. He was pitting his father, with the most filial pride and confidence, against his creditors.

Anderson held out his hand to Charlotte. "Good-night," he said, hastily, "and I hope you will feel no ill effects tomorrow from your fright." Then he was gone before Charlotte could say anything more.

"It's an awful shindy," Eddy said, still in that tone of strange glee, to his sister. To his great amazement, she caught him suddenly by his arm, the hurt one, but he did not flinch.

The girl began to cry. "Oh, Eddy!" she sobbed, pitifully. "Oh, Eddy dear!"

"What are you crying for, Charlotte?" asked Eddy, giving his head a rough caressing duck against hers. "Papa's enough for them; you know that. He ain't a mite scared."

CHAPTER XXIX

Anderson, as he went away that night, had before his eyes Charlotte's little face, the intensity of which had seemed to make it fairly luminous in the dim light, as she had turned it towards him. There was in that face at once unreasoning and childish anger that he was there at all, and in a measure a witness of the distress and disgrace of herself and her family, and a piteous appeal for help — at once a forbidding and a beseeching. For Anderson, naturally, the forbidding seemed most in evidence as an impulse to action. He felt that he must withdraw immediately and save them all the additional mortification that he could. So he hurried away down the road, with the girl's face before his eyes, and the sound of the scolding voice in the house in his ears. The voice carried far. In spite of the wrath in it, it was a sweet, almost a singing, voice, high-pitched but sonorous. It was the voice of little Willy Eddy's German wife, and it came from a pair of strong lungs in a well-developed chest, and was actuated by a strong and indignant spirit. Arthur Carroll, listening to her, was conscious of an absurdly impersonal sentiment of something like admiration. The young woman was really in a manner superb. The occasion was trivial, even ignoble. Carroll felt contemptuous both for her and for himself, and yet she dignified it to a degree. Minna Eddy was built on a large scale; she was both muscular and stout. Her short, blue-woollen skirt, increasing with its fulness her firm hips, disclosed generously her sturdy feet and ankles, which had a certain beauty of fitness as pedestals of support for her great bulk of femininity. She had come out just as she had been about her household tasks, and her cotton blouse, of an incongruous green-figured pattern, was open at the neck, disclosing a meeting of curves in a roseate crease, and one sleeve, being badly worn, revealed a pink boss of elbow. Minna Eddy had a distinctly handsome face, so far as feature and color went. It was a harmonious combination of curves and dimples, all overspread with a deep bloom, as of milk and roses, and her fair hair was magnificent. She had a marvellous growth both for thickness and length, and it was plaited smoothly, covering the back of the head as with a mat. She had come out with a blue handkerchief tied over her head, but she had torn it off, and waved it like a flag of battle in one fat, muscular hand as she lifted on high her voice of musical wrath. She spoke good English, although naturally tinctured by the abuses of the countryside. She had come to America before she could talk at all, and all her training had been in the country. The only trace of her German descent was in the sounds of certain letters, especially *d* and *v*. She said *t* for *d*, and *f* for *v*. Carroll noticed that as he noticed every detail. His senses seemed unnaturally acute, as possibly any animal's may be when at bay, and when the baiting has fairly begun.

A little behind Minna Eddy, and at her right, stood her husband, with a face of utter discomfiture and terror. Now and then he reached out a small, twitching hand and made an ineffectual clutch at her elbow as she talked on. At times he rolled terrified and appealing eyes at Carroll. He seemed even to be begging for his partisanship, although the absurdity of that was obvious.

"Oh, you other man," his eyes seemed to say, "see how terrible a woman can be! What can we do against such might as this?" The room was quite full of people, but Minna Eddy had the platform.

"You, you, you!" she repeated before every paragraph of invective, like a prelude and refrain. "You, you, you!" and she fairly hurled the words at Carroll — "you, you, you! gettin' my man" — with a fierce backward lunge of her bare right elbow towards her husband, who shrank away, and a fierce backward roll of a blue eye — "gettin' my man to take all his money and spend it for no goot. You, you, you! When I haf need of it for shoes and stockings for the children, when I go with my dress in rags. You, you, you!" She went on and on, with a curious variety in the midst of monotony. The stream of her invective flowed on like a river with ever-new ripples. There was a species of fascination in it for the man who was the object of it, and there seemed to be also a compelling quality for the others in the room. There had been no preconcerted movement among Carroll's creditors, but a number of them had that evening descended upon him in a body. In the parlor were the little dressmaker; the druggist; the butcher; Tappan, the milkman; the two stenographers, and Harrison Day, the clerk, who had come on the seven-o'clock train from New York; two men with whom he had dealings in a horse-trade; an old man who had made the garden the previous spring; and another butcher who had driven over from New Sanderson. In the dining-room door stood Marie, the Hungarian maid, and behind her was the coachman. Carroll stood leaning against the corner of the mantel-piece; some of the others were defiantly yet deprecatingly seated, some were standing. Anna Carroll, quite pale, with an odd, fixed expression, stood near her brother. When Charlotte entered the house, she took up a position in the hall, leaning against the wall, near the door. She could hear every word, but she was quite out of sight. She leaned heavily against the wall, for her limbs trembled under her, and she could scarcely stand. Her aunt had looked around as she entered, and a question as to where she had been had shaped itself on her lips: then her look of inquiry and relief had died away in her expression of bitter concentration upon the matter in hand. She had been alarmed about Charlotte, as they had all been. Mrs. Carroll had called softly down the stairs to know if Charlotte had come, and the girl had answered, "Yes, Amy dear."

"Where have you been, dear?" asked the soft voice, from an indistinct mass of floating white at the head of the stairs.

"I'll tell you by-and-by, Amy dear."

"I was alarmed about you," said the voice, "it was so late; about you and Eddy."

"He has come, too."

"Yes, I heard him." Then the voice added, quite distinctly petulant, "I have a headache, but it is so noisy I cannot get to sleep." Then there was a rustle of retreat, and Charlotte leaned against the wall, listening to the hushed turmoil surmounted by that voice of accusation in the parlor. Eddy stood full in the doorway, in a boyish, swaggering attitude, his hands on his hips, and bent slightly, with sharp eyes of intense enjoyment on Minna Eddy. Suddenly, Carroll turned and caught sight of him, and as if perforce the boy's eyes turned to meet his father's. Carroll did not speak, but he raised his hand and pointed to the hall with an upward motion for the stairs, and Eddy went, with a faint whimper of remonstrance. The scolding woman saw the little, retreating figure, and directly the torrent of her vituperation was turned into a new course.

"You, you, you!" she proclaimed; "dressin' your boy up in fine clothes, while mine children have went in rags since you have came to Banbridge! You, you, you! gettin' all my man's money, and dressin' up your boy in clothes that I haf paid for! You, you, you!"

But Minna Eddy had unwittingly furnished the right key-note for a whole chorus. Madame Griggs, who had been rocking jerkily in a small, red-plush chair which squeaked faintly, sprang up, and left it still rocking and squeaking.

"Yes," said she, "yes, that is so. Look at the way the whole family dress, at other people's expense!"

She was hysterical still, yet she had not lost her sense of the gentility of self-restraint. That would come later. Her face worked convulsively, red spots were on her thin cheeks, but there was still an ingratiating, somewhat servile, tone in her voice, and she looked scornfully at Minna Eddy. Then J. Rosenstein, who kept the principal dry-goods store in Banbridge, bore his testimony. His grievances were small, but none the less vital. His business dealings with the Carrolls had been limited to sundry spools of thread and kitchen towellings and buttons, but they were as lead in his estimate of wrong, although he had a grave, introspective expression, out of proportion to the seeming triviality of the matter in his mind. He held in one long hand a slip of paper, and eyed Carroll with dignified accusation.

"This is the fifth bill I have made out," he remarked, and he raised his voice to the pitch of his brethren of the Bowery when they hawk in the street. "The fifth bill I have made out, and it is only for one dollar and fifty-three cents, and I am poor."

His intellectual Semitic face took on an ignoble expression of one who squeezes justice to petty ends for his own deserts. His whine penetrated the rising chorus of the other voices, even of the butcher, who was a countryman of his own, and who said something with dolorous fervor about the bill for meat which had been running for six weeks, and not a dollar paid. He was of a more common sort, and rendered a trifle indifferent by a recent visit to a beer-saloon. He was also somewhat stupefied by an excess of flesh, as to the true exigencies of life in general. After he had spoken he coughed wheezily, settled his swelling bulk more comfortably in the red-velvet chair, and planted his wide-apart, elephantine legs more firmly on the floor, while he mentally appraised the Oriental rug beneath his feet, with a view to the possibility of his taking that in lieu of cash, and making a profitable bargain for its ultimate disposal with a cousin in trade in New York. Looking up, he caught Rosenstein's eyes just turning from a regard of the same rug, and the two men's thoughts met with a mental clash. Then the New Sanderson butcher, who was a great, handsome, blond man with a foam of yellow beard, German, but not Jew, strolled silently over to them, and with sharp eyes on the rug, conferred with the other two in low, eager whispers. From that time they paid little attention to what was going on around them. They talked, they gesticulated, they felt of the rug.

Madame Griggs, settling her skirts genteelly, spoke again. "I guess my bill has been running fully as long as anybody's here," she said, in her small, shrill voice. She eyed the two stenographers as she spoke, with jealous suspicion. There was a certain smartness about their attire, and she suspected them of being City dress-makers. She also suspected the strange young man with them of being a City lawyer, whom they had brought with them to urge their claims. Madame Stella Griggs had a ready imagination. The two stenographers had not spoken at all. From time to time the prettier wept, softly, in her lace-edged handkerchief; the other looked pale and nervous. Whenever she looked at Carroll her mouth quivered. The young man sat still and winked furiously. He had discovered Carroll's address and informed the girls, and they had planned this descent upon their employer. Now they were there, they were frightened and intimidated and distressed. They were a gentle lot, of the sort that are born to be led. Their resentment and sense of injustice overwhelmed them with grief, rather than a desire for retaliation. They were in sore straits for their money, yet all would have walked again into the snare, and they regarded Carroll with the same awed admiration as of old. No one but felt commiseration for him, and trust in his ultimate payment of their wages. They regarded the other creditors with a sort of mild contempt. They felt themselves of another kind, especially from the Germans and Jews. When Willy Eddy's wife had declaimed, one stenographer had whispered to the other, "How vulgar!" and the other had responded with a nod and curl of a lip of scorn. They met Madame Griggs's hostile regard with icy stares. The less pretty girl said to the young man that she thought it was mean for a dressmaker to come there and hound folks like that, and he nodded, winking disapprovingly at poor Madame Griggs, who was just then cherishing the wild idea of consulting him for herself in his supposed capacity of a lawyer. The stenographer, turning from her remark to the clerk, met the laughing but impertinent gaze of one of the horse-trading men, and she turned her back upon him with an emphasis that provoked a chuckle from his companion.

"Got it in the shoulder then, Bill," he remarked, quite audibly, and the other reddened and grinned foolishly. They were rough-looking men with a certain swagger of smartness. They regarded Carroll with a swearing emphasis, yet with a measure of reluctantly compelled admiration.

"I'll be damned if he ain't the first that ever got the better of Jim Dickerson," one had said to the other, as they had driven up to the house that evening. "I'll be —— damned if I see now how he got the better of me," the other rejoined, with a bewildered expression. As he spoke his mind revolved in the devious mesh of trap which he had set for Carroll, and realized the clean cutting of it by Carroll by the ruthless method of self-interest. Neither man had spoken besides a defiant response to Carroll's polite "Good-evening," when they had entered. They sat and watched and listened. Occasionally one raised a hand, and an enormous diamond glowed with a red light like a ruby. In the four-in-hand tie of the other a scarf-pin in the shape of a horse's head with diamond eyes caught the light with infinitesimal sparks of fire. Above it his clean-shaven, keen, blue-eyed face kept watch, sharply ready to strike anger as the diamonds struck light, and yet with a certain amusement. He had shown his teeth in a smile when Willy Eddy's wife pronounced her tirade. He did so again when she reopened, having regained her wind. When she spoke this time, she glared at Anna Carroll with a dazzling look of spite.

"There ain't no red silk dresses for me to rig out in," said she, and she pointed straight at Anna's silken skirts. "No, there ain't, and there won't be, so long as my man's money goes to pay for *hers*." She said "hers" with a harder emphasis than if she said "yours."

Anna never returned her vicious look, she never moved a muscle of her handsome face, nor changed color. She continued to stand beside her brother, with a curious expression of wide partisanship, and of regard for these people as objects of offence as a whole, rather than as individuals.

"Folks can pretend to be deaf if they want to," said Minna Eddy, "but they hear, an' they'll hear more."

"That was fifteen dollars beside the findings, and they amounted to twelve dollars and sixty-three cents more," said Madame Griggs, and this time she addressed the young man whom she took to be a lawyer. She met his nervous winks with a piteous smile of appealing confidence. She wondered if possibly he might not be willing to undertake her cause in connection with the other supposed dressmakers' at a reduced rate. Nobody paid the slightest attention when she spoke, Anna Carroll least of all.

Suddenly, Henry Lee tiptoed into the room. He came in smiling and nervous. When he saw the assembled company he started, and gave an inquiring glance at Carroll, who regarded him in an absent-minded fashion, as if he hardly comprehended the fact of his entrance. It was the glance of a man whose mind is too crowded to admit of more. But Lee went close to him, bowing low to Anna, and extending his hand with urbanity, flustered, it is true, yet still with urbanity.

"Good-evening, captain," he said, and even then, in sore distress of mind as he was, he looked about at the company for admiration for this proof of his intimacy with such a man.

"Good-evening," Carroll said, mechanically, and he shook hands. Anna Carroll also said "Good-evening," and smiled automatically.

"A fine evening," said Lee, but he got no rejoinder to that. He looked at the company, and his small, smug, fatuous face, which was somewhat pale and haggard, frowned with astonishment. Again he looked for information into Carroll's unanswering face. He looked at an empty chair near him; then he looked at Carroll and his sister standing, and did not seat himself. He also leaned against the mantel on the other corner from Carroll, and endeavored to assume an unconcerned air, as if it were quite the usual thing for him to drop into the house and encounter such a non-descript company. He looked across at the druggist and postmaster, and bowed with flourishing politeness. He said to Carroll, endeavoring to make his voice so unobtrusive that it would be unheard by the company, but with the non-success usual to a nervous and self-conscious man, that he had a word to say to him later on when he was at liberty, some matter of business which he wished to talk over with him.

"Very well," Carroll replied. Then Lee followed up his remark, which had in a measure reassured him.

"Got a cigar handy, captain?" said he. "I came off without one in my pocket."

Carroll took out his cigar-case and extended it to Lee, who took a cigar, bit the end off, and scratched a match. Carroll handed the case mechanically to the postmaster and Drake, who were near. They refused, and he took one himself, as if he did not realize what he was doing, and lit it, his calm, impassively smiling face never changing. He might have been lighting a bomb instead of a cigar, for all the actual realization of the action which he had. He accepted a light from Lee, who had lit his first with trembling haste. At the first puff which he gave, at the first evidence of the fragrant aroma in the room, one turbulent spirit, which had hitherto remained under restraint, burst bounds and overwhelmed all besides. Even Minna Eddy, who was fast warming to a new outburst, even Madame Griggs, who had both hands pressed to her skinny throat because of a lump of emotion there, and whose sunken temples were beating to the sight under the shade of her protuberant frizzes, looked in a hush of wonder and alarm at this furious champion of his own wrongs. Even the two butchers and the dry-goods merchant looked away from the glowing Oriental web upon which they stood. The weeping stenographer sat with her damp little wad of lace-edged handkerchief in her hand and stared at him with her reddened eyes; the other held her flaccid purse, and looked at the speaker. Now and then she nudged violently the friend, who did not seem to notice it.

Tappan, the milkman, arose to his feet. He had been sitting with a stiff sprawl in the corner of a small divan. He arose when the fragrance of that Havana cigar smote his nostrils like the odor of battle. He was in great boots stained with the red shale, for the roads outside Banbridge were heavy from a recent rain. He was collarless, his greasy coat hung loosely over his dingy flannel shirt. He was unshaven, and his face was at once grim and sardonic, bitter and raging. It was the face of an impotent revolutionist, who cursed his impotence, his lack of weapons, his wrong environments for his fierce spirit. He belonged in a country at war. He had the misfortune to be in a country at peace. He belonged in a field of labor wherein weapons and armed men, sown by the need of justice, sprang from the soil. He was in a bucolic pasture, with no appeal. He was a striker with nothing save fate against which to strike. He raged behind prison-bars of circumstance. Now, for once, was an enemy for his onslaught, although even here he was restricted. He was held in check by his ignoble need. He feared lest, in smiting with all the force at his command, the blow recoil upon himself. He feared lest he lose all where he might lose only part. But when he began to speak his caution left him. There was real fire in the grim, unshaven man; the honest fire of resentment against wrong, the spirit of self-defence against odds. He was big enough to disregard self-interest in his defence, and he was impressive. He sniffed as a preliminary to his speech, and there was in that sniff fury, sarcasm, and malignancy. Then he opened his mouth, and before the words came a laugh or the travesty of one. There was something menacing in his laugh. Then he spoke.

"Cigar!" he said. "Have a cigar? Will you have a cigar? Oh yes, a cigar." His voice was murderously low and soft. He even lisped slightly. "A cigar," he repeated. "A cigar. Oh, Lord! If men like me git a hand of chewing-tobacco once a month, they think they are damned lucky. Cigar, Lord!" Then the soft was out of his voice. He cut his words short, or rather he seemed to hammer them down into the consciousness of his auditors. He turned upon the others. "Want to know how that good-for-nothin' liar an' thief gits them cigars?" he shouted. "Want to know? Well, I'll tell you. I give 'em to him, an' you did. How many of you can smoke cigars like them, hey? Smell 'em. Ten or fifteen cents apiece; mebbe more. We give 'em to him. Yes, sir, that's jest what we did. He took the money he owed us for milk and meat and dress-makin' an' other things to buy them cigars. You got up early an' worked late to pay for 'em; he didn't. I got up at half-past three o'clock in the mornin' — half-past three in the winter, when he was asleep in his bed, damn him. The time will come when he won't sleep more than some other folks. I got up at half-past three o'clock, and I snatched a mouthful of breakfast, fried cakes and merlasses, that he'd 'a' turned up his nose at. He had beefsteak an' eggs at our expense, he did, an' I had a cup of damned weak coffee, cause I was too honest or too big a fool, whichever you call it, to buy any coffee I couldn't pay for. He'd 'a' turned up his nose at sech coffee. An' I went without sugar in it, an' I went without milk, so's to give it to him, so's he could git cigars. And as for cream, cream, cream! Lord! Couldn't git enough cream to give him. He was always yellin' for cream. Cream! My wife an' me would no more of thought of our puttin' cream in our coffee than we'd thought of putting in five-dollar gold pieces to sweeten it. No, we saved the cream for him. My wife don't look so young and fat as his wife. His wife has been fed on our cream." Tappan looked hard at Anna Carroll, whom he evidently took for Carroll's wife. He took note of her dress. "My wife never had a silk gown," said he. "Lord! I guess she didn't! She had to git up as early as I did, an' wash milk-pans, so we could give milk to that man, an' he could save money on us to git his wife a silk gown. Lord! Jest look —"

Then Madame Griggs spoke, her small, deprecatory snarl raised almost to hysterical pitch. She was catching the infection of this bigger resentment and sense of outraged justice.

"He didn't save money to git his wife that silk gown with your milk money," said she, "for I made that gown, an' I got the material, an' I ain't been paid a cent. That was one of the gowns I made when Ina was married. That silk cost a dollar and a quarter a yard. I could have got it at ninety-eight cents at a bargain, but that wa'n't good enough for her. He didn't take your milk money for that. He didn't take any money to pay anybody for anything he could run in debt for, I can tell you that. He must have paid somebody that wouldn't wait an' wouldn't be cheated."

"Must have been dealin' with a trust, then," said one of the horsemen, with a loud laugh. "Guess he's been cheatin' 'most everything else."

"And that lady ain't his wife, neither," said Madame Griggs to Tappan. "That's his sister. I made another gown for his wife, a lighter shade, an' I ain't been paid for that, neither." Suddenly she burst into a hysterical wail. "Oh, dear!" she sobbed. "Oh, dear! Here I've worked early an' late. Here I've got up in the mornin' before light an' worked till most dawn, an' me none too strong, never was, and always havin' to scratch for myself, a poor, lone woman, an' here I am in debt, an' they sendin' out for the money; an' I've worked so hard to build up my business, an' tried to make things nice, an' please, an' here I've got to fail. Oh, dear!" Suddenly she made a weak rush across the room, her silk petticoat giving out a papery rustle, her frizzes vibrating like wire under her hat, crested with ostrich plumes. She danced up to Carroll and looked at him with indescribable piteousness of accusation. "Why couldn't you, if you had to cheat, cheat a man an' not a woman like me?" she demanded, in her high-pitched tremolo.

Carroll took his cigar from his mouth and looked at her. His face was quite pale and rigid. Even Tappan stopped, watching the two. Madame Griggs held up, with almost a sublimity of accusation, her tiny, nervous, veinous hands. The fingers were long and the knuckles were slightly enlarged with strenuous pullings of needles and handling of scissors; the forefinger was calloused. "Look at my hands," said she. "See how thin they be. I've worked them 'most to the bone for your folks. I took a lot of pride in havin' your daughter look nice when she was married. If I was a man an' goin' to steal, I'd steal from somebody besides a woman with no more strength than I have, all alone in the world, and that's been knocked hard ever since she can remember." Then she brought a stiffly starched little handkerchief from the folds of a small purse, and she wept with a low, querulous wail like a baby. Standing before Carroll, "Oh, dear! Oh, dear! Oh — dear!" she wailed.

Carroll laid a hand on her shaking shoulder. It felt to him like a vibrating bone, so meagre it was. He bent over her and said something that the others did not hear, but her wild rejoinder gave them the key. She was fairly desperate; all her obsequiousness had disappeared. She was burning with her wrongs; she even took a certain pleasure in letting herself loose. She shook her shoulder free from his touch. She turned on him, her tearful, convulsed face uncovered, her frizzes tossing, as bold and unrestrained in her wrath as was Minna Eddy, who came forward to her side as she spoke.

"You needn't come wheedlin' around me," she cried. "I don't believe a word of it, not a word. I'll believe it when I see the color of your cash. You're dreadful soft-spoken, an' so is your wife an' your sister an' your daughters. Dreadful soft-spoken! Plenty of soft soap runnin' all over every time you open your mouth. I don't want soft soap. Soft soap won't buy me bread an' butter, nor pay my debts. Folks won't take any soft soap from me instead of money. They want dollars an' cents, an' that's what I want every time, dollars an' cents, an' not soft soap. Yes, it's dollars an' — cents — and not so-ft soa-p." Suddenly the dress-maker, borne high on a wave of hysteria, disclosing the innate coarseness which underlay all her veneer of harmless gentility and fine manners, raised a loud, shrill laugh, ending in a multitude of reverberations like a bell. There was about this unnatural metallic laughter something fairly blood-curdling in its disclosure of overstrained emotion. She laughed and laughed, while the room was silent except for that, and every eye was fixed upon her. Poor, little Estella Griggs, of all that accusing company of Arthur Carroll's petty creditors, had the floor. She laughed and laughed. She threw back her head. Her plumed hat was tilted rakishly one side; her frizzes tossed high above her forehead, revealing the meagre temples; her skinny throat seemed to elongate above her ribboned collar; her thin cheeks, folded into a multitude of lines by her distorting mirth, glowed with a hard red; her eyes gleamed with a glassy brilliance. Then, suddenly, that long, skinny throat seemed to swell visibly. She choked and gurgled, then came a wild burst of sobbing. Hysteria had reached its second stage. It was frightful.

"Good God!" said one of the horsemen, under his breath.

"That's so," said the other. "Let's git out of this."

They elbowed their way out of the room. "See you again," one of them said, curtly, to Carroll as he passed.

"See you tomorrow about that little affair of ours, an' by G—, you've got to pony up, you can take your oath on that, an' don't you forget it," whispered the other in Carroll's ear, with a fierce emphasis, and yet he half grinned with a masculine sympathy in this ultra crisis.

"It's gitting too thick," said the other horseman. "See you tomorrow, and, by G—, you've got to do somethin' or there'll be trouble."

Carroll nodded. He was ashy white. He had strong nerves, but he was delicately organized, man though he was, and with unusual self-control. He felt now a set of sensations verging on those displayed by the laughing, sobbing woman before him. He was conscious of an insane desire to join in that laugh, in those sobbing shrieks. His throat became constricted, his hands became as ice. The tragic absurdity of the situation filled him at once with a monstrous mirth and grief. The antitheses of emotion struggled together within him. He looked at the little, frantic creature before him, and opened his mouth to speak, but he said nothing. Anna Carroll caught his elbow.

"Come away, Arthur," she whispered.

She was trembling herself, but she had been braced to something of this kind from being a woman herself, and was not so intimidated. Carroll strove to speak again. Minna Eddy suddenly joined in her torrent of vituperation with the dress-maker's. She caught up the soft-soap idea with a peal of laughter more sustained than that of Madame Griggs, for she had a better poise of mentality, and her wrath was untempered with the grief and self-pity of a small, helpless woman who was fitted by nature for petting rather than for warfare.

"Soft soap!" shouted Minna Eddy, while her small husband vainly clutched at her petticoats. "Soft soap! Lord! I makes my own soft soap. I has plenty to clean with. I don't want no soft soap. I want money." She laughed loud and long, a ringing, mocking peal. Madame Griggs's loud sobbing united with it. The dissonance of unnatural mirth and grief was ghastly.

"Good God! Hear them!" whispered Sigsbee Ray to the druggist.

"I'd rather owe fifty men than one woman," the druggist whispered back.

Lee edged nearer the women and strove to speak. He had a purpose.

Carroll, gazing at the women in a fascinated way, again opened his mouth in vain, and again Anna dragged backward at his arm.

"For Heaven's sake, Arthur, come out of this," she whispered, and he yielded for the second. He let himself be impelled to the door, then suddenly he recovered himself and stepped forward with an accession of dignity and authority which carried weight even in the face of hysterical unreason. He raised his hand and spoke, and there was a hush. Madame Griggs and Minna Eddy remained quiet, like petrified furies, regarding the man's pale face of assertive will.

"I beg you to be quiet a moment and listen to me," he said. "I can do nothing for any of you tonight, and, what is more, I will not do anything tonight. It is impossible for me to deal with you in such an unexpected fashion as this, in such numbers. I have not gone into bankruptcy; no meeting of my creditors had been called. I have and you have no legal representative here. Now I am going, and I advise you all to do likewise. I beg you to excuse me. I know you all, I know the amount of my indebtedness to you all, and I promise you all, if I live, the very last dollar I owe you shall be paid. You must, however, give me a little time, or nobody will get anything. I will communicate with you all later on. Nobody shall lose anything, I say. Now you must excuse me."

"Look at him; he's sick," whispered the pretty stenographer to the other, whose soft, little sob of response alone broke the hush as Carroll went out with his sister at his side. Their shadows moved across the room as they ascended the stairs in the hall. The creditors, left alone, regarded one another in a hesitating fashion. The two women, Minna Eddy and Estella Griggs, remained quiet. Presently the two butchers and the dry-goods merchant, standing about the Oriental rug, quite a fine Bokhara, resumed their whispered colloquy regarding it, then they went out. Lee began talking to the druggist and the postmaster, with Willie Eddy at his elbow listening eagerly.

"Carroll's sick," said Lee, with a curious effect of partisanship towards himself, as well as Carroll. "He's sick, and it is too bad. His nerves are a wreck."

"Well, our nerves are becoming wrecks," the postmaster rejoined, dryly.

"That's so," said the druggist, with a worried look. "I don't know but I'll have to mortgage my stock. I've lost more than I can afford in that United Fuel."

"I don't like to own up I've been bit," said the postmaster, "but when it comes to being sick, and nerves being wrecks, there are others with full as much reason as Carroll."

"He'll pay up every cent," said Lee, eagerly.

"Maybe he will pay his debts," said the postmaster. "I am not going to say he won't. I suppose he means to. But when it comes to making things good, when he has simply led you by the nose into disastrous speculations, I don't know. Bigger men than Arthur Carroll don't do it."

"That's so," said Drew. "It's one thing to pay your butcher's bill in the long run, and be above stealing goods off the counter, but a man can cheat his fellow-men in a stock trade and think pretty well of himself, and other folks think well of him."

"That's so," said Sigsbee Ray.

"I haven't any doubt that he will arrange that," said Lee. "And, for that matter, the United Fuel may look up yet. I had a prospectus —"

"Prospectus be damned!" said the postmaster. He seldom used an oath, and his tongue made a vicious lurch over it.

The druggist gave an enormous sigh. "Well, it won't come up tonight, and I've left my little boy alone in the store," said he. "I've got to be going."

"So have I," said the postmaster. "My wife is alone."

"My wife always stands up for Carroll," said Lee, trotting nervously after the other men as they left the room. "Says she guesses he will end up by paying his bills as well as other men that are blaming him."

"Hope to God he will," said the postmaster.

The clerk and the two stenographers from Carroll's office had been having their heads together over a time-table. They also slipped out after the three men. The elder one still sniffed softly in her handkerchief.

The young man looked around at the stair up which Carroll had disappeared, and winked as he went out. There were left Carroll's coachman, the Hungarian girl, Madame Estella Griggs, Willy Eddy, and his wife. The coachman heard a noise of pounding in the stable and ran out. Marie remained in the doorway looking at the others with her piteous red eyes; Minna Eddy advanced towards her.

"They owe you your wages, don't they?" said she, with no sympathy, but rather a menace.

Little Marie shrank back. "Yis," said she, pursing her lips.

"You're a fool!" said Minna Eddy.

Marie smiled feebly at her.

Minna Eddy stood glaring around the room. Her husband was at her elbow, watching her anxiously.

"Come home now, Minna," he pleaded.

But she stamped her foot suddenly. "I ain't goin' to stand it!" she declared. "I'm goin' to take what I can get, I be." Her eyes rested first upon one thing, then another, then she looked hard at the Oriental rug, which the three tradesmen had discussed. Then she swooped upon it and began gathering it up from the floor.

"Oh, Minna! Oh, Minna!" gasped little Willy Eddy.

"You lemme be," she said, fiercely. "I see'd them men lookin' at this. It ain't handsome, but it's worth good money. I heard something they said. I ain't goin' to lose all that money. I'm goin' to take what I can git, I be."

"Minna, you —"

"Lemme be."

"It ain't accordin' to law, Minna."

"What do you s'pose I care about the law?" She turned to Estella Griggs, who was watching her eagerly, with a gathering light of fierce greed in her eyes. "If you take my advice you'll help yourself to something while you have the chance," said she.

"Oh, Minna, it's stealin'! You'll be liable —"

"Liable to nothin'. Stealin'! If folks don't steal no more 'n I do, I'll risk 'em. I'm a-takin' my lawful pay, I be. If you take my advice, you'll take somethin', too."

Minna Eddy moved from the room with the rug gathered up in a roll in her arms, but Marie had been gradually recovering herself. Now she came forward.

"You must not take that; that iss not your rug," said she. "You must not take that."

"Git out," said Minna Eddy. She thrust at the Hungarian with her rug-laden arms, but the little peasant was as strong as she. Marie caught hold of the rug and pulled; Minna also pulled.

"You lemme go," said Minna, with a vicious voice, but lowered, for obvious reason.

"You must not take that," said Marie. She was, however, rather fainter-hearted than the other woman.

Minna suddenly got the mastery. The Hungarian almost tumbled backward. Minna, with the rug, was out of the room, her trembling, almost whimpering husband at her heels. Madame Griggs looked at Marie. Her distorted face was at once greedy, anguished, and cunning. She began to gasp softly.

"Oh! Oh!" said she. "Oh!"

Marie regarded her in wondering agitation.

"Water! water! quick! Oh, get some water!" moaned Madame Griggs. "I am faint! Water!" She sank into a chair, her head fell back. She rolled her eyes at the terrified girl; she gasped feebly between her parted lips.

Marie ran. Then up rose Madame Estella Griggs. She swept the tea-table of its little Dresden service and some small, silver spoons. She gathered them up in a little, lace-trimmed table-cover, and she fled with that booty and a sofa-pillow which she caught from the divan on her way out.

When Marie returned she stood gaping with the glass of water. She was not over-shrewd, but she took in at once the situation. She understood that the second lady had fled like the first, with the teacups, the spoons, the table-cover, and the sofa-pillow. She stood looking desolately around the room, and her simple heart tasted its own bitterness.

CHAPTER XXX

Charlotte had followed her father and aunt up-stairs that night, starting up softly like a shadow from her place in the hall. She went silently behind them until they reached the open door of Anna's room; then her father turned and saw her.

"You here, Charlotte?" he said.

"Yes, papa," replied Charlotte, turning a pitiful but altogether stanch little face up to his.

He put his arm around her, drew her head against his shoulder, tipped up her face, and kissed her. "Go to bed now, darling," he whispered.

"Papa, I can't; I —"

"There is nothing you can do, sweetheart; there is nothing for you to worry about. Papa will take care of you always, whatever happens. Go to bed now, and go to sleep, honey."

"But, papa, I can't sleep. Let me stay and —"

"No, dear. There is nothing you can do. It will only worry me to have you stay. Go to bed, and put all this out of your mind. It will all come right in the end."

Carroll kissed Charlotte again, and put her gently from him, and she disappeared in her own room with a suppressed sob.

"I am glad Ina is out of the way," Anna said, but with no bitterness.

"So am I," Carroll agreed, simply.

"I wish Charlotte had as good a man to look out for her," said Anna.

Carroll straightened himself with quick pride. "I shall look out for her," he said. "You need not think I am quite out of the running yet, when it comes to looking out for my own flesh and blood."

"No, of course you are not, Arthur. I did not mean to imply any such thing," Anna rejoined, hastily. "I was only — Come into my room. Amy is fast asleep by this time, and if she is not she has a headache, and you might as well try to consult with an infant in arms as Amy with a headache. And something has to be done."

"Yes, you are right, Anna," Carroll replied, with a heavy sigh.

"Those people will all go when they get tired of waiting. There is no use in our bothering with them any more tonight. Come in."

Anna led the way into her room, and closed the door. A lamp burned dimly on the dresser amid a confusion of laces and ribbons. The whole room looked in a soft foam of dainty disorder. Anna did not turn the light up. She stood looking at her brother in the half-light, and her face was at once angry and tender.

"Well?" said she, with a sigh of desperate inquiry.

"Well?" rejoined Carroll.

"What next?"

"The Lord knows!"

"Something has to be done. We are up against a dead wall again. And for some reason it strikes me as a deader wall than ever before."

Carroll nodded.

"We cannot stay in Banbridge any longer?" Anna said, interrogatively.

"We may have to," Carroll replied, curtly.

"You mean?"

"There may be a little difficulty about getting out. We could not leave the State, anyhow, and —"

"And what? We can go somewhere else in the State, I suppose. I am not particularly in love with this section of the union, but it all makes little difference after one reaches a certain point."

"Poor old girl!" said Carroll.

Anna looked at him, and her eyes suffused and her mouth quivered. Then she smiled her usual smile of mocking courage, even bravado. "Oh, well," said she, "I have faced the situation and chewed my cud of experience for a good many years now, and I am used to it. I may even end up by tasting the sweet in the bitter."

"You had as hard an experience in another line as I had. I don't know but it was harder."

"No harder, I reckon," Anna replied, almost indifferently. "It was the same thing — the doll stuffed with sawdust, and all that; you with a friend, and I with a lover. Well, it is all over now."

"It isn't; that is the worst of it," Carroll said, gloomily.

"I don't see why."

"A sequence is never over. There is even all eternity for it."

"Well, the first of the sequence is over, anyhow. All we have to consider is the succeeding stages."

"That is about enough."

Anna laughed. "I agree with you there, dear. Well, I suppose the stage of the sequence for immediate consideration is the feasibility of emerging into the next stage. You think it is likely to be more difficult for the wandering tribe of Carroll to make their exodus with grace and dignity than usual?"

"It rather looks that way now."

"I suppose that promoting business, that business transacted in the New York office, got you into rather hotter waters than usual."

Carroll nodded.

"There *was* an office, I suppose."

Carroll nodded again, laughing a little. Anna laughed too. "One never knows," said she. "I suppose that was a delegation from the office, tonight, the two pretty girls and the winking young man."

"Yes," said Carroll.

Anna had flung herself into an easy-chair beside him. Carroll remained standing. She leaned her head back and crossed her hands behind her neck in a way she had. She was a thing of lithe grace in her soft red silk. The dim light obliterated all the worn lines in her face. Carroll regarded her even in the midst of the distressful stress of affairs with a look of admiration. It was an absent-minded regard, very much as a mourner might notice a stained-glass window in a church while a funeral was in progress. It was the side-light of grace on affliction involuntarily comprehended, from long training, by the exterior faculties. Carroll even said, half perfunctorily:

"You look well tonight. That red gown suits you, honey."

"The gown that that poor little beggar of a dress-maker is not paid for," said Anna.

Carroll frowned. "I did not have enough for that," he said. "It was impossible. I paid the other bills."

"All dressmakers have to be cheated," said Anna. "I never knew one that wasn't. I may as well reap the benefit of a universal law of cause and result, as some other woman." Her voice rang hard, but she looked up affectionately at her brother. Suddenly she reached out her hand, caught his, and kissed it. "There is one thing we Carrolls pay in full, and never run in debt for, and that is our affection for and belief in one another," said she. "We have our hearts full of one coin, anyway."

"I suppose the world at large would prefer our pockets full of the coin of the realm," answered Carroll, but he looked fondly down at his sister.

"I suppose so. If I had not worn this dress, I should send it back to that dressmaker."

"But you have worn it."

"Oh yes. Of course it is out of the question now. It is very pretty. Well, Arthur, if we go back far enough we are not responsible for this dress. We are responsible for none of the disasters which follow in our wake. That man down in Kentucky precipitated the whole thing. Arthur, you do look like a fiend whenever I mention that man!"

"I feel like one," Carroll replied, coolly.

"Well, that man was directly responsible for the whole wreck — the general wreck, I mean. My own wreck is an individual matter, and, after all, I never fairly lowered my sails for that especial gale. I never will own to it."

"You were a brave girl, Anna."

"But the other wreck, the whole wreck, that man of yours is responsible for. And we were not half a bad lot, Arthur."

"Maybe not; but when the ship breaks up, it does not make so much difference what the timbers were, nor how she was built."

"I suppose you are right. Well, what is to be done with the old masts and sails and things?"

"I know what is to be done with a part of it."

"What part of it?"

"Well, to depart from similes, the female contingency."

"The female contingency?"

"Yes, and the juvenile. You and Amy and Charlotte and Eddy."

"What do you mean, Arthur?"

"You are going down to Kentucky to the old place, to spend the winter with Aunt Catherine."

"Aunt Catherine wrote you?"

"Yes."

"When?"

"I got the letter day before yesterday."

"She invited us?"

"Yes, honey."

"Not you?"

"There was no reason why she should invite me."

"Aunt Catherine never had any feeling for you."

"Perhaps she has had as much as I deserve. You know I have, to put it frankly, rather broken the record of an honorable family for —"

"For what?"

"For honor, dear."

Then Anna broke out, passionately. "I don't care! I don't care!" she cried. "I don't care what she thinks; I don't care what anybody thinks! I don't care what you do or don't do, you are the best man that ever lived, Arthur." She began to weep suddenly, feeling blindly for her handkerchief.

Carroll pulled her head against his shoulder. "Dear," he whispered, don't; you must not, darling, you are worn out. You are not well."

"Arthur, are you sure — are you sure that you have not rendered yourself liable? Arthur, are you sure that they cannot arrest you for anything you have done this time?"

"Quite sure, Anna."

"You have looked out for that?"

"Yes."

"They can't arrest you?"

"No. Anna, you are nervous."

"Martin was impudent yesterday, when you were out, about his pay. He talked about going to a lawyer."

Carroll made an impatient movement. "If he does not stop coming to you about it —"

"He is afraid of you. Then Maria came and cried. She says she has lost her lover, because she did not have decent clothes to wear."

"Anna, they shall not trouble you again. Don't, dear. Why, I never knew you to fret so before!"

"I never did. I never minded it all so much before. I think I am ill. There is a dull pain all the time in the back of my neck, and I do not sleep at all well. Then my mental attitude seems suddenly to have changed. I was capable of defiance always, of seeing the humor in the situation, even if it was such an oft-repeated joke, and such a mighty poor one; but now, even if I start with a glimpse of the funny side of it, suddenly I collapse, and all at once I am beaten."

Carroll stroked her graceful, dark head. "There is nothing for it but you must go, honey."

"Arthur, I will not. It may be better for the others, but as for me, I will not."

"Yes, you will, Anna, honey."

"Arthur Carroll!"

"You must, dear. Frankly, Anna, you know how I shall feel about parting with you all, but it will be a load off my mind. If a man is not able to care for his own, it is better for him and for them that they should go where they will be cared for."

"You need not speak in that way, Arthur. You have done all you could. All this would never have been if it had not been for us, and your wanting us to have everything. We have been a helpless lot. None of us have ever blamed you or complained, not even Amy, baby as she is."

"I know it, dear, but it is better for you all to go."

"You have done all you could, always," Anna repeated, in a curious, sullen fashion.

"Well, we will leave that. If Aunt Catherine takes you all this winter, it will go hard if I do not pay her in some way later on; but the point is now, you must all go."

Anna shook her head obstinately.

Carroll bent down and kissed her. "Good-night, dear," he said. "Try to sleep."

"I wonder if those people are all gone."

"Yes, I think so. I heard Marie lock the door. Good-night."

Anna rose and threw her arms around her brother's neck. "Whatever happens, you have got your old sister left," she said, with a soft sob.

"Nobody is going to attach her for my debts," Carroll said, laughing, but stroking her head fondly.

"No, she is not an available asset. I never will go, Arthur. The others may do as they think best. I will not go."

"Not tonight, Anna, honey," Carroll said, as he went out of the room.

Anna Carroll, left alone, rose languidly, unfastened her red silk gown, and let it fall in a rustling circle around her. She let down her soft, misty lengths of hair, in which was a slight shimmer of white, and brushed it. Standing before her dresser, using her ivory-backed brush with long, even strokes, her reflected face showed absolutely devoid of radiance. The light was out of it — the light of youth, and, more than the light of youth, the light of that which survives youth, even the soul itself. And yet there was in this face, so unexpectant and quiescent that it gave almost the effect of dulness, a great strength and charm which were the result of an enduring grace of attitude towards all the stresses of life. Anna Carroll carried about with her always, not for the furbishing of her hair nor the embellishment of her complexion, but for the maintenance of the grace and dignity of her bearing towards a hard and inscrutable fate, a species of mental looking-glass. She never for a minute lost sight of herself as reflected in it. She had not been a happy woman, but she had worn her unhappiness like a robe of state. She had had a most miserable love-affair in her late youth, but no one except her brother could have affirmed with any certainty that it had occasioned her a moment's pang.

She was hopeless as regarded any happiness for herself in a strictly personal sense. She knew that her destiny as a woman had been unfulfilled, but she would rather have killed herself than pitied herself. She was as hard to herself and her own possible weakness as she was to anybody on earth, possibly harder. She cheated the dressmaker, she ate at the expense of others, as she would have cheated herself had she known how. It did not occur to her to go without anything which she could by any means get; not because she wanted it so keenly, as from another phase of the same feeling which had led Minna Eddy to appropriate the rug, and Estella Griggs the paraphernalia of the tea-table and the sofa-pillow. She had herself been duped in a larger sense; she was a creditor of Providence. She considered that she had a right to her hard wages of mere existence, when they came in her way, were they in the form of red silk gowns or anything else. She would admit no wrong in her brother, for the same reason, reserving only the right to condemn him at times on the boy's account. She began thinking about the boy as she went on with her preparations for bed. Her face lit up a little as she reflected upon the benefit it might be to Eddy to be in Kentucky. She thought of the dire possibility of serious complications for Arthur in this culminating crisis of his affairs.

"Better for the child to be out of it," she said to herself, and that singular anger with Arthur for the sake of the boy, which was like anger with him for his own sake, came over her. She identified the two. She saw in Eddy the epitome of his father, the inheritor of his virtues and faults, and his retribution, his heir-at-large by the inscrutable and merciless law of heredity. "Yes, it is better for Eddy to be out of it," she repeated to herself, with the same reasoning that she might have used had she been proposing to separate her brother's better self from his worse. But she resolved more firmly that she would not go herself. She would urge the others' going, but she would remain.

CHAPTER XXXI

But in spite of Anna Carroll's resolve, she went to Kentucky with the others in two weeks' time. She had had quite a severe attack of illness after that night, and it had left her so weakened in body that she had not strength to stand against her brother's urging. Then, too, Mrs. Carroll had displayed an unexpected reluctance to leave. She had evinced a totally new phase of her character, as people who are unconquerable children always will when least expected to do so. Instead of clinging to her husband and declaring that she could not leave, with an underlying submission at hand, she straightened herself and said positively that she would not go. She was quite pale, her sweet face looked as firm as her husband's.

"I am not going to leave you, Arthur," she said. "If your sister stays with you, your wife can. Your sister can go, and take Eddy, but your wife stays. I don't care what happens. I don't care if Marie and Martin do go. Marie is not cooking so well lately, anyway, and I never did like the way Martin went around corners. We can get new servants I shall like much better. I shall go into the City myself next week to the intelligence office. I am not afraid to go. I don't like to cross Broadway, but I can take a cab from the station. I will sit there in a row all day with those other women, until I get a good maid, if it is necessary. I don't care in the least if Marie and Martin do go. You can get another man who will turn the corners more carefully. And I don't mind because somebody took that rug — somebody — who was not paid. I think it was a very rude thing to do. I think when you take things that way it is no better than burglary, but I should not make any fuss about it. Let the woman have the rug. Although it does seem as if anybody had the rug, it ought to be that man we bought it of in Hillfield. You know he did not seem to like it at all, because he was not paid for it. But maybe he did not come by it honestly himself. He was a singular-looking man — a Syrian or Armenian or a Turk, and one never knows about people like that. I don't mind in the least; it is all right. And I don't care about the teacups and things. One of the cups was nicked, and I really like Sèvres much better than Dresden. I should have got Sèvres when I bought them, only the man who had the Sèvres I wanted would not give us credit. We had no charge account there. I don't mind in the least; but I think that dressmaker was very impolite to take the things, because, of course, we shall never feel that we can conscientiously give her any more of our custom; and we have given her a great deal of work, with dear Ina's wedding and everything, more than anybody in Banbridge. No, I don't mind in the least about these things. I can rise above that when it is a question of my husband. And when you talk of having to leave Banbridge, that does not daunt me at all. On the whole, I would rather leave Banbridge. I should like to live a little nearer the City, and I should like more grounds, and a house with more conveniences. For one thing, we have no butler's pantry here, and that is really a great inconvenience. Take it altogether, the house, and the distance from New York, I shall not be at all sorry to move. And" (Mrs. Carroll's sweet face looked hard and set, her gently pouting mouth widened into a straight line; she had that uncanny expression of docile and yielding people when they assume a firm attitude), "I shall not go away and leave you, Arthur," she repeated; "Anna shall not stay here with you and I go to Aunt Catherine's. If any one stays, I stay. I am your wife, and I am the one to stay. I know my duty."

"Amy, dear," said Carroll, "it will really make me happier to know that you are more comfortable and happy than I can make you this winter."

"I shall not be comfortable and happy," said she. "No, Arthur, you need not pet me; I am quite in earnest. You treat me always as if I were a child. You do, and all the rest, even my own children. And I think myself that two-thirds of me is a child, but one-third is not, and now it is the one-third that is talking, and quite seriously. It is I who am going to stay with you, and not Anna."

"Anna is not going to stay either, sweetheart," Carroll said.

A quick change came over Mrs. Carroll's face. She looked inquiringly at her sister-in-law. "Anna said she would not go," she said.

"She has thought better of it," Carroll said, quietly.

"Yes, Amy, I am going," Anna said, wearily, "and I don't think you had better decide positively tonight whether you will go or not. Leave it until tomorrow."

"But how could you get along without anybody to keep house for you all winter, Arthur?" asked Mrs. Carroll.

"As thousands of men get along," Carroll replied. "I can take my meals at the inn, and somebody could be got to come by the day and see to the furnace and the house."

"I suppose somebody could," Mrs. Carroll agreed, a frown of reflection on her smooth forehead.

She wept piteously when it came to parting, two weeks later, but she went.

They all started early in the morning. Carroll accompanied them to the station, and was well aware of an unusual number of persons being present to see the train start. He knew the reason: a rumor had gotten about that he as well as his family was to leave Banbridge and the State. He knew that if he had made a motion to get on the train, there might have been a scene, and he bade his family good-bye on the platform, before his covert audience of creditors. Lee was there, ostentatiously shaking hands with the ladies, but secretly watchful. Tappan was surlily attentive, leaving his milk-wagon tied in front of the station. Minna Eddy and Willy had driven down in their wagon from their little farm. Four children were huddled in behind. Minna had gotten out and stood on the platform. Willy sat on the seat holding the baby and the reins. There had been a thaw; the roads outside were heavy, and their old mule was harnessed up with their old horse. Willy had been somewhat afraid to come.

"Suppose he should make a fuss about that," he said, pointing to the Bokhara rug which adorned their little sitting-room.

"I ain't afraid of his making any fuss about that old mat," said Minna; "I guess he knows what he's about. It's him that's afraid, an' not me. An old mat that's worth about fifty cents! It ain't half so pretty as one that Frank Olsen's wife got in New Sanderson for four dollars and ninety-eight cents. I'm goin' to have some more of them things, an' he ain't goin' to git out of Banbridge, if I have to hang on to his coat-tails. You lemme go, Willy Eddy."

Therefore they came, starting before daylight in the frosty morning. Carroll was conscious of them all, of the druggist and the postmaster; of the two horsemen with whom he had had a half-settlement, and who were now about to force the remainder; of the two butchers and the dry-goods merchant, who had been exceedingly nasty about the rug, and persisted in thinking that the Carrolls were responsible for its disappearance. They had now other chattels in view, and were only delayed from taking prompt measures by the uncertainty as to what belonged to Carroll, or to his wife, or to the owner of the house. There was also lurking around the corner of the station, but quite ready for immediate action should it be necessary, another man, who represented the arm of the local law. There was also Madame Estelle Griggs, and, curiously enough, the sight of that little, meagre-bedecked figure and that small, rasped, piteous face of nervous suspicion affected Carroll more forcibly than did any of the others. He was conscious of a sensation of actual fear as he caught sight of the waving plume, of the wiry frizzes, of the sharp, frost-reddened face, of those watchful, unhappy eyes. He realized that if she should make a scene there, if he should hear again that laugh and those wailing sobs, he could not answer for what he might do. There even flashed across his mind a mental picture of the on-rush of the train, and of a man hurling himself before it, to get for once and all out of sight and sound of the unspeakable, grotesque, unmanning shame of the thing. It was when he saw her that he resolved that he would not put his foot on the train, lest she might think he meant to go. However, she would probably have made no manifestation. She was herself in mortal terror of retribution because of the things which she had confiscated in payment of her debt. She had little of Minna Eddy's strength of confidence in her own proceedings. She had, however, consoled herself by the reflection that possibly nobody knew that she had taken them. She had hidden them away under her mattress, and slept uneasily on the edge of the bed, lest she break the cups and saucers. If it had not been so early in the morning, presumably too early for visitors from the City, she would not have dared show herself at the station. In these days she sewed behind closed doors, with her curtains down. She went to her customer's houses for tryings-on, instead of having her patrons come to her. She was always ready, working with her eyes at the parting of the curtains, to flee down a certain pair of outside back-stairs, and cut across the fields, should men be sent out from the City to collect money. Rosenstein's store was under her little apartment, and she knew she could trust him not to betray her. The dressmaker was in these days fairly tragic in appearance, with a small and undignified, but none the less real, tragedy. It was the despair of a small nature over small issues, but none the less despair. Carroll would have paid that bill first of all, had he had the money, but none but himself knew how little money he had. Had the aunt in Kentucky not sent the wherewithal for the railway fares, it was hard to be seen how the journey could have been taken at all. It had even occurred to Carroll that some jewelry must needs be sacrificed. He had made up his mind, in that case, that Anna would be the one to make the sacrifice. She had an old set of cameos from her grandmother, which he knew were valuable if taken to the right place. Anna had considered the matter, and would have spared him the suggestion had not the check come from the aunt to cover all the expenses of the trip, with even some to spare. With the extra, Mrs. Carroll insisted upon buying a new hat for Charlotte. Charlotte that morning showed little emotion. She was looking exceedingly pretty in the new hat and her little, blue travelling-gown. Madame Griggs eyed that and reflected that she had not made it herself, that it must have been a last winter's one, although it had kept well in style, and she wondered if the dressmaker who made it had been paid. Charlotte in parting from her father showed no emotion. He kissed her, and she turned away directly and entered the train. There was an odd expression on her face. She had not spoken a word all the morning except to whisper to Eddy to be still, when he remarked, loudly, on the number of people present at the station.

"All this crowd isn't going, is it?" he demanded.

"Hush!" Charlotte whispered, peremptorily, and he looked curiously at her.

"What is the matter with you this morning, anyhow?" he inquired, loudly. Eddy had in a leash a small and violently squirming puppy, which had lately strayed to the Carroll place, and been found wagging and whining ingratiatingly around the stable. Eddy had adopted it, and even meditated riding in the baggage-car to relieve its loneliness should the conductor prove intractable concerning its remaining in the passenger-coach. Eddy, of the whole party of travellers, was the only one who pre-sented an absolutely undisturbed and joyously expectant countenance. He had the innocent selfishness of childhood. He could still be single-eyed as to the future, and yet blameless. He loved his father, but had no pangs at parting, when the wonders of the journey and the new country were before him. His heart also delighted in the puppy, leaping and abor-tively barking at his side. He kissed his father good-bye as the train approached, and was following the others, with the little dog straining at his leash, when his onward progress was suddenly arrested, another grimy little hand tugged at the leash.

"Say, what you goin' off with my dog for?" demanded the owner of the hand, another boy, somewhat older than Eddy, and one of his school-mates.

Eddy, belligerent at once, faced about. He caught up the wriggling puppy with such a quick motion that he was successful and wrenched the other boy's hand from the leash.

"It isn't your dog. It's my dog. What you talking about?" he growled back.

"You lie!"

"Lie yourself!"

"Gimme that dog!"

"It's my dog!"

"Where'd ye git it?" sneered the other, making clutches at the puppy.

"My papa bought him for me in New York."

"Hm! All the way your father could git a dog like that is to steal him. Your father ain't got no money. You stole him. You steal jest like your father. Gimme the dog."

The claimant boy laid such insistent hands on the puppy, and Eddy so resisted, that the little animal yelped loudly.

Carroll stepped up. His lips were ashy. This last idiotic episode was unnerving him more than all that had gone before. "Give that boy his dog," he commanded Eddy, sternly.

Eddy clung more tightly to the little dog, and began to whimper. "But, papa —"

"Do as I tell you."

"He came to our stable, and he didn't have any collar on, and a dog without any collar on —"

"Do as I tell you."

But Eddy had found an unexpected ally. Anderson had come on the platform as the train approached. He was going on business to New Sanderson, and he had furtively collared the owner of the puppy, thrust something into his hand, whispered something, and given him a violent push. The boy fled. When Carroll turned, the boy who had been imperiously aggressive at his elbow was nowhere to be seen. Several of the bystanders were grinning. Anderson was moving along to be at the side of his car, as the train approached. It had all happened in a very few seconds. Eddy clung fast to the puppy. There was no time for anything, and the female Carrolls were pressing softly about for the last words.

"I don't think the puppy belonged to that boy," Mrs. Carroll said. "He was just a little, stray dog."

She had seen nothing of what Anderson had done, and neither had the others. There was manifestly nothing more to be done. It was an absurdity for Carroll to load himself up with that squirming puppy, when the ownership seemed so problematic. He bade them all good-bye again, and they got on the train. The women's pretty, wistfully smiling faces appeared at windows, also Eddy's, and the innocently wondering visage of the puppy. Anderson was in the smoking-car. As the train passed, Carroll saw his face at a window, and bowed, raising his hat half-mechanically. Anderson was conscious of a distinct sensation of pity for him, the more so that he was helpless and rebelliously depressed himself. He meditated upon the advisability of going into the other car, the Pullman, before the arrival of the train at New Sanderson, and bidding Charlotte farewell. He finally decided not to do so. He had no reason to think that she would care especially to have him, and while his self-respect, in spite of his perfect cognizance of the disadvantages of his position, was sufficient not to make him hesitate on that account, he had had a feeling against intruding upon the possible sadness of the ladies when making what they must recognize as a forced exit from their home under humiliating circumstances. It did not occur to him that they might possibly not feel so.

Carroll, left on the platform while the train steamed out of sight, in its backward trail of smoke full of rainbow lights in the frosty air, turned to go home. He was going to walk. Martin had driven the family to the station, and had himself gotten on the rear car of the train. He was about seeking employment in New Sanderson. One of the horsemen had driven off with the rig; the other was waiting for a word with Carroll. The discussion was short, heated, and profane on one side; calm, low, and imperturbable on the other.

"You'll have it in the end," Carroll said, as he turned to go.

"The end has got to come pretty darned quick," the other retorted, jumping into his little trotting-gig and spinning off.

The others of the crowd had melted away rather quickly. Minna Eddy had clambered into the wagon and gathered up the reins, while her husband retained the wailing baby. In truth, in spite of her bravado, she had some little doubts as to the wisdom of her confiscation of the rug. Madame Griggs, actuated by a similar doubt, also fluttered away swiftly down the street. The men also, upon making sure that Carroll was not intending to abscond, retreated. Carroll was quite alone when the horseman spun away in his gig, with its swift spokes flashing in blinding rings of light as he disappeared around the curve. It was one of those mornings in the fall when the air is so clear that the sunlight seems intensified. There had been a hard frost the night before, and a delicate rime was still over the ground, only melting in the sunniest spots. Only the oak leaves, a brownish-red shag mostly on the lower branches, were left on the trees. The door-yards were full of dried chrysanthemums, the windows gay with green-house plants. The air was full of the smell of smoke and coffee and frying things, for it was Banbridge's breakfast-hour. Men met Carroll on their way to the next train to the City, walking briskly with shoulders slightly shrugged before the keen wind. They bowed to him with a certain reserve. He met one young girl carrying a music-roll, who wore on her face an expression of joy so extreme that it gave the effect of a light. Carroll noticed it absently, this alien joy with which he had no concern. As the girl passed him, he perceived a strong odor of violet from her dainty attire, and it directly, although he was unaware of the connection, caused him to remember the episode of his discovering the two women, Mrs. Van Dorn and Mrs. Lee, spying out the secrets in his house. That same odor had smote his nostrils when he entered the door. He reviewed from that starting-point the succeeding stages of his stay in Banbridge, the whole miserable, ignominious descent from a fictitious prosperity to plain, evident disgrace and want. He was returning to his desolate house. Martin had gone, wretchedly and plainly incredulous of Carroll's promise to finally pay him every cent he owed him. Maria had packed her box, and tied two gay foreign handkerchiefs into bags to contain her ragged possessions. He was to be entirely alone. He could remain in the house probably only for a short time, until the owner should find a new tenant. He walked along with his head up, retaining his old stately carriage. As he turned the street corner on which his house stood, he saw a figure advancing, and his heart stood still. He thought he recognized Charlotte, incredible although it was, since he had just seen her depart on the train. But surely that was Charlotte approaching, although she carried strange parcels. The girl was just her height, she even seemed to walk like her, and she surely wore a dress of which Charlotte was very fond. It was of a dusky red color, the skirt hanging in soft pleats. The hat was also red with a white wing. There was fur on the coat, and Carroll could see the fluff of it over the girlish shoulders. He could see the stiff white gleam of the wing. Then he saw who it was — Marie, with a yellow handkerchief gathered into a bag in one hand, and a little kitten which she had cherished, in a paper bag in the other. The kitten's black head protruded, and it was mewing shrilly. Marie was radiant with smiles, and she wore Charlotte's dress. She had stolen up-stairs and viewed herself in the mirror in Mrs. Carroll's room, and she had hopes of herself in that costume even without any money in her pocket. She was dreaming her humble little love-dream again. She smiled up at Carroll in a charming fashion as they met.

"Good-bye," said she, with her pretty little purse of the mouth. They had already had an interview concerning her wages that morning.

Carroll said good-bye with a stiff motion of his mouth. He realized that Charlotte had given Marie her dress. Somehow the sight of Marie in that dress almost made a child of the man.

CHAPTER XXXII

Carroll, when he reached his house, went up to the front door, unlocked it, and entered. At once there smote upon his consciousness that strange shock of emptiness and loneliness which has the effect, for a sensitive soul entering a deserted house, of a menacing roar of sound. He went through the hall to the little smoking-room or den on the right, opposite the dining-room, and the first thing which he saw on the divan was Charlotte's little chinchilla muff which she had forgotten. He regarded it with the concern of a woman, reflecting that she would miss it; and he must send it to her, and was wondering vaguely about a suitable box, when he became aware of a noise of insistent knocking mounting in a gradual crescendo from propitiatory timidity to confidence. The knocking was on the kitchen door, and Carroll went hurriedly through the house. When he reached the door it was open, and a tramp was just entering, with head cautiously thrust forward. When he saw Carroll, the unshaven, surly face manifestly became dismayed. He turned to go, with a mutter which savored of appeal, excuse, and defiance, but Carroll viciously accelerated his exit with a thrust between the shoulders.

"What the devil are you doing here?" demanded Carroll.

The man, rolling surly yet intimidated eyes over his shoulder, after a staggering recovery from a fall, muttered something in an unintelligible *patois*, the grovelling, slurring whine of his kind.

"Well, get out of this!" shouted Carroll.

The man went, shuffling along with a degree of speed, lifting his clumsily shod feet with a sort of painful alacrity as if they were unduly heavy. His back, in its greenish-brown coat, was bent. He was not a very young man, although vigorous. Carroll stood looking at the inglorious exit of this Ishmael, and he was conscious of a feeling of exhilaration. He felt an agreeable tingling in his fists, which were still clinched. The using of them upon a legitimate antagonist in whose debt he was not, and never had been, acted like a tonic. Then suddenly something pathetic in that miserable retreating back struck the other man, who also had reason to turn his back on and retreat from his kind; a strange understanding came over him. He seemed to know exactly how that other man, slinking away from his door, felt.

"Hullo, you!" he called out.

The man apparently did not hear, or did not think the shout meant for him. He kept on.

Carroll shouted again. "Hullo, you! Come back here!"

Then the man turned, and his half-scared, half-defiant face fronted Carroll. He growled an inarticulate inquiry.

"Come back here!" repeated Carroll.

The tramp came slowly, suspiciously, one hand slyly lifted as one sees a wary animal with a paw ready for possible attack.

"Wait here," said Carroll, indicating the stoop with a gesture, and I will see if I can find something for you to eat."

The man reached the door and paused, and remained standing, still with that wary lift of hand and foot in readiness for defence or flight, while Carroll rummaged in the pantry, which was a lean larder. At last he emerged with half a pie and a piece of cake. He extended them to the tramp, who viewed them critically and mumbled something about meat.

"Take these and clear out, or leave them and clear out!" shouted Carroll, and again the sense of exhilaration was over him.

The man took the proffered food and slunk rapidly out of the yard.

Carroll laughed, and closed and bolted the kitchen door, which Marie had left unlocked. Then he returned to the den and sat down with the morning paper and a cigar. He skimmed over the contents, the rumors of wars, and cruelties, the Wall Street items, the burglaries, the fires, the defalcations, the suicides, the stresses of the world, creation old, enduring in their fluctuations and recurrences like the sea, beating with the same force upon the hearts of every new generation. Carroll, as he sat there idly smoking, fell to thinking abstractedly in that vein. He had a conception of a possible ocean of elemental emotion, of joy and passion, of crime and agony and greed, ever swelling and ebbing upon the shores of humanity. He had a mind of psychological cast, although it had been turned of a necessity into other channels. Finally he turned wholly to himself and his own difficulties, which had reached possibly the worst crisis of his life. He had never been in such a hard place as this. He had heretofore seen a loop-hole out, into another labyrinth in the end, it is true, still a way out. Now he saw none except one; that was into a fiery torture, and whether it was or was not the torture of beneficial sacrifice he could not tell.

As he sat there his face grew older with the laboring of his mind over the track of his failures and over the certain difficulties of the future. He sat there all the morning. Noon came, but he did not think of food, although he had eaten little that morning. He lit another cigar and took up the paper again, and read an account of the suicide of a bank defaulter by shooting himself through the brain. He fell to thinking of suicide in his own case, as a means of egress from his own difficulties, but he thought idly, rather as a means of amusement, and not with the slightest seriousness. He had a well-balanced brain naturally, and maintained the balance even in the midst of misfortune. However, a balance, however perfect, indicates by its very name something which may be disturbed. He thought over, idly, various means of unlawful exit from the world, and applied them to his own case. He decided against the means employed by the desperate bank cashier; he decided against the fiery draught of acid swallowed by a love-distracted girl; he decided against the leap from a ferry-boat taken by an unknown man, whose body lay unidentified in the morgue; he decided against illuminating gas, which had released from the woes of life a man and his three children; he thought rather favorably of charcoal; he thought also rather favorably of morphine; he thought more favorably still of the opening of a vein, employed by fastidious old Romans who had enough of feast and gladiators and life generally and wished for a chance to leave the entertainment. All this was the merest idleness of suggestion, a species of rather ghastly amusement, it is true, but none the less amusement, of an unemployed and melancholy mind. But suddenly, something new and hitherto unexperienced was over him, a mood which he had never imagined, a possibility which he had never grasped. His brain, tried to the extreme by genuine misery, tried in addition by dangerous suggestion, lost its perfect poise for the time. A mighty hunger and thirst — a more than hunger and thirst — a ravening appetite, a passion beyond all passions which he had ever known, was upon him, had him in its clutches. He knew for the first time the most monstrous and irresistible passion of the race, the passion for release from mortal existence, the passion for death. At that moment he felt, and probably felt truly, that had he been in dire peril, he would not have lifted a finger in self-preservation. He turned his eyes inward upon himself with greed for his own life, for his own blood, and back of that was the ravening thirst for release from the world and the flesh and the miseries which appertained to them, as one suffocating might thirst for air. He realized suddenly himself, stifling and agonizing, behind a window which he had no need to wait for an overruling Providence to open, which was not too heavy for his own mortal strength, which he could open himself. He realized that whatever lay outside *was* outside; it was air outside this air, misery outside this particular phase which was driving him mad. His imagination dwelling upon the different means of suicide, now became judicial. He thought seriously upon the drawbacks to one, the advantages of another. Then since the man was essentially unselfish and fond of his own flesh and blood, he began to reflect upon the horror of a confessed suicide to them. He began to study the feasibility of a suicide forever undiscovered. He began to plan how the thing might distress his family as little as possible. His cigar went out as he sat and studied. The furnace fire was low and the room grew cold. He never noticed it. He studied and studied the best means of suicide, the best means of concealing it, and all the time the greed for it was increasing until his veins seemed to run with a liquid fire of monstrous passion, the passion of a mortal man for his own immolation upon fate, and all the time that sense of intolerable suffocation by existence itself, by the air of the world, increased.

He had now arrived at a state of mind where every new phase was produced by suggestion. He was, in a sense, hypnotized. Everything served to swing him this way or that, up or down. The sight of a little perfume-bottle on the table, a dainty glass thing traced over with silver, set him thinking eagerly of another little bottle, of glass with a silver stopper, his wife's vinaigrette which she was fond of using when her head ached. From that, the contemplation of inhaling aromatic salts, he went naturally enough to the inhaling of more potent things which assuage pain, and could assuage, if taken in sufficient quantities, the pain of life itself. He remembered the exaltation which he had experienced once when given chloroform for a slight operation. Directly the idea of repeating that blissful sensation seized upon him he was mad for it. To go out of life like that, to take that way of opening the window into eternity, into another phase of existence or into oblivion, what ecstasy! He remembered that when under the chloroform, a wonderful certainty, a comprehension, seemingly, of the true import of life and death and of the hereafter, had seized him. He remembered a tremendous assurance which he had received under the influence of the drug, of the ultimate joy beyond this present existence, of the ultimate end in bliss of all misery, of the tending of death to the fulness of life. He remembered a rapture beyond words, an enthusiasm of gratitude for such an immortal delight for the power which he had sometimes rebelled against and reviled for placing him in the scale of existence. He remembered how all his past troubles seemed as only stepping-stones to supernal heights, how he could have kissed them for thankfulness that he had been forced by an all-wise Providence over the agony of the ascent to such rapture. Immediately his thoughts centred upon chloroform. He looked across at the divan with its heaped-up pillows, and his mind, acting always from suggestion, became filled with the picture of his peaceful bed up-stairs, and himself lying thereon, oblivious to all his miserable cares and worries, passing out of reach of them on an ecstatic flight propelled by the force of the winged drug. He began to consider the possibility of obtaining chloroform. At once the instinct of secrecy asserted itself. He decided that he could not, under the circumstances, go into the drug-store in Banbridge and ask for a quantity of the drug sufficient for his purposes. He realized that to do so would be to incur suspicion. He doubted if he could maintain a perfectly unmoved countenance while asking for it. He felt that his face would bear evidence to his wild greed. He heard, as he sat there, the whistle, then the rumble of a heavy freight-train a quarter of a mile distant, and at once he thought of the feasibility of going to New York for the chloroform. He looked at his watch and reflected that he had lost the noon train. He also reflected as to the possible suspicion which he might awaken of going to join his family, and making his final exodus from the town and his creditors. He placed his watch in his pocket, and his eyes fell on the electric-light fixture, with a red silk shade over the bulb, and at once his mind conceived the idea of his going somewhere on the trolley-cars. He thought of going to New Sanderson; then dismissed that as not feasible. He knew too many people in that place, and had too many creditors. Then he thought of going to Port Willis, which was also connected with Banbridge by a trolley-line, and was about the same distance. Again he looked at his watch. It was nearly two o'clock. He wondered absently where the day had gone, that it was so late. He had not the least idea as to the times and seasons of the Port Willis trolley-cars, but he directly arose to make ready. As he did so he heard a distressful mew, and the black kitten which Marie had essayed to carry with her that morning made a leap to the window-sill. The little animal looked in, fixed his golden, jewel-like eyes on the man, and again uttered an appealing, accusatory wail. Then she rubbed her head with a pretty, caressing motion against the window-glass. She had evidently escaped from the Hungarian and sped home. Carroll opened the window, and the cat arched her back and purred, hesitating. Carroll waited patiently. Finally she stepped across the sill, and he closed the window. Then he called the cat into the kitchen, but he could find no milk for her, nothing except a tiny scrap of beefsteak. The cat followed him around the kitchen, slinking with her furry stomach sweeping the floor, and mewed loudly, with alert eyes of watchful fear, exactly as if she were in a strange place. The strangeness in the house intimidated her. She missed the wonted element of the human, and the very corners of her familiar kitchen looked strange to her. She would not even eat her meat, but ran under the table and wailed loudly, with wild eyes of terror on Carroll. He went out, shutting the door behind him, and her loud inquiring wail floated after him.

Carroll brushed his overcoat and hat carefully, and put them on. He went out of the house and took the road to the trolley-line. It was still very cold, and the rime of the morning lay yet on the shaded places. In the road, in the full glare of the sun, were a few dark, damp places. The sky was very clear, with a brisk wind from the northwest. It was at Carroll's back and urged him along. He walked quite rapidly. He had a curious singleness of purpose, as unreasoning and unreflective as an animal in search of food. He was going to Port Willis for chloroform to satisfy a hunger keener than any animal's, to satisfy the keenest hunger of which man, body and soul together, is capable, a hunger keener than that of love or revenge, the hunger for the open beyond the suffocating fastnesses of life. He met several people whom he knew, and bowed perfunctorily. One or two turned and looked after him. Two ladies, starting on a round of calls, Mrs. Lee and Mrs. Van Dorn, again looked forth from the window of Samson Rawdy's best coach, and at the intent man hurrying along the sidewalk.

"I wonder where's he going," Mrs. Lee said, in a hushed tone. She was just approaching a house where they meditated calling, and she was rubbing on her violet-scented white gloves. Mrs. Lee looked worn and considerably thinner than usual, and she was uncomfortably conscious of her last season's bonnet. "My bonnet doesn't look very well to make calls," she had remarked, when she entered the coach, hired, as usual, at her companion's expense.

"It looks very well indeed," said Mrs. Van Dorn, in a covertly triumphant voice. She herself wore a most gorgeous new bonnet with a clump of winter roses crowning her gray pompadour. "It isn't the one you wore last winter, is it?" asked she.

"Yes," admitted Mrs. Lee.

"You don't mean it! I thought it was new," said Mrs. Van Dorn, lying comfortably.

"No, it's my old bonnet. I thought maybe it would do a while longer," said Mrs. Lee, meekly.

"I heard yesterday that a good many folks in Banbridge had been losing money through Captain Carroll," said Mrs. Van Dorn, with appositeness.

Mrs. Lee colored. "Have they?" said she.

"I heard so."

"Who is that man coming?" said Mrs. Lee, quickly, striving to turn the conversation. Then she directly saw that the man was Carroll himself.

"Why, it's Captain Carroll himself!" said Mrs. Van Dorn, and then Mrs. Lee wondered, in her small, hushed voice, where he was going.

Samson Rawdy, driving, looked sharply at him. He even leaned far out from the seat after he had passed, and watched to make sure he did not take the road to the railroad station. Then he began, for the hundredth time mentally, calculating the amount that was still owing him. It was not much, only a matter of two dollars and some cents, but his mind dwelt upon it.

"Seems to me he looked queer," Mrs. Lee remarked, thoughtfully, after Carroll had passed.

"How do you mean?"

"I don't know. There was something about the way he was walking made me think so. I suppose he doesn't know what way to turn."

"Well, I don't pity him," said Mrs. Van Dorn, with subdued vindictiveness. "I don't see what a man is thinking of to come into a place and conduct himself as he has done. They say he is in debt everywhere, and has cheated everybody who didn't know any better than to be cheated."

Mrs. Van Dorn spoke with point. She had heard on very good authority that Mrs. Lee's husband had lost heavily through his misplaced confidence in Carroll. Mr. Lee knew that she knew, but she stood up bravely for the maligned man hurrying towards the Port Willis trolley-car.

"Well, I don't know," said she. "You can't always tell by what people say. It always seems to me that Banbridge folks are pretty ready to talk, anyway. We don't know how much temptation the poor man has had, and maybe he never meant to cheat anybody."

"Never meant!" repeated Mrs. Van Dorn, sarcastically. "Why, that is the way he has been doing right along everywhere he has lived. Why, I had it straight from a lady I met who had visited in Hillfield, New York, where they used to live before they came here. Never meant!"

"Maybe he didn't," persisted Mrs. Lee. She was a grateful soul, and, even if capable of small and petty acts, was of fine grain enough to bear no rancor towards the discoverer of them; but the other woman was built on a different plan.

"I don't take any stock in him at all," she said, with a species of delight. She looked out of the small, rear window of the coach as she spoke. "He's going to Port Willis," she said. "He's getting in the trolley-car."

Samson Rawdy also turned his head and saw with a strained side glance Carroll getting into the Port Willis trolley-car. Then he said: "G'lang!" to his horses, and they turned a corner with a fine sweep, while the ladies began getting their cards ready.

"I wonder what he's going to Port Willis for," said Mrs. Van Dorn, reflectively and malignantly. "I suppose he's looking out for somebody to cheat over there."

"Well, I pity him, poor man!" said Mrs. Lee. "If a man does cheat other folks, he can't do it without cheating himself worst of all, and it always turns out so in the end."

As is often the way with a simple tongue, hers spoke more wisdom that it wot of. It was indeed quite true that poor Arthur Carroll, seating himself in the Port Willis trolley-car, had in the bitter end cheated himself worse than he had any of his creditors. He was more largely in his own debt than in that of any other man; he had, in reality, less of that of which he had cheated than had any of his victims. Hardly one of them all was in such sore straits as he, for in addition to his immediate personal necessities there was always the incubus of the debts. And he was starting forth upon this trip with the purpose in his overstrained, distorted brain of spending his last reserve, and incurring a debt to himself which should never be paid to all eternity.

Carroll seated himself in the car, which was already quite well filled;

there was not much time to spare before its scheduled departure. He found a corner seat empty, and settled himself into it with a bitter little sense of self-gratulation for at least that minor alleviation of the situation. The corner seat in a Port Willis trolley-car had distinct advantages aside from the physical comfort, owing to the frequent crowding and the uncertain nature of the component elements of the crowd.

Carroll settled back in his corner and surveyed his fellow-passengers, waiting with a kind of stupid patience for the starting of the car. There was a curious look of indifference to remaining or going, on most of the faces, the natural result of the universality of travel in America, the being always on the road for all classes in order to cover the enormous distances in this great country between home and work or amusement. All excitement over the mere act of transit has passed; there is stolidity and acquiescence as to delays and speed, unless there are great interests at stake. As a rule, the people in the Port Willis trolley-car had not great interests at stake; they were generally not highly organized, nervously, and were to all appearances carried as woodenly from one point to another as were the seats of the car. That afternoon a German woman sat nearly opposite Carroll. She was well-dressed in a handsome black satin skirt, with an ornate, lace-trimmed waist showing between the folds of her seal cape. There were smart red velvet roses and a feather in her hat. She sat with her feet far apart, planted squarely to prevent her enormous slanting bulk from slipping on the high seat. Her great florid face, a blank of animal cognizance of existence, stared straight ahead, her triple chins were pressed obstinately into the fur collar of her cape. She was the wife of a prosperous saloon proprietor of Port Willis, which was a city of saloons. She had herself been nourished on beer, until her naturally strong will had become so heavy that it clogged her own purposes. Her absently set face had a bewildered scowl as if at some dimly comprehended opposition. Carroll surveyed her with a sort of irritated wonder. No mathematical problem could present for him difficulties as insuperable as this other human being, who, in a similar stress to his own, would think of beer instead of chloroform, and of sleep instead of death — indeed, for whom a similar stress could not exist, so cushioned was both soul and body with stupidity and flesh against the pricks and stabs of life.

Beside Carroll sat, sprawling his ungainly sideways length over the seat, a lank countryman in top-boots red with the earth of the country roads. His face, lantern-jawed, of the Abraham Lincoln type, lacking the shrewd intelligence of the trained brain, was painfully apathetic. He had scarcely looked up when Carroll took his seat beside him. His lantern jaws worked furtively and incessantly with a rotary motion over his quid of tobacco, which he chewed with the humble and rudimentary comfort of an animal over its cud. He was half-starved on his poor country fare, and the tobacco furnished his stomach with imagination in lieu of solid food. Now and then he rose and slouched to the door, and returned. At the other end of the car, opposite, were two Hungarian women, short, squat, heavily oscillating as to hips, clad in full, short skirts, aprons, and gay handkerchiefs over strange faces, at once pitiful, stern, and intimidating. One of the women was distinctly handsome, with noble features closely framed by a snow-white kerchief. She had the expression of the pure and unrelenting asceticism of a nun, but four children nearly of an age were with her — one a baby in her arms, one asleep with heavy head on her shoulder, the other two, a boy and girl, sitting on the seat with their well-shod little feet sticking straight out, and their little Slav faces, softened by infancy, looked unsmilingly out of the opposite window. The baby in her lap was also strangely sullen and solemn, with an intensely repellent little face in a soft, white hood. The face of the baby looked like an epitome of weary, even vicious, heredity. He looked older than his mother. Now and then she bent, and her severe face took on an expression of majestic tenderness. She pressed her handsome face close to the little, elfish, even evil face of the child, and kissed it. Then the baby smiled a fatuous, toothless smile, and he also was transformed; his little glory of infancy seemed to illuminate the face marked with the labors and sins and degradation of his progenitors. The other Hungarian woman, who had with her one child, older than the baby, very large and heavy, caught it up and kissed it with fervor, and the child stared at her in return with a sort of patient wonder. Then the two women exchanged smiles of confidence. Carroll watched, remembering Amy with their children. She had been very charming with the children, and, after all, there was not such a difference as might appear at first. The thought flashed into Carroll's mind that here was a little, universal well-spring of human nature which was good to see, but the deadly pessimism and despair of his own mood made him straightway corrupt the spring with his own dark conclusions.

"What is it all for?" he asked himself, bitterly. "look at the handsome alien creature there, with four young around her, and the other with that unresponsive little brat. Any one of those children, from the looks of their faces, is capable, if left to its own unguided proclivities, of murdering the very parent who is now caressing him; any one of them is hardly capable of doing anything in life for his own good or happiness, or the good and happiness of the world, if left to himself, as he will be. What does either of those women know about training a child with those features, a child distorted from birth?"

Beyond Carroll, on the same seat, sat two quite pretty young girls with smart hats, and protuberant pompadours over pink-and-white faces. They had loosened their coats, revealing coquettish neckwear. They sat with feet crossed, displaying embroidered petticoats, at which now and then the Hungarian women glanced with the hopeless admiration with which one might view crown jewels. The two girls covertly now and then reached forward their pretty heads and regarded Carroll with half-bold, half-innocent coquettishness, but he did not notice it. One whispered to the other how handsome he was, and did she know who he was.

A rumble and jar became audible, and the New Sanderson car came up at right angles on the track on the other road. The two cars connected. Then passengers alighted from the New Sanderson car and entered the waiting one. There was a distinct stir of excitement as they entered, for it was evidently a bridal party. They were all Hungarians, and on their way to Port Willis for the ceremony. There were the prospective bride and groom and several friends of both sexes. They settled themselves in the car, the girls huddled close together, the young men by themselves. The bride was quite evident from the bridal whiteness of her hat, a pitiful cheap affair bedecked with thin white ribbon and a forlorn white plume; but although the bridegroom was as unmistakable, it was difficult to tell how. Carroll decided that it was because of the intensified melancholy and abjectness and shame of his expression. Not one of the young men, who numbered as many as the girls, but had it. They were all ignoble, contemptible, their faces above their paper collars and hideous ties stained with miserable imaginations. There was not a self-respecting face among them; but the girls were better. There was in their faces an innocent gayety like children. Instead of the painful, restrained grins of the young men, they giggled artlessly when their eyes met. They were innocently conscious of their flimsy and gaudy dresses of the cheapest lawn or muslin on that cold day, with a multitude of frills of cheap lace and bows of cheap ribbon, with bare hands adorned with blue or red stoned rings protruding from their poor jacket-sleeves. The bride, afraid of crushing her finery, had nothing over her shoulders in her thin white muslin except one of the gay Hungarian kerchiefs. It was of an exceedingly brilliant green color, a green greener than the grass of spring. Above it her homely, downcast face showed beneath the flapping white hat, which had a cluster of blue roses under the brim next the dark streaks of her coarse hair. The face of the bride was simple and rude in contour and line, the face of a peasant from a long line of peasants, and it was complex with the simple complexity of the simplest and most primal emotions, with love and joy and wonder, the half-fearful triumph of swift inertia, attained at last in the full element of life. The others were different; they were dimpling and laughing and jesting in their unintelligible guttural. Their faces knew nothing of the seriousness of the bride's. One of them was exceedingly pretty, with a beauty unusual in her race. Her high cheek-bones were covered with the softest rosy flesh, her wide mouth was outlined by curves. She wore her cheap muslin with an air, gathering up her petticoat, edged with the coarsest lace, daintily from the muddy floor, revealing her large feet in heavy shoes and white stockings. All the young men of the party except the prospective groom, who sat entirely wrapped in his atmosphere of grinning, shamefaced consciousness, glanced furtively at her from time to time. She was quite aware of their glances, but she never returned them. When a young man looked at her, she said something to one of the girls, and laughed prettily, striking another pose for admiration. She never, however, glanced at Carroll as did the two pretty girls beyond him on the same seat. She seemed to have no consciousness of any one in the car outside of those of her own race. Indeed, the whole party, travelling in a strange land, speaking their strange tongue, gave a curious impression of utter aliency. It was almost as if they lived apart in their own crystalline sphere of separation, as if they were as much diverse as inhabitants of Mars, and yet they were bound on a universal errand, which might have served to bring them into touch with the rest if anything could. Carroll gathered an uncanny impression that he might be himself invisible to these people, that, living in another element, they actually could not see or fairly sense anything outside. He looked from them to the two older women of the same race with their children, and again his pessimistic attitude, evolved from his own misery, set his mind in a bitterly interrogative attitude. He looked at the bride and the mistakenly happy mother caressing the evil-looking child, and a sickening disgust of the whole was over him.

The car started, and proceeded at a terrific speed along the straight road. Carroll stared past the bulk of the German woman at the flying landscape. Since noon the sky had become clouded; it threatened snow if the wind should go down. The earth, which had been sodden with rain a few days before, the mud from which showed dried on the countryman's boots, was now frozen in a million wrinkles. The trees stood leafless, extending their rattling branches, the old corn-fields flickered with withered streamers; a man was mournfully spreading dung over a slope of field. His old horse stood between the shafts with drooping head. The man himself was old, and moved slowly and painfully. A white beard of unusual length blew over his right shoulder. Everything seemed aged and worn and weary, and full of knowledge, to its undoing. To Carroll, in this mood, even the bridal-party, even the children, seemed as old as age itself, puppets evolved from the ashes of ages, working out a creation-old plan of things.

The car was very close and hot — in fact, the atmosphere was intolerable — but he felt chilly. He pulled his coat closer. Two young men, countrymen, who had entered from the New Sanderson car, and sat next the German woman, eyed him at the gesture, and their eyes fell with a sort of dull dissent upon his handsome coat. One said something to the other, and both laughed with boorish malice. Then one, after glancing at the conductor, whose back was turned as he talked to one of the pretty girls with pompadours, bent his head hastily to the floor. Then he scraped his foot, and looked aloft with an innocent and unconcerned expression. One of the pretty girls had observed him, and said something to the conductor, pointing to a printed placard over the man's head. The conductor looked at him, but the man did not notice. He gave his fare, when it was demanded, surlily. Then he bent his head again, when the conductor had turned again, scraped his foot, and gave a sharp glance at the same time at Carroll's long coat, which was almost within range. The German woman suddenly awoke to nervous life and pulled her satin skirt aside, with a look at the offender, to which he was impervious.

Then the car stopped in response to a signal, and a tiny, evidently aged, woman with the activity of a child sprang on board. She had a large bag which she bore on one meagre little arm as if it had been a feather. Her wrinkled little face, rosily colored with the cold air, peeped alertly from under quite a fine, youthful hat trimmed with smart bows and a wing, but set crookedly on the head. Her sparse gray hair was strained tightly back from her thin temples and wound tightly at the back. Although she was undoubtedly old, her face could no more be called old than could that of a bird. She kept it in constant motion, bringing bright eyes to bear upon the different passengers. She did not travel very far. She stopped the car, springing alertly to her feet and pulling the bell-rope. Then she hopped off as spryly as a sparrow, on her thin ankles, moving with nervous haste. Then it was that Carroll noticed the boy for the first time, although he was seated directly opposite, and the child looked long and intently at the man. When the strange, agile old woman ran through the car, the boy looked across with a look of innocent fun at the man, and for the first time the two pairs of eyes met. It was not in Carroll, whatever his stress of mind, to meet a smile like that without response. He smiled back. Then the boy ducked his head with fervor, and off came his little cap, like a gentleman.

He was a handsome little fellow, younger than Eddy by a year or two, fair-haired and blue-eyed, with a most innocent and infantile expression. He was rather poorly dressed, but he looked well cared for, and he had the confident and unhesitating regard of a child who is well-beloved. He had a little package of school-books under his arm.

Carroll, after returning the child's smile, turned away. He did not look again, although he felt that the blue eyes with a look of insistent admiration were steadfastly upon his face. The country through which the car was now passing was of a strange, convulsive character. It was torn alike by nature and by man. Storms and winds had battered at the clayey soil, spade and shovel had upturned it. It was honey-combed and upheaved. There were roughly shelving hills overhung with coarse dry grass like an old man's beard, there were ragged chasms and gulfs, and all in raw reds and toneless browns and drabs, darkened constantly by the smoke which descended upon them from the chimneys of the great factories to the right. Over this raw red and toneless drab surface crawled, on narrow tracks, little wagons, drawn by plodding old horses, guided by plodding men. Beyond, the salt river gleamed with a keen brightness like steel. The sky above it was dull and brooding. The wind was going down. The whole landscape was desolate, and with a strange, ragged, ignominious desolation. The earth looked despoiled, insulted, dissected, as if her sacred inner parts were laid bare by these poor pygmies, the tools of a few capitalists grubbing at her vitals for the clay which meant dollars.

In the most desolate part of this desolate country, the car was stopped, and two Syrians laden with heavy grips got on. These tall, darkly gaunt men, their sinister picturesqueness thinly disguised by their Western garb, these Orientals in the midst of the extremest phase of the New World, passed Carroll with grace, and seated themselves, with a weary air, and yet an air of ineffable lengths of time at command, suggestive of anything but weariness. There was actually, or so Carroll fancied, a faint odor of attar of rose and sandal-wood evident in the horribly close car. The men had in their grips rosaries, and Eastern stuffs or Eastern trinkets of the cheapest description.

To Arthur Carroll, regarding them, the fancy occurred, as it had often occurred, of himself following a similar pursuit. He had revolved in his mind all possible schemes of money-making, of winning an honest living. All the more dignified methods, the methods apparently suited to himself, seemed out of his reach. He pictured himself laden with a heavy grip, with two of them, one painfully poised on the hip, the other dragging at the hand, going about the country, concealing his rage with abjectness and humility, striving to dispose of his small and worthless wares for money enough to keep the machinery going.

"I believe I would make a very good peddler," he thought. Although his grace of address was involuntary, like any keenly intelligent and retrospective man, he could not avoid being aware of it. He felt that he could outstrip that saturnine Syrian in his own field.

Looking away from them, his eyes met the little boy's, also returning from a sober, innocent contemplation of them, and the boy's eyes again smiled at him with an odd, confidential expression. So clearly wise and understanding was their direct regard, that it almost seemed as if the child guessed at the man's thoughts; but that was, of course, impossible. Carroll smiled at him again, and the little face blushed and dimpled like a girl's with admiration and grateful delight. He was a daintily built little boy, with nothing of Eddy's little dash of manner, but he was charming. The car reached Port Willis and proceeded along the principal street. Carroll suddenly reflected that he must soon get off; he would reach the end of the line. Again his errand loomed up before him. The necessity for immediate action removed the paralyzing effect which the very horror of it had had upon him for a time. Curiously enough, during the half-hour in the car he had held, as it were, a little truce with this fell appetite which had seized upon him. He had thought very little of it. The strange inertia of passivity in motion of the other passengers had seized upon him, but now was coming a period of wakening. The passengers began to drop off. The bridal-party went out chattering and laughing, the prospective bride with ugly red spots of agitation on her high cheek-bones, the pretty girl holding up her laced petticoats with the air of a princess. The stout German woman got off in front of her husband's saloon. The Syrians stopped in front of a store. Carroll rode through to the end of the line, and there was then nobody left except himself, the two pretty girls, and the little boy. The girls swept off before him, with a consciousness of their backs in his sight. Carroll got off, and, to his utter amazement, the little boy, pressing close to his heels, lifted a small voice. It was an exceedingly small and polite little voice, as sweet as a girl's, a thin treble.

"Be you Eddy Carroll's father?" asked the little voice.

Carroll looked down from his height at the small creature beside him. The little, upturned face looked very far down. The little cap was pushed back and the fair hair clung to the innocent forehead damply like a baby's.

"Yes, my little man," said he, affably. "Who are you?"

"I go to school with him," said the little boy.

"Oh!" said Carroll.

"Has he went?" further inquired the little boy, wistfully. He was a little scholar, but he had not learned as yet the practical application of English. It was "has gone" in the book and "has went" on the tongue.

"Yes; this morning," replied Carroll.

"I was in his classes," said the little voice.

"Why, you are younger than he is!" said Carroll.

"I guess I got my lessons better," admitted the little voice, but with no conceit, rather with a measure of apology.

Carroll laughed. "You must have," said he. The boy had, undoubtedly, a rather intellectual head, a full forehead, and eyes full of thought and question.

"You go to school in Banbridge?" said Carroll, walking along the street by the boy's side.

"Yes. I live here. My papa is dead and my mother dressmakes."

"Oh!" said Carroll. Suddenly, to his utter amazement, the small hand which was free from the books was slid into his, and he was walking up the street with the strange small boy clinging to his hand. Carroll was conscious of a feeling of grotesque amusement, of annoyance, and at the same time of pleasure and of exquisite flattery. There was, strangely enough, in the child, nothing which savored of the presuming or the forward. There was no more offence to be taken than if an exceedingly small, timidly ingratiating, and pretty dog had followed one. There was the same subtle compliment implied, that the dog and the child considered him a man desirable to be followed, a man to be trusted by such helplessness and ignorance and loving admiration.

Carroll asked no more questions, but walked up the street with the boy clinging to his hand. He thought of Eddy, but the touch of this child was very different; the hand was softer, not so nervous. Carroll, walking up the street, became forgetful of the child, who remained silent, only glancing up at him now and then, timidly and delightedly and admiringly. It was, in fact, to the boy, almost as if he were walking hand in hand with a god. But to the man had returned in full force the abnormal passion which had sent him thither. He looked for a drug-store where he could buy chloroform. His mind was as set upon that one end as a hunting-dog's upon his quarry. He could not seem to grasp anything very intelligently but that one idea, which crowded out every other for the time. The two passed store after store, markets, beer-saloons, fruit-stalls, and dry-goods. There were several blocks before the first drug-store was reached. Carroll saw the red, green, and blue bottles in the windows, and turned towards the door.

"Mr. Willard keeps this store; he's a nice man," volunteered the boy, in his sweet treble.

Carroll looked down and smiled mechanically. "Is he?" he said.

"Yes. My mamma makes Mis' Willard's dresses. She's real good pay."

Carroll entered the store, the boy still keeping close hold of his hand.

There was no one behind the counter, on which stood an ornate soda-fountain with the usual appliances for hot and cold beverages. A thought struck Carroll. He put his hand in his pocket and looked down at the boy.

"Do you like chocolate?" he asked.

The boy blushed and hung his head.

"Do you?" persisted Carroll.

"I didn't ask for any," the boy said, in an exceedingly shamefaced voice.

Carroll laughed as a man came from the rear of the store and paused inquiringly behind the counter. "Give this little boy a cup of hot chocolate, and make it pretty sweet," he said.

When the boy was seated, blissfully sipping his chocolate, Carroll asked calmly for his chloroform. The druggist himself gave it to him without any demur. There was that about Carroll's whole appearance which completely allayed suspicion. It seemed inconceivable that a man of such appearance, benevolently and genially treating a pretty little boy to a cup of chocolate, should be essaying to purchase poison for any nefarious purpose. The druggist put up the chloroform in a bottle marked poison in red letters, changed the bill which Carroll gave him in payment, and remarked that it was a cold day and looked like snow. The boy was hurrying to finish his chocolate, that he might follow again this object of his admiration, but Carroll caught sight of the Banbridge car coming up the street, after having made an unusually long wait at the terminus of the line.

"Take your time, my boy. I have to go," he said, and hurried out to the car, leaving the boy staring wistfully after him with the chocolate sweet upon his tongue.

Carroll, with his chloroform in his pocket, boarded the car, and speeded again over the road to Banbridge. The way home seemed to him like a dream. He was not conscious of much about him; his mind now seemed concentrated on that small bottle in his pocket. He noticed nobody in the car, but sat in his corner, with eyes fixed absently on the flying landscape. The conductor had to speak twice before he realized that he was asking for his fare. When the car reached the end of the line in Banbridge, he sat still for a few seconds before he collected himself enough to understand that the end of his journey was reached, and it was time for him to get off the car and walk home.

Walking along the familiar way, his apathy began to fail and his nervous excitement returned. He began to realize everything, this hideous end to his failure of a life which was so rapidly approaching. He realized that he was walking alone to his deserted home, cold and cheerless, dark and silent. It was already dusk, the days were short and the sky heavily clouded. The raw wind from the northeast smote him hard in the face like a diffused flail of wrath. He thought of his wife and children and sister speeding along to their old home in the cheerful Pullman-car. He reflected that about this time they would be thinking of going to the dining-car for their dinner. He reflected that after the chloroform had done its work, they would be well cared for in Kentucky, much better off than they had ever been under his doubtful protection; that Eddy might grow up to be a better man than his father, that Charlotte would marry down there, that they would all be comfortable, and in the intense and abnormal self-centredness of the mood which was upon him, that mood which leads a man to escape from his own agony of life by the first exit, that awful hunger for the beyond of his own soul, he never gave a thought to the possible sufferings of his family, to their possible grief at the loss of him. He actually hugged himself with the contemplation of their comfort and happiness, which would follow upon his demise, as he hugged himself upon the prospective ecstasy and oblivion in the bottle in his pocket.

He came in sight of his house, and a bright light shone in the dining-room window. He looked at it in bewilderment. His first thought was an unreasoning one that some of his creditors had in some unforeseen way taken possession. He went wearily around to the side door. There was a light also behind the drawn curtain of the kitchen. He opened the door and smelled broiling beefsteak and tea. Then Charlotte, warm and rosy, laughing and almost weeping at the same time, ran towards him with her arms held out.

"I have come back, papa," said she.

CHAPTER XXXIII

For the first time in his life Arthur Carroll had a perfect sense of the staying power, of the impregnable support, of love and the natural ties of humanity. Charlotte's slender arms closed around his neck; she stood, half-weeping, half-laughing, leaning against him, but in reality he leaned against her, the soul of the man against the soul of the girl, and he got from it a strength which was stronger than life or death. He felt that it bent not one whit before his terrible weight of misery and perplexity. He was stayed.

"I came back, papa," Charlotte repeated. She was herself a little terrified by what seemed to her a daring action; then, too, she dimly perceived something beneath the surface which made her tremble. She felt the despairing weight of the other soul against her own. She stood still, clinging to her father, saying in her little, quivering voice that she had come back, and he was quite still, until at last he made a little sound like a dry sob, and Charlotte straightened herself and took his hand firmly in her little, soft one. The girl became all in a second a woman, with the full-fledged instincts of one. She knew just what to do for a man in a moment of weakness. She towered, by virtue of the maternal instinct within her, high above her father in spiritual strength.

"Papa, come into the house," said she, and her voice seemed no longer Charlotte's, but echoed from the man's far-off childhood. "Come into the house, papa," she said; "come." And Carroll followed her into the house, like a child, his hands clasped firmly and commandingly by the little, soft one of his daughter.

Charlotte led her father into the dining-room, which was warm and light. There was a Franklin stove in there, and a bright fire burned in it.

"The furnace fire had gone out, and I could not do anything with that, so I made a fire in this stove," Charlotte explained. "I made it burn very easily." She spoke with a childish pride. It was, in fact, the first time she had ever made a fire. "The fire in the kitchen-range was low, too," she said, but I put some coal on and I poked it, and there is a beautiful bed of coals to cook the beefsteak." Then Charlotte caught herself up short. "Oh, the beefsteak will burn!" she cried, anxiously. "Do sit down, papa, and wait a minute. I must see to the beefsteak."

With that Charlotte ran into the kitchen, and Carroll dropped into the nearest chair. He felt dazed and happy, with the happiness of a man waking to consciousness from an awful incubus of nightmare, and yet a deadly sense of guilt and shame was beginning to steal over him. That bottle of chloroform in his pocket stung his soul like the worm, which gnaweth the conscience unceasingly, of the Scriptures. He thought vaguely of removing it, of concealing it somewhere. He looked at the china-closet, the door of which stood ajar; he looked at the sideboard with its glitter of cut glass and silver; but reflected that Charlotte might directly go to either and discover it, and make inquiries. He kept it in his pocket.

He heard Charlotte running about in the kitchen. He continued to smell the broiling beefsteak and tea, and also toast. He became conscious of a healthy hunger. He had eaten nothing since morning, and very little then. Then he gathered his faculties together enough to wonder how this had come about; how and why Charlotte had returned. But he sat still in the chair beside the Franklin stove. He gazed steadily into the red glow of the coals, and a strange dimness came over his vision. A species of counter-hypnotism seemed to overcome him. He had been in an abnormal state, superinduced by unhealthy suggestions of the imagination acting upon a mind ill at ease; now his natural state gradually asserted itself. His mind swung slowly back to its normal poise. When Charlotte entered, bearing a platter of beefsteak, he turned to her quite naturally.

"How did it happen, darling?" he asked.

Charlotte looked at him, and her face, which had been anxious and puzzled, lightened. She laughed. "I had my mind all made up, papa," she replied, in a triumphant little voice.

"That you would come back?"

"Yes, papa. I knew there was no use in saying I would not go. I knew if I did, Amy would directly declare that she would not go either, and I should spoil everything. So I decided that I would start with the rest, and come back."

"How far did you go?"

"I went to Lancaster. I did not mean to go so far. I meant to get off at New Sanderson, but I could not manage it. Amy wanted to play pinochle, and I could not get away. But when we got to Lancaster, we stopped awhile, and Amy was having a nap, and Anna was reading, and the train made a long stop, and Eddy and I got out, and I told Eddy what I was going to do, and gave him a little note. I had it all written before I started. I said in the note that I was coming back, that I did not want to go to Kentucky; that I was coming back and would stay with you a little while, and then we would both go to Kentucky and join the others. I said they were not to worry about me."

"What did you tell Eddy?"

"I told Eddy that you could not be left alone with nobody to cook for you, and he must get on the train and not make any fuss, and tell the others, and be a good boy, and he said he would. I saw him safely on the train."

"How did you get here from Lancaster, child?"

"I took the trolley," Charlotte said. "There is a trolley from Lancaster to New Sanderson, you know, papa."

Charlotte did not explain that the trolley from Lancaster to New Sanderson was not running, and that she had walked six miles before connecting with the trolley to Banbridge. "I got the meat in New Sanderson," said she. "I got some other things, too. You will see. We have a beautiful supper, papa."

Carroll looked at her, and she answered the question he was ashamed to ask. "Aunt Catherine sent me a little money," she said. "She sent me twenty-five dollars in a post-office order. She wrote me a letter and sent me the money for myself. She said the shops were not very good down there — you know they are not, papa — and I might like to buy some little things for myself in New York before coming. I said nothing about the money to Amy or the others, because I had this plan. I even let Amy take that extra money and buy me the hat. I was afraid I was mean, but I could not tell her I had the money, because I wanted to carry out this plan, and I did not see how I could get back or do anything unless I kept it, for I had no money at all before. I have written a letter to Aunt Catherine, and she will get it as soon as they get there. I don't think she will be angry; and if she is, I don't care." Charlotte's voice had a ring of charming defiance. She looked gayly at her father. "Come, papa," said she, "the beefsteak is hot. Sit right up, and I will bring in the tea and toast. There are some cakes, too, and a salad. I have got a beautiful supper, papa. I never cooked any beefsteak before, but just look how nice that is. Come, papa."

Carroll obediently drew his chair up to the table. It was daintily set; there was even a little vase of flowers, rusty red chrysanthemums, in the centre on the embroidered centrepiece. Charlotte spoke of them when she brought in the tea and toast. "I suppose I was extravagant, papa," she said, "but I stopped at a florist's in New Sanderson and bought these. They did not cost much — only ten cents for all these." She took her seat opposite her father, and poured the tea. She put in the lumps of sugar daintily with the silver tongs. Her face was beaming; she was lovely; she was a darling. She looked over at her father as she extended his cup of tea, and there was not a trace of self-love in the little face; it was all love for and tender care of him. "Oh, I am so glad to be home!" she said, with a deep sigh.

Carroll looked across at her with a sort of adoration and dependence which were painful, coming from a father towards a child. His face had lightened, but he still looked worn and pale and old. He was become more and more conscious of the chloroform in his pocket, and the shame and guilt of it.

"Why did you come back, honey?" he asked.

"I didn't want to go," Charlotte said, simply. "I wasn't happy going away and leaving you alone, papa. I want to stay here with you, and if you have to leave Banbridge I will go with you. I don't mind at all not having much to get along with. I can get along with very little."

"You would have been more comfortable with the others, dear," said Carroll. He did not begin to eat his supper, but looked over it at the girl's face.

"You are not eating anything, papa," said Charlotte. "Isn't the beefsteak cooked right?"

"It is cooked beautifully, honey; just right. All is. I am glad to see you come back. You don't just know what it means to me, dear, but I am afraid —"

Charlotte laughed gayly. "I am not," said she. "Talk about comfort — isn't this comfort? Please *do* eat the beefsteak, papa."

Carroll began obediently to eat his supper. When he had fairly begun he realized that he was nearly famished. In spite of his stress of mind, the needs of the flesh reasserted themselves. He could not remember anything tasting so good since his boyhood. He ate his beefsteak and potatoes and toast; then Charlotte brought forward with triumph a little dish of salad, and finally a charlotte-russe.

"I got these at the baker's in New Sanderson," said she. She was dimpling with delight. She looked very young, and yet the man continued to have that sense of dependence upon her. She exulted openly over her supper, her cooking, and her return. "I don't know but I was very deceitful, papa," she said, but with glee rather than compunction. "Amy and Anna had no idea that I did not mean to go with them to Aunt Catherine's, and oh, papa, what do you think I did? What do you?"

"What, dear?"

"My trunk was packed with, with — some old sheets and blankets and newspapers — and all my clothes are hanging in my closet up-stairs." Charlotte laughed a long ring of laughter. "I knew I was deceitful," she said again, and laughed again.

Carroll did not laugh. He was thinking of the Hungarian girl in Charlotte's red dress, but Charlotte thought he was sober on account of her deceit.

"Do you think it was very wrong, papa?" she asked, with sudden seriousness, eying him wistfully. "I will write and tell Amy tonight all about it. I couldn't think of any other way to do, papa."

"I met Marie as I was coming home from the station this morning," Carroll said, irrelevantly.

Charlotte looked at him quickly, blushed, and raised her teacup.

"I thought at first, though I knew it could not be, that I saw you coming," said he; "something about her dress —"

"Papa," said Charlotte, setting down her cup, and she was half-crying — "papa, I had to. Marie was so shabby, and she said that her lover had deserted her because she was so poorly dressed; and though of course he could not be a very good man, nor very loyal to desert her for such a reason as that, yet those people are different, perhaps, and don't look at things as we do; and Marie has got another place; but — but she — didn't have any money, you know, and she didn't really have a dress fit to be seen, and that dress I gave her I did not need at all — I really did not, papa. I have plenty besides, and so I gave it to her, and my little Eton jacket, and I told her she would certainly have every cent we owed her, and she seemed very happy. She is going to a party tonight and will wear that dress. She thinks she will get her lover back. Those Hungarian men must be queer lovers. Marie said he would not marry her, anyway, until she had some money for her dowry, but she thinks she may be able to keep him until then with my red silk dress, and I told her she should certainly have it all in time." Charlotte's voice, in making the last statement, was full of pride and confidence without a trace of interrogation.

"She shall if I live, dear," said Carroll. All at once there came over him, stimulated with food for heart and body, such a rush of the natural instinct for life as to completely possess him. It seemed to him that as a short time before he had hungered for death, he now hungered for life. Even the desire to live and pay that miserable little Hungarian servant-maid was a tremendous thing. The desire to live for the smallest virtues, ambitions, and pleasures of life was compelling force.

"I have something beautiful for breakfast tomorrow morning, papa," said Charlotte, "and I know how to make coffee." And he felt that it was worth while living for tomorrow morning's breakfast alone. No doubt this state of mind, as abnormal in its way as the other had been, was largely due to physical causes, to the unprosaic quantity of food in a stomach which had been cheated of its needs for a number of days. The blood rushed through his veins with the added force of reaction, supplying his brain. He was not happier — that could scarcely be said — but he was swinging in the opposite direction. Whereas he had wanted to die, because of his misery and failures, he now wanted to live, to repair them, and the thought was dawning upon him, to take revenge because of them. In this mood the consideration of the bottle of chloroform in his pocket became more and more humiliating and condemning. The sight of the girl's innocent, triumphant, loving little face opposite overwhelmed him with a stinging consciousness of it all. He felt at one minute a terrible fear lest those clear young eyes of hers could penetrate his miserable secret, lest she should say, suddenly: "Papa, what did you go to Port Willis for? What have you in your pocket?"

Charlotte went to bed early, after she had cleared away the table and washed the dishes, unwonted tasks for her, but which she performed with a delight intensified by a feeling of daring.

"Papa, I have washed the dishes beautifully; I know I have," she said, and she looked at him for praise, her head on one side, her look half-whimsical, half-childishly earnest. "I don't see why it is at all hard work to be a maid," said she.

"There are other things to do, dear, I suppose," Carroll said.

"I think I could easily learn to do the other things," said she. "I don't quite know about the washing and ironing, and possibly the scrubbing and sweeping." Charlotte surveyed, as she spoke, her hands. She looked at the little, pink palms, made pinker and slightly wrinkled by the dish-water; she turned them and surveyed the backs with the slightly scalloping joints, and the thin-nailed fingers. She shook her head. "I don't know," said she, again.

"I know," Carroll said, quickly. "Your father is going to take care of you, Charlotte. It has not yet come to that pass that he is quite helpless."

Charlotte did not seem to notice his hurt, indignant tone. She went on reflectively. "It does seem," said she, "as if there were a great many ways of being crippled besides not having all your arms and legs; as if it were really being very much crippled if you are in a place where there is work to be done, and your hands are not rightly made for doing it. Now here I am, and I can't do Marie's work as well as Marie did it, because she was really born with hands for washing and ironing and scrubbing and sweeping, and I wasn't. A person is really crippled when she is born unfitted to do the things that come her way to be done, isn't she, papa?"

"There is no question of your doing such things, Charlotte," Carroll said again, and Charlotte looked at him quickly.

"Why, papa!" said she, and went up to him and kissed him. She rubbed her cheek caressingly against his, and his cheek felt wet. She realized that with a sort of terror. "Why, papa, I did not mean any harm!" she said.

"I will get a servant for you tomorrow, Charlotte," he said, brokenly. "It has not yet come to pass that you have to do such work." He spoke brokenly. He did not trust himself to look at the girl, who was now looking at him intently and seriously.

"Papa, listen to me," said she. "Really, there is no scrubbing nor sweeping nor washing nor ironing to be done here for quite a time. Marie has left the house in very good condition. There is enough money to pay for the laundry for some time, and as for the cooking, you can see that I shall love to do that. You know Aunt Catherine used to let me cook, that I always like to."

Carroll made no reply.

"Papa, you are not well; you are all worn out," Charlotte said. "Let us go into the den, and you smoke a cigar and I will read to you."

Carroll shook his head. "No, dear, not tonight," he said.

"We will have a game of cribbage."

"No, dear, not tonight. You are tired, and you must go to bed. Take a book and go to bed and read. You are tired."

"I am not very tired," said Charlotte, but therein she did not speak the entire truth. Her spirit was leaping with happy buoyancy, but she could scarcely stand on her feet, she was so fatigued with her unaccustomed labor and the excitement of it all. There was a ringing in her ears, and her eyelids felt stiff; she was also a little hoarse. "Will you go to bed, too, papa?" said she, anxiously.

"I will go very soon, dear."

"Won't you want anything else before you go?"

"No, darling."

Charlotte stood regarding him with the sweetest expression of protection and worshipful affection, and withal the naïveté of a child pleased with herself and what she has done for the beloved one. "You *did* have a good supper, didn't you, papa?" she asked.

"A beautiful supper, sweetheart."

"You never had a better?"

"Never so good, never half so good," said Carroll, fervently, smiling down at her eager face.

"You are glad I came back, aren't you, papa?"

"Glad for my own sake, God knows, dear, but —"

"There are no buts at all," Charlotte cried, laughing. "No buts at all. If you don't think I am happier and better off here with you than I would be rattling down to Kentucky on that old railroad, and I am always carsick on a long journey, you know, papa."

Charlotte lit a lamp and bade her father good-night. She kissed him and looked at him anxiously and with a little bewilderment. He had seated himself, and was smoking with an abstracted air, his eyes fixed on vacancy.

"Now, papa, you will go to bed very soon yourself, won't you?" she urged. "You look sick, and I know you are tired out."

"Very soon, honey," Carroll replied.

After Charlotte had gotten into bed, and lay there with her lamp on a stand beside her and her book in hand, she listened more than she read. When in the course of half an hour she heard her father come up the stairs and enter his own room, she gave a sigh of relief. "Good-night, papa," she called out.

"Good-night, dear," he responded. Then Charlotte fell asleep with her light burning and her book in her hand, and she did not hear her father go softly over the stairs a second time.

As was said, his mind, in regaining its normal balance, had swung too far to the opposite direction. His desire to live, that possessed him, was as much too intense as his previous desire to die. He had for the time being another fixed idea, not as dangerous in a sense as the other, at least not to himself, but still dangerous. The miserable little bottle of chloroform became, in this second abnormal state of his mind, the key-note on which his strenuous thoughts harped. It seemed to him that that bottle with its red label of "Poison" was as horrible a thing to have as a blood-stained knife of murder. It was in a sense blood-stained. It bore the stigma of the self-murderer. It bore evidence to his hideous cowardice, his unspeakable crime of spirit. He felt that he must do away with that bottle; but how? After he was in his room, and the door locked, he took the bottle from its neat wrapper of pink paper and looked at it. It seemed like an absurdly easy thing to dispose of; but it did not, when he reflected, seem easy at all. It was not a thing to burn, or throw away. He thought of opening the window and giving it a fling; but what was to hinder some one finding it in the morning under the windows? The man actually sat down and gazed awhile at the small phial of death with utter helplessness and horror; and as he did so, the always smouldering wrath of his soul towards that man in Kentucky, that man who had wronged him, swelled to its height. He had always hated him, but his hate had never assumed such strength as this. He became conscious, as he had never been before, that that man was responsible for it all, even to the crowning horror and ignominy of that bottle. He reflected that no man of his name had ever, so far as he knew, stained it as he had done by his life; that no man of his name had ever so stained the record of his race by the contemplation of such a dastardly death. He felt, gazing at that bottle, every whit as guilty as if he had drained the contents, and he told himself that that man was responsible, that that man had murdered him in the worst and subtlest way in which murder can be done; he had caused him to do away with his own honor. He felt himself alive to his furthest fancy with hate and a desire for revenge.

"I will live, and I will have the better of him yet," he muttered to himself.

Every nerve tingled; his fingers clutched the bottle like hot wires — that bottle which that other man had caused him to buy, and which he could not get rid of, this palpable witness to his crime and disgrace.

Finally he got up and threw up the window; then he put it down again. It did not seem to him, in his unreasoning state, that he could probably empty the chloroform out of the window without the slightest danger of detection, and then scrape the label from the bottle. It did not seem possible to him that Charlotte would not immediately perceive the fumes of the drug which would cry to her from the ground. Her room was next his own. He sat down again and gazed at the bottle with the absurd bewilderment of a drunken man. Then he tried stowing it away in a drawer of the dresser, behind a pile of shirts. He even, after doing that, began to undress, but that did not satisfy him. It seemed certain to him that Charlotte would find it in the morning, and say, "Why, papa, what is this bottle marked 'Poison' in your drawer?"

At last he unlocked his door, opened it, and stole softly down-stairs. He unfastened the kitchen door, and went across the field and garden behind the house, to the little pond beside the rustic arbor, the little sentimental Idlewild of the original dwellers in the house. It was a dark, waving night. It still did not storm, and was warmer. It would probably rain before morning. The wind smote his face damply. He had come out in his shirt-sleeves. He moved slyly, like a thief; he felt like one, like a thief and a murderer — a self-murderer, and a murderer, in will, of the man who had caused him to commit the crime. He felt burning with hate as he slunk across the field, of hate of the man who had brought him to this, who had caused his financial and moral downfall. At that time, had the man been near, his life would have been worth nothing. Carroll thought, as he hurried on, holding fast to the bottle, how he could overthrow him, uncork the bottle and hold it to his face, that he might inhale the death he had meted out to him. It seemed to him like the merest instinct of self-defence. He stumbled now and then over the tangle of dry vines in the garden, among the corn-stalks. He went like a guilty thing, instead of moving with his usual confident state, the state of a gentleman from a long line of gentlemen. He had become alive to his own shame, his own ignominy, and he had turned at bay upon the one who had caused him, as he judged, to fall.

When he reached the little pond, he paused and looked about him for a second. It was a desolate spot at that time of year and that hour. The little sheet of water gleamed dully like an obscured eye of life. The trees waved their slender arms over it. Something about the summer-house creaked as a damp wind blew on his face. He saw through the trees a faint gleam of light from a house window farther down the road. He heard a rustle in the undergrowth on his right, probably a stray cat or a bird. He stood there holding the bottle of chloroform and hating that man; then he raised his arm and flung the thing into the pond. There was a splash which sounded unnaturally loud, as if it could be heard a long distance.

Then Carroll turned and went home across the field; the evidence of his guilt was hidden away out of sight, but the memory and consciousness of it was in his very soul and had become a part of him, and his hate of the man who had brought him to it stalked by his side like a demon across the fields.

CHAPTER XXXIV

The next morning Carroll looked ill, so ill that Charlotte regarded him with dismay as she sat opposite him at the breakfast-table. She was full of delight over her meal. She had gotten up early and made the fire and cooked the breakfast; in fact, Carroll had been awakened from the uneasy sleep into which he had fallen towards morning by the fragrance of the coffee. He opened his eyes, and it took him some time to adjust himself to his environment, so much had happened since the morning before. He awoke in the same room, in the same bed, but spiritual stresses had made him unfamiliar with himself. It took him some time to recall everything — the departure of his family, his journey to Port Willis, Charlotte's return, the chloroform — but that which required no time to return, which was like a vital flame in him from the first second of his consciousness, was his hatred of the man who had done him the wrong. As he lay there reflecting he became aware that he had always hated in just such measure as this, from the very first moment in which he had become aware of the wrong, only he had not himself fairly sensed the mighty power of the hate. He had not known that it so permeated his very soul, so filled it with unnatural fire. At last he arose and dressed and went downstairs, and greeted Charlotte, radiant and triumphant, and seated himself opposite her at the table, when her face fell.

"You are certainly ill, papa," said she.

"No, dear," said Carroll. "I am not ill at all." This morning he tried to eat, to please her, for his appetite of the night before had gone. He was haggard and pale, and his eyes looked strained.

"You look very ill," said Charlotte. "Let me call the doctor for you, papa, dear."

Carroll laughed. "nonsense," he said. "I am as well as ever I was. You make a baby of your old father, honey."

"Have another chop, then," said Charlotte.

And Carroll passed his plate for the chop, and ate it, although it fairly nauseated him. He looked at the child opposite as he ate, and she looked as beautiful as an angel, and as good as one to him. He thought how the little thing had come back to him, her unfortunate father, who had made such a muddle of his life, who had been able to do so little for her; how she had given up the certainty of a happy and comfortable home for uncertainty, and possibly privation, and the purest gratitude and love that was so intense possessed him. Looking at Charlotte, he almost forgot the hatred of the man who had brought this upon him, and then the hatred awoke to fiercer life because of the love.

Then, all unconsciously, Charlotte herself, seemingly actuated by a species of mental telegraphy, spurred him on. "Papa," said she, viewing him with approbation as he ate his second chop, "is that man in Acton who treated you so dreadfully still living there?"

Carroll's face contracted. "Yes, dear," he said.

"If I had gone down there, and had seen that man, I should have been afraid of the way I would have felt when I saw him," said Charlotte. Her innocent girl's face took on an expression which was the echo of her father's. "I suppose he is prosperous," she said.

"I think so, honey."

"I feel wicked when I think of him," said Charlotte, still with the look which echoed her father's, "when I think of all he has made you suffer, papa."

Carroll made no reply; the two looked at each other for a second. The girl's soft face became almost terrible.

"I think if I were a man, and met him, and — had a pistol, I should kill him," she said, slowly.

Carroll made an effort which fairly convulsed him. His face changed. He sprang up, went over to Charlotte, took hold of her head, bent it back, and kissed her. "For God's sake, honey, don't talk in that way!" he said. "All this is not for you to meddle with nor trouble your little head with."

"Yes it is, if it troubles you, Papa."

"I can manage my own troubles, and I don't want any little girl like you trying to take hold of the heavy end," Carroll said, and laughed quite naturally.

"Then you must not look so ill, papa."

"I am going to have another cup of coffee," Carroll said, and showed diplomacy.

Charlotte delightedly poured out the coffee. "Isn't it very good coffee?" she said.

"Delicious coffee."

"I am going to get a beautiful dinner for you," Charlotte said. The second cup of coffee had reassured her. She began to think her father did not look so ill, after all. She was herself in a state of perfect content and happiness. She felt a sense of triumph, of daring, which exhilarated her. She adored her father, and how cleverly she had managed this coming back. How impossible she had made it for any one to gainsay her! After breakfast her father went out, telling her he should be home by noon, and she busied herself about the house. She was an absolute novice about such work, but she found in it a charm of novelty, and she developed a handiness which filled her with renewed triumph. She kept considering what would her father have done if she had not returned.

"He would have had no supper when he came home last night," Charlotte said — "no supper, for he evidently was not going to the inn, and the fire was out. How dreadful it would have been for him!" She imagined perfectly her father's sensations of delighted surprise and relief when he espied her, to welcome him, when he felt the warmth of the fire, when he smelled the supper. The pure delight of a woman over the comfort which she gives a child or a man whom she loves was over her. She realized her father's comfort as she had never realized any of her own. She fairly danced about her work. She put the bedrooms in order, she washed the breakfast dishes. Then she meditated going down-town and buying a fish for dinner. Carroll was very fond of baked fish. About ten o'clock she had finished her work, and she put on her hat and coat and set forth. She ordered the fish, and paid for it. She gave the man a five-dollar note to change. He looked at it suspiciously. When she had gone out, he and two other men who were standing in the little market looked at one another.

"Guess the world's comin' to an end," he said, laughing, "when they pay cash with five-dollar bills."

"Sure it was a good one?" said one of the other men.

"I thought all Carroll's family had went," said the third man.

"Guess they didn't have enough money to take this one, and you can't beat the Pennsylvania Railroad nohow," said the fishman.

Charlotte went on to the butcher's, bought and paid for some ham, then to Anderson's for eggs. The old clerk came forward as she entered, and answered her question about the eggs.

"Do you want them charged?" he asked.

"No, I will pay for them," replied Charlotte, and took her little purse, and just then Anderson, having heard her voice, looked incredulously out of his office, his morning paper in hand. Charlotte laid some money on the counter, and stepped forward at once. She saw with a sort of wonder, and an agitation within herself for which she could not account, that the man was deadly white, that he fairly trembled.

"Good-morning, Mr. Anderson," she said.

Anderson was a man of self-control, but he gazed down at her fairly speechless. He had been telling himself that she had gone as certainly out of his life as if she were dead, and here she was again.

"I thought," he stammered, finally.

Charlotte's face of innocent wonder and disturbance flushed. "No, I did not go, after all," she said, like a child. "That is, I started, but I went no farther than Lancaster. They thought I was going — they all did — but I could not leave papa alone, and so I came back." She was incoherent. Her own confusion deepened. She tried to look into the man's face, but her own eyes fell; her lips quivered. She was almost crying, but she did not know why. She turned to the counter, behind which stood the man with the package of eggs and the change.

"Send that package," Anderson said, brusquely.

"The wagon has gone."

"Send it as soon as it comes back. There will be time enough."

"I can manage if I don't have the eggs until noon," said Charlotte.

The clerk turned to put away the parcel in readiness for the delivery-wagon, and again Anderson and the girl looked at each other. Anderson had caught up his hat with his newspaper as he came out of the office, and Charlotte looked at it.

"Were you going out?" she asked, timidly, and yet the question seemed to imply a suggestion. She glanced towards the door.

Anderson muttered something about an errand, and went out with her. They walked along the street together. Suddenly Charlotte looked up in his face and began confiding in him. She told the whole story.

"You see, I couldn't leave papa," she concluded.

Anderson looked down at her, and the look was unmistakable. Charlotte blushed and her face quivered.

"Then you are going to stay here all winter?" he said, in a low voice.

"Oh, no, I think not," she replied. "I think we shall go away."

Anderson's face fell. She had spoken very eagerly, almost as if she were anxious to go.

She made it worse. "I don't think I should have come back if it had not been for that," she said. "I did not see what poor papa could do all alone, trying to move. I don't think I should."

"Yes," said Anderson, soberly.

"Perhaps I should not have," said she. She did not look at him. She kept her eyes fixed on the frozen ground, but the man's face lighted.

They kept on in a vague sort of fashion and had reached the post-office. They entered, and when Anderson had unlocked his box and taken out his mail, and Charlotte had gotten some letters which looked like bills for her father, he realized the he had no excuse to go any farther with her. He bade her good-morning, therefore. Charlotte said good-morning, and there was a little uncertainty and wistfulness in her look and voice. She was very unsophisticated, and she was wondering whether she should ask him to call, now her mother and aunt had gone. She resolved that she would ask her father. As for Anderson, he went back to the store in a sort of dream. He suddenly began to wonder if the impossible could be possible. At one moment he ridiculed himself for the absurdity of such an imagination, even, and then the imagination returned. He reflected that he would have had no such doubt if it had not been for his lack of success in his profession. He charged himself with a lack of self-respect that he should have doubts now.

"After all, I am a man," he told himself. "I am as good as ever I was."

Then he considered, and rightly, that it was not his own just estimate of himself which was to be taken into consideration in a case of this sort, but that of the people. He realized that a girl brought up as Charlotte Carroll had been might, knowing, as she must finally know, her own father to be little better than a common swindler, not even dream of the possibility of marrying a grocer. He had to pass his old office on his way home to dinner that noon, and he looked at it with more regret than he had ever done since leaving it. The school was out and the children were streaming along the street. The air was full of their chatter. Henry Edgecomb came up behind him with a good-morning. He looked worn and nervous. Anderson looked at him sharply after his greeting.

"What is the matter?" he asked.

"Nothing, only I am tired out," Edgecomb replied, wearily. "Sometimes I envy you."

"Don't," said Anderson.

"I do. This friction with new souls and temperaments is wearing my old one thin. I would rather sell butter and cheese."

"Rather do anything than desert the battle-field you have chosen, because you are beaten," said Anderson, with sudden bitterness.

"Nonsense! You are not beaten."

"Yes, I am."

"You have simply taken up new weapons."

"Weights and balances," said Anderson, but his laugh was bitter.

He left Edgecomb at the corner, and, going up his own street, reflected again. He began to wonder if possibly he would not have done better to have stuck to his profession; if he could not have left Banbridge and tried elsewhere — in the City. He wondered if he had shown energy and manly ambition, if he had not been poor-spirited. When he reached home his mother eyed him anxiously and asked if he were ill.

"No," he said, "but I met Henry, and he looks wretchedly."

"He hasn't enough to eat," Mrs. Anderson said. "Harriet does not give him enough to eat. It is a shame. If I were in his place I would get married."

"He says he is tired out teaching. He talks about the friction of so many natures on his."

"Of course there is a friction," said Mrs. Anderson, "but he could stand it if he had more to eat. Let us have a dinner next Sunday night; let us have a roast turkey and a pudding. We will have lunch at noon. Henry is very fond of turkey, and it is late enough to get good ones."

"Shall we ask Harriet?" inquired Anderson, with a lurking mischief.

His mother looked at him with quick suspicion. "You don't want her asked?" she said.

"Why should she be asked? She never is."

"I don't know but with an extra dinner —"

"She has her mission," Mrs. Anderson said, with firmness. "You are eating nothing yourself, Randolph." Presently she looked at her son with an inscrutable expression. "Are the Carrolls all gone?" she asked.

Anderson cut himself a bit of beefsteak carefully before replying. "Some of them, I believe," said he.

"I heard Mrs. Carroll and her sister and daughter and the boy all went yesterday morning. Josie Eggleston came in about the Rainy Day Club meeting, this morning, and she told me." There was something so interrogative in his mother's tone that Anderson was obliged to say something.

"They all went except the daughter, I believe," he said.

"The girl who was here?"

"Yes."

"Then she didn't go?"

"She went as far as Lancaster, but she came back?"

"Came back?"

"Yes. She didn't want to leave her father alone, and — under a cloud, as he seems to be, and she knew if she declared she was not going there would be opposition — that, in fact, her mother would not go."

"I don't think much of her for going, anyway," said Mrs. Anderson. "Leaving her husband all alone. I don't care what he had done, he was her husband, and I dare say he cheated on her account, mostly. She ought not to have gone."

"They wanted her to go; she is not very strong; and the sister is really ill," said Anderson, "and so the daughter planned it. She went as far as Lancaster, then she got off the train."

"Why, I should think her mother would be crazy?"

"She sent word back, a letter by Eddy. He got off the train with her; the train stopped there a few minutes."

"Then she came back?"

"Yes."

"And she is going to stay with her father?"

"Yes."

"Oh!" said Mrs. Anderson.

After dinner Anderson sat beside the sitting-room window with his noon mail, as was his custom, for a few minutes before returning to the store, and his mother came up behind him. She stroked his hair, which was thick and brown, and only a little gray on the temples.

"She is a very pretty girl, and I think she is a dear child to come back and not leave her father alone," she said.

Anderson did not look up, but he leaned his head caressingly towards his mother.

"I have been thinking," said she. "I am a good deal older; she is only a little, young girl, and I am an old lady, and I have never called there. You know I never call on new people nowadays, but she must be very lonely, all alone there. I think I shall go up there and call on her some afternoon this week, if it is pleasant. I have some other calls I want to make on the way there, and I might as well."

"I will order the coach for you any afternoon you say, mother," replied Anderson.

CHAPTER XXXV

It was the next day but one that Mrs. Anderson, arrayed in her best, seated in state in the Rawdy coach, was driven into the grounds of the Carroll house. Charlotte answered her ring. The elder woman's quick eye saw, with both pity and disapproval, that the girl was unsuitably arrayed for housework in a light cloth dress, which was necessarily stained and spotted.

"She had on no apron," she told her son that night. "I don't suppose the poor child owns one, and of course she could not help getting her dress spotted. Her little hands were clean, though, and I think she tries hard. The parlor was all in a whirl of dust. She had just been sweeping, and flirting her broom as people always do who don't know how to sweep. The poor child's hair was white with dust, and I sat down in a heap of it, with my best black silk dress, but of course I wouldn't have seemed to notice it for anything. I brushed it off when I got in the carriage. I said, 'You are doing your work?' And she said, 'Yes, Mrs. Anderson.' She laughed, but she looked sort of pitiful. The poor little thing is tired. She isn't cut out for such work. I said her hands and arms didn't look as if she could sweep very easily, but she bristled right up and said she was very strong, very much stronger than she looked, and papa wanted to get a maid for her, but she preferred doing without one. She wanted the exercise. The way she said *preferred!* I didn't try to pity her any more, for that. Randolph —"

"What is it, mother?"

"How much has that child seen of you?"

"Not so very much, mother. Why?"

"I think she thinks a great deal about you."

"Nonsense, mother!" Anderson said. It was after tea that night, and the mother and son sat together in the sitting-room. They had a fire on the hearth, and it looked very pleasant. Mrs. Anderson had a fine white apron over her best black silk, and she sat one side of the table, knitting. Anderson was smoking and reading the evening paper on the other. He continued to smoke and apparently to read after his mother made that statement with regard to Charlotte. She looked at him and knew perfectly well that he was not comprehending anything he read.

"She is a very sweet girl," she said, presently, in an inscrutable voice. "I don't like her family, and I must say I think her father, from what I hear, almost ought to be in prison, but I don't think that child is to blame."

"Of course not," said Anderson. He turned his paper with an air of pretended abstraction.

"She says she thinks her father will leave Banbridge before long," said Mrs. Anderson, further.

Her son made no response. She sat thinking how, if Carroll did leave Banbridge and the rest of the family were in Kentucky, why, the girl could be judged separately; and if Randolph should fancy her — she was not at all sure that he did — of Charlotte she had not a doubt. She had never had a doubt of any woman's attitude of readiness to grasp the sceptre, if it were only held out by her son. And she herself was conscious of something which was almost infatuation for the girl. Something about her appealed to her. She had an almost fierce impulse of protection, of partisanship.

Anderson himself had not the least realization of his mother's actual sentiments in the matter. It was the consequence in inconsequence of a woman, which a man can seldom grasp. From what he had known of his mother's character heretofore, a girl coming from such a family would have been the last one to appeal to her for a daughter-in-law. She had been plainly hostile to young women with much superior matrimonial assets. He had often surmised that she did not wish him to marry at all. He did not understand the possibility there is in some women's natures of themselves falling in love, both individually and vicariously, with the woman who loves their sons, or who is supposed to love their sons.

"Captain Carroll came into the yard just as I drove out," said Mrs. Anderson. "He is a very fine-looking man. It is a pity." Then she added again, with an obscure accent of congratulation, "Well, if he goes away nobody need say anything more against him."

Anderson reflected, without expressing it aloud, that it was doubtful if Carroll's exit was possible, and, if possible, would be conducive to silence from his creditors, but he apparently continued to read.

"He is a very handsome man," said his mother again, "and he has the air of a gentleman. He bowed to me like a prince. He is a very fine-looking man, isn't he?"

Before Anderson could reply the door-bell rang.

"I wonder who it is," Mrs. Anderson said, in a hushed voice.

"Somebody on business, probably," replied Anderson, rising. The maid had gone out. As he went into the front hall his mother rustled softly into the dining-room. She was always averse to being in the room when men came on business. Sometimes commercial travellers infringed upon Anderson's home hours, and she was always covertly indignant. She was constantly in a state of armed humility with regard to the details of business. She felt the incongruity of herself, the elderly gentlewoman in the soft, rich, black silk, with the scarf of real lace fastened with a brooch of real pearls at the throat, with the cap of real lace, with the knots of lavender ribbon, on her fluff of white curls, remaining in the room while the discussion as to the rates of tea and coffee or sugar or soap went on. So she slipped with her knitting-work into the dining-room, but she dropped her ball of white wool, which remained beside the chair which she had occupied in the sitting-room. She was knitting a white shawl. She sat beside the dining-table, and continued to knit, however, pulling furtively on the recreant ball, while her son ushered somebody into the sitting-room, asked him politely to be seated, and then closed the door. That prevented her from knitting anymore, as the wool was held taut. So she finally laid her work on the table and went out into the hall on her way up-stairs. The door leading from the hall into the sitting-room was closed, and she stopped and eyed curiously the hat and coat on the old-fashioned mahogany table in the hall. She stood looking at them from a distance of a few feet; then she wrapped her silk draperies closely around her and slid closer. She passed her hand over the fine texture of the coat, which was redolent of cigar smoke. She took up the hat. Then she spied the top card on the little china card-basket on the table, and took it up. It was Arthur Carroll's. She nodded her head, remained standing a moment listening to the inaudible murmur of conversation from the next room, then went up-stairs, to sit down in her old winged arm-chair, covered with a peacock-pattern chintz, and read until the visitor should be gone. She was fairly quivering with astonishment and curiosity. But she was no more astonished than her son had been when he had opened the front-door and seen Arthur Carroll standing there. He had almost doubted the evidence of his eyes, especially when Carroll had accepted his invitation to enter, and had removed his coat and hat and followed him into the sitting-room.

"It is a cold night," Anderson said, feeling that he must say something.

"Very, for the season," replied Carroll, "and I have not yet, in spite of my long residence North, grown sufficiently accustomed to the heated houses and unheated out-of-doors to keep my top-coat on inside, even if I remain only a few minutes."

The sumptuous lining of the coat gleamed as he laid it on the hall-table; there was something unconquerable, sumptuous, genial, undaunted yet about the man. He had the courtesy of a prince, this poor American who had lived by the exercise of his sharper wits on his neighbor's dull ones, if report said rightly. And yet Anderson, as he sat opposite Carroll, and they were both smoking in a comrade-like fashion, doubted. There was something in the man's face which seemed to belie the theory that he was a calculating knave. His face was keen, but not cunning, and, moreover, there was a strange, almost boyish, sanguineness about it which brought Eddy forcibly to mind. It was the face of a man who might dupe himself as well as others, and do it with generous enthusiasm and self-trust. It was the face of a man who might have bitter awakenings, as well as his dupes, but who might take the same fatuous, happy leaps to disaster again. And yet there was a certain strength, even nobility, in the face, and it was distinctly lovable, and in no weak sense. He looked very like Eddy as he sat there, and, curiously enough, he spoke almost at once of him.

"I believe you were a friend of my son, Mr. Anderson," he remarked, with his pleasant, compelling smile.

Anderson smiled in response. "I believe I had that honor," he replied. Then he said something about his having gone, and how much his father must miss him. "He is a fine little fellow," he added, and was almost surprised at the expression of positive gratitude which came into Carroll's eyes in response. He spoke, however, with a kind of proud deprecation.

"Oh, well, he is a boy yet, of course," he said, "but there is a man in him if fate doesn't put too many stumbling-blocks in his way."

"There is such a thing," said Anderson.

"Undoubtedly," said Carroll. "Moral hurdles for the strengthening of the spirit are all very well, but occasionally there is a spirit ruined by them."

"I think you are right," said Anderson; "still, when the spirit does make the hurdles —"

"Oh yes, it is a very superior sort, after that," said Carroll, laughing; "but when it doesn't — Well, I hope the boy will have tasks proportioned to his strength, and I hope he will have a try at them all, anyhow."

"He seems to me like a boy that would," Anderson said. "What do you think of making of him?"

"I hardly know. It depends. His mother has always talked a good deal about Eddy's studying law, but I don't know. Somehow the law has always seemed to me the road of success for the few and a slippery maze to nowhere for the many."

A sudden thought seemed to strike Carroll; he looked a little disturbed. "By-the-way," he said, "I forgot. You yourself —"

Anderson smiled. "Yes, I studied law," said he.

"And gave it up?"

"Yes. I could not make a living with it."

Carroll regarded the other man with a curious, wistful scrutiny. He looked more and more like Eddy. His next question was as full of naïveté as if the boy himself had asked it, and yet the charming, almost courtly state of the man never for one instant failed. "And so," he said, "you tried selling butter and eggs instead of legal wisdom?" The question might have been insolent from its purport, but it was not.

Anderson laughed. "Yes," he replied. "People must eat to live, but they can live without legal wisdom. I found butter and eggs were more salable."

Carroll continued to regard him with that pathetic, wondering curiosity. "And you have never regretted the change?" he asked.

"I don't say that, but, regret or not, I had to make it, and — I am not exactly sure that I do regret it."

"But this — this new occupation of yours cannot be — precisely congenial."

"That does not disturb me," Anderson said, a little impatiently.

Carroll looked at him with understanding. "I see you feel as I do about that," he said. "It is rather proving one's self of the common to hold back too strenuously from it, and yet" — he hesitated a moment — "it takes courage, though," he said. Suddenly his eyes upon the other man became full of admiration. "My daughter tells me, or, rather, my son told me principally, that you are interested in entomology?" he said.

"Oh, I dabble a little in it," Anderson replied, smiling.

Carroll's eyes upon him continued to hold their wistful questioning, admiring expression. Anderson began to wonder what he had come for. He was puzzled by the whole affair. Carroll, too, seemed to present himself to him under a new guise. He wondered if his reverses had brought about the change.

"I do not wish," said Carroll, "to display curiosity about affairs which do not concern me, and I trust you will pardon me and give me information, or not, as you choose; but may I ask how you happened, when you became convinced that you were not to make a success in law, why you chose your present business?"

"I have not the slightest objection to answering," said Anderson, although he began to wonder if the other had called simply for the purpose of gratifying his curiosity about his affairs — "not the slightest. I simply tried to think of something which I should be sure to sell, because people would be sure to buy, and I thought of — butter and cheese. It all seems exceedingly simple to me, the principle of obtaining enough money wherewith to live and buy the necessaries of life. It is only to look about and possibly within and see what wares you can command, for which people will be willing to give their own earnings. It is all a question of supply and demand. First you must study the demand, and then your own power of supply. If you can interpret law like Rufus Choate, why, sell that; if you can edit like Horace Greeley, sell that; if you can act like Booth or sing like Patti, sell that; if you can dance like Carmencita, sell that. It all remains with you, what you can do, sing or dance, or sway a multitude, or sell butter and eggs; or possibly, rather, it remains with the public and what it decides you can do — that is better for one's vanity."

"Decidedly," agreed Carroll, with an odd, reflective expression.

"If the public want your song or your novel or your speech, they will buy it, or your dance, and if they don't they won't, and you cannot make them. You have to sell what the public want to buy, for you yourself are only a unit in a goodly number of millions."

"And yet how extremely all-pervading that unit can feel sometimes," Carroll said, with a laugh.

He was silent again, puffing at his cigar, and again Anderson, leaning back opposite and also smoking, wondered why he was there. Then Carroll removed his cigar and spoke. His voice was a little constrained, but he looked at Anderson full in the face.

"Mr. Anderson," he said, "I want to know if you will kindly tell me how much I owe you, for I am one of the consumers of butter and eggs."

Anderson continued to smoke a second before answering. "I cannot possibly tell you here, Mr. Carroll," he replied then.

"Of course I know I should have written and asked for the bill," Carroll said, "but I knew some had been paid, and — you have been most kind, and —"

Anderson waited.

"In short," said Carroll, speaking quickly and brusquely, "I am under a cloud here, and — your mother called to see my daughter this after-noon, and I thought that possibly you would pardon me if I put it all on a little different basis."

Carroll stopped, and again Anderson waited. He was becoming more and more puzzled.

Then Carroll spoke quite to the point. "I could have sent for the bill which you have so generously not sent, which you have so generously allowed my poor, little daughter to think was settled," said he, "but if you had sent it I simply could not have paid it. I could have written you what I wished to say, but I thought I could say it better. I wish to say to you that I shall be obliged if you will let me know the extent of my indebtedness to you, and if you will accept my note for six months."

"Very well," said Anderson, gravely.

"If you will have the bill made out and sent me tomorrow, I will send you my note by return mail," said Carroll.

"Very well, Mr. Carroll," replied Anderson.

Carroll arose to go. "You have a pleasant home here, Mr. Anderson," he said, looking around the room with its air of old-fashioned comfort, even state.

"It has always seemed pleasant to me," said Anderson. An odd, kindly feeling for Carroll overcame him. He extended his hand. "I am glad you called, Captain Carroll," he said. He hesitated a moment. Then he added: "You will necessarily be lonely with your family away. If you would come in again —"

"I cannot leave my daughter alone much," Carroll answered, "but otherwise I should be glad to. Thank you." He looked at Anderson with evident hesitation. There was something apparently which he was about to say, but doubted the wisdom of saying it.

"Your daughter is still with you?" Anderson said.

"Yes."

Then Anderson hesitated a second. Then he spoke. "Would you allow me to call upon your daughter, Captain Carroll?" he asked, bluntly.

Carroll's face paled as he looked at him. "On my daughter?"

"Yes. Captain Carroll, will you be seated again for a few minutes. I have something I would like to say to you."

Anderson was pale, but his voice was quite firm. He had a strange sensation as of a man who had begun a dreaded leap, and felt that in reality the worst was over, that the landing could in no way equal the shock of the start. Carroll followed him back into the sitting-room and sat down.

Anderson began at once with no preface. "I should like to marry your daughter, if she can love me well enough," he said, simply.

"Does she know you at all, Mr. Anderson?" Carroll said, in a dazed sort of fashion.

"She knows me a little. I have, of course, seen her in my store."

"Yes."

"And once, as you may remember, she came here."

"Yes, when she had the fright from the tramp."

"She cannot know me very well, I admit."

"I don't see that you know her very well, either, for that matter."

"I know her well enough," said Anderson. "I have no doubt as far as I am concerned. My only doubt is for her, not only whether she can care sufficiently for me, but whether, if she should care, it would be the best thing for her. I am much older than she. I can support her in comfort, but not in luxury, probably never in luxury; and you know my position, that I have been forced to abandon a profession which would give my wife a better social standing. You know all that; there is no need of my dwelling upon it."

Anderson said that with an indescribable pride, and yet with a perfect acquiescence in the situation. He looked at Carroll, who remained quite pale, looking at him with an inscrutable expression of astonishment. Finally he smiled a little.

"As they say in the comic column, this is so sudden, Mr. Anderson," he said.

"I can well imagine so," Anderson replied, smiling in his turn. "It is rather sudden to me. Nothing was further from my intention than to say this tonight."

Carroll looked at him soberly. "Mr. Anderson, it all depends upon the child," he said. "If Charlotte likes you, that is all there is to be said about it. You are a good man and you can take care of her. As far as the other goes, I have no right to say anything. Frankly, I should prefer that you had succeeded in your profession than in your present business, on her account."

"So should I," said Anderson, gloomily.

"But it is all for her to decide. Come and call, and let matters take their course. But — I shall say nothing to her about this. A girl like Charlotte is a sensitive thing. Call and see. As far as I am concerned —" Carroll paused a second. Then he rose and held out his hand. "I have no reason whatever to object to you as a husband for my daughter, and my son-in-law," he said.

"Thank you," said Anderson.

Carroll had gone out of the door, and Anderson was just about to close it after him, when he turned back. "By-the-way, Mr. Anderson," he said, and Anderson understood that he was about to say what had been on his mind before and he had refrained from expressing. "I want to inquire if you have any acquaintance with the large grocery house of Kidder & Ladd, in the City?" he asked.

"A slight business acquaintance," replied Anderson, wonderingly.

"I saw," said Carroll, in an odd, breathless sort of voice, "an advertisement for a — floor-walker in that house. I wondered, in the event of my applying for it, if you would be willing to give me a letter of introduction to one of the firm, if you were sufficiently acquainted."

"Certainly," said Anderson, but he was aware that he almost gasped out the answer.

"I saw the advertisement," said Carroll again. "I have to make some change in my business, and" — he essayed a laugh — "I have to think, as we have agreed is the thing to do, of some salable wares in my possession. It did occur to me that I might make a passable floor-walker. I have even thought of a drum-major, but there seems no vacancy in that line. If you would."

"Certainly," said Anderson again. "Would you like it now?"

"If it is not too much trouble."

Anderson hastened to the old-fashioned secretary in the sitting-room and wrote a line of introduction on a card while Carroll waited.

"Thank you," Carroll said, taking it and placing it carefully in his pocket-book. The two men shook hands again; Carroll went with his stately stride down the street. It was snowing a little. Anderson thought idly how he had not offered him an umbrella, as he saw the flakes driving past the electric light outside as he pulled down the window-curtains, but he was as yet too dazed to fully appreciate anything. He was dazed both by his own procedure and by that of the other man. It was as if two knights in a mock tourney had met, both riding at full speed. He had his own momentum and that of the other in the shock of meeting.

His mother's door opened as he went up-stairs with his night-lamp, and her head in a white lace-trimmed cap, for she still clung to the night-gear of her early youth, peered out at him.

"Who was it?" she asked, softly, as if the guest were still within hearing.

"Captain Carroll."

"Oh!"

"He came on business."

"He stayed quite awhile. You had a little call with him?"

"Yes, mother."

She still looked at him, her face, of gentle, wistful curiosity, dimly visible between the lace ruffles of her nightcap, in the door.

"He spoke of your calling there this afternoon, and he seemed much pleased," Anderson said.

"Did he?"

"Yes."

"Well, good-night, dear," said Mrs. Anderson, with an odd, half-troubled but rather enjoyable sigh. Her son kissed her, and she disappeared. She got back into bed, and put her lamp out. The electric light outside streamed into her room and brought back to her mind moonlight reveries of her early maidenhood. She remembered how she used, before she ever had a lover, to lie awake and dream of one. Then she fell to planning how, in the event of Randolph's marrying, the front chamber could be refurnished, and the furniture in that room put in the northwest chamber, which was sparsely furnished and little used except for storage purposes. Then the northwest room could be the guest-chamber, and Randolph's present room would answer very well for his books, and would be a study when the bed was taken down.

She had the front chamber completely refurnished when she fell asleep, and besides had some exciting and entirely victorious feminine tilts with sundry women friends who had ventured to intimate that her son had made an odd matrimonial choice. It was quite a cold night, and she wondered if that child had sufficient clothing on her bed. She was in reality, in her own way, as much in love with the girl as her son.

CHAPTER XXXVI

Carroll, in the ensuing weeks, living alone with Charlotte, endured a species of mental and spiritual torture which might have been compared with the rack and wheel of the Inquisition. It seemed to Arthur Carroll in those days as if torture was as truly one of the elements incumbent upon man's existence as fire, water, or air. He got an uncanny fancy that if it ceased he would cease. He had all his life, except in violent stresses, that happy, contented-with-the-sweet-of-the-moment temperament popularly supposed to be a characteristic of the butterfly over the rose. But deprive the butterfly of the rose and he might easily become a more tragic thing than any in existence. Now Carroll was deprived of his rose, he could get absolutely none of the sweets out of existence from whence his own individuality manufactured its honey. Even Charlotte's presence became an additional torment to him, dearly as he loved her and as thoroughly as he realized what her coming back had done for him, from what it had saved him. She had given him the impetus which placed him back in his normal condition, but, back there, he suffered even more, as a man will suffer less under a surgical operation than when the influence of the anesthetics has ceased. There was absolutely no ready money in the house during those weeks except the sum which Charlotte's aunt had sent her, which was fast diminishing, and a few scattering dollars, or rather, pennies, which Carroll picked up in ways which almost unhinged his brain when he reflected upon them afterwards. Whatever he had done before, the man tried in those days every means to obtain an honest livelihood, except the one which he knew was always open, and from which he shrank with such repugnance that it seemed he could not even contemplate it and his mind retain his balance. In his uneasy sleep at night he often had a dream of that experience which had yielded him money, which might yield him money again. He saw before him the sea of faces, of the commonest American type, of the type whose praise and applause mean always a certain disparagement. He saw his own face, his proud, white face with the skin and lineaments of a proud family, stained into the likeness of a despised race; he heard his own tongue forsaking the pure English of his fathers for the soft thickness of the negro, roaring the absurd sentimental songs; he saw his own stately limbs contorted in the rollicking, barbaric dance — and awoke with a cold sweat over him. He knew all the time that that was all was left to him, but he snatched at everything. He could not obtain the floor-walker position of which he had spoken to Anderson. He thought that possibly his fine presence and urbane manner might recommend him for a place of that sort, but it was already filled. He went to several of the great department stores and inquired if there was a vacancy. He felt that the superintendents to whom he applied regarded his good points as he might have regarded the good points of a horse. One of them told him that if he would give his address, he would be given the preference whenever a vacancy occurred. Carroll knew that he was mentally appraised as a promising person to direct ladies to ribbon and muslin counters. He looked at another floor-walker strutting up and down the aisle, and felt sure that he could do better, and all this amused contempt for himself deepened and bored its way into his very soul. He always asked himself, with the demand of an unpitying judge, if he could not have done better for himself if he had begun at once; if he had not at the first failure drifted with no resistance, with the pleasant, easy, devil-may-careness which was in his nature along with the sterner stuff which was now upheaving and asserting itself, and taken what he could, how he could. He had not, after all, had an absolutely unhappy home, although it had been founded on the sands, and although that iron of hatred of the man who had done him the wrong had been always in his soul. The life he had led had been not one of active and voluntary preying upon his fellow-men; it had been only the life of one who must have the sweets of existence for himself and those he loved, and he had gotten them, even if the flowers and the fruit hung over the garden-walls of others. Now it suddenly seemed to him that he could no longer do it, as he had done, even if the owners of the fruit and flowers should be still unawares. Curiously enough, the old *Pilgrim's Progress* which he had read as a child was very forcibly in his mind in these days. He remembered the child that ate the fruit that hung over the wall, and how the gripes, in consequence, seized him. Something very like the conviction of sin was over the man, or, rather, a complete consciousness of himself and his deeds, which is, maybe, after all, the true meaning of the term. It was true that the self-knowledge had seemed to come, perforce, because it was temporarily out of his power to transgress farther; in other words, because he was completely found out; but all the same, the knowledge was there. He saw himself just as he was, had been — a great man goaded on always by the small, never-ceasing prick of hatred, with the sense of injury always stinging his soul, living as he chose, having all that he could procure, utterly careless whether at the expense and suffering of others or not. Now, for the first time, he began to adjust himself in the place of others, and the adjusting produced torment from the realization of their miseries, and worse torment from realization of his own contemptibility. It really seemed as if all positions which might have been in some keeping with the man and his antecedents were absolutely out of his reach. Not a night but he read the advertising columns until he was blind and dizzy. Every morning he went to New York and hunted. The first morning he had taken the train, he had actually to assure some of his watchful creditors that he was going to return. Then all day he wandered about the streets, making one of long lines of applicants for the vacant positions. One morning he found himself in the line with William Allbright. He recognized unmistakably the meek, bent back of the old clerk three ahead of him in the line. A book-keeper had been advertised for in a large wholesale house, and there were perhaps forty applicants all awaiting their turn. His first impulse, when he caught sight of his old clerk, was to leave the line himself; then the nobility which was struggling for life within him asserted itself and made him ashamed of his shame. He stood still with his head a little higher, and moved on with the slowly moving line of men which crawled towards the desk like a caterpillar. He saw Allbright turn away rejected with a feeling of pity; the old man looked dejected. Carroll reflected with a sensation of pride that at least he did not owe him. He himself was rejected promptly after he had owned to his age. The man four behind him was chosen. He was a very young man, scarcely more than a boy, unless his looks belied him. He was distinctly handsome, with the boy-doll style of beauty — curly, dark hair, rosy cheeks, and a small, very carefully tended mustache. He wore a very long and fashionable coat, and was evidently pleasantly conscious of its flop around his ankles. His handsome face wore an expression of pert triumph as he passed on into the inner office. ... Carroll, who had lingered with an idle curiosity to ascertain who was the successful applicant, heard a voice so near his ear that it whistled. The voice was exceedingly bitter, even malignant.

"That's the way it goes, these times; that's the way it always goes," said the voice.

Carroll turned and gazed at the speaker, a man probably older than himself; if not, he looked older, since his hair was quite white and his carriage not so good.

"The employers nowadays are a pack of fools, a pack of fools!" said the man. His long, rather handsome face, a face which should have been mild in its natural state was twisted into a thousand sardonic wrinkles. "A pack of fools!" he repeated. "Here they'll go and hire a little whippersnapper like that every time, instead of a man who has had experience and knows how to do the work, just because he's young. Young! What's that? You'd think what they wanted was a man to keep their books straight. I can keep books if I do say so, and that young snip can't. Lord! He was in Avin & Mann's with me. Why, I tell you he can't add up a column of figures three inches long straight, to save his neck. The books will be in a pretty state. I'll give him just ten days before they'll have to get an expert in to straighten out things. Hope they will; serve 'em right. Here I am, can't get a job to save my life, because my hair has turned and I've got a few more years over my head, and I can keep books better than I ever could in my life. Good Lord! You'd think it was what was inside a man's head they'd be after, instead of the outside." He looked at Carroll. "Guess I've got a little the advantage of you in age," he said, "but I suppose that's the matter why you were given the cold shoulder."

"I shouldn't be surprised if you were right, sir," replied Carroll, rather apathetically. He was going through all this without the slightest hope, but only for the sake of feeling that he had done his utmost before he took up with the alternative which so dismayed his very soul. He himself looked old that morning. He had retained his youthful appearance much longer than men usually do, but as he had viewed his reflection in the glass that morning he had said to himself that he at last was showing his years. His hair had turned visibly gray in the last few weeks; lines had deepened; and not only that, but the youthful fire had given place to the apathy and weary resignation of age.

"But you look as if you could do more and better work in an hour than that young bob-squirt could in a month," said the man at his side.

"Very likely," replied Carroll, indifferently.

"You don't seem to care much about it," the other man said. The two had gone out of the building, and were walking slowly down the street.

"If they want young men, they do, I suppose," Carroll said.

"Been trying long?"

"Quite a time."

"Well, the employers are a set of G. D. fools!" said the other man. An oath sounded horribly incongruous coming from his long, thin, benevolent mouth.

"I don't see what you are going to do about it if they are," Carroll replied, still with that odd patience. It seemed to him as if he was getting a sort of fellow-feeling and intense personal knowledge of his fellow-beings, which united him to them with ties stronger than those of love. He felt as if he more than loved this rebellious wretch beside him, as if he were one with him, only possessed of that patience which gave him a certain power to aid him. "I suppose men have the right to employ whom they choose," said Carroll. "If they prefer young men who don't know how to do the work, to old men who do, I suppose they have a right to engage them. And they may have some show of reason for it. I don't see what can be done, anyway."

"I'll tell you what has got to be done, sir, and how we can help ourselves," returned the other, with a ranting voice which made people turn and stare at him. "I'll tell you. We've got to form a union. There are unions for everything else. We have got to have a union of older men qualified to work, who are shouldered out of it by boys. Once that is done, we are all right. Today in this country a man can't hire whom he pleases in most things. The unions have put it out of his power. The people have risen. We belong to a part of the people who haven't risen. Now we must rise. Let us form a union, I say. If they engage young men before us, there are ways of making them smart for it, the employers as well as the employés. I tell you that has got to be done."

Suddenly the men heard a laugh behind them. It was a woman's laugh, shrill and not altogether pleasant — not the laugh of a young woman, but the woman who came up with and immediately began to speak looked quite young. She was undeniably pretty. Her blond pompadour drooped coquettishly over one eye, her cheeks were pink, her face smooth, her figure was really superb, and she was very well dressed, in a tailor-made gown, smart furs, and a hat evidently of the English-tailor make.

"Excuse me," she said, with perfect assurance, and yet with nothing of offensive boldness, rather with an air of *camaraderie*, "but I heard you talking, you two, and I thought I would give you a few points. I don't know whether you know it or not, but I have recently secured the position of cashier there, in Adkins & Somers's." She motioned with one nicely gloved hand back towards the place they had just left. "I got it in preference to about a dozen young girls, too," she said, with triumph, "but I shouldn't have if —" She hesitated a minute. The color on her cheeks deepened under the floating veil, and there was, in consequence, a curious effect of two shades of rose on her cheeks. "See here," she said, walking along with them, "I don't know you two men from Adam, and I needn't take the trouble, and if you don't like it you can lump it, but I'm going to say something. I know I look young. I ain't fishing for a compliment. I know it. I've got a looking-glass in a good light, and I've got my eyes in my head, and, what's more, I'm spunky enough to own it to myself if I don't look young; but I ain't young. I ain't going to say how old I am, but I will say this much, I ain't young. I've been married twice and I've had three children. My first husband died, the second went off and left me. I've got a daughter fourteen years old I'm keeping in school. She ain't going into a department store, if I work my fingers to the bone." She said the last with a fierce air that made her for a second really look younger. "Well," she went on. "I'll tell you, too. I had a good place for a number of years, but the man died in September, and the man that took the business put his sister in my place. Then I was out of a job. I hadn't saved a cent, and I didn't know what I was going to do. Mildred — that's my daughter — is big of her age and good-looking, and she wanted to leave school and go to work, but I wouldn't let her. Well, I studied up all the advertisements and I tried, and I couldn't do a thing. Then I set my wits to work. I ain't one to give up in a hurry; I never was. As I said before, I didn't have much money, but I hire our little flat of a woman, and she's a good sort, and she's willing to wait, and a month ago I took every cent I could raise and I went through a course of treatment with a beauty-doctor. I had my hair (it was turned some) dyed, and I was massaged until I felt like a currant-bun, but I always had a good skin, and there was something to work on, and I took my figure in hand; that wasn't very bad, anyway, but I got new corsets, awful expensive ones, and had a tailor suit made. I had to raise some money on a little jewelry I had, but I made up my mind it was neck or nothing, and, sir, a month ago I got that place in Adkins & Somers's at a thousand a year. They are good men, too. You needn't think there's any-thing wrong." She looked at them with an expression as if she was ready to spring at the slightest intimation of distrust on their part. "It is only just that people think they want young help and they are going to have it. I've got the place and I'm in clover, and it's worth something looking so much better, though it don't make much difference to me. All I care about now-adays is my daughter."

The two men looked at the woman, Carroll with a courteous sym-pathy, and the interest of an observer of human nature. She was of a pro-nounced American type, coarse, vulgar, strident-voiced, smart, with a shrewdly working brain and of an unimpeachable heart. She was gener-osity and honesty itself, as she looked at the two men in a similar strait to the one from which she had extricated herself.

The other man, who had a bitter, possibly a dangerous strain devel-oped by his misfortunes, laughed sardonically. "How long do you think you can keep it up?" said he. "Hm?" Had he been less worn and weary, and apparently even starved, his laugh and question would have evoked a sharper response. As it was, the woman replied with the utmost good-nature.

"Any old time," said she. "Lord! I ain't setting up for a kid. I ain't fool enough to put on short skirts and pigtails, but I am setting up for a young lady, and I can keep it up, anyhow. Lord! I ain't so very old, anyhow. If I didn't look the way I do now, I couldn't get a position, because they'd put me down for a back-number; but I had something left for that beauty-doctor to work on." Then she gazed critically at the two men. "It wouldn't take much to make you into a regular dude," said she to Carroll. "You are dressed to beat the band as it is. Say!" She gave him a confidential wink.

"Well?" said Carroll.

"You are dressed most too well. It's all very well to look stylish, to look as if you had been earning twenty-five hundred a year, but, Lord! you look as if you had been getting ten! The bosses might be a little afraid of you. They might say they didn't see how a man could have dressed like you do, unless he had helped himself to some of the firm's cash. See? I don't mean any offence. You look to me like a real gentleman."

"Thank you," replied Carroll.

"If I was you I'd put on a pair of pants not quite so nicely creased, and I'd sell that overcoat and get a good-style ready-made one. Your chances would be a heap better — honest."

"Thank you," said Carroll, again. He was conscious of amusement and a curious sense of a mental tonic from this loud-voiced, eagerly helpful female.

"I'm right, you bet," said she. "But otherwise it wouldn't take much. You go and have a little something put on your hair, and have your face massaged a little, and if I was you I'd buy a red tie. You can get a dandy red tie at Steele & Esterbrook's for a quarter. That one you have on makes you look kinder pale. Then a red tie is younger. Say, I'll tell you, if you would only have your mustache trimmed, and wax the ends, it would make no end of difference."

"What are you going to do when you are asked how old you are? Lie?" inquired the other man, in his bitter, sardonic voice.

This time the woman regarded him with slight indignation. "Say," said she, "you'll never get a place if you don't act pleasanter. Places ain't to be got that way, I can tell you. You've got to act as if you'd eat nothin' but butter an' honey for a fortnight. If you feel mad, you'd better keep it in your insides." Then she answered his questions. "No, I ain't goin' to lie, and I ain't goin' to tell anybody else to lie," said she. "Lying ain't my style. But it ain't anybody's business how old you are, anyhow. I don't know what right a man that I go to get a place from has got to ask how old I be. All he has any right to know is whether I ain't too old to do my work. I don't lie; no, siree. All I say is, and kinder laugh, 'Well, call it twenty-five,' or you might call it thirty, and with some, again, you might call it thirty-two or three. That ain't lyin' if I know what lyin' is." As the woman spoke her face assumed precisely the mischievous, challenging smile with which she had replied to similar questions. Carroll laughed, and the other man also, although grudgingly.

"Well," he said, "there's different ways of looking at a lie."

"It wouldn't be any manner of use for you to say you wouldn't see twenty-eight again, no matter how much you got fixed up," the woman retorted. "But I guess you can get something, if it ain't quite so good. I have a gentleman friend who is over fifty and who said he was thirty-seven, and he got a dandy place last week. But I tell you you'll have to hustle more'n this other gentleman. You're bald, ain't you?"

"I don't know what that has got to do with it," growled the man, and he tried to quicken his pace; but she kept up with him.

"It's got a good deal to do with it," said she. "I know a place on Sixth Avenue where you can get an elegant front-piece that nobody could ever tell, for three dollars and forty-nine cents. Another gentleman friend of mine — he's a sort of relation of mine; my sister was his first wife — got one there. Yes, sir, you'll have to get one, and you'll have to get your face massaged and your eyebrows blacked, and, Lord! you'll have to have that beard shaved off and have a mustache, if you get anything at all. Lord! you look as if you'd come right out of the Old Testament. I don't see why you're wasting your time hanging around offices for, without you see to that, first of all. I should think your wife would tell you, but I suppose she's the same sort. Now as for you," she added, turning again to Carroll, "if you just get polished up a little bit — say, here's the card of my beauty-doctor" (she produced a card from an ornate wrist-bag) — "you'll look dandy."

Suddenly the woman, with a quick good-bye, turned to cross Broadway, but her good-nature and sympathy had something fine and inexhaustible, for even then she turned back to look encouragingly upon the older, soured, bitter, ungrateful man with Carroll, and she said: "You go 'long with him, and I guess you'll get a place, too. Good-bye."

With that she was gone, passing as straight as if she owned an unassailable right of way through the press of vehicles. Just as she gained the opposite sidewalk a fire-engine thundered up.

"She had a close call from that," Carroll said. His face had altered. He still looked amused.

"That woman couldn't get run over if she tried," said the other man.

"There ain't nothing made in the country that can run over her. It's women like her that's keeping men out of the places that belong to them by right."

"I am afraid there was some truth in her theory and her advice," Carroll said, laughing, and looking after the second engine clanging through the scattering crowd.

"Well, I guess when I go to buying women's frizzes to wear to get a place, she'll know it," said the other man. "Good lord! if it's the outside of the head they want, why don't they get dummies and done with it? I tell you what is needed is a new union."

Just at that moment they reached a restaurant from which came an odor of soup. Carroll turned to his companion. "I am going in here to get some lunch," he said. "I don't know what kind of a place it is, but if you will go with me, I shall take pleasure in —"

But the man turned upon him fiercely. "I ain't got quite so low yet that I have to eat at another man's expense," he said. "You needn't think, because you wear a better coat than I do, that —" The man stopped and nodded his head, speechless, and went on, and was out of sight, but Carroll had seen tears in the angry eyes.

He went into the restaurant, took a seat at a table, and ordered a bowl of tomato-soup. As he was sipping it he heard a voice pronounce his name, and, glancing up, saw two pretty girls and a young man at a nearby table. He recognized the young man as the one who had been lately in his employ. About the girls he was not so sure, but he thought they were the same who had come to Banbridge to plead for their payment. They all bowed to him, and he returned the salutation. They all had a severe and, at the same time, curious expression. One of the girls whispered to the other, and although the words were not audible, the sharp hiss reached Carroll's ears.

"Wonder what he's doing in this place," she said.

The other girl, the elder, craned her neck and observed what Carroll was eating. "He hasn't got anything but a bowl of tomato-soup," she replied.

"S'pose he's goin' through the whole bill," said the young man. The three were themselves lunching frugally. One of the girls had also a bowl of tomato-soup, the other a large piece of squash-pie. The young man had a ham sandwich and a cup of coffee. Smoking was allowed in the place, and the atmosphere was thick with cigarette smoke, and a warm, greasy scent of boiling and frying. Carroll continued to eat his soup. The three at the other table had nearly finished their luncheons when he entered. Presently they rose and passed him. The young man stopped. He paled a little. His old awe of Carroll was over him. In spite of himself, the worshipful admiration he had had for the man still influenced him. The poor young fellow, whose very pertness and braggadocio were simple and childlike, really felt towards the older man who had been his employer much as a faithful retainer towards a feudal baron. His feeling towards him was something between love and an enormous mental worship. His little, ordinary soul seemed to flatten itself like an Oriental before his emperor when he spoke to Carroll sipping his bowl of tomato-soup in the cheap restaurant. He had, after all, that nobility of soul which altered circumstances could not affect. He was just as deferential as if Carroll had been seated at a table in Delmonico's, but the fact remained that he was about to ask him again for his money. He was horribly pressed. He had obtained another position in one of the department stores, which paid him very little, and he was in debt, while his clothes were in such a degree of shabbiness that they were fairly precarious. The very night before he had sat up until midnight mending a rent in his trousers, which he afterwards inked; and as for his overcoat, he always removed that with a sleight-of-hand lest its ragged lining become evident, and when ladies were about he put it on in an agony lest his arms catch in the rents. He had even meditated cutting out the lining altogether, although he had a cold. He was so in debt that he had stopped eating breakfast; and the leaving off of breakfast for other than hygienic reasons, and when it has not been preceded by a heavy dinner the night before, is not conducive to comfort. So he bent low over Carroll and asked him in a small voice of the most delicate consideration, if he could let him have a little on account.

Carroll had turned quite white when he approached him, but his regard of him was unswerving. "It is impossible for me today, Mr. Day," he replied, "but I assure you that you shall have every cent in the end."

The tears actually sprang into the young fellow's nervously winking eyes. "It would be a great accommodation," he said, in the same low tone.

"You shall have every cent as soon as I can possibly manage it," Carroll repeated.

"I have a position, but it does not pay me very much yet," said the young fellow, "and — and — I am owing considerable, and — I need some things."

His involuntary shrug of his narrow shoulders in his poor coat spoke as loudly as words.

Carroll was directly conscious in an odd, angry, contemptuous sort of fashion, and whether because of himself, or of that other man, or of an overruling Providence, he would have been puzzled to say, of his own outer garment of the finest cloth and most irreproachable make. "As soon as I can manage it, every cent," he repeated, almost mechanically, and took another sip of his soup. The young fellow's winking eyes, full of tears, were putting him to an ignominious torture.

The two girls had stood close behind the young man, waiting their turns. Now the younger stepped forward, and she spoke quite audibly in her high-pitched voice.

"Good-morning, Mr. Carroll," said she, with a strained pertness of manner.

"Good-morning," Carroll returned, politely. He half arose from the table.

The girl giggled nervously. Her pretty, even beautiful face, under her crest of blond hair and the scoop of a bright red hat, paled and flushed. "Oh, don't stop your luncheon," said she. "Go right on. I just wanted to ask if you could possibly —"

"I am very sorry," Carroll replied, "but today it is impossible; but in the end you shall not lose one dollar."

The girl pouted. Her beauty gave her some power of self-assertion, although in reality she was of an exceedingly mild and gentle sort.

"That is very well," said she, "but how long do you think it will be before we get to the end, Mr. Carroll?"

"I hope not very long," Carroll said, with a miserable patience.

"It had better not be very long," said she, and suddenly her high voice pitched to tragedy. "If — if — I can't get another place that's decent for a girl to take," said she, "and if I don't get what's owing me before long, I shall either have to take one of them places or get a dose." She said the last word with an indescribably hideous significance. Her blue eyes seemed to blaze at Carroll.

Then the other girl pressed closer. "You needn't talk that way," said she to the girl. "You know that I —"

"I ain't goin' to live on you," returned the other girl, violently. People were beginning to look at the group.

"Now, you know, May," said the other girl, "my room is plenty big enough for two, and I'm earning plenty to give you a bite till you get a place yourself, and you know you may get that place you went to see about yesterday."

"No, I won't," said May. "It seems to me it's pretty hard lines that a poor girl can't get the money she's worked as hard for as I have."

The other girl pushed herself in front of May and spoke to Carroll, and there was something womanly and beautiful in her face. "I have a real good place," she said, in a low voice, and she enunciated like a lady. "A real good place, and I'll look out for May till she gets one, and I can wait until you are able to pay me."

"I will pay you all as soon as possible. I give you all my word I will pay you in the end," said Carroll.

He seemed to see the three go out in a sort of dream. It did not really seem to him that it was he, Arthur Carroll, who was sitting there in that smoking, greasy atmosphere, before that table covered with a stained cloth, over which the waiter had ostentatiously spread a damp napkin, with that bowl of canned tomato-soup before him, and that thick cup of coffee, with those three unhappy young creditors, who had reviled and, worse than reviled, pitied him, passing out, with the open glances of amused curiosity fastened upon him on every side.

"Guess that dude is down on his luck," he heard a young man at his left say.

"Guess he put the money he'd ought to have paid that young lady with into his overcoat," his companion, a girl with a picture-hat, and a wide lace collar over her coat, responded.

Carroll felt that he was overwhelmed, beaten, at bay before utter ignominy. The thought flashed across him, as he tried to swallow some more of the soup, that in some respects, if he had been a murderer or a great bank defaulter with detectives on his track, the situation would at least have been more endurable. The horrible pettiness of it all, consti-tuted the maddening sting of it. While he was thinking this the girl they called May came flying back, her blond crest bobbing, her cheeks blazing. She looked like a beautiful and exceedingly vulgar little fury. She came close to Carroll, while the other girl's voice was heard at the door pleading with her to come back.

"I won't come back till I have said my say, so there!" she called back. Then she addressed Carroll very loudly. She was transformed for the time. Hysteria had her in its clutch. She was half-fed, half-clothed, made desperate by repeated failures. There was also a love affair in the back-ground. She was, in reality, not so very far removed from the carbolic-acid crisis. "I say," said she. "I say, you! You'd better look out! You'd better pony up pretty quickly or you'll get into trouble you don't count on. There was a man at the office that morning after you quit, and if he should happen to walk in here and see you, you'd have a policeman after you. You'd better look out!"

Carroll felt his face flush hot. For the first time in his life he was con-scious of being actually down. He realized the sensation of the under dog, and he realized his utter helplessness, his utter lack of defence against this small, pretty girl who was attacking him. Everybody in the place seemed listening. Some of the people at the farther tables came nearer, other's were craning their necks. The girl gave her head an indescribable toss, at once vicious, coquettish, and triumphant. Her blond crest tossed, the scoop of her red hat rocked.

"I thought I'd just tell you," said she. Then she marched, holding her skirts tightly around her, with a disclosure of embroidered ruffles and the contour of pretty hips, and there was a shout of laughter in the place. Carroll pushed away his bowl of soup and turned to a grinning waiter near him.

"My check," he said.

"I ain't your waiter," replied the man, insolently.

"Bring me my check for this soup and coffee," repeated Carroll, and the man started. There was something in his look and tone that com-manded respect even in this absurdity. In reality, for the time, he was almost a madman. His fixed idea reasserted itself. At that moment, if it had been possible that his enemy, the man who had precipitated all this upon him, could have entered the room, there would have been murder done, and again for the moment his mind overlapped on the wrong side of life, and the desire for death was upon him. There was that in his face which hushed the laughter.

"They had better not hound that man much farther," one man at the table on the right whispered to his companion, who nodded, with sharp eyes on Carroll's face. They were both newspaper-men.

When Carroll had paid his bill and passed out, one of the men, young and clean-shaven, pressed close to his side.

"Pardon me, sir," he said, "but if you would allow me to express my regrets and sympathy —"

"No regrets nor sympathy are required, thank you, sir," replied Carroll.

"If I could be of any assistance," persisted the man, who was short in his weekly column and not easily daunted.

"No assistance is required, thank you, sir," replied Carroll.

The man retreated, and rejoined his companion at the table.

"Get anything out of him?" asked the other.

"No, but I can make something out of him, I guess."

"Poor devil!" said the other man.

"It might have paid to shadow him," said the first man, thoughtfully. "I shouldn't wonder if he took a bee-line for a drug-store. He looked desperate."

"Or perhaps the park. He looks like the sort that might have a pistol around somewhere."

This man actually, after a second's reflection, left his luncheon and hastened after Carroll, but he did not find him. Carroll had recovered himself and had taken the Elevated up-town to answer another advertisement. That was one for a book-keeper, and there was also unsuccessful. Coming out, he stood on the corner, looking at his list. He had written down nearly every want in the advertising columns. Actually he had even thought of trying for a position as coachman. He certainly could drive and could care for horses, and he considered quite impartially that he might make a good appearance in a livery on a fashionable turn-out. He had left now on his list only two which he had not tried; one was for a superintendent to care for a certain public building, a small museum. He had really a somewhat better chance there, apparently, for he had at one time known one of the trustees quite well. For that very reason he had put it off until the last, for he dreaded meeting an old acquaintance, and, too, there was a chance, though not a very good one, that the acquaintance might work harm instead of advantage. Still, the trustee had been in Europe for several years past, and the chances were that he would know nothing derogatory to Carroll which would interfere with his obtaining the position.

He reached the building, took the elevator to the floor on which was situated the offices, and, curiously enough, the first person he saw, on emerging from the elevator, was the man whom he knew, waiting to ascend. The man, whose name was Fowler, recognized him at once, and greeted him, but with constraint. Carroll immediately understood that in some unforeseen way the news which travels in circles in this small world had reached the other. He saw that he knew of his record during the last years.

"I have not seen you for a number of years, Mr. Carroll," said Fowler.

"No," replied Carroll, trying to speak coolly, "but that is easily accounted for; you have been abroad most of the time, living in London, have you not?"

"Yes, for seven years," replied the other, "but now I am home in my native land to end my days." Fowler was quite an elderly man, and remarkably distinguished in appearance, clean-featured and white-haired — indeed, he had cut quite a considerable figure in certain circles on the other side. He was even taller than Carroll, and portly in spite of the sharpness of his features.

"You are glad to be back in America?" Carroll said; he was almost forgetting, for the moment, the object of his visit to the place. He had years ago been on terms of social intimacy with this man.

"If I were not I would not say so," replied Fowler, with a diplomatic smile. "I do not disparage my country nor give another the preference in my speech, until I deliberately take out naturalization papers elsewhere."

Carroll smiled.

"By-the-way," said Fowler, whose handsome face had hard lines which appeared from time to time from beneath his polished surface-urbanity, "I have not seen you for perhaps ten years, Mr. Carroll, but I heard from you in an out-of-the-way place — that is, if anything is out of the way in these days. It was in a little Arab village in Egypt. I was going down the Nile with a party, and something went wrong with the boat and we had to stop for repairs; and there I found — quartered in a most amazing studio which he had rigged up for himself out of a native hut and hung with things which looked to me like nightmares, and making studies of the native Egyptians — and I must say he seemed to be doing some fine work at last — Evan Dodge."

Carroll understood then, perfectly, but he took it calmly. "I always felt that Dodge had genuine ability," he said.

"He has the ability to strike twelve, but not to strike it often," said Fowler. "However, all his models in that place striking twelve made it easier for him. His work was good, and I think it will be heard from. He had some good tea, and a tea-kettle, and he made us a cup, and we talked over the home news, Dodge and I and two other gentlemen and three ladies of the party. You see, Dodge was comparatively fresh from home. He had only been quartered there about a month."

"Yes," said Carroll.

"He spoke of seeing you quite recently. He said he had had a studio the summer before in Hillfield, where I believe you were living at the time." Nothing could have excelled the smoothness and even sweetness of Fowler's tone and manner; nothing could have excelled the merciless-ness of his blue eyes beneath rather heavy lids, and the lines of his fine mouth.

"Yes, he did have a studio there," assented Carroll.

"I believe that is quite a picturesque country about there."

"Quite picturesque."

"Well, Dodge did not make a mistake going so far afield, though, for, after all, his specialty is the human figure, and here it is only trees that are not altered in their contour by the fashions. Yes, he was doing some really fine work. There was one study of a child —"

"He made one very good thing in Hillfield," said Carroll, "a view from the top of a sort of half-mountain there. I believe he sold it for a large price."

"Well, I am glad of that," said Fowler. "Dodge has always been hampered in that way. Yes, he told me all the news, and especially mentioned having lived in the same village with you."

"Yes," said Carroll, with the dignity of a dauntless spirit on the rack.

"I hope your wife and family are well," said Fowler, further.

"Quite well, thank you."

"Let me see — you are living in New York now?"

"No, I am at present in Banbridge."

"Banbridge?"

"In New Jersey."

"Let me see — your family consists of your wife and a daughter and son?"

"Two daughters and a son. One daughter married, last September, Major Arms."

"Arms? Oh, I know him. A fine man." Fowler regarded Carroll with a slight show of respect. "But," he said, "I thought — Major Arms is nearly quite your age, is he not?"

"He is much older than Ina, but she seemed very fond of him."

"Well, she has a fine man for a husband," said Fowler, still with the air of respect. "Your son is quite a boy now?"

"He is only ten."

"Hardly more than a child."

"My wife and son and my sister are at present in Kentucky with my wife's aunt, Miss Dunois; only my younger daughter is with me in Banbridge."

"Catherine Dunois?"

"Yes."

"I used to know her very well. She was a beauty, with the spirit of a duchess."

"The spirit still survives," said Carroll, smiling.

"She must be quite old."

"Nearly eighty."

The elevator going up stopped in response to a signal from Fowler. He extended his hand. "Well, good-day," said Fowler. "I am glad we chanced to meet."

"Well, it is a small world," replied Carroll, smiling. "The chances for meeting are much better than they would be, say, in Mars."

"Much better, and for hearing, also. Good-day."

"Good-day."

Carroll saw the elevator with its open sides of filigree iron, ascending, and the expression upon Fowler's calm, handsome face, gazing backward at him, was unmistakable. It was even mocking.

Carroll touched the electric button of one of the downward elevators, and was soon carried rapidly down to the street door. He felt, as he gained the street, that he would rather starve to death than ask a favor of

Fowler. He did not ask for pity, or even sympathy, in his downfall, but he did ask for recognition of it as a common accident that might befall mankind, and a consequent passing by with at least the toleration of indifference from those not actively concerned in it; but in this man's face had been something like exultation, even gloating, Carroll thought to himself, as he went down the street, in the childish way that Eddy might have done, with a sort of wonder, reflecting that he never in his life, that he could remember, had done Fowler, even indirectly, a bad turn. He might easily have been totally indifferent to his misfortunes, to his failings, but why should they have pleased him?

Carroll walked rapidly along the street until he reached Broadway again. It was a strange day; a sort of snow-fog was abroad. The air was dense and white. Now and then a mist of sleet fell, and the sidewalks were horribly treacherous. The children enjoyed it, and there were many boys and a few girls with tossing hair sliding along with cries of merriment.

Carroll thought of Eddy as one little fellow, who did not look unlike him, fairly slid into his arms.

"Look out, my boy," Carroll said, good-humoredly, keeping him from falling, and the little fellow raised his cap with a charming blush and a "Beg your pardon, sir." A miserable home-sickness for them came over Carroll as he passed on. He longed for the sight of his boy, or his wife and Anna. He had grown, in a manner, accustomed to Ina being away. There is something about marriage and the absence it causes that brings one into the state of acquiescence concerning death. But he longed for the others, and he thought of his poor little Charlotte at home all day, and her loneliness. He looked at his watch, and realized that he must hurry if he caught the train which would take him to Banbridge at six o'clock. He had one more place on his list, and that was far up-town. He crossed to the Elevated station and boarded the first up-town train. What he was about to do was, in a way, so monstrous, taking into consideration his antecedents, his bringing-up, and all his forebears, that it had to his mind the grotesqueness of a gargoyle on his house of life. He was now going to apply for the last position on his list, that of a coachman for a gentleman, presumably of wealth, in Harlem. The name was quite unknown to him. It was German. He thought to himself in all probability the owner was Jewish. This was absolutely his last venture. He chose this as he would choose anything in preference to the one which was always within reach. As the train sped along he fell to thinking of himself in this position for which he was about to apply. He imagined himself in livery sitting with a pair of sleek bays well in hand. He reflected that at least he could do his work well. He wondered idly about the questions he would be asked. He considered suddenly that he must have a reference for a place of this sort, and he tore a leaf out of his note-book, took out his stylo-graphic pen, and scribbled a reference, signing his own name. He reflected, as he did so, that it was odd that he, who had employed so many doubtful methods to gain financial ends, should feel an inward qualm at the proceeding. Still, he was somewhat amused at the thought that Mr. A. Baumstein might write to him at Banbridge, and he should in that case reply, repeating his own list of qualification for the place. He wondered if they would ask if he were married, if they would prefer him married, if he drank, if he would be forbidden to smoke in the stables. He considered all the questions which he should be likely to ask himself, in a similar case. He got a curious feeling as if he were having an experience like Alice in Wonderland, as if he were in reality going in at the back of his own experiences, gaining the further side of his moon. He began to be almost impatient to reach his station and see the outcome of it all. Strangely enough, he never reflected on the good advice which the young woman that morning had given him as to the undesirable gentility of his general appearance. He never considered that as a drawback. When he reached his station he got off the train, went down the stairs, crossed the avenue, and up a block to the next street. When he found the number of which he was in search he hesitated a second. He wondered at what door he should apply. It manifestly could not be the front door. He therefore went farther down the street and gained the one running parallel, by which means he could reach the rear entrance of the house. It had no basement entrance under the front door. It was a new building, and quite pretentious, the most pretentious of a new and pretentious block. He traversed the small back yard, bending his stately head under a grove of servants' clothes which were swinging whitely from a net-work of lines, and knocked on the door. His knock was answered by a woman, presumably a cook, and she looked like a Swede. Unaccountably to him, she started back with a look of alarm and nearly closed the door, and inquired in good English, with a little accent, what he wanted. Carroll raised his hat and explained.

"I saw an advertisement for a coachman," he said, briefly, "and I have come to apply for the place if it is not already filled."

To his utter amazement the door was closed violently in his face, and he distinctly heard the bolt shot. He was completely at a loss to account for such a proceeding. He remained standing, staring at the blank front of the door, and a light flashed across the room inside and caused him to look at the windows. The light had been carried into a room at the back, but he saw in the pale dimness of the kitchen a group of women and one boy, and they were all staring out at him. Then the boy started on a run across the room, and he heard a door slam. Carroll waited. He could not imagine what it was all about, and a feeling of desperation was coming over him. It seemed to him that he must find something to do, that he could not go home again. The position of coachman began to seem desirable to him. Charlotte need not know what he was doing; no one need know. He had resolved to give another name, and he would soon find another position. This would be a makeshift. In this he could at least keep himself to himself. He need associate with nothing except the horses, and they were likely to be thorough-breds. It would not, after all, be half so bad as some other things — guiding superb horses through the streets and waiting at doors for his employers. To his mind, a coachman — that is, a City coachman — wears always more or less of a mask of stiff attention to duty. He could hide behind this mask. In reality, Carroll was almost at the end of his strength. His pride had suddenly become a forgotten thing. He was wretchedly worn out, and, in fact, he was hungry, almost famished. He had eaten very little lately, and poor Charlotte, in truth, knew little about cookery. He, in reality, became for the time what in once sense he was impersonating. He became a coachman in dire need of a job. Therefore he waited. He reflected, while he waited, that if they did not hurry he would miss his train and Charlotte would worry. In case he secured the position she would certainly have to join the others in Kentucky; there would be no other way, for he would be obliged to remain in the City over night.

All at once the door before him was swung violently open and a gentleman stood there. Carroll felt at once that he was Mr. A. Baumstein.

"What do you want, sir?" inquired the gentleman, and his tone was distinctly hostile, although he looked like a well-bred man, and it seemed puzzling that he thus received an answer to his application.

"I saw your advertisement, sir —" Carroll began.

"My advertisement for what, pray?" repeated Mr. Baumstein.

"For a coachman," replied Carroll, "and I thought if you had not already secured one —"

"Clear out, or I will call a policeman!" thundered Mr. Baumstein, and again the door was slammed in his face.

Carroll then understood. A gentleman who would have been presentable at the Waldorf-Astoria, at a gentleman's area door applying for a position as coachman, was highly suspicious. He understood readily how he would have looked at the matter had the cases been reversed. He made his way out of the little yard, dodging the fluttering banners of servants' clothes, and was conscious that his progress was anxiously watched by peering eyes at the windows. He reflected that undoubtedly that house would be doubly bolted and barred that night, and he would not be surprised if a special policeman were summoned, in view of the great probability that he was a gentleman burglar spying out the land before he descended upon it in search of the spoons and diamonds. Somehow the fancy tickled him to that extent that he felt almost as hysterical as a woman. He laughed aloud, and two men whom he met just then turned round and looked at him suspiciously.

"Dopey, I guess," one said, audibly, to the other.

It was now in Carroll's mind to gain the Elevated as soon as possible, and hurry down-town to his ferry and catch his train. He consulted his watch, and saw that he had just about time, if there were no delays. As he replaced his watch he remembered that he had, besides his railroad book, very little money, only a little silver. The helplessness of a cripple came over him. He recalled seeing a man who had lost both his legs shuffling along on the sidewalk, with the stumps bound with leather, carrying a little tray of lead-pencils which nobody seemed to buy. He felt like that cripple. A man living today in the heart of civilization, where money is in reality legs and wings and hands, is nothing more than a torso without it, he thought. He felt mutilated, unspeakably humiliated. It seemed more out of his ability to get any honest employment than it had ever done before. A number of laborers with their dinner-satchels, and their pick-axes over their shoulders, passed him. They looked at him, as they passed, with gloomy hostility. It was as if they accused him of having something which of a right belonged to them. He fell to wondering how he would figure in their ranks. He was no longer a very young man. However, his muscles were still good and supple; it really seemed to him that he might dig or pick away at rocks, as he had seen men doing in that apparently aimless and hopeless and never-ending fashion. He thought in such a case he should have to join the union, and he really wondered if they would admit him, if he pawned his clothes and should buy some poorer ones. He decided, passing himself before himself in mental review, that he might be treated by the leaders of a labor union very much as he had just been treated by Mr. Baumstein at his area door. He also decided that men like those who had just met him regard him with even worse suspicion and disfavor. He remembered stories he had read of gentlemen, of students, voluntarily joining the ranks of labor for the sake of information, but it seemed somehow impossible when it was attempted in earnest. Decidedly, his appearance was against him. He had the misfortune to look too much like a man who did not need to dig to easily obtain, in labor's parlance, a job to dig. Yet, while he thought of it, such was the man's desperation, his rage against his odds of life, that it seemed to him that a purely physical attack on the earth, to which he was fastened by some indissoluble laws of nature which he could not grasp, would be a welcome relief. He felt that with a heavy pick in his hand he could strike savagely at the concrete rock, the ribs of the earth, and almost enjoy himself. He felt that it would be like an attack, although a futile and antlike one, at creation itself. All this he thought idly, walking, even hurrying, along the slippery pavement through the pale, sleety mist. He walked as rapidly as he could, some of the time slipping, and recovering himself with a long slide. He came to a block of new stone houses, divided from another by a small space taken up by a little, old-fashioned, wooded structure that might have been with propriety in Banbridge. He noticed this, and the thought came to him that possibly it was the property of some ancient and opinionated mortal who was either holding it for higher prices or for the sake of some attachment or grudge. And just as he reached it he saw coming from the opposite direction his old book-keeper, William Allbright. Allbright, moving with a due regard to the dangerous state of the pavement, had still an alacrity of movement rather unusual to him. As he came nearer it was plain to see that his soberly outlined face, long and clean-shaven, was elated by something. He started when he recognized Carroll, and stopped. Carroll felt, meeting him a sensation of self-respect like a tonic. Here was at least one man to whom he owed nothing, whom he had not injured. He held out his hand.

"How do you do, Mr. Allbright?" he said.

"Quite well, thank you, Mr. Carroll," replied Allbright, then his delight, which makes a child of most men, could not be restrained. "I have just secured a very good position in a wholesale tea-house — Allen, Day & Co.," he said.

"That is good," said Carroll, echoing the other's enthusiasm. He really felt a leap of joy in his soul because of the other's good-fortune. He felt that in some way he himself needed to be congratulated for his good-fortune, that he had been instrumental in securing it. His face lit up. "I am delighted, Mr. Allbright," he repeated.

"Yes, it is a very good thing for me," said Allbright, simply. "I was beginning to get a little discouraged. I had saved a little, but I did not like to spend it all, and I have my sister to take care of."

"I am very glad," Carroll said, still again.

Allbright then looked at him with a little attention, pushing, as it were, his own self, intensified by joy, aside. "You are not looking very well, Mr. Carroll," he said, deferentially, and yet with a kindly concern.

"I am very well," said Carroll. Then he pulled out his watch again, and Allbright noticed quickly that it was a dollar watch. He remembered his suspicion. "I must hurry if I am to get my train," said Carroll. "You live here, Mr. Allbright?"

"Yes. I have lived here for twenty years."

"Well, I am very glad to hear of your good-fortune. Good-day, Mr. Allbright."

Carroll had not advanced three paces from Allbright before his feet glissaded on the thin glare of the pavement, he tried to recover himself, and came down heavily, striking his head; then he knew no more for some time.

CHAPTER XXXVII

Charlotte had expected her father home at a little after six o'clock that night. That was the train on which he usually arrived lately. She had not the least idea what he was doing in the City. She supposed he was in the office as he had been hitherto. She never inquired. With all the girl's love for her father, she had a decided respect. She was old-fashioned in her ways of never interfering or even asking for information concerning a man's business affairs.

Charlotte went down to the station to meet her father, as she was fond of doing. She had her dinner all ready. It was pretty bad, but she was innocently unaware of it. In fact, she had much faith in it. She had a soup which resembled greatly a flour paste, and that was in its covered tureen on the range-shelf, keeping hot and growing thicker. She had cooked a cheap cut of beef from a recipe in the cook-book, and that was drying up by the side of the soup. Poor Charlotte had no procrastination, but rather the failing of "Haste makes waste" of the old proverb. She had her cheap cut of beef all cooked at three o'clock in the afternoon, and also the potatoes, and the accompanying turnips. Salad at that time of the year she could not encompass in any form, but she had a singular and shrunken pudding on the range-shelf beside the other things. She set the coffee-pot well back where it would only boil gently, and the table was really beautifully laid. The child's cheeks were feverishly flushed with the haste she had made and her pride in her achievements. She had swept and dusted a good deal that day, also, and all the books and bric-à-brac were in charming arrangement. She felt the honest delight of an artist as she looked about her house, and she said to herself that she was not at all tired. She also said that she was not at all hungry, even if she had only eaten a cracker for luncheon and little besides for breakfast. She realized a faintness at her stomach, and told herself that she must be getting indigestion. Her little stock of money was very nearly gone. She had even begun to have a very few things charged again at Anderson's. Sometimes her father brought home a little money, but she understood well enough that their financial circumstances were wellnigh desperate. However, she had an enormous faith in her father that went far to buoy her up. While she felt the most intense compassion for him that he should be so hard pressed, it never occurred to her that it could be due to any fault or lack of ability in him, and she had, in reality, no doubt whatever of his final recovery of their sinking fortunes. She wrote her mother that papa was going to the City every day, that they were getting on very well, and while they had not yet a maid, she thought it better to wait until they were perfectly satisfied before engaging one. The letters she had received at first from Mrs. Carroll had been childishly amazed and reproachful, although acquiescent. Her aunt had written her more seriously and with great affection. She told her to send for her at once if she needed her, and she would come.

Charlotte, going down the street towards the station that night, expected a letter by the five-o'clock train. She reached the post-office, which was near the station, at a quarter before six, and she found, as she anticipated, letters. There were several for her father, which she thought, accusingly towards the writers, were bills. It was odd that Charlotte, while not really morally perverted, and while she admitted the right of people to be paid, did not admit the right of any one to annoy her father by presenting his bill. She looked at the letters, and, remembering the wretched expression on her father's face on receiving some the night before, it actually entered into her mind to tear these letters up and never let him see them at all. But she put them in her little bag, and opened her own letters and stood in the office to read them. The train was not due for fifteen minutes yet, and was very likely to be late. She had letters from her mother, Ina, and aunt. They all told of the life they were leading there, and expressed hope that she and her father were well, and there was a great deal of love. It was all the usual thing, for they wrote every day. There were also letters from them all for Carroll. The Carroll family, when absent from one another, were all good correspondents, with the exception of Carroll. There was even a little letter from Eddy, which had been missent, because he had spelled Banbridge like two words — Ban Bridge.

Charlotte read her letters, smiling over them, standing aloof by the window. The post-office was fast thinning out. There had been the customary crowd there at the arrival of the mail — the pushing and shrieking children and the heavily shuffling loungers — all people who never by any possibility got any letters, but who found a certain excitement in frequenting the office at such times. Just as Charlotte finished her last letter and replaced it in the envelope, Anderson came in for his mail. He did not notice her, but went directly to his box, which had a lock, opened it, and took out a pile of letters. Charlotte stood looking at him. He looked very good and very handsome to her. She thought to herself how very much better-looking he was than Ina's husband. There was something about the manly squareness of his shoulders, as he stood with his back towards her, examining his letters, which made her tremble a little, she could not have told why. Suddenly he looked up and saw her, and she felt that the color flashed over her face, and was ashamed and angry. "Why should I do so?" she asked herself. She made a curt, stiff little bow in response to Anderson's greeting, and he passed her going out of the office with his letters. Then she felt distressed.

"I need not have been rude because I was such a little idiot as to blush when a man looked at me," she told herself. "It was not his fault. He has always been lovely to us." She reviewed in her mind just her appearance when she had given him that stiff little bow, and she felt almost like crying with vexation. "Of course he does not care how I bow to him," she thought, and somehow that thought seemed to give her additional distress, "but, all the same, I should have been at least polite, for he is very much a gentleman. I think he is much better bred, and he certainly knows much more than Ina's husband, even if he does only keep a grocery store; but then army officers are not supposed to know much except how to fight."

The heavy jar of a passing freight train made her look at the post-office clock, and with her usual promptness, although it was fully seven minutes before the train was due, even if it were on time, and she was only about one minute's walk from the station, she reflected that she must start at once if she were to meet her father. So she stowed away her letters in her little bag, and fairly ran across the icy slope between the office and the station. She saw, as she hurried along, a child tumble down, and watched him jump up and run off to make sure he was not hurt. When she reached the station she did not go in the waiting-room, which seemed close and stuffy, but remained out on the platform. The sun had set, but the western sky, which was visible from that point, was a clear expanse of rose and violet. Charlotte stood looking at it, and for a minute she was able to find that standing-point outside her own little life and affairs which exists for the soul. She did not think any more of the money troubles, of her bowing so stiffly to Mr. Anderson. She forgot not only her petty worries, but her petty triumphs and pleasures. She forgot even the exceeding becomingness of a new way in which she had dressed her hair. She forgot her coat, which she had herself trimmed with fur taken from an old one of her mother's, and in which her heart delighted. She forgot her supreme dinner warming on the range-shelf at home. She forgot the joy she would soon have in seeing her father alight from the train. The little, young, untrained creature saw and knew for the moment only the eternal that which was and is and shall be, and which the sunset symbolized. Her young face had a rapt expression looking at it.

"Dandy sunset, ain't it?" said a voice at her ear. She looked and saw Bessy Van Dorn, her large, blooming face, rosy with the cold, smiling at her from under a mass of tossing black plumes on a picture-hat. The girl was really superb in a long, fur-lined coat. She had driven in a sleigh to the station, and she expected Frank Eastman on the train, and was, with the most innocent and ignorant boldness in the world, planning to drive him home, although she was not engaged to him and he was not expecting her. Her face, turning from the wonderful after-glow of the sunset to Charlotte's, had also something of the same rapt expression in spite of her words.

"Yes, it is beautiful," replied Charlotte, but rather coldly. She was a friendly little soul, but she did not naturally care for girls of Bessy Van Dorn's particular type. She was herself too fine and small before such a mass of inflorescence.

"It's cold," said Bessy Van Dorn, further, "but, land, I like it! Have you been sleigh-riding?"

"No, I haven't," replied Charlotte.

"Oh, I forgot," said Bessy.

Charlotte knew what she had forgot — that the horses had gone for debt — and she reddened, but the other girl's voice was honest.

"I'd like to take you sometime," said Bessy.

"Thank you," said Charlotte.

"I'd offer to take you home tonight," said Bessy, "but I've arranged to take somebody else."

"Thank you. I could not go, anyway," said Charlotte. "I am down to meet my father."

"Oh!" said Bessy. "Well, then you couldn't. A sleigh ain't quite wide enough for three, unless one of 'em is your best young man," she giggled. Charlotte felt ashamed.

"My father is," she said, sternly. She fairly turned her back on Bessy Van Dorn, but she did not notice it, for the train was audible in the distance, and Bessy began calculating her distance from the car in which Frank Eastman usually rode, that she might be sure not to miss him.

Charlotte stood on the platform, and also ran along by the side of the train scanning anxiously the men who alighted. To her great astonishment, her father was not among them. She could scarcely believe it when the train went slowly past the station and her father had not got off.

Bessy Van Dorn, driving Frank Eastman in her sleigh, with the fringe of fur tails dangling over the back, looked around at Charlotte slowly retreating from the station. "Why, her father didn't come!" said she.

"Whose father?" asked young Eastman. He looked admiringly and even lovingly at the girl, and yet in a slightly scornful and shamed fashion. He hated to think of what some of the men he knew would say about her meeting him at the station.

"Why, that poor little Charlotte Carroll's!" said Bessy. "Say," she added, after a second's hesitation.

"What?" asked young Eastman.

"I've a good mind to ask her to ride. We're goin' her way. You don't mind?"

"Not a bit," said young Eastman, but he did think uncomfortably of Ina's sister seeing him with Bessy Van Dorn.

Bessie promptly stopped. They had not yet made the turn from the station to the main road, and Charlotte was just behind them.

"Say," she called out, "get in here. I'll take you home — just as soon as not."

"Thank you," replied Charlotte. "I have an errand. I am not going home just yet."

"All right," replied Bessy, touching her horse. "I'd just as soon have taken you as not, if you'd been going home."

"Thank you," Charlotte said, again.

"I declare, she looked as if she was just ready to cry," said Bessy to Eastman, as they drove up the street.

She was quite right. Charlotte was horribly frightened by her father's non-arrival on the train. He had never come on a later train than that since the others had gone. The thought of returning alone to her solitary home was more than she could bear. She remembered that there was another train a half-hour later, and she resolved to remain down for that. She thought that she would go to Mr. Anderson's store and purchase some cereal for breakfast, that she might have that charged. She was conscious, but she tried to stifle the consciousness, of a hope that Mr. Anderson would be there, and she might tell him that her father had not arrived on that train, and he would reassure her. But Mr. Anderson had naturally gone straight home from the post-office to supper. Charlotte ordered her cereal, and also a few eggs. Then she went back to the station. It was nearly twenty minutes before the train was due. She walked up and down the platform, which extended east and west. The new moon was just rising, a slender crescent of light, and off one upper horn burned a great star. It was a wonderful night, cold, with a calmness and hush of all the winds of heaven which was like the hush of peace itself. Charlotte noticed everything, the calm night and the crescent moon, but she came between herself and her own knowledge of it. Her mind was fixed upon the train and the terrible possibility that her father might not arrive on that. It seemed to her that if he did not arrive on that it was simply beyond bearing. The possibility was too terrible to be contemplated with reason, and yet she could not have told just why she was in such a panic of fear. A thousand things might happen to keep any business-man in the City later than he had expected. He had often been so kept while the others were home; but now she was alone, and she felt that he would certainly come unless something most serious had detained him. Charlotte had naturally a somewhat pessimistic turn of mind, and her imagination was active. She imagined many things; she even imagined the actual cause of Carroll's detention, among others, that he had slipped on the ice and injured himself. The falling of the boy on her way to the six-o'clock train had directly swerved her fancy in that direction. But she imagined everything. That was only one of many casualties. The train was a little late. She stood staring down the track at the unswerving signal-lights, watching for the head-light of the locomotive, and it seemed to her quite certain that there had been an accident on that train. A thought struck her, and she went into the waiting-room and asked the ticket-agent if the train was very late. The agent was quite a young man, and he looked at her with a covert masculine coquettishness as he replied, but she was oblivious of that. All she thought of was that, if there had been an accident on the line and the train was late on that account, he would surely be apt to know. Her heart was beating so fast that she trembled; but he said ten minutes, and said nothing about an accident, and she was reassured. She turned to go, after thanking him, and he volunteered further information.

"There is a freight ahead delaying the train," he said.

"Oh, thank you," replied Charlotte. Then she went out on the platform again and watched for the head-light of the locomotive, staring down the track past the twinkle of the signal-lights. Suddenly it flashed into sight far off, but she saw it. She waited. Soon she heard the train. A gateman crossed the tracks from the in-station, padlocking the gates carefully after him. A baggage-master drew a trunk to the edge of the platform. A few passengers came out of the waiting-room.

Charlotte waited, and the train came majestically around the curve below the station. She moved along as it came up, keeping her eyes on the cars. She seemed to have eyes with facets like a cut diamond. It was really as if she saw all the car doors at once. But she moved with a strange stiffness, and could not feel her hands nor feet; her heart beat so fast and thick that it shook her like the pulse of an engine. She moved along, and she saw every passenger who alighted. Then the train steamed out of the station with slowly gathering speed, and her father had not come on it.

Charlotte, when she actually realized the fact, the possibility of which had seemed incredible, gained a little strength. It was like the endurance of disaster which is sometimes more feasible than the contemplation of it. She thought at once what to do. In the event of her father having been delayed by some unforeseen business he would surely telegraph. She at once crossed the slope from the station and went to Andrew Drake's drug-store, where the telegraph-office was. She asked if a telegram had come for her, if one had been sent to the house. When the boy in charge answered no, she felt as if she had received a stunning blow. She had then no doubt whatever that something had happened to her father, some accident. The boy, who was young and pleasant-faced, watched her with a vague sympathy. In a moment she recovered herself. He might have sent a telegram which had not arrived. It might come any moment. The boy directly had the same thought. "The minute the telegram comes I'll get it up to you," he said, earnestly. "I expect Mr. Drake back every minute, and I can leave."

"Thank you," said Charlotte.

It was an hour and a half before the next train. She went out of the store and walked miserably along the street to her deserted home.

CHAPTER XXXVIII

There is, to a human being of Charlotte Carroll's type, something unutterably terrifying about entering, especially at nightfall, an entirely empty house. The worst of it is it does not seem to be empty. In reality, the emptiness of it is the last thing which is comprehended. It is full to overflowing with terrors, with spiritual entities which are much more palpable, when one is in a certain mood, than actual physical presences. Charlotte approaching the house, saw, first, glimmers of light on the windows, which were merely reflections ostensibly from the electric light in the street, not so ostensibly from other lights.

"Oh, there is some one in there," Charlotte thought to herself, and again that horrible, pulsing, vibrating motion of her heart overcame her. "Who is there?" she asked herself. She remembered that terrible tramp whom she had seen asleep in the woods that day. He might have been riding on some freight-train which had stopped at Banbridge, and stolen across and entered the vacant house. She stood still, staring at the cold glimmers on the windows. Then gradually she became convinced that they were merely reflections which she saw. Aside from her imagination, Charlotte was not entirely devoid of a certain bravery, or, rather, of a certain reason which came to her rescue. "What a little goose I am!" she told herself. "Those are only reflections. They are the reflections of the light in the street." As she studied it more closely she saw that the light, being intercepted by the branches of the trees on the lawn, swaying in a light wind, produced some of the strange effects at the windows which had seemed like people moving back and forth in the rooms. Then all at once she saw another glimmer of light on the front window of her father's room which she could not account for at all. She moved in front of a long, fan-shaped ray cast by the electric light in the street, and, looking at the window, the reflection was still there. She could not account for that at all, unless it was produced by a light from a house window — which was probably the case. At all events, it disquieted her. Still, she overcame her disinclination to enter the house because of that. She reasoned from analogy. "All the other lights are reflections," she told herself, "and of course that must be." However, the main cause of her terror remained: the unfounded, world-old conviction of presences behind closed doors, the almost impossibility for a very imaginative person to conceive of an entirely empty room or house — that is, empty of sentient life. She had hidden the front-door key under the mat before the front door; she had lived long enough in the country to acquire that absurdly innocent habit. She groped for it, thought for a second, with a gasp of horror, that it was not there. Then she felt it with her gloved hand, fitted it in the lock, opened the door, and went in, and the inner darkness smote her like a hostile crowd.

It was actually to the child as if she were passing through a thick group of mysterious, inimical things concealed by the darkness. It was as if she heard whispers of conspiracy; it was even as if she smelled odors of strange garments and bodies. Every sense in her was on the alert. She even tasted something bitter in her mouth. It was all absurd. She reiterated in her ears that it was all absurd, but she had now passed the point wherein reason can support. She had come through an unusually active imagination into the unknown quantities and sequences of life. She put out her hands and groped her way through the darkness of the hall, and the fear lest she should touch some one, some terrible thing, was as bad as the reality could have been. She knew best where to find matches in the dining-room, so she went through the hall, with a sort of mad rush in spite of her blindness, and she gained the dining-room and felt along the shelf for a little hammered-brass bowl where matches were usually kept. In it she felt only two. The mantel-shelf was the old-fashioned marble monstrosity, the perpetuation of a false taste in domestic architecture, but it was excellent as to its facilities for scratching matches. She rubbed one of the two matches under the shelf on the rough surface, but it did not ignite. It evidently was a half-burned match. She took the other. It seemed to her that if that failed her, if she had to grope about the kitchen for more in this thick blackness — for even the street-light did not reach this room — she should die. She rubbed the last match against the marble, and it blazed directly. She shielded it carefully with her hand from the door draught, and succeeded in lighting a candle in one of a pair of brass candlesticks which stood on the shelf. She then held the flaring light aloft and looked fearfully around the room. Everything was as usual, but, strangely enough, it did not reassure her. The solitariness continued to hold terrible possibilities for her as well as the darkness, and with the light also returned what had been for a few minutes in abeyance before her purely selfish fear, the anxiety over her father. She moved about the house with the candle, going from room to room. It seemed to her that she could not remain one minute if she did not do so. Every time before entering a room she felt sure that it was occupied. Every time after leaving it she felt sure that something unknown was left there. She went into the kitchen, and saw her miserable little dinner drying up in the shelf of the range, and then for the first time self-pity asserted itself. She sat down and sobbed and sobbed.

"There, I got that nice dinner, that beautiful dinner," she said to herself, quite aloud in a pitiful wail like a baby's, "and perhaps poor papa will never even taste it. Oh dear! Oh dear!"

She rocked herself back and forth in the kitchen-chair, weeping. She had set the candle on the table, and a draught of wind from some unknown quarter struck it and the strangest lights and shadows flared and flickered over the room and ceiling. Presently, Charlotte, looking at them, became diverted again from her grief. She looked about fearfully. Then she made a tremendous effort, rose, and lighted a lamp. With that the room was not so frightful, yet it was still not normal. The familiar homely articles of furniture assumed strange appearances. She saw something on the range, a little object which filled her with such unreasoning horror that it was almost sheer insanity. It was simply because she could not for the moment imagine what the little object, which had nothing in the least frightful about it, could be. Finally she rose and looked, and it was only a little iron spoon which she must have dropped there. She removed it, but still the horror was over her. She lifted the cover from the dish of meat, and again the tears came.

"Poor papa! poor papa!" she said.

Then she carried the lamp into the dining-room, and went into the parlor. She had made herself quite satisfied that there was in reality nothing menacing in the house except her own fears. She would sit beside one of the front windows in the parlor, in the dark, in order that she might not be seen, and she would watch for her father, and she would also watch for any one who might approach the house with any harmful intent.

Charlotte curled herself up in a large chair beside the window which commanded the best view of the grounds and the drive. With the light of the young moon there was really no possibility that anything could approach unseen by her, unless by way of the fields from the back. But that she did not think of. Her mind became again concentrated upon her father and the possibility of either his return on the next train or a telegram explaining his absence. She knew that the next train from New York was due in Banbridge at a few minutes after eight. She had no time-table, but she remembered Major Arms arriving once, and she was quite certain that the train was due at eight-seventeen. It might, of course, be late. She reflected, with a sense of solid comfort, that the trains were rather more apt to be late than not. She need not give up hope of her father's arriving on this train until even nine o'clock, for besides the possibility of the lateness there was also that of his walking rather than taking a carriage from the station. In fact, he would probably walk, since he was still in Samson Rawdy's debt. She might allow at least twenty minutes for the walk from the station. She might allow more even than that. She sat at the window, and waited, peering out. There was a singular half-dusk rather than half-light from the new moon. The moon itself was not visible from where she sat, for the window faced north, but she could see over everything the sweet influence of it. There was no snow on the lawn, which was a dry crisp of frost-killed grass, as flat as if swept by a broom, and here and there were the faintest patches and mottles of silver from this moon, aside from a broad gleam of the garish light from the street-lamp. The bushes and trees showed lines of silver. The moon was so young that the stars were quite brilliant. Taking all the lights together — the electric light in the street, the new moon, and the stars — the lawn was quite visible, and even, because the leaves were now all gone from the trees, the road for quite a distance beyond. Charlotte had a considerable vista in which to watch for her father. The time passed incredibly in this watching. She had upon her such a fear and even premonition that he might not come, that the minutes passed with the horrible swiftness that they pass for a criminal awaiting execution. The first time she slipped out in the dining-room — with a last look at the lawn and road, to be sure that he would not be there in the mean time — to see what time it was by the clock on the shelf, she was amazed. It was already eight o'clock. She had not dreamed it was more than half-past seven. She crept back to her place by the parlor window, with the feeling that much of her time of reprieve had passed, and that she was so much the nearer the certainty of tribulation. Instead of impatience she had rather the desire to defer approaching disaster. While she watched, she had less and less hope that her father would come on that train, and yet she kept her heart alive by picturing her rapture when she should see his tall, dark figure enter the lawn path, when she should run and unlock and unbar the door and throw her arms around his neck. She made up her mind that she should not confess to him what a panic she had been in because of his non-arrival. She planned how she would run and set the dinner, in which she still believed, on the table, and how hungry he would be for it. She was quite sure that her poor father did not in these days provide himself with sumptuous lunches in the city. But all the time she reared these air-castles, she saw for a certainty the dark sky of her trouble through them. For some premonition, or a much modified form of prophecy, the rudimentary expression of a divine sense in reality exists. It existed in Charlotte watching for her father at the window, and yet so bound up was she in the probabilities and present sequences of things that she still watched. now and then she made sure that she saw her father turn from the road into the lawn, but the figure, to her horror, would remain standing still in one place. It was simply a slender spruce which had seemed to start out of a corner of the night with a semblance of life. Now and then she actually did see a figure coming up the road, approaching the entrance to the lawn, and her heart leaped up with joy. She watched for it to enter, but that was the end. Whoever it was, it had passed the house and gone farther up the road. Those were the cruellest moments of any — the momentary revival of hope and then the dashing it to the ground. By-and-by her eyes, strained with such watching, began to actually deceive her. She saw, as she thought, shadows, approach and enter the house. Several times she ran to the door and opened it, and no one was there.

After she had gone out in the dining-room and seen that it was eight-seventeen, the time when the train was due in Banbridge, she watched for the train. She knew that she could hear the rush of the train after it left the station; she could even catch a glimpse of the rosy fire of the locomotive through the trees, since the track was elevated. She therefore watched for that, but it was very late. That was unmistakably a great solace for her. She actually had a prayerful mood of thankfulness for the lateness of the train. It was that much longer that she need not give up hope. There was a few minutes that she felt quite easy. Suddenly she remembered how foolish she had been to watch for her father, anyway, before she heard the arrival of the train. She realized that her head was overstrained, her reason failing her. "How could papa come before the train?" she asked herself. But after a few minutes her fears reasserted themselves. She watched for something inimical to appear crossing the lawn instead of her father. And then she heard a train, and she felt faint, but in a second she became aware that it was a long freight. No passenger-train ever moved thus with the veritable chu-chu of the children, the heavy panting of two engines. Then after that she started again, for she heard a train, but it was as if she had been let fall by some wanton hand from a cruel height, for that train was clearly a fast express which did not stop at Banbridge. Then she heard a faint rumble of another freight on the Lehigh Valley road. Then at last came the train for which she had been looking, the train on which her father might come, the train on which he surely would come unless some terrible thing had happened. She heard distinctly, with her sharpened ears, the stop of the train at the station, the letting off of steam. She heard the engine-bell. She heard it resume its advance with slowly gathering motion. She saw a rosy flash of fire in the distance from the engine. Then she waited for carriage-wheels, or for the sight of her father coming up the road. It was quite soon that she heard carriage-wheels on the frozen ground, and she ran to the door and opened it, but the carriage passed. Samson Rawdy was taking home the next neighbor. "It will take papa considerably longer if he walks," she told herself, and she locked the door and returned to her station at the window. She saw again a dark figure approaching on the road outside, and she thought with a great throb of joy that he had surely come, but the figure did not enter the grounds. She allowed twenty-five minutes for him to walk from the station. She said to herself if, when twenty-five minutes had elapsed, he had not come, she should certainly know that he had not come on that train. She did not dare look at the clock, but after a while, when she did so, she found it was twenty-seven minutes after eight. Still that clock often gained. She ran out in the kitchen and looked at the clock there, but that had stopped at half-past seven. It was very seldom that anybody remembered to wind up the kitchen-clock since Marie went. Her own little watch was at the jeweller's in New Sanderson for repairs. She had nothing to depend on except the dining-room clock, which, to her great comfort, so often gained. She decided that she might wait until ten minutes of nine by that clock before she gave up hope, but the next time she went trembling out to look at it it was only three minutes before nine. Then it occurred to her that her father might easily have had an errand at one of the stores before coming home. The post-office would be closed; she had no hope for that, but he might have had some business. She thought that she might allow until half-past nine before she entirely gave up her father having come on the eight-seventeen train. It was then that she began running out on the lawn to the entrance of the drive to watch for him. She put a Roman blanket, which was kept on the divan in the den, over her head, and she continually ran out across the lawn, and stood close to a tree, staring down the road for some sign of her father. Curiously enough, she was not nearly so terrified out-of-doors as in the house. The strain of returning to that vacant house was much worse for her than going across the lawn in the lonely night. She watched and watched, and at last when she returned to the house and looked at the dining-room clock, it was half-past nine, and she completely gave up all hope of her father having come on that train.

A species of stupor, of terror and anxiety, seemed to overcome her. She sat by the parlor window, still staring out from mere force of habit. She knew that the next and last train that night was not due until one-thirty, presumably nearly two o'clock. She knew that there was not the slightest chance of her father's coming until then, but her mind now centred on the telegram. It did seem as if there must be a telegram, at least. All at once a figure appeared in the road and swiftly turned into the drive. She thought at once that the boy in the drug-store was bringing the telegram; still, she resolved not to open the door until she was sure who it was. She peered closely from the window, and it was unmistakably the drug-store boy who emerged from the tree shadows and came up on the stoop. She ran to the door and unfastened it, not waiting for him to ring.

She held out her trembling little hand for the telegram, but he kept his at his side. He looked at her, grinning half-sympathetically, half-sheepishly. He was an overgrown boy, perhaps three years younger than she, whom a pretty girl overwhelmed with an enormous self-consciousness and admiration.

"Where is it?" asked Charlotte, impatiently.

"I ain't got nothing'," said the boy.

"Then why —"

"I was going home from the store, and I thought I'd jest stop an' let you know there wa'n't no telegrams yet. It wa'n't much out of my way."

Charlotte gasped.

"I thought it might be a relief to your mind to know," said the boy. "I thought you might be watchin'. I saw your father didn't come on that other train. I was up at the station on an errand."

"Thank you," said Charlotte, feebly.

The boy lingered a second with bashful eyes on her face, then he said again that he thought he would just stop in and let her know. He was going down the path, and she was just closing the door, when he called back that she might have a telegram if her father sent it by the postal-telegraph system.

"You won't get none from our place after now," he said, "for Mr. Drake won't bring up none so late; but if your father sends that way, you could get one, mebbe."

"Thank you," replied Charlotte, and the boy went away.

When Charlotte re-entered the house and locked the door, a loneliness which was like a positive chill struck over her. It was much worse now since she had been in communication with another human being.

"If he had only been a girl I would have gone down on my knees to him to stay all night with me," she thought.

She tried to think if there was anybody in Banbridge whom she could ask to stay with her, but she could think of none. She thought of Marie, but she did not even know where she was. There was no woman whom she could call upon. She resumed her seat beside the window. She did not dream of going to bed. She had now to watch for the possible postal telegram; it would not be time for the last train for hours yet. She had the telegraph-messenger and some possible marauder to watch for. She kept her eyes glued to the expanse of the lawn and small stretch of road visible between the leafless trees. Now and then a carriage passed; very seldom a walking shadow. She always started at the sight of these, thinking the telegram might be about to arrive. If the telegram should arrive she expected fully that it would be of some terrible import. A thought struck her, something that she might do. If her father was injured, if she were to be sent for from the City, she resolved that she would have everything in readiness for instant departure. There was a train which Banbridge flagged after the arrival of the last train from New York. She lit a lamp, went up-stairs, and packed a little travelling-bag with necessaries, and made some changes in her dress, and felt a certain relief in so doing. She had very little money, and a book with two or three railroad tickets. She felt that she could start at a moment's notice should the telegram arrive. All the time she was packing she was listening for the door-bell. It became quite firmly fixed in

294 ☞ MARY E. WILKINS FREEMAN

her mind what the telegram would be: that her father was terribly injured and had been carried to a hospital, that she should at once go to the hospital. It sometimes occurred to her that he might be even dead, but that idea did not so take hold on her fancy as the other.

She left the lamp burning up-stairs, thinking suddenly that it would be well to have the house present the appearance of being well inhabited. She took her hat and coat and her little travelling-bag, and she went back to the place by the parlor window and stared out at the lawn again. It was growing very late. Soon it would be time for her to watch for the last train. It really seemed to the girl an incredible supposition of disaster that that train could pass by and her father not appear, and that in the face of her morbid and pessimistic conclusions. She was a mass of inconsistencies, of incoherencies. She at once despaired and hoped with a hope that was conviction. At last, when she saw by the clock that it only wanted a few minutes before the time when the last train was due, her spirits arose as if winged. She even went out in the kitchen and examined the wretched dinner to make sure it was still hot. She put more coal on the range. The house was growing very cold, and she knew that the furnace fire needed attention, but she absolutely dared not go down cellar alone at that time. They had very little coal, also, and had been in the habit of letting the furnace fire die down at night. She put on her coat when she returned from the kitchen, and sat again by the window. She felt now an absolute certainty that her father would arrive on this train. She felt that it was monstrous to assume that her father would not come home all night and leave her alone with no message. She felt even quite radiantly happy sitting there. She said to herself what a little goose she had been. Even a noise made by some coal falling in the kitchen-range failed to startle her. She now hoped that the train would not be late, and it was, in fact, very nearly on time. Then she watched for her father with not the slightest doubt that he would come. It had come to that pass that her credulity as to disaster had failed her. It was simply out of her power to credit the possibility of his not coming on this train when he had sent no telegram. She knew that there would be no carriage at the station at that hour, unless he had telegraphed for one from New York, and she questioned, in the state of their finances, if he would do that. She was therefore sure of seeing his figure appear, coming, with the stately stride which she knew so well, into view on the road below the lawn.

She allowed twenty-five minutes for his appearance after she had seen the train pass. She knew nothing could detain him in the village at that time of night, and she was sure he would come within that time. She looked at the dining-room clock and found that she had, if she allowed that twenty-five minutes, just fifteen minutes to wait. She sat shrugged up in her little fur-trimmed coat, for the house was growing very cold, and stared intently at the pale glimmer of the road. After the twenty-five minutes had passed, she went out in the dining-room and looked at the clock. The time was more than passed; there was no doubt. Her father had not come. The panic seized her.

She was now dashed from the heights of hope, and the shock was double. She realized that her father had not come, would not come that night; that she would probably have no telegram. She realized that she was all alone in the house. Now again unreasoning fear as well as the anxiety for her father seized her. Again the conviction of the awful population of the empty rooms was upon her. She sat down again by the window, and she tried to make her reasoning powers reassert themselves.

"If anything comes this way, I shall see it in time, and I can run out the back door and across to the neighbors," she told herself. "If anything comes in the back way, I shall hear and have time to run out the front door; and I know there is nothing in the house." But she could not reassure herself, since what terrified her, and even temporarily unbalanced her, was fear itself.

Fear multiplied, growing upon itself, spreading out new tentacles with every throb of her imagination, filling the whole house. All her life she had thought what a frightful thing it would be if ever she were left alone by herself in a house, all night; and now worse than that had come to pass, for she was not alone; the house was peopled by fear and the creatures of fear. She heard noises constantly that she could not account for, and she also saw things which she could not account for. Again the small and trivial, acutely stinging horror of some ordinary object in a new and awful guise possessed her. She was almost paralyzed at the sudden glimpse of something on the divan across the room. It was a long time before she could possibly totter to investigate, and ascertain it was one of her own gloves. But it did not strike her as at all funny. There was still something frightful to her about the glove. She went back to the window, and soon she distinctly heard a noise up-stairs, and then a shadow crossed the ceiling. A new horror seized her — a horror of herself. She felt that in another moment she might herself become a very part and substance of the fear that was oppressing her. She had an imagination of jumping up, of running about and screaming, of breaking something. Then with that clutch at life and reason which is life itself, which all dying and despairing things have at the last, she thought again that there must be somebody, somebody in the whole place to whom she could turn, somebody who would help her, who would pity her. She had heretofore only thought of the possibility of somebody who would come and stay with her; it now occurred to her that she herself might be the one to go, and that she might escape from this house of fear. It was suddenly to her as to a prisoner who realizes that all the time his prison doors have been unbarred.

"What am I staying here for in this awful house by myself?" she suddenly thought. When that idea came to her, the idea of escape, the action of her mind became involuntary. There was only one to whom she could run for aid. She remembered so vividly that the experience seemed to repeat itself, her terror of the tramp in the woods, and how she had seen Anderson. She sprang up. It became sure to her that she must get away from that house, that she must not remain. The imaginative girl, whom anxiety and want of food had weakened, as well as fear, was fairly at the point of madness, or that hysteria which is the border-land of it. She distinctly heard herself laugh as she ran out of the room and out of the house. Her head was bare, but she did not think of that. She had on her coat which she had worn because of the coldness of the house. She fled across the lawn to the street. Once on the road, she was saner, she felt only the natural impulse of flight of any hunted thing. She fled down the road past the quiet village houses, in which the people slept in their beds. The electric lights were out, the moon was low. It was quite dark. Nobody except herself was abroad in the night. A great pity for herself, a pity that she might have felt for a little lonely child out by herself at night, when everybody else was safe in their homes, came over her. She sobbed as she ran; she even sobbed quite loudly. She did not feel so afraid, as wild for somebody to take her in and comfort her. She ran down the main street and turned up the one on which the Andersons lived. When she reached the house it was quite dark, except for a very faint glimmer in one of the upper front rooms. It was from the little night-lamp which Mrs. Anderson always kept burning. The sight of that light seemed to give Charlotte strength to get up the steps. She had run so weakly that all the way she had a thought of the terraces of steps leading to the Anderson house, if she could climb them. She went up the steps, and then she pressed hard the electric button on the door; she also raised the superfluous old brass knocker which Mrs. Anderson cherished because it was a relic from her husband's time; then she clanged that. Then she sank down on the step in front of the door.

CHAPTER XXXIX

Almost at once a light flashed from an upper window in response to Charlotte's knock and ring. Anderson himself had been in New York that night with Henry Edgecomb to the theatre. A celebrated play was on, in which a celebrated actress figured, and the two had taken one of their rather infrequent excursions. Consequently, Anderson had not been in the house more than an hour, and during that hour had been writing some letters which he wished to get off in the early mail. His room was at the back of the house, a long room extending nearly the whole width, consequently his own brightly shining light had not been visible to Charlotte coming up the street.

As he was not undressed, he lost no time in opening his door and entering with his lamp the front hall. As he did so his mother's door opened, and her delicate, alarmed old face, frilled with white cambric, appeared.

"Oh, who is it at this time of night, do you suppose, Randolph?" she whispered.

"I don't know, mother dear; don't be frightened."

But she came quite out in her white night draperies, which made her appear singularly massive. "Oh, do you suppose there are burglars in the store?" she said.

"No. Don't worry, mother."

"Do you suppose it is fire?"

"No; there is no alarm."

"Randolph, you won't open the door until you have asked who it is. Promise me."

"It is nobody to be afraid of, mother."

"Promise me."

"It is probably Henry come back for something. Harriet may have locked him out, and he forgotten his night-key." That was actually what had flashed through Randolph's mind when he heard the knock and ring.

"Well, I shouldn't wonder if it was," said Mrs. Anderson, in a relieved tone.

"Go back to bed, mother, or you will catch your death of cold."

"But you will ask?"

"Yes, yes."

Anderson hurried down-stairs, and in consideration of his mother's listening ears of alarm, he did call out, "Who is there?" at the same time unlocking the door. It was manifest to his masculine intelligence, unhampered by nerves, that no one with evil intent would thus strive to enter a house with a clang of knocker and peal of bell. He, therefore, having set the lamp on the hall-table, at once unlocked the door, and Charlotte pulled herself to her feet and her little, pretty, woe-begone face, in which was a new look for him and herself, confronted him. Anderson did not say a word. He somehow — he never remembered how — laid hold of the little thing, and she was in the house, in the sitting-room, and in his arms, clinging to him.

"Papa didn't come. Papa didn't come home," she sobbed, but so softly that Mrs. Anderson, who was listening, did not hear.

Anderson laid his cheek down against the girl's soft, wet one, as if it were the most natural thing in the world, as if he had been used to so doing ever since he could remember anything. There was no strangeness for either of them in it. He patted her poor little head, which felt cold from the frosty night air.

"There, there, dear," he said.

"He didn't come home," she repeated, piteously, against his breast, and it was almost as if she were accusing him because of it.

"Poor little girl!"

"Not on the last train. Papa didn't come on the last train, and — there was no telegram, and I — I was all alone in the house, and — and — I came." She sobbed convulsively.

Anderson kissed her cheek softly, he continued to smooth the little, dark, damp head. "You did quite right," he whispered — "quite right, dear. You are safe now. Don't!"

"Papa!"

"Oh, some business detained him in the City."

"What has happened to papa?" demanded Charlotte, in a shrill voice, and it was again as if she were unconsciously accusing Anderson. When a heart becomes confident of love, it is filled with wonder at any evil mischance permitted, and accuses love, even the love of God. "What has happened to papa? Where is he?" she demanded again. And it was then that Mrs. Anderson, unseen by either of them, stood in the doorway with an enormous purple-flowered wrapper surging over her nightgown.

"Hush, dear!" whispered Anderson. "I am sure nothing has happened."

"Why are you sure?"

"If anything had happened I should have heard of it. I came out on the last train myself. If there had been an accident I should certainly have heard."

"Would you?"

"I surely should have. Don't, dear. Your father has just been detained by business."

"Then why didn't papa telegraph?"

"He did not get it in the office in season. The office closes at half-past eight," said Anderson, lying cheerfully.

"Does it?"

"Of course! There is nothing for you to worry about. Now I'll tell you what we will do. My mother is awake. I will speak to her, and you must go straight to bed, and go to sleep, and in the morning your father will be along on the first train. He must have been as much worried as you."

"Poor papa," said Charlotte.

"So you were all alone in the house, and you came down here all alone at this time," said Anderson, in a tone which his mother had never heard. But it was then that she spoke.

"Didn't her father come home?" she asked.

When the girl turned like a flash and saw her she seemed to realize for the first time that she had been, and was, doing something out of the wonted. A great, burning blush surged all over her. She shrank away from the man who held her. She cowered before the other woman.

"No, papa didn't come," she stammered, "and — I didn't know what to do, and I came here."

"You did quite right, you precious child," said Mrs. Anderson, suddenly, in a voice of the tenderest authority. She held out her arms and Charlotte fled to them. Mrs. Anderson looked over the girl's head at her son with the oddest and most inexplicable reproach. "You go up and see if the heat is turned on in that little room out of mine," she commanded, and then you go into the kitchen and see if you can't find the milk, and set some on the stove to warm. You can pour a little hot water in it to hurry it. If the fire isn't good, open the dampers. And, Randolph, you get my hot-water bag out of my bed, and fill it from the tea-kettle — that water will be hotter than the bath-room, this time of night — and you bring it right up; be as quick as you can." Then all in the same breath she was comforting Charlotte. "Your father is all right, dear child. Don't you worry one mite — not one mite. I remember once, when I was a girl, my father didn't come home, and mother and I were almost crazy, and he came in laughing the next morning. He had lost his last train because there was a block on account of the ice. The river was frozen over. There is nothing for you to worry about. Now come right up-stairs and go to bed. There is a little room out of mine, as warm as toast, and you won't be a bit afraid. There you were all alone in that great house, you poor, blessed child."

Charlotte sobbed, but now with a certain comfort.

"I should have been so afraid, I should have lost my senses, all alone in a house at your age," said Mrs. Anderson, all the time gently impelling the girl along with her. "Of course there is nothing to be afraid of, but one imagines things; and you came here all alone at this time of the night!"

"Yes," responded Charlotte, with a gasp of the intensest self-pity, sure of an echo.

Randolph ran up-stairs before his mother and Charlotte and snatched the hot-water bottle out of his mother's bed, and was out the opposite door, which connected with the back stairs leading to the kitchen. As he went out he heard his mother say: "All that way alone this time of night, you poor, precious child!" and Charlotte's little, piteous, yet comforted sob in response, exactly as a hurt baby might respond to commiserations. He felt his own knees tremble as he went down-stairs, carrying the hot-water bottle, which had always struck him as a rather absurd article, to be regarded with the concessions which a man should make to the little, foolish devices for the comfort of a softer and slighter sex. He hunted up the milk in the ice-box, and warmed it with solicitude in a china cup, which, luckily, did not break. The fire was still very good, and the water in the tea-kettle quite boiling. It was not long before he knocked at his mother's door, bearing the water-bottle dangling on one wrist, and carrying the cup of milk. His mother opened the door just wide enough to receive the articles.

"Is the milk hot?" she asked.

Randolph meekly replied that it had almost boiled.

"The water-bottle is hot, too," said his mother, in a satisfied tone. "She is undressed. I got one of my nightgowns for her, and it is quite warm in the little room. Now I am going to take this in to her, and make her drink the milk, and I hope she will get to sleep."

"I hope she will," replied Randolph, in a sort of dazed fashion, and there was a foolish radiance over his face, and he did not meet his mother's eyes.

"I'm coming into your room a minute, after I see to her," said his mother, and if the man had been a child the tone would have sounded ominous.

"All right, mother," replied Anderson. He crossed the hall to his room lined with books, with the narrow couch. It hardly seemed like a bedroom, and indeed he spent much of his time, when not at the store, there. He resumed his seat in the well-worn easy-chair beside his hearth, upon which smouldered a fire, and waited. He still felt dazed. He had that doubt of his own identity which comes to us at times, and which is primeval under stress of a great surprise. The old nursery rhyme of the old woman who had her petticoats clipped and was not sure of herself, has a truth in it which dates from the beginning of things. Anderson, sitting precisely as he had been sitting before in the same chair by the same hearth — he had even taken up the same book in which he had thought to read a chapter after his letters were finished, before retiring — was as completely removed from his former state as if he had been translated into another planet. He looked around the long room, which had a dark, rich coloring from the backs of old books, and some dark red hangings, and even that had a curious appearance of unsubstantiality to him. Or was it substantiality. Suddenly it seemed to him that heretofore he had seen it all through a glass, and now with his natural eyes. He had attained a height a nature whence the prospect is untrammelled by imaginations and shows in the clear light of reality. He thought of the girl whom his mother was coddling, tucking into bed as if she were a baby, and such a wave of tenderness and protection came over him that he felt newly vivified by it. It was as if his very soul put forth arms and wings of love and defence.

"The dear little girl!" he thought to himself — "the dear little girl!"

The thought that she was safe under his roof, away from all fancied and real terror, filled him with such a joy that he could scarcely contain it. He imagined her nestling in that warm little bed out of his mother's room, and the satisfaction that he might have felt had she been his child instead of his sweetheart, filled him with pure delight. He tried to imagine her terrors, her young-girl terrors, alone in that house, her panic running alone through the night streets, and he even magnified it through inability to understand it. He said to himself that she might have almost gone mad, and again that sublime joy, that immense sense of the protection and tenderness of love, filled his soul, which seemed to put forth wings. Then the door opened and his mother entered softly, slipping through in her voluminous, purple-flowered draperies, with glimpses of white frills and large padding feet in purple-knitted slippers. She still wore her frilled nightcap, and her face confronted him from the white setting with a curious severity. Her hair was put up on crimping-pins, and her high forehead gave her a rather intellectual and stern appearance, and she looked much older.

Randolph rose. "Sit down, mother," he said.

"No; I am not going to stop a minute. I am going back to her. She seemed real quiet, and I think she'll go to sleep, but if she should wake up and find herself alone she might be frightened."

Mrs. Anderson spoke as if of a baby in arms.

"Yes, she might; she has had a terrible shock," Anderson said, in what he essayed to render a natural tone.

"Terrible shock! I should think she had, poor child!" said Mrs. Anderson, and she seemed to reproach him.

"It was a long way for her to come alone," said Anderson, as if he were trying to excuse himself.

"I should think it was. It's a good mile, and that wasn't the worst of it. Worrying about her father, and all alone in the house! I was always scared to death alone in a house, and I know what it means." She still seemed reproachful.

"She must have been frightened."

"I should rather think she would have been." Suddenly his mother's face regarding his took on a different expression; it became shrewd and confidential. "Do you suppose her father has taken this way of —?" she said.

"No," answered Randolph, emphatically.

"You don't?"

"No, I do not. I don't know the man very well, and I don't suppose his record is to be altogether justified, but, if I know anything, he would no more go voluntarily and leave that child alone all night to worry over him than I would."

"Then you think something has happened to him?"

"I am afraid so."

"Do you think there has been an accident?"

"I don't know, mother."

His mother continued to look at him shrewdly. "Do you suppose he has got into any trouble?" she asked, bluntly.

"I don't know, mother."

Then Mrs. Anderson's face suddenly resumed its old, reproachful expression. "Well, I don't care if there has," said she. She whispered, but her voice was intense. "I don't care if there has. I don't care if he is in state-prison. That child has got to caring about you, and you ought to —"

Anderson turned and looked at his mother, and her severe face softened and paled. He looked to her at that moment more like his father than himself. He was accusing her.

"Mother, do you think, if she cares, that I would ever desert her, any more than father would have deserted you?" he demanded.

It was her turn to excuse herself. "I know you are honorable, Randolph," she said, "but I saw when I came in, and I don't see how you have seen enough of her to have it happen; but I know girls, and I can see how she feels, and I didn't know but you might think if her father —"

"What difference do you think her father makes to me, mother?" asked Anderson.

CHAPTER XL

When Carroll came to himself that night after his fall, his first conscious motion was for his dollar watch. He was in William Allbright's bed. There were only two sleeping-apartments in the little tenement. William was seated beside him, watching him with his faithful, serious face; there was also a physician, keenly observant, still closer to the injured man's head; and the sister, Allbright's sister, was visible in the next room, seated in a chair which commanded a good view of the bed. It was Allbright who had rescued Carroll from the station-house; for when he did not rise, the usual crowd, who directly attribute all failures to recover one's self from a manifestly inappropriate recumbent position, had collected, and several policemen were on the scene.

"I know this gentleman," Allbright said, in his rather humble, still half-respectful, voice, which carried conviction. "I know this gentleman. I have been a book-keeper in his office. He slipped on the ice. I saw him fall. He is not drunk."

One of the policemen, who had been long in the vicinity and knew Allbright, as from the heights of the law one might know an unimportant and unoffending citizen, responded.

"All right," he said, laconically. "Hospital?"

"Guess he's hurted pretty bad," remarked another policeman, who was a handsome athlete.

"Hospital?" inquired the first, who was a man of few words, of Allbright.

"I guess we'd better have him taken to my house. It's right here," replied Allbright. "Then we'll call in Dr. Wilson and see how much is the matter with him. Maybe he's only stunned. The hospital is apt to be a long siege, and if there isn't any need of it —"

"His house is right here," said the first policeman to the second, with a stage aside.

"All right," said the second.

A boy pulled Allbright by the sleeve. "Say, I'll go for the doc," he cried, eagerly. He was enjoying the situation keenly.

"Well," replied Allbright, "be quick about it. Tell him there's a man badly hurt at my house."

The boy sped like a rocket, and three more with him. They all yelled as they ran. They were street gamins of the better class, and were both sympathetic and entertained. They lived in a tenement-house near Allbright, and knew him quite well by sight.

Meantime the two policemen carried Carroll the short distance to William Allbright's house. He was quite unconscious, and it was an undertaking of considerable difficulty to carry him up the stairs, since the Allbrights lived in the second story.

The clerk in the department store, and his mother, who lived on the first floor, came to their door in undress and offered their hospitality, but Mr. Allbright declined their aid.

"No," he said. "I know him. It is Mr. Carroll. He had better be taken up to my rooms."

When at last they laid the unconscious man on Allbright's bed, which his sister, pale, and yet with a collectedness under such surprising circumstances which spoke well for her, had opened, the policeman who was not an athlete, and was, in fact, too stout, wiped his forehead and said, "Gee."

The other remained looking at the injured man soberly.

"Guess he's hurted pretty bad," he remarked again.

"You bet," said the first. "Gee!"

Allbright's sister came with the camphor-bottle, which she kept in a sort of folk-lore fashion, as her mother had used to do in the country. Allbright brought the whiskey, of which he kept a small supply in the house in case of dire need, and stood over Carroll with that and a tea-spoon, with a vague idea of trying to insinuate a few drops into his mouth.

The two policemen clamped heavily down-stairs, agreeing that they would remain until the doctor came, and see if it was to be the hospital after all.

"Guess he's hurted pretty bad," remarked the handsome policeman for the third time.

The doctor came quickly, almost on a run. He lived within a block, and had not a large practice. He was attended by a large throng of boys, for the three had served as a nucleus for many more. He turned around to them with an imperative gesture as he entered the house door.

"Now you scatter," said he. He was a fair man, but he had at once an appeal of good-fellowship and a certain force of character. Besides, there were the two policemen hovering near. The boys withdrew and remained watching in the dark shadows cast by an opposite house. In case the injured man was carried to the hospital, and the ambulance should come, they could not afford to miss that. They had not so many pleasures in life.

The doctor mounted the stairs; he had been there before, for All-bright's sister was more or less of an invalid, and he at once abetted Allbright's purpose of the few drops of stimulant on the teaspoon, which the patient swallowed with a pathetic, gulping passiveness like a baby's.

"He swallows all right," remarked Allbright's sister, in an agitated voice. She stood aloof, waving the camphor-bottle; her eyes were dilated, and her face had a pale, gaping look.

"You go out in the other room and stay there," said the doctor to her, with the authority which a hysterical woman defers to and adores.

Allbright's sister was a very good woman, but she had sometimes imagined, then directly driven the imagination from her with a spiritual scourge like a monk of old, what might have happened if the doctor were not already married.

Carroll's forehead was dripping with camphor, and there was danger should he open his eyes. The doctor wiped the pale forehead gently and spoke to him.

"Well, you had quite a hard fall, sir," he said, in a loud, cheerful voice, and directly Carroll answered, like a somnambulist:

"Yes, quite a fall."

Then he seemed to lapse again into unconsciousness. The doctor and Allbright remained working over him, but it was within fifteen min-utes before the time when the last train for Banbridge was due to leave

New York that he made the first absolutely conscious motion.

"He is feeling for his watch," said Allbright, in an agitated whisper. His wits were sharpened with regard to Carroll's watch. Carroll's coat and vest had been removed, and were hanging over a chair. Allbright at once got the dollar watch from its pocket and carried it over to the sick man. "Here is your watch, Mr. Carroll," he said, and his voice was full of both respectful and tender inflections.

A sob was distinctly heard from Allbright's sister out in the sitting-room. The woman from down-stairs, the department clerk's mother, was now with her.

"He wants to see if his watch is safe, poor man," said she, in a tearful voice, and Allbright's sister whimpered again.

"It's a wonder some of them kids didn't swipe it," said the down-stairs woman, and Allbright's sister was conscious of a distinct thrill of disgust in the midst of her excitement and pity. She was of a superior sort to the down-stairs woman, and she often told her brother she could not get used to folks using such language.

Poor Carroll was looking dimly at his watch, and Allbright at once divined that he could not distinguish the time without his eye-glasses. He therefore leaned over him — his own spectacles were on his nose — and told him the time.

"It's almost seventeen minutes past twelve, Mr. Carroll," he said.

Carroll made a movement to rise, then subsided with a groan. "Where am I?" he inquired, feebly, with a bewildered stare around the strange room. Directly opposite him hung a large crayon portrait of Allbright's father, a handsome man with a reverend beard like a prophet, and his eyes became riveted upon that.

"You are in my house, Mr. Carroll," said Allbright, with a tender, caressing motion of his hand towards him, like a woman.

"You had a fall on the ice, Mr. Carroll," said the physician, in a tone of soothing explanation, "but you will soon be as good as new."

"How far up-town?" inquired Carroll, still gazing at the portrait, which had an odd hardness of outline, and appeared almost as if carved out of wood.

"You are at One Hundred and Twenty-fifth Street," replied Allbright. "You are at my house, Mr. Carroll. You fell right out here, and I had you carried in here."

Carroll tried again to rise, and made a despairing gasp. "Oh, my God!" he said. "I have lost the last train out. There isn't time to get down to the ferry, and there is that poor child all alone there, and she won't know —"

"You can send a telegram," suggested the doctor. "Now, Mr. Carroll, don't get excited."

"She will be all right," said Allbright.

"What is it?" asked the down-stairs woman, coming to the door.

"His daughter is all alone in the house, I guess, and he's worried about her," explained Allbright.

"There ain't nothin' goin' to eat her, if she is, is there?" inquired the down-stairs woman.

"I'll run with a telegram," said Allbright, eagerly, to the doctor.

But at that moment Carroll lapsed into unconsciousness. The excitement had been too much for him. He lay as if asleep.

"Where does he live?" asked the doctor, of Allbright.

"I don't know exactly. Somewhere out on the Pennsylvania Railroad."

"You don't know?" repeated the doctor, with a faint accent of surprise.

Allbright shook his head.

"You were book-keeper in his office?"

"Yes, but I haven't been there for some time. I never asked any questions."

The doctor turned and looked at Carroll. Then he went out of the room, with Allbright following, and gave him some directions. He asked for a glass two-thirds full of water and poured some dark drops into it.

"The minute he gets conscious again give him a spoonful of this," he said, "and you had better sit beside him and watch him." Then he turned to Allbright's sister, who was trembling from head to foot with a nervous chill. "You take a dose of that whiskey your brother gave him," he said, jerking his shoulder towards the inner room, "then go to bed, and don't worry your head about him."

"Oh, doctor, he isn't going to die here?"

"Die here? No, nor nowhere else for one while. There is nothing the matter with the man except he bumped his head rather too hard for comfort."

"How long is he likely to be here on their hands?" inquired the down-stairs woman.

"He will be able to go home in the morning, I think," said the doctor.

"Oh, doctor, you aren't going to go away and leave us with a strange man as sick as he is?" asked Allbright's sister, hysterically. She shook so that she could scarcely speak.

"You won't have to worry half so much over a strange man as you would over one you know," replied the doctor, jocosely, "and he is not very sick. He will be all right soon. Now you take some of your brother's medicine and go to bed, for I have six cases to visit tonight before I go home, and I don't want another."

Allbright's sister bridled with an odd, inexplicable pride. She did not like to be a burden on her brother, nor make trouble, but there was a certain satisfaction in having the down-stairs woman, who, she had always suspected, rather made light of her ailments, hear for herself that she was undoubtedly delicate. Even the minor and apparently paradoxical pretensions of life are dear to their possessors in lieu of others.

"Very well. I suppose I've got to mind the doctor," she replied, and even smiled foolishly and blushed.

The doctor turned to Allbright.

"I think he will be all right in the morning," he said; "a bit light-headed, of course, but all right. However, don't let him go home before noon, on your life. I will look in in the morning before he goes." And then he turned to Allbright's sister. "On second thought, I will let you make a good big bowl of that gruel of yours before you go to bed," he said; "then he can take it in the course of the night if he is able; and beat him up some eggs in the morning."

"I'll make the gruel if she ain't able," said the down-stairs woman, in a tone vibrating between kindness and scorn.

"Thank you. I am quite able to make it," said Allbright's sister, and she was full of small triumph and persistency. Yes, she would make the gruel, even if she was so very delicate that she ought to go at once to bed. It was quite evident that she thought that the down-stairs woman could not make gruel good enough for that man in there, anyway.

"Well, I guess I'll go," said the down-stairs woman, "as long as I don't seem to be of any use. If there was anything I could do, I'd stay." And she went.

"The idea of her coming up here and trying to find out what was going on!" Allbright's sister said to her brother as she was getting the meal ready for the gruel. "I never saw such a curious woman."

"If we hadn't got so attached to the place we would move," said Allbright, who was leaving his patient momentarily, to change his shoes for slippers.

"I know it," said the sister, "but I can't help feeling attached to the place, we have lived here so long; and there is that beautiful cherry-tree out in the yard, and everything."

"That is so," said Allbright.

"I am glad Mr. Carroll didn't have to be carried to a hospital."

"I suppose he would have been if I had not happened to be right on the spot," said Allbright, reflectively, to his sister.

"You think he'll be all right in the morning, don't you?"

"Oh yes, the doctor said so!"

Outside, the watching boys in the shadow of the church disappointedly vanished, cheated of their small and grewsome excitement, when they saw the doctor quietly walk towards his house and realized that there was to be no ambulance and no hospital.

"Gee! I've had knocks harder 'n that, and never said nothin' about it," said one boy as he scurried away with the others towards his home in the high tenement-house.

CHAPTER XLI

It was quite early the next morning when Charlotte received the telegram that her father had had a fall on the ice, was not badly injured, and would be home on the noon train. Anderson had gone very early to the telegraph-office. It was being ticked off in Andrew Drake's drug-store when he inquired, and the boy viewed him with intense curiosity when he took the message, but did not dare ask any questions. Anderson hurried home with it to Charlotte, who was not yet up. Mrs. Anderson had insisted upon her having her breakfast in bed, and she had yielded readily. In fact, she was both too confused and too ashamed to see Anderson. She dreaded seeing him. She was as simple as a child, and she reasoned simply.

"He held me in his arms and kissed me last night, the way Major Arms would have done with Ina," she told herself, "and of course I suppose I must be engaged to him; but I don't know what he must think of me for coming here the way I did. It was almost as if I asked him first." She wondered if Mrs. Anderson had seen. But Mrs. Anderson's manner to her was of such complete and caressing motherliness that she could not have much fear of her. In reality, the older woman, who had an active imagination, was slightly jealous, in view of future possibilities.

"I wonder if they will think they ought to sit by themselves evenings," she reflected. She looked at the girl's slight grace in the bed, and the little, dark head sunken in the pillow, and she wondered how in the world the mother of a girl like that could stay one minute in Kentucky and leave her. "She must be a pretty woman!" she thought to herself. Already she hated the other mother-in-law, and she felt almost a maternal right to the girl. She recalled what she had seen the night before, and thrills of tender reminiscence came over her. "Randolph will make just such a good husband as his father," she thought to herself, and then she rather resented his superior right over the girl, as she might have done if it had not been a question of her own son, and Charlotte had been her own daughter. She loved her as she loved the daughter she had never had. She stroked her hair softly as it curled over the pillow.

"You have such pretty hair, dear," she said, with positive pride. The little, flushed face looked up at her.

Charlotte had just finished her breakfast. Anderson had brought the telegram and gone, and the two were alone. It was arranged that Charlotte was to get up in an hour, and that Mrs. Anderson was to go home with her in one of Samson Rawdy's coaches.

"We will take my maid, and she can get the furnace fire started," she said, "and help about the dinner."

"I had such a nice dinner all ready last night," Charlotte said, "and I am afraid it must be spoiled now."

"Never mind. We will get another," said Mrs. Anderson.

Both Anderson and his mother had succeeded in quieting Charlotte's lingering fears concerning her father.

"He probably got stunned," Anderson said; "and he cannot be very bad or he would not be coming home on the noon train." He was talking to Charlotte from his mother's room, with the door ajar.

There was something conclusive in Anderson's voice which reassured Charlotte.

"My son would not say so unless he thought so," said Mrs. Anderson. "He never says a thing he does not mean." She spoke with a double meaning which Charlotte wholly missed. It had not occurred to her that Mr. Anderson would have taken her in his arms last night and kissed her and comforted her, if he had not been thoroughly in earnest and in love with her. She supposed, of course, he wished to marry her. All that troubled her was her own course in practically proposing to him. Presently, after she and Mrs. Anderson were alone together, she tried to say something about this to the other woman.

"I don't know as I ought to have come here last night," she said, "but —"

"Where else would you have gone?" inquired Mrs. Anderson.

Charlotte looked up at her piteously. "I hope Mr. Anderson didn't think I — I — ought not to," she whispered, and she felt her cheeks blazing with shame. She did not know if Mrs. Anderson really knew, but she was as much ashamed.

Mrs. Anderson stooped over her and laid her soft old cheek against the soft young one. "My precious child!" she whispered. "I could not help seeing last night, and this was just the place for you to come, for this is your home, or is going to be; isn't it, dear?"

Charlotte put up her soft little arms around the other woman's neck, and began to cry softly. "Oh," she sobbed, "I don't want him to think that I —"

"Hush, dear! He will think nothing he ought not to think," said Mrs. Anderson, who did not, in reality, know in the least what the girl was troubled about, but rather thought it possible that she might fear lest her son was not in earnest in his attentions, on her father's account. She did not imagine Charlotte's faith and pride in her father. "My son cares a great deal for you, dear child, or he would never have done as he did last night," she said, "and some day we are all going to be very happy."

Charlotte continued to sob softly, but not altogether unhappily.

"My son will make a very good husband," Mrs. Anderson said, with a slight inflection of pride. "He will make a good husband, just as his father did."

"He is the best man I ever saw, except papa," cried Charlotte then, with a great gulp of blissful confession, and the two women wept in each other's arms. "I will try and make him a good wife," Charlotte whispered, softly.

"Of course you will, you precious child."

But suddenly Charlotte raised herself a little and looked at Mrs. Anderson with a troubled face. "But I can't leave papa all alone," she said, "and your son would not want to leave you."

"Of course my son could not leave me," Mrs. Anderson said, quickly.

"I could not leave papa all alone."

"Well, we won't worry about that now, dear," Mrs. Anderson replied, although her forehead was slightly knitted. "Your mother and aunt will be back; some way will be opened. We will not worry about that now."

Charlotte blushed painfully at the thought that she had been hasty about making preparations for the marriage, and had shocked Mrs. Anderson. "You don't think papa is very badly hurt?" she said.

"Why, of course not, dear. Didn't you hear what Randolph said? He probably was stunned. It is so easy to get stunned from a fall on the ice. My husband got a bad fall once, one icy Sunday as we were coming home from the church. They had to carry him into Mr. John Bemis's house, and he did not come to for several hours. I thought he was killed. I never was so frightened except once when Randolph had the croup. But he got all over it. His head was a little sore, but that was all. I presume it was black and blue under his hair. Randolph's father had beautiful thick hair just like his. I dare say he was not hurt so badly, because of that. Your father has thick hair, hasn't he?"

"Yes."

"Well, I dare say he struck on his head, just as my husband did, and was stunned. I dare say that was just what happened. Of course he did not break any bones, or he would not be coming home on the noon train. I don't believe they would let him out from the hospital so soon as that, even if he had only broken his arm."

"Oh, do you think they carried him to a hospital?"

"They took him somewhere where he was taken care of, or he would not be coming home on the noon train," said Mrs. Anderson. "It is almost time for you to get up, and I want you to drink another cup of coffee. You came here without any hat, didn't you, poor child?"

"Yes."

"Well, I haven't got any hat, and you can't wear one of my bonnets, but I have a pretty white head-tie that you can wear; and nobody will see you in the closed carriage, anyway."

"I am making so much trouble," said Charlotte.

"You precious child!" said Mrs. Anderson; "when I think of you all alone in that house!"

"It was dreadful," Charlotte said, with a shudder. "I suppose there was nothing at all to be afraid of, but I imagined all kinds of things."

"The things people imagine are more to be afraid of than the things they see, sometimes," Mrs. Anderson said, wisely. "Now, I think perhaps you had better get up, dear, and you must drink another cup of coffee. I think there will be just about time enough for you to drink it and get dressed before the carriage comes."

Mrs. Anderson took the pride in assisting the girl to dress that she had done in dressing her son when he was a child. She even noticed, with the tenderest commiseration instead of condemnation, that the lace on her undergarments was torn, and that there were buttons missing.

"Poor dear child, she never had any decent training," she said to herself. She anticipated teaching Charlotte to take care of her clothes, as she might have done if she had been her own girl baby. "I guess her clothes won't look like this when I have had her awhile," she said to herself, eying furtively some torn lace on the girl's slender white shoulder.

When they were at last driving through the streets of Banbridge, she felt unspeakably proud, and also a little defiant.

"I suppose there are plenty of people who will say Randolph is a fool to marry a girl whose father has done the way hers has," she told herself, "but I don't care. There isn't a girl in Banbridge to compare with her. I don't care; they can say what they want to." She was so excited that she had put on her bonnet, which had a little jet aigrette on top, awry. After a while Charlotte timidly ventured to speak of it and straighten it, and the tenderest thrill of delight came over the older woman at the daughterly attention.

She told Randolph that noon, after she had got home, that she was really surprised to see how well the poor child, with no training at all, had kept the house, and she said it, remembering quite distinctly a white shade of dust in full view on the parlor-table.

"Her dinner was all dried up, of course," she said, "but I thought it looked as if it might have been quite nice when it was first cooked."

Already Mrs. Anderson was becoming deceptive for the sake of the girl. She had carried a box of provisions to the house, and they had stopped at the fish-market and bought some oysters; and Mrs. Anderson had taught Charlotte how to make a stew, and retreated before it was quite time for Carroll to arrive. She felt in her heart of hearts that she could not see him yet. Even her love for the girl did not yet reconcile her to Carroll. Charlotte was so glad that her little purse was in her coat-pocket and that she had enough money to pay for the oysters. She felt that she could not have borne it had she been obliged to borrow money of Mrs. Anderson. She felt that it would reflect upon her father. Already she had an instinctive jealousy on her father's account. She loved Mrs. Anderson, but she felt vaguely that not enough was said, even there was not enough anxiety displayed, with regard to her father. She reflected with the fiercest loyalty that even although she did love Mr. Anderson, although she had let him kiss her, although at the mere memory thrills of delight overwhelmed her, she would not ever admit even to herself that he was any better than her father — her poor father who had been hurt and whom everybody was blaming and accusing. Directly after Mrs. Anderson and the maid had gone, she began making the oyster-stew. It would not be quite so good as if she had waited until her father had really arrived, and Mrs. Anderson had told her so, but Charlotte could not bear to wait. She wished him to have something nice and hot the minute he came in. The water boiled and she made the tea. Mrs. Anderson had said that the tea might be better for him than coffee, and she also made toast. Then she went again into the parlor to the window, as she had done the night before; but it was all so different now. She was so happy that she was confused by it. She had not been brought up, as one would say, religiously, although she had always gone to church, but now she realized a strange uplifting of her thoughts above the happiness itself, to a sense of God. She was conscious of a thankfulness which at once exalted and humbled her. She sat down beside the window and looked out, and everything, every dry spear of grass and every slender twig on the trees, was streaming like rainbows in the frosty air. It came to her what an unspeakable blessing it was that she had been allowed to come into a world where there were so many rainbows and so much happiness, and how nothing but more rainbows and happiness could come of these. That there was nothing whatever to dread in the future. And she thought how her father was coming home, and she thought of all her horrible imaginations of the night before as she might have thought of a legion of routed fiends. And soon Samson Rawdy drove her father into the grounds, and she ran to the door. She opened it and went to the carriage with her arms extended, but he got out himself, laughing.

"Did you think I wanted help, honey?" he said, but though he laughed, he walked weakly and his face was very pale.

He paid Samson Rawdy, who opened his mouth as if to say something, then looked at Carroll's pale face and changed his mind, getting rather stiffly up on his seat — he was growing stout — and driving away.

"Oh, papa!" Charlotte said, slipping her arm through his and nestling close up to him as they went into the house.

Carroll bent down and kissed her. "Papa's poor little girl!" he said. "It was mighty hard on her, wasn't it?"

"Oh, papa, you are not hurt very badly?"

"Not hurt at all, sweetheart. I, to put it simply, tumbled down on the ice and hit my head, and was so stunned that I did not come to myself until it was too late for the last train."

"Oh, papa, where were you? Did they carry you to a hospital?"

"No, dear. I was very near a man who used to keep my books before I gave up my office, and he had me carried to his house, which was near by, and he and his sister did everything for me, they and their doctor."

"They must be such good people!" said Charlotte.

"Such good people that I can never pay them," said Carroll, in an odd voice. They had entered the house and were going through the hall. "Not in other ways than money," he added, quickly. "I owe him nothing." It was the first time that Carroll had ever attempted to justify himself to his child, but at that moment the sting of thinking that she might suspect that he owed Allbright money was more than he could bear.

When they were in the dining-room, Carroll turned and looked at Charlotte. "My poor little girl! What did you think, and what did you do?" said he.

She threw her arms around his neck again and clung to him. "Oh, papa, when you didn't come, when the last train went by and you didn't come, I thought —"

"Poor little sweetheart!"

"I went down to the six-o'clock train, and then I waited for the next, and then I came home, and I watched, and the telegraph-boy came to tell me there was no telegram, and I had the dinner keeping warm on the back of the range; it was beefsteak cooked that way in the cook-book, and there was a pudding," said Charlotte, incoherently, and she began to weep against her father's shoulder.

In reality, the girl's nerves were nearer the overstrained point now than they had been before. She was so glad to have her father home, she was so dazed by her new happiness, and there was something about her father's white face which frightened her in a subtle fashion. There was a changed meaning in it beside the sick look.

"Poor little girl!" Carroll said again. "Did you have to stay here alone all night?"

"No, papa. I stayed just as long as I could, and then I went out, and I ran —"

"Where, dear?"

"I ran to —"

Carroll waited. Charlotte had turned her face as far away from him as she could as she leaned against him, but one ear was burning red.

"I ran to the — Andersons'. You know Mr. Anderson, that time when I was so frightened by the tramp — You know I stayed there to tea, that — Mrs. Anderson was very kind," said Charlotte, in a stammering and incoherent voice.

"Oh," said Carroll.

Suddenly Charlotte raised her head, and she looked at him quite bravely, with an innocent confidence. "Papa," said she, "you needn't think I am ever going to leave you, not until Amy and the others come back, because I never will. You never will think so?"

"No, darling," said Carroll. His face grew paler.

"But," continued Charlotte, "when I went to the Andersons' last night, I rang the bell, and I pounded with the knocker, too, I was so frightened, and Mr. Anderson came right away. He had been to New York himself, to the theatre, and he had not been home long, and —"

Carroll waited.

"I am never going to leave you, papa," said Charlotte, "and I love you just as much. I love you just as much as I do — him, only, of course, it is different. You needn't think I don't. There is nobody like you. But he — if you don't mind, papa, I think I will marry Mr. Anderson sometime, the way Ina did Major Arms."

Carroll did not speak for a moment. He continued looking at her with an expression made up of various emotions — trouble, relief, shame.

"He is a very good man," said Charlotte, in a half-defensive tone. "He is the best man I ever saw, except you, papa."

Carroll bent down and kissed her. "You are very sure you love him, are you, dear?" he said.

"Why, papa, of course I am! I never could see how Ina could love Major Arms enough to marry him, but I can see how anybody could be glad to marry Mr. Anderson."

"Then I am very glad, sweetheart," Carroll said, with a curious quietness, almost weariness.

"His mother is lovely, too," said Charlotte.

"That is nice, dear, for I suppose you will live with them."

"When Amy and the others come back," said Charlotte. "I am not ever going to leave you, papa. You know it, don't you?"

"Yes, sweetheart," said Carroll, still with the same curious, weary quiet.

Charlotte looked at him anxiously. "Does your head ache now, papa?" she asked.

"No, dear."

"But you don't feel well. You are very pale."

"I feel a little weak, that is all, dear."

"You will feel better when you have had dinner. Mrs. Anderson came home with me, she and her maid, and she gave me some lovely thin slices of ham, and there is an oyster-stew, and some tea. Sit down, papa dear, and we will have dinner right away."

Carroll made a superhuman effort to eat that dinner, but still the look whose strangeness rather than paleness puzzled Charlotte never left his face. She kept looking at him.

"You won't go to New York again tomorrow, will you, papa?" said she.

"No, dear. I don't think so."

"I wish you wouldn't go again this week, papa. Today is Thursday."

"Perhaps I won't, dear."

After dinner Carroll lay down on the divan in the den and Charlotte covered him up, and after a while he fell asleep; but even asleep, when she stole in to look at him, there was the same strange expression on his face. It was the face of a man whose mind is set irrevocably to an end. A martyr going to the stake might have had that same look, or even a criminal who was going to his doom with a sense of its being his just deserts, and with the bravery that befitted a man.

That evening Anderson came to call, and Carroll answered the door-bell. He took him into the parlor, and spoke at once of the subject upper-most in the minds of both.

"Charlotte has told me," Carroll said, simply. He extended his hand with a pathetic, deprecatory air. "You know what you are doing when you ask for my daughter's hand," he said. "You know she might have a par-entage which would reflect more credit upon her."

"I am quite satisfied," Anderson replied, in a low voice. All at once, looking at the other man, it struck him that he had never in his life pitied any one to such an extent, and that he pitied him all the more because Carroll seemed one to resent pity.

"This much I will say — I can say it confidently now," said Carroll, "I shall meet all my indebtedness. You will have no reason to hesitate on that account," but he paused a moment. "I am driven to resorting to any honest method which I can find to enable me so to do," he continued. He made a slight emphasis upon the word honest.

"I can understand that as fully, possibly, as any man," Anderson replied, gravely.

Carroll looked at him. "Yes, so you can," he said — "so you can. Well, this much I will say for myself, Mr. Anderson. I am proud and glad to confide my daughter to your keeping. I am satisfied, and more than satis-fied, with her choice."

"Thank you," replied Anderson. He felt a constraint, even embar-rassment, as if he had been a very young man. He was even conscious of blushing a little.

"Sit down," said Carroll, placing a chair for him, and offering him a cigar.

Then he went to call Charlotte. It was at that moment rather a hard experience for Charlotte that it was not her mother instead of her father who called her to go down and see her lover. She had thought, with a pas-sion of yearning, of her mother who had done the same thing, and would understand, as she fluffed out her pretty hair around her face in front of the glass in her room. When her father called her she ran down, but instead of going at once into the parlor, where she knew her lover was waiting for her, she ran into the den. She felt sure that her father had retreated there. She found him there, as she had thought, and she flung her arms around his neck.

"I am never going to leave you alone, you know, papa," she whispered.

"Yes, dear."

"Papa, come in there with me."

Carroll laughed then. "Run along, honey," he said, and gave her a kiss, and pushed her softly out of the room.

CHAPTER XLII

Carroll, left alone, lighted another cigar from force of habit. It was one of the abominably cheap ones which he had been smoking lately when by himself. He never offered one to anybody else. But soon the cigar went out and he never noticed it. He sat in a deep-hollowed chair before a fireless hearth, and the strange expression upon his face deepened. It partook of at once exaltation and despair. He heard the soft murmur of voices from the parlor where the lovers were. He reflected that he should tell Anderson, before he married Charlotte, the purpose in his mind; that he owed it to him, since that purpose might quite reasonably cause a man to change his own plans with regard to marrying her. He decided that he would tell him that night before he left. But he felt that it would make no difference to a man of Anderson's type; that it was only for his own sake, the sake of his own honor, that it was necessary to tell him at all. Then he fell to thinking of what was before him, of the new life upon which he would enter the next Monday, and it was actually to this man of wrong courses but right instincts, this man born and bred of the best and as the best, as if he were contemplating the flames of the stake or the torture of the rack. He felt, in anticipation, his pride, his self-respect, stung as with fire and broken as upon the wheel. He was beset with the agonies of spiritual torture, which yet brought a certain solace in the triumph of endurance. He had at once the agony and the delight of the fighter, of the wrestler with the angel. What he had set himself to do for the sake of not only making good to others what they had lost through him, but what he had lost through himself, was unutterably terrible to him. But while his face was agonized, he yet threw back his head with the motion of the conqueror. And he owned to himself that the conquest was even greater because it was against such petty odds, because both the fight and the triumph savored of the ignoble, even of the ridiculous. It would be much easier to be a hero whom the multitude would applaud and worship than a hero whom the multitude would welcome with laughter. When comedy becomes tragedy, when the ignominious becomes victorious, he who brings it about becomes majestic in spite of fate itself. And yet withal the man sitting there listening to the soft murmur from the other room felt that his own life, so far as the happiness which, after all, makes life worth living for mortal weakness, was over. He thought of his wife and sister and children, who would be all safely sheltered, and, he hoped, even happy in time, although separated from him; and while his soul rejoiced over that, he yet could not help thinking of himself. Listening to the voices of the lovers in the parlor, he thought how he and Amy used to make love, and how it was all over, perhaps forever over. He smiled a little as he remembered how his Charlotte had asked him to go with her to meet her lover. Gentle and affectionate to his family as he was, Carroll was essentially masculine. He could not in the least understand how the girl felt. He felt a little anxious lest the child should not really love Anderson, because she hesitated, since he could see no other reason for her hesitation. However, when, about eleven o'clock, he heard the stir of approaching departure, and went hurriedly into the hall in order to intercept Anderson before he went, one glimpse of the girl's little face reassured him. She seemed to at once have grown older and younger. She was reflective, and fairly beaming with utmost anticipations. She looked at Anderson as he had never seen her look at any one. He had doubted a little about Ina; he had no doubt whatever about Charlotte. "She is in love with him, fast enough," he said to himself. He spoke to Anderson, and asked to have a word with him before he went.

"Come back into the parlor a moment, if you please," he said. "I have a word to say to you."

Anderson followed him into the room. He already had on his overcoat. Carroll stood close to him and spoke in a low voice. His face was ghastly when he had finished, but he looked proudly at the other man.

"Now it is for you to say whether you will advance or retreat, for I think that, under the circumstances, nobody could say that you did not do the last with honor," he concluded.

Anderson, who had also turned pale, stared at him a second, and his look was a question.

"There is absolutely nothing else that I can do," replied Carroll, simply; "it is my only course."

Anderson held out his hand. "I shall be proud to have your daughter for my wife," he said.

"Remember she is not to know," Carroll said.

"Do you think the ignorance preferable to the anxiety?"

"I don't know. I cannot have her know. None of them shall know. I have trusted you," Carroll said, with a sort of agonized appeal. "I had, as a matter of honor, to tell you, but no one else," he continued, still in his voice which seemed strained to lowness. "I had to trust you."

"You will never find your trust misplaced," replied Anderson, gravely, "but it will be hard for her."

"You can comfort her," Carroll said, with a painful smile, in which was a slight jealousy, the feeling of a man outside all his loves of life.

"When?" asked Anderson, in a whisper.

"Monday."

"She will, of course, come straight to my mother, and it can all be settled as soon as possible afterwards. There will be no occasion to wait."

"Amy may wish to come," said Carroll, "and Anna."

"Of course."

The two men shook hands and went out in the hall. Carroll went back to the den, and left Charlotte, who was shyly waiting to have the last words with her lover. Pretty soon she came fluttering into the den.

"You do like him, don't you, papa?" she asked, putting her arms around her father's neck.

"Yes, dear."

"But I am never going to leave you, papa, not for him nor anybody, not until Amy and the others come back."

"You will never forget papa, anyway, will you, honey?" said Carroll, and his voice was piteous in spite of himself.

"Forget you, papa? I guess not!" said Charlotte, "and I never will leave you."

That was Thursday. The next afternoon Mrs. Anderson came and called on Charlotte. She was glad that Carroll was not at home. She shrank very much from meeting him. Carroll had not gone to New York, but had taken the trolley to New Sanderson. He also went into several of the Banbridge stores. The next Sunday morning, in the barber's shop, several men exhibited notes of hand with Carroll's signature.

"I don't suppose it is worth the paper it is written on," said Rosenstein, with his melancholy accent, frowning intellectually over the slip of paper.

"He gave the dressmaker one, too," said Amidon, and she is tickled to death with it. The daughter had already asked her to take back a silk dress she had made for her, and she has sold it for something. The dressmaker thinks the note is as good as money."

"I've got one of the blasted things, too," said the milkman, Tappan.

"It's for forty dollars, and I'll sell out for ten cents."

"I'd be willing to make my davyalfit that Captain Carroll's notes will be met when they are accentuated," said the little barber, in a trembling voice of partisanship, looking up from the man he was shaving; and everybody laughed.

Lee, who was waiting his turn, spoke. "Captain Carroll says he will pay me the price I paid for the United Fuel stock, in a year's time," he said, proudly. "The stock has depreciated terribly, too. A pretty square man, I call him."

"He's got more sides than you have, anyhow," growled Tappan, who was bristling like a pirate with his week's beard; and everybody laughed again, though they did not altogether know why.

However the recipients of Carroll's notes doubted their soundness, they folded them carefully and put them in their pocketbooks. When Carroll took the eight-o'clock train to New York the next morning, several noticed it and thought it looked well for the payment of the notes.

"Guess he's goin' to start another cheat," said the milkman, who had stopped at the saloon opposite Rosenstein's. "I seed him git on the eight-ten train."

Charlotte had been told by her father that he was going to New York that morning, and she had risen early and prepared what she considered a wonderful breakfast for him. She was radiant. Anderson had called upon her the evening before. She had never been so happy. Her father seemed in very good spirits, but she wondered why he looked so badly. It was actually as if he had lost ten pounds since the night before. He was horribly haggard, but he talked and laughed in a manner rather unusual for him, as he ate his breakfast. Charlotte watched jealously that he should do that. When he took his second badly fried egg, she beamed, and he concealed his physical and mental nausea.

When they were eating breakfast, much to Charlotte's amazement, the village express drove into the yard.

"Why, there is the express, papa!" she said.

"Yes, honey," replied Carroll, calmly. "I have a trunk I want to send to New York."

"Oh, papa, you are not going away?"

"Sending a trunk does not necessarily imply you are going yourself, honey. I have a trunk to send in connection with some business."

"Oh!" said Charlotte, quite satisfied.

Carroll rose from the table and showed the expressman the way to his room, and the trunk was brought down and carried away, and Charlotte asked no more questions and thought no more about it. Carroll walked to the station. When it was time for him to start, he went to Charlotte, who was clearing away the breakfast dishes, and held her in his arms and kissed her.

"Good-bye, papa's blessing," he said, and in spite of himself his voice broke. The man had reached the limit of his strength.

But Charlotte, who was neither curious nor suspicious, and was, besides, dazzled by her new happiness, only laughed. "Why, papa, I should think you were going away to stay a year!" said she.

Carroll laughed too, but his laugh was piteous. He kissed her again. "Well, good-bye, honey," he said. Just as he was going out of the door he stopped, and said, as if it were a minor matter which he had nearly forgotten, "Oh, by-the-way, sweetheart, I want you, at exactly half-past nine, to go into the den and look in the third volume of the *Dutch Republic*, and see what you will find."

Charlotte giggled. "A present!" said she. "I know it is a present, but what a funny place to put it in, papa, the third volume of the *Dutch Republic*."

"At exactly half-past nine," said Carroll. He kissed her again and went away.

Charlotte stood watching him go out of the yard. It came into her head that he must have had some very good luck, and had taken this funny way of making her a present of some money. Of course it could only be money which was to be hidden in such a place as a book. Poor Charlotte's imaginations were tainted by the lack of money.

She could hardly imagine a pleasant surprise unconnected with money. She hurried about her household tasks, and at exactly half-past nine, for she was obedient as a child, she went into the den and got from the case the third volume of the *Dutch Republic*. In it she found an envelope. She thought that it contained money, but when she opened it and found a letter, suddenly her heart failed her. She sat down dizzily on the divan and read the letter. It was very short. It only told her that her father loved her and loved them all; that he was writing the others just what he was writing her; that he loved her, but he was forced to go away and leave her, and not even let her know where he was nor what he was doing — not for a long time, at least; but that she was not to worry, and she was to go at once to Mrs. Anderson, who would take care of her until she was married. Then he bade God bless her, and said he was her loving father. Charlotte sat with the letter in her lap, and the room looked dim to her. She heard the door-bell ring, but she did not seem to realize what it was, not even when it rang the second and the third time. But the front door had been left unlocked when Carroll went, and Anderson came in presently, and his mother was with him. Mrs. Anderson knew nothing except that Carroll had gone, and nobody was to know where, or why, but that there was nothing dishonorable about it, and Charlotte was to come to them. She was quite pale herself when she saw Charlotte sitting on the divan with the letter in her lap.

"I have a letter from papa," Charlotte said, piteously, in a trembling voice. Then Anderson had her in his arms and was soothing and comforting her, and telling her he knew all about it. It was all right, and she was not to worry.

Mrs. Anderson stood watching them. "Where are your coat and hat, child?" said she, presently. She, in reality, felt that she was the proper person to have comforted the girl, under such circumstances, and not a man who knew nothing about girls, nor how they would feel when deserted, in a measure, by a father. When they were in the carriage, she sat on the seat with Charlotte and kept her arm around her, and looked across almost defiantly at her son.

"It is a terrible strain on the poor little thing, and if we are not careful she will be down with a fever," she told Randolph, privately, when they were home.

He laughed. "Take care of her all you want to, mother," he said.

After dinner he went up to the Carroll place. He had his instructions from Carroll what to do. Some of the creditors were partly satisfied with the things belonging to the Carrolls; some were taken to the Anderson house for Charlotte. As for Charlotte herself, she was, in reality, not so far from the fever which Mrs. Anderson had predicted. She adored her father. Every day she watched for a letter. At last Anderson told her as much as he could and not break his word to her father.

"Your father is perfectly safe, dear," he said, "and he is earning a great deal of money."

"What is he doing?" asked Charlotte, and her manner showed for the first time suspicion of her father.

"Something perfectly honest, dear," Anderson replied, simply, "but he does not want you to know and he does not want the others to know. You just be contented and brave and make the best of it all."

That was not long before they were married. It had seemed best to them all that they should not delay long. Mrs. Carroll did not come to the wedding, because Ina was ill. Anna knew as well as Anderson what her brother was doing. She had somehow comforted her sister-in-law without telling her anything, but she did not think it best to visit Banbridge. She had at times a feeling as if she herself were doing what her brother was, and the shame and pride together stung her in the same way. She wrote by every mail to Carroll, and posted it in another town, and nobody knew. In one of the letters she told him with an unconcealed glee that his old enemy, the man who had brought about all this, had had a shock of paralysis.

"He will never speak again," she wrote. "He has become dead while he is alive. After all, the Lord is just."

Carroll got that letter a few weeks after Charlotte was married. One Sunday night he made a trip to Banbridge. He was close-shaven; he had grown very thin; nobody would have recognized him, nobody did recognize him, although he met several Banbridge people whom he used to know on the train. It was after dark, but the winter sky was full of stars, which seemed very near as he took his way up the street towards the Anderson house. He walked slowly when he approached the house, and frequently cast a look behind him, as if he were afraid of being seen.

When he reached the house he saw the curtains in the sitting-room were not drawn, and a warm glow of home seemed to shine forth into the wintry night. Carroll cautiously went up the steps, very softly. He went far enough to see the interior of the room, and he saw Charlotte and her husband sitting there. Mrs. Anderson was there also. She was reading the Bible, as befitted a Sunday night. Now and then she looked at Charlotte with a look of the utmost love and pride. Anderson, who was reading the paper, looked up, and the watching man saw him, and his eyes and Charlotte's met. The man watching knew that no anxiety about him seriously troubled her then, that she was entirely happy, and a feeling of sublime content and delight that it should be so, and he quite outside of it all, came over him.

He went softly down the steps and along the street to the station, where he could get a train back to the City in a few moments. To his own amazement, he was quite happy, he was even more than happy. A species of exaltation possessed him. Even the thought of himself, Arthur Carroll, posing nightly as a buffoon before the City crowds, did not daunt him. He realized a kind of joyful acquiescence with even that. He felt a happy patience when he considered the time that might elapse before he could see his family again. He passed the butcher's shop, and reflected with delight that he should be able to meet the note which was due next day. He remembered happily that he had been able to send Charlotte a little sum of money for her *trousseau*, and that perhaps a part of it had bought the pretty, rose-colored dress which she was wearing that night. Still, all this did not altogether account for the wonderful happiness which seemed to fill him as with light. He hurried along the street frozen in ridges like a sea, and he remembered what Anna had written about the man who had wronged him, and all at once he understood what filled him with this exaltation of joy, and he understood that underneath all the petty dishonors of his life had been a worse dishonor which took hold of his very soul and precipitated all the rest, and that he was now rid of it. He had no sense of triumph over his enemy, no joy that the Lord had at last wreaked vengeance upon the man who had injured him; but he was filled with an exceeding pity, and a sense of forgiveness which he had never in his life felt before. He had never forgiven before; now he forgave. He remembered, going along the streets, the words of The Lord's Prayer, "Forgive my debts as I forgive my debtors," and his very heart leaped with the knowledge that forgiveness was due him because of his forgiveness of another, and that the debt of honor to God and his own soul was paid.

THE END

www.ingramcontent.com/pod-product-compliance
Lightning Source LLC
Chambersburg PA
CBHW032205030726
47494CB00020B/626